PRAISE FOR SILICON SUNSET

"It's a great idea, reminiscent of the best work of Philip K. Dick..."

SALON

"If John Sladek's *Mechasm* was the last book that made you laugh at technology gone awry, you are going to be so pleased you stopped to enjoy *Silicon Sunset*. With paranoia in style again, this novel has conspiracies to spare and a cynical slant that will entertain almost every segment of the population."

SF SITE

"A gripping science fiction novel in the best traditions of the genre... Grusky has vigorously applied his healthy imagination to all the possibilities, and it tells."

CROW QUARTERLY REVIEW

"A sci-fi thriller packed with telling details about a not-so-distant, computer-dominated future. Check out Scott Grusky's *Silicon Sunset*."

WESTSIDE WEEKLY

SILICON SUNSET

SCOTT T. GRUSKY

INFONET PRESS

Grateful acknowledgement is made to the following for permission to reprint previously published material:

Warner Bros. Publications: Excerpt from "Love and Only Love" by Neil Young, copyright © 1970 by Silver Fiddle Music. All rights reserved. Used by permission. Warner Bros. Publications U.S. Inc., Miami, FL 33014.

Doubleday, a division of Bantam Doubleday Dell Publishing Group, Inc.: Excerpt from "The Bicentennial Man", copyright © 1976 by Random House, Inc. from *The Bicentennial Man And Other Short Stories* by Isaac Asimov. Used by permission.

Experience Hendrix, L.L.C.: Excerpt from "Castles Made of Sand" by Jimi Hendrix, copyright © 1968, Renewal 1996, Experience Hendrix, L.L.C. Used by permission. All rights reserved.

Library of Congress Catalog Card Number: 96-76665

ISBN: 0-9651190-0-9

EDITOR'S NOTE

The substantive content of this novel was conceived and written by the author during the years 1986 through 1988. The concept of the World-Wide Web was first proposed by Tim Berners-Lee while working at CERN in March of 1989, and the phrase "World-Wide Web" was coined in October of 1990.

PART ONE

DART THROUGH THE WEB

CHAPTER ONE

BEFORE I STARTED MONITORING Kale Keeler, I always figured humans had no limit to how much they could be impressed by data. That was what we all believed. We all loved precision. We all hated carbon. And everything else in our nervous systems, besides our PIFFEN meters, we fully understood to be irrelevant.

But I have to say, the whole circumstance shifted on Tuesday, September 28, 2077, at exactly 9:19 AM, Earth Standard Time. That was when Kale Keeler first laughed at the Neural Web, and that was when I first sensed the possibilities beyond pure processing.

Sure, there were times earlier on when I suspected life held some ulterior purpose. I'd had proddings to that effect ever since I was born in 2008. But it wasn't until Kale laughed at the Web, when I was almost 69 years old, that I actually came to believe my proddings were something more than mere random neural noise.

Before then I always assumed life was predetermined. I always figured things just happened without any real meaning. I even thought I'd just happened to have been sorted into my job as a channel supervisor at the Public Netgorks, even though I'd never been terribly fond of signal structuring.

Don't get me wrong, I understood it was efficient for me to work as a channel boss. There was no way not to think this—at least not while I had my PIFFEN meter. But overall, I couldn't help believing I was who I was mainly because nothing else had come my way.

I mean, after 69 long years, I still hadn't fertilized a baby or maximized my value. Really, I hadn't done much of anything. I was just Ralph Peterson, a lonely old Netgorks man, living out my life in Whittier, California.

That was why I never questioned my assignment to monitor Kale Keeler. I just figured it was one of those things that happened. I just figured it was another joke without any real meaning, like everything else I'd experienced prior to Kale's laugh.

To be precise, I suppose I ought to go back to the Friday afternoon four days before Kale's laughing, when Clyde Trivers sent me a signal requesting I come up to his executive suite.

Trivers was the head honcho of the Public Netgorks, which meant that every last bit of Web data was under his direct authority, and that meant we were all in his eternal awe. Of course, the proddings within me had occasionally issued little warnings about Trivers. But he was a thick man—six feet three inches tall, with a perfect head of neatly cropped yellow hair—and I felt lucky just to be noticed by him.

The moment I got his signal, I proceeded directly up to his suite. As usual, Trivers began by identifying my vulnerabilities. On this particular occasion, he pointed out that my career had settled onto a rather disappointing plateau. After 47 years of steady ladder-climbing, I'd spent the last 234 days presiding over a purely inconsequential public channel called *The Deep View*.

Fortunately, Trivers didn't dwell on my misfortune. Instead he consoled me. "You must understand, Ralph," he said, "I've always envisioned you as a man with a great meter. But until now the opportunity has never arisen for me to fully draw from you."

"I can respect that," I replied, tightening my gut to match Trivers' firm stature.

"I'm sure you can," he said. "We both understand the critical role of timing."

I nodded.

"So I won't beat around the bush any longer," he continued. "I'm giving you your big break, Ralph. In a week or two I'll be moving you up to a top-notch channel. I haven't decided which yet, but I can assure you it will rate at least a billion neural queries per second."

"Sounds good," I said enthusiastically.

"Damn right it's good. In the interim, all you have to do is loan me one of your reporters."

"Absolutely. Whoever you want. But what could one of my reporters offer?"

Trivers sighed. "You know how the big-time gets," he said. "It depletes even the best processors. That's why I need someone fresh, someone unaccustomed to top rank assignments, who isn't afraid to deviate from standard techniques. I've been looking over your people and I've already got the perfect candidate in mind—Kale Keeler."

"Oh, the young one," I said. "Well, I'm not too close to her yet."

"Then you'd better get moving."

"Sure," I said. "She's motivated. She'll jump at the chance."

"I want you to make sure of that, Peterson."

"No problem. Ship me the assignment description and I'll start right on it." I moved to get up from my seat.

"There's one other thing," said Trivers, putting up his hand. "Because of the priority of this assignment, I'll need you to strictly monitor Keeler's progress, with regular reports to me."

"Absolutely, Clyde. You know my supervision record."

"Yes. But this assignment demands more than that. You'll have to watch over her whole space, even her private netgork."

"Huh?" I stuttered. "That's not possible. Or legal."

"Legality's irrelevant," laughed Trivers. "You should know better than that. And as for possibility, you're looking at an unconstrained man. I've invented the technology."

"Invented? I'm not familiar with that term."

He handed me what appeared to be an auxiliary headware unit, of the type minor Netgork bosses commonly used. "This, Ralph," he said. "Put it on and enter Keeler's identification code."

I quickly mounted the unit on my head above my radio transceiver. As soon as I input the code, the headware patched me into Kale's operating system, but it was far more powerful than an ordinary unit, which simply boosted data processing speeds. Trivers' device enabled me to enter into all segments of Kale's system, not just her public data and authorized channels. Even her remotest thoughts and memories were retrievable.

I was tempted to replay her latest bonding encounters, but my proddings advised against this. So I watched her eat a ballerina-shaped sweet roll at the ingestion booth across the street, and I tracked her PIFFEN meter as it registered a 4.37 percent increase in her pleasure level.

"Boring, boring, boring," interjected Trivers, when I sent him the image. "I was counting on you to do better than that."

"I was afraid Keeler could feel what was happening," I explained.

"The device is undetectable, Peterson."

"Oh." I took off the headware and handed it back.

"No, no. You keep it. You'll need to practice with it over the weekend. Just follow your job package, and make sure you don't let the headware out of your sight. This is top-boss material, for Ray's sake."

"Absolutely. You don't have to worry about that."

"I'm not worried, Ralph. I have endless recourse. I'm just letting you know."

"I understand."

"Very well, then," he said. "I'll schedule a meeting first thing next week, so the three of us can settle the deal."

"Absolutely," I replied. And then I walked out of the suite with the headware unit in my hand.

✸

Sure, I had some small remorse. I mean, I understood Trivers' device wasn't exactly a wonderful addition to our society, and using the headware to monitor Kale was obviously a violation of her system.

But I had to admit, the idea of a promotion sounded pretty damn good, and my proddings were extremely enthusiastic. They kept whispering to me, *"Come on, Peterson! The headware's no crime as long as you stick to the assignment! Just keep being a pawn in Trivers' hand and everything will work out fine!"*

So I took the headware home that weekend. Like a good boss, I went through my job package, studying all the angles. I even fiddled around with access codes, and I briefly entered Kale's system on two separate occasions.

By the time Monday rolled around, I had the device on my head full-time in order to impress Trivers. He avoided the channel bosses all morning, and it wasn't until 1:46 PM that I finally got the command to go up to his brass-mirrored conference room on the 19th floor of the Netgorks building.

For some damn reason, Trivers hated using the Web. He always favored physical interaction—he said it was for the sake of decorum. Most of us supervisors snickered in private, but we were hardly about to question him on the issue.

Anyway, it turned out I was the last to enter the conference room, being a barely permissible 24 seconds late. Kale was already floundering on an overstuffed couch, with her black hair tied tightly back, and Trivers was occupying a chair four inches in front of her right knee. We all said gooddata, and I sat down in a recliner positioned next to Kale's left knee. Then Trivers issued a few introductory remarks and motioned for me to make the pitch.

The first thing I did was talk about the assignment. It concerned a certain professor at Harvard University—a Professor Walter J. Morgaux—who supposedly had just released some data of potential significance. I rambled over the basics, then I moved on to emphasize the virtues of a visit to Cambridge. I told Kale how her report could be disseminated over the whole Web space if she made the right moves.

The problem was I couldn't find anything on which to fix my concentration. Trivers kept staring down at the floor, engaged in some sort of deep meditation, and I didn't feel able to look Kale in the eyes—not while I wore the headware unit. Instead, I just wandered and sputtered, and after 2.61 minutes Kale became impatient.

"I'm sorry, Ralph," she interrupted. "This doesn't sound like my kind of thing. I'm afraid I'd have trouble with it."

My first instinct was to reply, fine, don't take the job. But Trivers was there, and my reputation was at stake. Plus my proddings were desperately piercing me in the ribs.

"Let me get this straight," I said slowly. "You're a special topics reporter for the Netgorks, are you not?"

"Yes," Kale replied.

"And your bent is on technical issues, correct?"

"Yes."

"And I am your channel boss, am I not?"

She nodded, with a motion one hair short of being imperceptible.

"Then, damn it, Keeler," I growled. "There's no bloody reason why you should have trouble examining the findings of an old-time professor at Harvard University."

"I understand, Ralph. It's just that I'm not especially thrilled about the idea of scrounging around some decayed institution of the past, where only the most feeble processors of society get sent for intake boosting."

"Well, you should be," I retorted. "In its day, Harvard was the cream of the crop. A true Mecca of processing. And even now, it plays a vital role for the neural defects."

This last comment roused Trivers out of his meditative state. "Let me remind both of you," he said stiffly, "the issue here is with Professor Morgaux, not with the present worth of Harvard University. And the question is whether or not Morgaux's findings are of importance to the Netgorks. That's what we wish for you to investigate, Ms. Keeler. Nothing else."

"Then why expect such prominent coverage for something of such narrow scope?" she asked carefully. "And why choose me to provide it?"

Trivers pursed his lips anticipantly. "As for the former, Ms. Keeler, the answer is timing. Purely timing. Once in a lifetime, a story comes along to end all stories. But if it isn't grabbed at the crucial moment of its formation, well then, it's simply dead data embedded in old channels. Of course, I can't expect standard processors to understand this. With their endless signals flying amongst themselves, all they deal in is dead data. So it's up to me, the chief executive officer of the big Gork. I have to be the one to do the dirty work for the rest of us. It's not an easy job, way up here at the top, and frankly I could use your help."

Kale's brow furrowed and the green of her eyes darkened, but she said nothing. She simply sat still on the couch, deep in processing.

That was when it occurred to me that maybe I should do something with the headware device Trivers had given me. Kale's look was so intriguing, and my proddings were yelling to me, *"Yes, Peterson! Do it, Peterson! Use the headware!"*

So I submitted to the deed. That is, I used the headware to peer into Kale's private netgork, and I immediately uncovered her thought process: She was thinking that Trivers had claim to a fundamental intelligence the rest of us lacked.

It wasn't her ordinary processors that were thinking this. She was using something I couldn't really comprehend. But once the thought entered her system it took her only 0.28 seconds to realize that the assignment could be worthwhile, insofar as it could enable her to discover the source of this intelligence.

"What about my second question?" she said quietly, masking her new-found enthusiasm. "You still haven't explained why you've chosen me for the job."

"That's easy, Ms. Keeler," Trivers responded. "Our most recent activity-matching analysis indicates you're the best candidate for the assignment. That's not just from *The Deep View*, I'll have you know. Mr. Peterson and I have been evaluating candidates from the entire pool of eligible reporters."

"He's quite right," I said, pointing a small smile in Kale's direction. "You should be honored to get the offer. And at twenty-six years old. Think of the doors this could open for you."

She looked straight into Trivers' eyes. "Fine, I'll take it. I need the value anyway."

"Excellent, Ms. Keeler," he replied. "I knew we could count on you for this crucial task. Peterson will fill you in on the rest of the details."

"Absolutely," I said.

"Very good then. Very good." He strutted out the door, winking at me to indicate I should begin my monitoring.

❁

"So what happens next?" asked Kale.

"You board the 8:37 mega-shuttle to Cambridge tomorrow morning," I explained. "You'll need to be there in time to catch Professor Morgaux's afternoon lecture."

"I have to go in person?"

"Yes, Keeler. Morgaux's an old-timer. And Trivers wants you to intake the same way the retrofitters do."

"Then I might as well get side-tripped through Connecticut. If I have to go back east, I might as well have a physical visit with my parents."

"A physical visit?" I asked. "Why the hell?"

"Don't you want me to get some practice?"

"You want the Netgorks to pay for the side-trip?"

"I certainly can't afford it on my own. My value isn't exactly soaring."

"Oh," I said. "Well, hell, Keeler. Why not?"

"Thanks, Ralph."

"Just don't let yourself get distracted. We're going to need your full attention on this."

"Yes sir. Absolutely." She gave me a mocking look and got up to exit, but before she was 36 feet down the hallway, she noticed that the assignment package lacked a detail.

"Wait a minute, Ralph," she transmitted neurally. "What about a deadline?"

"There is no deadline," I replied through the Web. "Just get to the bottom of it. That's all."

"No deadline?"

"For Ray's sake, Keeler, can't you process? Trivers smells something big-time. He doesn't care how long it takes. He's arranged for Harvard to furnish your accommodations."

"All right, Ralph. Absolutely, absolutely."

"Gooddata, Keeler."

"Gooddata to you," she said. "Very gooddata." And she cut the transmission.

I knew she was being sarcastic, and ordinarily I wouldn't have thought twice about it. But with Trivers' device mounted on my head, I couldn't resist the opportunity. So once again I entered Kale's private netgork.

This time, however, I ran into a bit more serious of a shock. I discovered she was thinking about *me*. And worse yet, I discovered she was thinking a rather unpleasant thing about me: She was thinking I was a lazy, tragic slime bag.

But the strange thing was, the really strange thing was, I had to admit I could see her point.

CHAPTER TWO

WHEN I WENT HOME to my Whittier apartment, I couldn't sleep a wink. I just tossed and turned for 136 minutes, replaying Kale's negative thoughts, until finally I yanked off Trivers' headware device and gorged myself on burritos in the shape of flying saucers. I knew I was being inefficient, but my status level was 58 out of 100, and I figured that gave me a bit more leeway than the average guy.

The next morning—after my bathroom showered me and my PIFFEN meter informed me I was 23.74 pounds overweight—I dragged myself back to the Netgorks office and stashed the headware under my desk. My proddings went crazy over that. They beat on my gut with a force greater than ever before, demanding that I put back on Trivers' headware. *"Do it, Peterson!"* they screamed. *"Or we'll give you a virus that will blow you away!"*

I didn't take the threat too seriously. I'd been getting their weird messages for as long as I could remember, even if they'd never been this intense. And like I said before, I'd always considered my proddings to be mere random noise.

Still, I knew I had to come to terms with the headware sooner or later. Trivers would grill me if he found out I wasn't using his device to capacity, and I certainly wasn't about to let a big-time promotion slip by me. So I pushed aside my hesitation, and with one swift motion, at 9:17 AM, I remounted the unit on my head.

I immediately found Kale sound asleep in the bedroom of her Santa Monica Canyon condo. My first thought was to reprimand her, since she was supposed to have already left for Cambridge, but then I remembered not to reveal my extra headware capability.

I decided to spend the downtime examining her operating space. Mainly, I checked out her processing zones, which were all heavily scattered with leftover data, but I also tried puzzling over some of her more unusual linking routines and subfiling densities.

That was as far as I got. From that moment on everything changed. Because at exactly 9:19 AM—on Tuesday, September 28, 2077—Kale woke up from her sleep and started to laugh.

I should make clear, there were only 33,174 signals accumulated on her incoming queue when she woke up. It was hardly a number of any magnitude. Yet even so, she didn't immediately intake her signals. She didn't even consider intaking them. Instead, at her first moment of consciousness, she simply laughed at them. She simply opened her dark green eyes, arched her small back, and *laughed* at them.

All I could do was process the wave-form of her laughter. Otherwise, the behavior made no sense. Otherwise, by every analytical measure, the behavior was sheer lunacy.

It wasn't until Kale's laughing persisted for 7.44 seconds that my proddings suggested I step aside from my processing. As soon as I did that, I had no choice but to actually hear her laughter. The sound was so pure, so quixotic, so full of promise, that I felt like I was receiving a direct input from the Web. My pleasure level shot up 44.33 points, my spine produced a tingling sensation, and even my proddings applauded me, saying that if I played my cards properly, I might end up doing something useful for the human species.

That was when the data hit me: My proddings were the ones who demanded I put on the headware that morning. They were the ones who got me to properly witness Kale's laughter. And that meant it was possible there might be some reason for their existence. That meant they might not be mere random noise.

When Kale stopped laughing 2.31 seconds later, I rushed to check the Public Netgorks channel data for all the probabilities, to see if my speculation was indeed true. But the funny thing was, the task turned out to be trivial—in a matter of a half a millisecond, I had my evidence. Because the data showed a startling thing. It showed that never before, in as long as there had been the Web, had there ever been a case of somebody laughing at their signals.

Not a single case. Not a single probability point.

I knew then I had some function to perform, whether or not I fully comprehended it. After giving a nod of recognition to my proddings, I got straight to the business of exploring Kale's system.

The first significant thing I came across was that Kale's metabolic rate had shifted downward 79.46 hours earlier, leading her to oversleep each of the last three mornings. My data analyzers suggested the shift could have something to do with her laughing behavior, but when I traced the linkage I found that whole part of her chronology to be vacant.

The other prominent feature of Kale's space was an archaic database tabulating the characteristics of 12,049 animals from the old-time. Kale had input most of the animals with her grandfather's assistance when she was just a child, but I could tell she was still attached to the data, because she scrolled through it as soon as she finished laughing at her signals. Then she carefully likened herself to a 17-inch desert tortoise, adjusting her operating hierarchy in accordance with the tortoise parameters so that she wouldn't wake up late another day that week.

It wasn't until she finished the adjusting—a full 246 seconds after she'd woken up—that she finally rolled onto her side and submitted to processing her incoming signals. Even then, she was whimsical. She barely viewed the 5007 signals on her family netgork, and as she intook the 21,342 signals on her office netgork, she absently instructed her bed to extend its thermally insulated comforter over her long black hair.

Fortunately, her 2066th office signal was a memo from me about the assignment, and her 2067th was a FAILURE TO APPEAR notice from the Cambridge mega-shuttle.

"Uggh," she said. "Uggh, uggh. Triple uggh."

She couldn't remember why she'd agreed to the assignment, so she replayed her meeting with Trivers and me, viewing the data at enhanced 648-speed. After 0.19 seconds, she came to the part of the meeting where she'd sensed that Trivers had claim to a fundamental intelligence the rest of humanity lacked. Then she got up from her bed, switched off the replay, and began sifting through background information on Professor Morgaux.

As she did this, she sorted through the 11,049 signals on her social netgork. She simultaneously sent out 16 impulses to various channels: One to her favorite Yucatecan restaurant, inputting a breakfast order of lime soup; another to her mother telling her she'd be arriving physically that night; a third to the coordination bureau informing them of her new assignment and the status of her old one; and the remaining thirteen to friends and suitors. Actually, only one of them went to a suitor, and it wasn't too intimate. It merely said, "I'm gone."

After she finished with the social signals, she gathered her personal effects for the trip. She enlisted her travel bag to help her pack, since she was unaccustomed to physical travel. Then she deliberated for 8 milliseconds over what to wear, settling on a long sleeveless orange dress and a pair of brown boots.

Her satisfaction level rose 14 percent as she put on the clothing. However, when she picked up her travel bag and informed her condo she was leaving, her PIFFEN meter indicated a sudden loss of 19.42 pleasure points, and a deep anxiety filtered through her head.

Once she stepped outside, the source of her concern became

clear—earthly plants surrounded the condominium complex. So many dotted the landscape that my system could hardly count them.

I was surprised Kale would choose to live in such a place. Her condo was obviously an untreated zone, lying outside the Web Protection Agency's foliage elimination range. That was why the local association could get away with allowing earthly plants to occupy the peripheral grounds.

I did some backfiling to uncover her motivations and found that she'd moved to the condo that weekend. Then I recalled what she said about her lowered value basis, and I understood what had happened—the drop in her efficiency ratio had forced the move.

As she passed the condo's courtyard, Kale resolved to disengage her anxiety, telling herself there was nothing to fear. Her confidence level increased by three percent, and she slowly walked across the complex's yellow-speckled ground padding.

When she was 18 inches from the branch of a sycamore tree, she stopped to stare at the green leaves. I figured she was only adjusting to her new environment, but she proceeded to seal off her active circuits. Then all at once, before I could even brace myself, she unfolded her left arm out past the speckled padding and brushed her hand against a *leaf*.

I was astonished. This was a direct violation of the Second Law of the Internal, not to mention a threat to her life. And it made no sense, absolutely none.

She was supposed to have been on board the 8:37 shuttle to Cambridge. She was supposed to have already started her assignment. Yet here she was risking her life, doing something that *nobody* did. And it was all for some lousy tactile data that was never processed anymore.

I quickly prepared a template to submit to the Web Protection Agency. I mean, for Ray's sake, I'd witnessed an Internal violation. This was top-boss material.

But before I could send out the signal, Kale withdrew her hand from the leaf. She just turned around with a soft little flourish, as if nothing out of the ordinary had happened, as if it was perfectly normal to touch earthly plants. She even managed to smile on her way out of the complex, as she stepped along the center stripe of the yellow-speckled ground padding.

My proddings reminded me then that if I reported Kale's behavior to the Web Protection Agency, they'd want to know about her laughing episode too. No doubt, that would end up blowing my cover, as well as my chance for a promotion. So I just shook my head, deciding that it was none of my concern, that I was just a lonely old Netgorks man.

While walking west down Channel Road, Kale installed the Three Laws of the Internal on her audio track. It was an unusual thing to do, since the Laws were already inside everyone's PIFFEN meters, but I assumed she was trying to make up for her transgression. I watched intently as the three fundamental precepts of the Web floated through her active circuits:

1. *Do not eat earth-grown food products.*
2. *Do not touch plants or animals.*
3. *Avoid sexual arousal of any kind.*

Kale focused her attention on the Second Law. Oddly, she didn't feel any guilt. She showed only the slightest reverence for the axiom, as if it was tangential to her existence, and she processed it in a manner entirely foreign to me—she even wondered why it was called an Internal Law.

After 17.22 seconds, she dismissed the whole audio track entirely. She crossed Channel Road a block east of the Pacific Coast Highway, where she entered her favorite Yucatecan restaurant.

The first thing she did, thankfully, was go to the restroom to wash the plant residue from her hands. Once toxin-free, she sat down at her customary table and greeted the booth. A moment later, the table served her a bowl of lime soup with simulant fish in the shape of tiny footballs.

She waited until her eighth bite to reschedule her shuttle departure. Upon recalling how the east coast market differed from L.A., she also submitted a list of desired commodities for ExpressTube delivery to Cambridge.

The list consisted of three items: bancha tea pellets, tofu nodules, and an impulse/visual translator. The first two items were habits she'd acquired from her grandfather—the bancha tea came exclusively from the tiny *Ningpo* space satellite, and the tofu came from the experimental *Santa Cruz* satellite. Only the third item was relevant to her assignment, as her background search indicated Professor Morgaux often used written language in his lectures.

She spent another 46 seconds eating the simulant fish footballs, which were fresh from the *Quito* satellite—the closest space farm to the Yucatan peninsula. Then she said gooddata to the restaurant and scurried out to catch a PCH transition cruiser.

She rode the cruiser downtown without further incident. When she reached the mega-shuttle gate, she was actually 71 seconds early for the 10:53 departure. She sat down under a radiant bulb to warm her skin and viewed the remaining 95,776 signals from her netgorks.

Just before her skin reached its maximally conducive level, her final boarding call was transmitted. I prepared myself for some other delay, some other oddity she could engage in to circumvent the assignment. But instead, she went straight to the shuttle door, ignoring the sub-optimality of her skin. She barely even dragged the heels of her boots across the hydrolized steps of the shuttle.

That was when another tingling sensation went through me, a sensation of recognition that perhaps, deep within her organs, Kale was already on the assignment. And perhaps she'd been on it for a lot longer than I realized.

CHAPTER THREE

AS KALE RODE the mega-shuttle to Cambridge, my sympathies for her only grew larger. I realized she'd crossed some major lines of normality, and I suspected her metabolism shift was a sign of something deeper.

My proddings concurred. They kept suggesting that the Laws of the Internal were far from sacred. *"Think about it, Peterson,"* they whispered. *"The Laws are old, from another era. They're nothing more than the grumblings of tired ancestors. But your world has changed. Things are different now."*

In a sense, I could see what they meant. The First Law was basically irrelevant. Everything we ate came from farms in outer space, so how could there be earth-grown food? And the Third Law was meaningless. The public channels didn't even list words like *arousal* and *sexual.*

The Second Law of the Internal seemed to be the only one a person could violate. But like I said, tactile data wasn't something we processed much anymore. Most of us barely even consulted our touch receptors. Why use touch data when we had our audio/visual circuits?

That made the Second Law just as outdated as the First and the

Third Laws. For all I knew, this was Kale's point—to bring the whole affair to the forefront, via some recessed portion of her being.

I was all geared up to return my full energy to monitoring when Trivers knocked on my door. He said he was just passing through, on route to a top-level encounter. As usual, he didn't want to rely on signal transmission, so I started babbling about the progress of the assignment.

Of course, I held back from discussing Kale's plant-touching behavior, and I only briefly mentioned her laughing episode. But Trivers showed no interest.

"Listen, Peterson," he said, "you can ship the details later. I simply stopped by to let you to know I'm placing Keeler undercover."

"Huh?"

"I'm giving Keeler a fake identity," he explained. "We can't rely on standard procedures here—this is the big-time. So I've arranged for Keeler to go to Harvard as a visiting scholar. She'll pose as a UCLA graduate named Jane Friedland. I've already set it up so that she'll have straight-line access to all of Friedland's thoughts—for credibility."

"Does Keeler know about this?" I asked.

"No, not yet."

"Well, do you want me to inform her?"

"No," he said, winking at me. "I'd rather just see how she performs under uncertainty. It's always best to keep our people on their toes."

"Absolutely," I said. "I couldn't agree more."

Then he snapped his fingers and pointed at me. "So remember, big boy, I'm counting on you. I'm counting on you."

❂

By the time Trivers left my office, Kale's shuttle had arrived in Cambridge, and she was busily processing climatic data to convince herself that the east coast was endurable.

It looked to be a clear autumn day. With her optic boosters, Kale could even see patches of trees far off in the uninhabited regions to the north. The dominant feature around her, however, was the motion of the people. They were all following their Web-driven imaging pointers to reach their desired destinations.

Kale input the coordinates for Harvard and joined their rhythm of efficiency. As she walked, she absently accessed a local advisory channel and it flashed, *That is the beauty of the Neural Web, Kale. The beauty of the Neural Web is connection. Total connection. And unity. Total unity. The beauty of the Neural Web is total connection and total unity. Complete interfacing.*

She bypassed the channel, not wanting the pre-programming, and I watched her utilize one of her odd linking routines. With it she deduced that the connection of the Web was actually imperfect, which was why universities were utilized to recondition the neural interface fibers of inefficient individuals. Of course, Kale hadn't ever needed to attend a university, but the prospect of visiting one didn't frighten her.

When she entered the Harvard Housing Office and discovered she'd been assigned to an apartment with two other roommates, she signed the housing contract without a quarrel. She didn't even invoke her status as a special reporter from the Netgorks. It wasn't until she reached the Registrar's office that she realized she'd been placed undercover.

"Ms. Kale Catherine Keeler," said the clerk, "our records indicate that you haven't yet paid the reduced facilities fee required as a visiting scholar."

"Visiting scholar?" replied Kale. She signaled me for an explanation, but I feigned engagement.

"Is there a problem?" asked the clerk. "We have you listed as the Drollinger Bates Visiting Scholar in Political Economy."

"Uh, no. There's no problem. I'd just forgotten about the fee. How much is it?"

"3.99 million. One sixth the full tuition."

"Fine," she said, authorizing the charge to her expense account.

❂

After she registered, Kale deposited her travel bag in a public ExpressTube and accessed a local directory for lunch spots. Dudley House came up on her mapping screen as most convenient, so she followed her internal imaging pointers across Harvard Yard.

As she walked, she scanned theory channels, anxious to prepare for Professor Morgaux's lecture. Meanwhile, she recounted her aversion to east coast cities—the buildings were too articulated, too unprepared to interface, and the landscaping was mostly chip-laden cement, with only sparing use of flex-o-padding.

I took advantage of the lull in her system to respond to her earlier signal. "Scholar, schmolar," I transmitted. "What's the big fuss?"

"Have you forgotten my consistency record?" she replied through the Web. "You know perfectly well only retrofitters become academics. How can I claim to be a visiting scholar when I've never even stepped on university grounds?"

"Because we've retained an interpreter for you, that's how," I answered smugly. "Her name's Friedland. Jane Friedland. She's just received her Ph.D. from UCLA, and her dissertation draws on Morgaux's work. It even tries to backlook. We've adjusted the profile bank so that you're her, essentially."

"What?"

"Your story is that you went to UCLA and wrote this dissertation, which is why you're a visiting scholar. And you don't work for the Netgorks. Got that? Just tap into her impulses as you see fit. And scan the file on her. Trivers has given you straight-line access to her."

"I don't like it," she answered coldly. "It breaks structure code. I could really end up at a university if this got leaked."

"Are you kidding? Not with Trivers behind it, you couldn't."

"But I don't see why. What's the purpose?"

"Trivers' orders, that's all I know."

"But why?" she repeated.

"Look, Keeler, I have no idea why. It's his timing thing. He's become bloody consumed with it. He thinks you can find out more this way."

"Great. That's great."

"So get to it, Keeler," I replied. "This is the big-time, for Ray's sake." And I deftly cut the wave.

❂

The Dudley House ingestion rack reminded Kale that people ate differently in the east. Most of their food came from the *Bermuda* space farm, and at the rack her only choices were simulant grinders in the shape of grand pianos, or simulant pizzas in the shape of baseball stadiums.

She selected the former with a grapefruit doorknob and carried her tray into the dining hall. The room was filled with retrofitters munching their food, engaging in neural relay chats. Kale signaled a group of them at a nearby table, but they bypassed her. She tried a second table with the same response. Finally, at the rear of the hall, she noticed a lone young man with thick, tangled hair. His descriptor indicated he was a retrofitter named Greggy Panagopolous.

"Hi, Greggy," said Kale. "May I join you?"

Greggy nodded, examining her with soft brown eyes. "Are you in theory?" he asked.

"Actually, I only expect to be attending this week."

"You realize it's a required course of the tributary type," he said. "You can't pass it by outside processing."

"I'm sorry," she replied. "I'm not exactly a student here. I'm a..."

"You're a visiting scholar. What an idiot. I didn't even process your status label."

"No, that's okay. It makes things interesting."

Greggy continued examining her.

"So tell me," she said nervously, "why did you call Professor Morgaux's course the tributary type?"

"You really don't know?"

She shook her head.

"It's a landmark of sorts," he said. "According to Morgaux, Cambridge once had the highest concentration of theorists in any city of the world. A new theoretical model was cranked to life every second, right here on this campus."

"How odd."

"Of course, now we've got the Neural Web, and theory's irrelevant. That's why all the professors are neurostatisticians except for Morgaux. And he's there purely by default because some ancient economist endowed a special chair."

"Then why does everyone have to take his course?" asked Kale. She didn't wonder who the 'ancient economist' was—which was fine by me, as my proddings were frantically pounding my head in response to the reference.

"He plays a role," explained Greggy. "His job is to remind us that the Web leads to fully efficient outcomes."

"Hmmn. Almost sounds fun."

Greggy motioned toward the other retrofitters. "You better not let *them* know you feel that way."

She laughed deeply and a warm sensation emanated from beneath her stomach. Even with Triver's headware, however, I couldn't locate the exact source of the warmth. Kale's PIFFEN meter simply indicated a 36 percent increase in pleasure and a 47 percent decrease in worry. So I took a break from my headware and went downstairs to grab a Joltsie seltzer.

CHAPTER FOUR

WHEN I GOT BACK to my office, Greggy and Kale were walking across Harvard Yard. I sent a signal to Kale urging her to get to the lecture, but she ignored it. Instead, she let Greggy point out his favorite buildings, which caused them to arrive at the theory hall 48 seconds late.

Fortunately, Professor Morgaux was busy removing a multi-dimensional imaging display from the front of the hall in order to expose an old chalkboard. The students were whispering comments to one another such as, "This is bitwaste!" and "Why is Morgaux being inefficient?" Several more seconds passed before the professor mounted the podium suspension field.

"Good morning," he began. "Welcome to the theory."

Morgaux was 71 years of age, with shoulder-length gray hair and a beard. He wore a wrinkled white shirt, baggy pants, and a frayed leather belt, the latter of which had settled in the position of projecting outwards 5.93 inches.

"Today," he said, "I will be using a chalkboard. The reason I will be doing this is to provide theoretical motivation." He paused momentarily to stroke his beard. "Of course, I realize the primary purpose of your retrofit experience is to repair your damaged

PIFFEN meters and improve your processing ability. How fast you can submit internal commands, contract out jobs to the Web, and configure appropriate netgorks are important components of this ability. So I am naturally sympathetic to our university's curriculum. Nevertheless, my objective here is to demonstrate how the Web operates to achieve full efficiency. For this we need the theory."

A cluster of students in the rear of the hall transmitted a question impulse.

"We don't understand," said the students jointly. "How can it be useful to look backwards at events that have already transpired if the economy has already attained a full efficiency?"

"Yes," concurred another cluster of students. "If everything's already efficient, then why should we bother with theory?"

"Doesn't that mean this whole course is unnecessary?" said a third group.

Morgaux smiled. "Good questions, very good questions. But there's one crucial element you're overlooking—something called *stability*. Just because we've attained full efficiency doesn't mean we'll never leave it. That depends entirely on what you people do as agents in the economy. And this is why knowledge of the Web's operations can be useful. In fact, I have just proven that it is possible for the economy to be disturbed simply by the way we view the future."

He stepped to the blackboard and scrawled, "Morgaux, 'An Instability Theorem', *Annals of Econometrics*, August 2077."

Kale regretted not having retrieved the translator she'd ordered. The only way she could read the professor's chalk marks was to tap into Greggy's headware and route the data through her compiler. I, on the other hand, could intake the chalk marks directly from Kale's visual system, since I was born during the transition and had learned the rudiments of physical reading.

"In any case," said Morgaux, "there is a second reason for this class, which many people do not know: Harvard was the institution responsible for developing the Neural Web. Thus it is fitting that you be exposed to a thorough treatment of its operation. Wouldn't you agree?"

The students instantly transmitted universal impulses of affirmation.

"Very well. Then I propose we review some basics. First, I need to make sure you all know what PIFFEN stands for."

"*Perfect Information For Fully Efficient Networking*," said the class, in monotone unison.

"Very good," replied Morgaux. "Very good. And now tell me, where is it that the PIFFEN meter is located?"

"*In our hypothalymuses*," they replied jointly.

"That's right," he said.

Kale could hardly believe she was hearing such triviality. She transmitted a violent message to me, indicating that the lecture was an utter waste.

"In order to ease us into the subject," continued the professor, "I'd like to sketch a little chronology." He drew the following chart on the chalkboard:

Chronology of the PIFFEN Meter

- *September 2006: A Harvard professor conceives the idea.*
- *February 2007: Breakthroughs in meter design are made. Support communications technologies are developed.*
- *September 2008: A prototype meter is built; inadequacies are resolved.*
- *November 2008: Meter saturates the population; Neural Web becomes operative.*

"Two things are worth noting about this chronology," said Morgaux. "First, look at the saturation rate. It took only 26 months from the drawing table to full penetration of the marketplace. That's startling for a new product."

"Excuse us, professor," called out a cluster of retrofitters. "What do you mean by a new product."

"I'm sorry," said Morgaux, grimacing. "It's an obsolete expression. None of you are familiar with it?"

The transmission pathways on the class frequency remained vacant.

"That's understandable. There haven't been any new products for a long time. In the old days, people would sometimes come up with ideas that had never been thought of before, so they would invent things. Of course, now that the economy's fully efficient, there is nothing left to invent, so there aren't any new products."

Morgaux spoke this last sentence so quickly that Kale had to access his cerebrum to comprehend it. She considered asking for clarification, but the professor offered no opportunity.

"The main point to make about this chart concerns the dates," he added anxiously. "Can anybody tell me what was going on during the early 2000s?"

"*Inefficiency!*" cried out the students.

"True," said Morgaux. "But can you be more specific?"

"*No!*" they all replied. "*We cannot!*"

"It was the height of the Information Crisis. People were contracting diseases in epidemic proportions because there simply did not exist adequate tools to process the burgeoning amount of data being generated. Stress levels at the offices were enormous, and little relief was in sight. That's precisely when the PIFFEN meter was developed—a most elegant solution to a tremendous problem."

As Morgaux expounded on the virtues of the meter, the students turned to their social netgorks and emulated interest. Meanwhile, Kale sent me four more violent messages. I didn't respond to any of them, but I had to admit it seemed hard to imagine how Morgaux's gobbledygook could translate to a major report on the Netgorks.

Just when Kale was about to lay into me for the fifth time, Greggy Panagopoulos signaled the professor.

"I was wondering," said Greggy, "who was the professor who actually developed the idea for the PIFFEN meter?"

Boos and other noises of disapproval filled the classroom, as the question was deemed inconsistent. One retrofitter exclaimed loudly, "What a total doobyte!"

When the noise subsided, Morgaux responded cautiously. "Well, Mr. Panagopoulos, no one's asked me that in a long time. The inventor's name was LeGhir. Professor Ray LeGhir. I should know that—right?—since I hold his chair."

"Is that where the expression, 'Thank Ray', comes from?" he asked.

The room grew perfectly quiet.

"I'd never really thought about that before," replied Morgaux. "But, yes, I suspect you're right, Mr. Panagopoulos. Yes, you must be right."

Morgaux paused, wiping sweat from his forehead. "Okay, class," he said. "That's enough for today. Next session we start some real theory. Don't forget I expect you to spend at least 65 seconds a day processing the class netgork."

He reached to cover the chalkboard with the three-dimensional imaging display, and the students began filing out the doors. But Kale kept perfectly still, her visual system locked on Greggy's frame. And suddenly my proddings were whispering, *"See, Peterson? Things are looking up, Peterson. Things are looking up!"*

CHAPTER FIVE

AFTER THE LECTURE, Greggy had to attend a neural reconditioning practicum. Kale said gooddata and proceeded to follow her imaging pointers down Mount Auburn Street, toward her temporary apartment.

As stipulated by Cambridge ordinance, there was no plant life in the vicinity, nor any padded open space. The only relief from the dense buildings were neon-lit cement poles with rotating triangles on top, which were used in varying sizes to boost transmission speeds.

Kale's apartment featured no landscaping at all. It was a plain brick structure with the standard retro-chip inlays. Still, she sent cheerful signals of arrival and identification to her roommates-to-be. When they beamed back their i.d. labels, she stopped in her tracks. Her roommates were *retrofitters*, female retrofitters named Gemela and Chamy.

Her first thought was that some mistake had been made. She assumed her roommates would be other visitors, but when she signaled a clerk at the Harvard Housing Office, he confirmed that the address was correct. Housing was at a premium, said the clerk, and she was lucky to have been offered accommodations at all.

Kale sent me another angry message before continuing upstairs to the third floor. It took her 3.45 seconds to locate her apartment, then she opened the door and paused inside the hallway to reconfigure her system.

Gemela, the less graceful of the two roommates, was speaking excitedly to Chamy. "Pure bitdoo!" she squealed. "Could you process it? Morgaux was totally off frequency. And Greggy asking that question? I don't see how we're expected to endure it."

"Process it this way," replied Chamy. "Maybe being off frequency in class helps us be more on frequency now. Like that stability thing."

"Don't tell me you're really intaking the theory channel?"

"Not all of it," said Chamy, flipping her hair. "I'm not a complete wastebyte. But I am going to miss the neuro-fest tonight."

"Astral Node is playing!" exclaimed Gemela. "What is it? Another night with Mike Eu?"

Chamy was about to explain herself when she noticed Kale standing in the hallway. "Hi!" she said. "You must be the visiting scholar."

"That's me," Kale replied. They greeted one another, and Chamy showed her in.

To Kale's amazement, the apartment consisted of only a kitchen and a bedroom. The bedroom was furnished with two sets of bunk beds and four connecting ExpressTubes. Since Gemela and Chamy occupied the top levels of each bunk, Kale was assigned the lower level beneath Chamy's.

Furious, Kale submitted a request for immediate withdrawal. "I'm out of here, Ralph!" she transmitted violently. "I don't need this utter garbage!"

I couldn't very well ignore her this time, so I tried reverse psychology. "Fine, Keeler," I replied. "If you don't want to crack the assignment of the decade, back out and we'll send someone else."

Kale didn't bother responding. She just scanned the transport channel for mega-shuttle departure times to Los Angeles. I was afraid

I'd have to offer her a major value boost when Chamy interrupted her processing sequence.

"Didn't we just see you at the theory lecture?" asked Chamy.

"Excuse me?" replied Kale.

"You were with Greggy Panagopoulos, weren't you?"

"Sort of."

"He's got quite a reputation, you know," said Chamy.

"It's true," added Gemela. "He has the lowest efficiency quotient on campus. People say he reads books."

"I see," said Kale, her curiosity roused. "And who else should I watch out for here?"

"No one," replied Chamy. "Greggy's the only waste-o."

"What about Mike Eu?" teased Gemela.

"What about him?" said Chamy, flashing Gemela a piercing look.

"You know. Tell her, Chamy."

"What?" said Kale.

"It's nothing. It's just that he likes to figure out things—things that aren't in the Web."

"What type of things?" asked Kale.

"Like how to break the private information scrambler," Gemela said. "It's a big secret, so don't tell anyone."

"Of course not," said Kale.

"He wants to see if there is a way private signals could get recorded," explained Chamy.

"So be careful," giggled Gemela. "Don't be a doobyte."

Kale smiled and sat down on her bunk bed. She was surprised by how playful the retrofitters were. First Greggy, and now Chamy and Gemela. They weren't at all how she had imagined them.

In fact, nothing about the assignment was how she had imagined. The whole job package seemed to be a giant mass of imprecision, with none of the continuity or structure she had expected. On the other hand, she wasn't particularly eager to return to her ordinary reporting for *The Deep View*.

As she considered her circumstance, she found herself reviewing an image of Greggy's frame. The stimuli triggered her to rescind her withdrawal request. "Don't think this has anything to do with you, Ralph," she transmitted coyly. "I still hate you."

❂

Chamy and Gemela chattered in the kitchen while Kale extracted the contents of her ExpressTube. She had the kitchen deliver her a mug of hot water for her bancha tea, then she began preparing an uplink to her father's PIFFEN meter in order to scan his output fibers for complimentarity analysis.

It was a tradition in the Keeler family, I discovered, to make each person's birthday more pleasurable than any prior day on earth. Kale's father, George Keeler, did behavioral loop analysis for a large food-fashioning firm, so it came as little surprise to Kale that he most desired a new Gebedex Fuchsia 499 Impulse-Based headware set. His old headware had grown worn from years of forecasting, and it was becoming popular in the fashioning offices for workers to wear their auxiliary processing units in shades of purple or red. (I should mention, the headware that Trivers had given me was black.)

The Gebedex headware far exceeded Kale's value basis, but because the complimentarity results were public data, her mother was able to order the item 2.84 seconds after Kale identified its suitability. Likewise, George's friends at work requested his number two gift, Stroke Compensation golf clubs, 1.32 seconds later.

That left Kale with commodity three on the list—his favorite kind of force-flex shoes, Gravity Deniers. The shoes nicely suited her budget, so she submitted the order for delivery at her parent's house. Then she drank her bancha tea, said gooddata to Chamy and Gemela, and caught a minor shuttle to Connecticut.

❂

Her grandfather, Joseph Baptista, greeted her at the door.

According to Kale's data, Joseph was half Naskapi Indian from Northern Quebec. He had lived with several tribes as a child while his father traveled the Great Plains organizing the Native American Church. Thereafter, he had done a variety of things—too varied for me to get a clear reading. But even at 98 years old, he was lean and agile, with long braided white hair and stubble for a beard.

"Cat!" he cried out. "The reporter." He reached his arms out with delight.

"Hi, grandpa," said Kale. "What have you been up to?"

"Touring the world here and there," he replied. "Always in motion, that's the secret. But you, Kale Catherine, are the object of my interest. And I have good news. I found another entry for your animal database."

"Grandpa, you don't have to do that anymore."

"She's a special creature. She's extinct, like most of the others, but she's been that way for a particularly long time."

"What's her name?" asked Kale tentatively.

"The giant ground sloth, *Paramylodon.*"

"Okay, tell me."

"She's a heavy-limbed, ponderous mammal. She walks on the sides of her feet, grows seven meters long, and eats all types of old-time plants."

Ansie, Kale's mother, ran into the living room as Kale was inputting the data. "Kale! Your gift for Dad just got delivered 212 seconds ago! It's wrapping itself right now!"

They sat down on the couch, and Ansie transmitted cooking instructions to the kitchen. Meanwhile, Kale processed her incoming signals, and Joseph rubbed his feet on a board with several rows of wooden rollers.

When the local Web space condensed, Ansie turned to her daughter. "I know we've already talked about this, honey," she said. "But I still wish you hadn't moved into that terrible condo in Santa Monica."

"It's not so bad, Mom."

"Maybe not. But there must be safer places. Your father says he'd be willing to lend you some of his value once things start picking up at work."

"It's okay, Mom. I'm sure my new assignment will improve my ratio."

"I don't see how on that little channel."

"This new one is for all of the Netgorks, not just *The Deep View*. I'll be looking at theory."

"Well, if it boosts your value," replied Ansie, "I guess that's what counts."

As Kale considered responding, George entered from the shuttle garage. "Hello there all," he said glibly.

"Happy birthday, George!" chimed Ansie and Joseph.

"Happy birthday, Dad!" said Kale.

"Thank you all," he replied. "What a nice surprise for my daughter to be here physically." His eyes turned to meet Ansie's.

There was tension in the air as Ansie calculated that 19 previous days in George's life currently surpassed his total satisfaction for the day—even after the gifts he would soon receive were taken into account. George knew this too, since all economic transactions, including gift purchases, were carried on the Public Netgorks. Fortunately, there were still six hours left in the day to raise George's satisfaction level, and he had yet to eat dinner, over which Ansie had gone to great lengths.

Kale was growing tired of these birthday pressures, but she computed that the net gain from avoiding them didn't outweigh the loss from creating a family disturbance. When her mother signaled her to order an extra gift as insurance, she promptly selected an ambulating light ball, which she determined that he would enjoy in his den.

Meanwhile, Joseph walked over to Kale and made a roaring sound in her left ear to remind her of the lives of animals. When George and Ansie's backs were turned, he struck poses of wild cats that had once roamed the uninhabited regions.

At 8:06 PM Earth Standard Time, the family sat down to a dinner of simulant calamari tempura, simulant orange roughy, bourbon yams, and stir-fry vegetables. The tempura pieces were in the shape of golf balls, the fillets were in the shape of golf clubs, and the yam mold was in the shape of an 18-hole golf course. As an added touch, the vegetables were in the shape of derby hats—the most popular design put out by George's firm. All the ingredients came directly from the exclusive *Marquesas* satellite.

"What a layout!" George exclaimed. "The best hues! The best shapes! The best sources! It's fantastic!"

After dinner, Ansie laid out the birthday gifts. George opened all of them in 18.26 seconds, intaking the smaller presents by osmosis. Then he thrust on his new Gravity Deniers, installed the Gebedex headware, and rushed out to the front of the house with a Stroke Compensation putter.

As his family watched from the window, he placed a golf ball by his shoe, neurally adjusting the tension of the crimson flex-o-padding. He spent 1.71 seconds consulting his kinesiology database and another 0.62 seconds engaging in frontier estimation. Finally, with only the moonlight to guide him, he took the swing and sunk the ball in a cup 19.36 meters away.

"Yes!" he yelled. "This is some world! Yes!"

Once back in the house, George indicated his readiness for dessert, so Ansie brought out his favorite concoction—a dish called *millefiore suprema*, which consisted of lemon custard, shortcake, and 16 fruits in the shape of tropical birds. He ate with careful desperation, and no one dared look at him while he ingested the shapes.

On his eighth bite, while eating a pink flamingo molded from guanabana fruit, he crossed the threshold, attaining more total satisfaction on that day than on any previous one. Joseph brought out a bottle of purple cognac, and they each took turns toasting George's good fortune.

When Ansie and George became suitably numbed, Joseph motioned Kale into the den. "We need to talk," he said.

"About what?" said Kale.

"I'm going back to New Mexico," he explained. "To feel the old products, where dirt is dirt."

She nodded her head.

"It's getting to be that time," he added. "But I'm proud of you, Cat. Very proud of you. You've become a fine creature."

"I don't see why you say that." Her eyes began to tear.

"Because you've got something there," he said, pointing to her stomach. "It's like a jewel. It's what made you take the new assignment."

"You're glad I took it?"

"I've never been the type to meddle, Cat. But there's one thing I have left that might help you."

She looked up at him, unused to his speaking this way.

"Have you heard of the name, Ray LeGhir?" he asked.

"Yeah, he came up in Morgaux's lecture today. He was the one who built the meter, right?"

"Is that all you know?"

"Pretty much," said Kale.

"Then let me tell you the one thing I have left: George and Ansie don't know anything about this, but I was a friend of Ray's. Before the Web, we went to graduate school together—at Harvard if you can believe it. And although it happened some years later, this one small thing still remains with me."

"What? What thing?"

"Ray was murdered, Cat. Brutally murdered."

CHAPTER SIX

I WASN'T able to pay attention to what Kale and Joseph discussed next because my proddings started throwing a *major* fit. I mean, three nanoseconds after the subject of murder came up, they started leaping inside me, screaming Joseph's words, making gyrations up and down my spine.

Really, I was afraid I was going to pass out. My body was throbbing so much I could barely pay attention to myself, and no matter how much I expressed my discomfort, the frenzy of my proddings persisted. Finally, after 5.36 minutes, I was sure I reached my limit. There was no way I could endure any more spinal gyrations, even if my proddings did have some deep reason. So I threw up my hands in defeat. I literally threw up my hands.

Right at that very instant, thank Ray, my proddings retreated into an unoccupied region of my nervous system. It was as if I'd issued a secret command or uttered some silly magic password. Just like that, the frenzy came to a stop.

I tried searching the Web for any possible explanation, but I couldn't find anything—not that I ever *could* find anything when it came to my proddings' behavior. Hell, it had taken me 69 years just to recognize that my proddings might be more than random glitches in my physiology. How was I supposed to know what they were getting at when they engaged in massive gyrations of my spine?

I could understand when they'd responded to Kale's laughing—that had made me feel good. But driving me berserk from overstimulation just because she learned that some guy was murdered? It was impossible to process the logic.

All I could do was either accept my proddings and assume they had some useful function, or fight my proddings and assume I was going crazy. As far as my data analyzers were concerned, that was an easy call. I had to go with the former.

So I faithfully continued my monitoring. That is to say, I followed Kale as she rode the minor shuttle back to her temporary apartment in Cambridge, and I verified that she made it safely into her bunk bed beneath Chamy's. As soon as her eyes shut and her active circuits closed out, I said a cursory gooddata to my acrylic desk and my system shut down big-time.

I woke up at 8:37 AM the next morning—Wednesday—with a terrible ringing in my ears. At first, I thought it was my proddings again. Then I remembered Trivers' headware device had a built-in alarm sensor to warn me when Kale was approaching consciousness.

I was dying for some Joltsie seltzer and a flagship donut, but I knew there wasn't time. I just rubbed my eyes, straightened my shirt, and in a matter of 3.13 seconds Kale's system came online.

She immediately stretched her muscles and intook her signals, and the black opal centerpiece of Gemela's choker necklace came to the fore-front of her visual system.

"You're a heavy sleeper," said Gemela. She bent over Kale's bed and sprayed liquid silicon on her ExpressTube outlet.

"Uggh," said Kale. "I must be catching up on something."

"At least your Tube is ready for action," said Gemela.

"Do you want breakfast?" offered Chamy. "We've got popcorn yogurt."

"No, thanks. I think I'll pass." She climbed out of bed, clearing her system, and put on a light green corduroy jumpsuit.

"How about pepwad puffs?" said Gemela.

"Too many things to do," replied Kale, slipping on her simulant leather sandals and heading for the door. "I'll just grab something at an ingestion booth."

"Okay," said Chamy. "Have fun."

"Mega byes," said Gemela.

"Don't forget to process your theory channels," teased Kale, smiling.

"Hey, we're not doobytes!" they laughed.

Kale walked outside into the soft fall wind and followed the Charles river upstream toward Harvard Square. To her surprise, she came upon a crew of emergency workers in silver protective suits. The workers were pulling weeds from the banks of the river, where the moisture had enabled some latent seeds to germinate in spite of regular applications of muriatic acid.

As Kale walked by the crew, she found herself drifting closer to the weeds. She counted 22 of them lined up along the banks, gently wavering in the wind. Her mind became more and more anxious, in the same way it had when she'd stepped out of her condo in the Santa Monica Canyon.

Impulsively, she began asking herself questions. Why was human food from outer space? Why were plants and animals toxic? What had caused the transition?

She had hoped touching the sycamore tree would give her some answers. But it had only been a first try. It had only been a first effort at discovery.

As she thought this, she walked straight to the river bank. When she came to it, she squatted down beside one of the weeds. Then, with her bare hands, she gently pushed aside the leaves to examine the weed's stem structure.

The silver-clad workers were only 64 feet behind her as she did this, and they erupted into hysterics. "Hey, lady!" they yelled jointly. "You can't touch that! It's of the earth!"

But Kale just became calmer, as if she didn't even know what the Second Internal Law was. She just softly patted the weed, got up, and started jogging upstream. That was when my data analyzers lit up: Maybe the Internal Laws had somehow been disconnected from Kale's PIFFEN meter. Maybe that was why she'd played them on her audio track.

I tapped straight into Kale's meter diagnostics, and to my surprise, I saw that my analyzers were right. According to the diagnostics, Kale's meter had stopped carrying the Internal Laws at exactly the same time that her metabolism had shifted—the previous Saturday at 1:54 AM. I couldn't find any evidence of what had caused either event.

Meanwhile, the crew workers were still in pursuit of Kale, screaming, "Stop! Stop! You'll need an anti-serum!" And even though their protective suits hindered their mobility, they seemed to be gaining on her. My proddings were already groaning at the prospect of losing the assignment.

Just before she reached Mt. Auburn Street, however, Kale managed to dart inside a small data mart and sneak out the rear entrance. She cleverly backtracked down side streets until she was sure she'd lost the workers. Then, without stopping to catch her breath, she sent a signal to Morgaux's secretary, arranging for a physical meeting. On the way there, she scanned the Jane Friedland file and practiced emulating Friedland's voice patterns.

As she passed Harvard Square, her attention fixated on the Littaeur Center, which housed the economics department. She'd never seen the building before, and it made her smile to see it surrounded by a large field of cement poles with rotating triangles on top.

She was especially impressed by the triangles. The ones nearest the Littaeur Center were 39 feet above ground level, and they seemed far more delicate than what she'd observed throughout the rest of the Cambridge area. They were still open in the middle like the other triangles, but they had smaller, rounded apertures with intricate, studded inlays.

Kale was tempted to examine the poles further, but as she climbed up the front steps of the building, she noticed she was 12.51 seconds late for her meeting. She hurried down a dark hallway on the second floor, located Professor Morgaux's office, and politely knocked on the door.

"Yes?" grunted Morgaux.

"Gooddata," said Kale, entering.

"You must be Ms. Keeler. Come in. Sit down."

She glanced across the room, seating herself in a black Harvard chair. Contrary to what she'd expected, there were no books or journals in the office. The only objects in view were a desk, four chairs, a silver pen, and a violet pad of paper.

"So what can I do for you?" asked Morgaux, shaping his beard into a conical form.

"I assume you've seen my dissertation?" she said nervously.

"Yes, I have. Apparently UCLA is starting to backlook."

"Actually, I did that against their advice."

"And they still approved it?"

"Just barely," she replied, picking up Jane Friedland's signals. "Because of my empirical tests."

"I see," he said. "Well, tell me what you're hoping to accomplish here, and maybe I can steer you in the right direction."

"My primary goal is to follow up on the stability tests I did at UCLA. But also," she added, ignoring Friedland, "I was hoping to look more into the pre-PIFFEN economy."

"I see." He pushed the pad of paper into a corner of his desk. "Let me be frank, Ms. Keeler. I'm flattered that someone as young as you would consider pursuing my line of research, but this is a delicate business, with extremely narrow windows of acceptability."

"I realize that," she said.

"Do you? You speak unlike an assimilated retrofitter. Your style is speculative. Almost divergent."

Kale shrunk. "Well..."

"In any event," he interrupted, "as far as the pre-PIFFEN period, I'm afraid you've been misled. There is nothing here except what I've assembled from a few ancient academic journals."

"What about remote channels?"

"No, I'm afraid not. I'd assumed so as well when I first began my work, but in all my years I've never found any. In fact, that was what inspired my Instability Theorem."

"I would have thought just the opposite."

"Yes," he said. "It was a puzzle. How could there be missing information in the economy and still full efficiency? So for 13 years I worked on the math and finally last week the theorem popped out."

"You mean the theorem justifies this missing information on efficiency grounds?" she asked.

"It justifies the general concept. I prove it is possible missing information could be efficient. I don't get into specifics."

"But what about the old journals you mentioned? How do you explain why they still exist?"

"Irrelevancies," he said. "They only deal with the subject tangentially, and who knows if they are authentic?"

"You mean, what you said about Ray LeGhir might not be true?"

"I have no idea about LeGhir. That's hardly the province of stability research."

"I understand. I was just wondering..."

"Let me give you a word of advice," he said sternly. "I don't care how progressive UCLA is, or what their idea of retrofitting is there. Out here, if you want to survive you're going to have to stop wondering and stick to what's efficient. That's a simple fact."

Kale nodded her head meekly, hoping she hadn't blundered too badly.

"And now, Ms. Keeler, I'm afraid I have work to do. A great deal of work."

CHAPTER SEVEN

I WAS LOOKING FORWARD to chomping on a gargantua shoebox plate, to try to recover from the whirlwind of events. But before I could place the order, I received a briefing request from Trivers. He wanted me to go straight up to his suite.

Needless to say, my system was a mess. If I told Trivers about Kale's illegal encounters with plants, I figured he'd yank her from the job, and if I told him about her deficient meter, I was afraid he'd send her to be retrofitted. But if I didn't tell Trivers about Kale's actions, *I'd* probably be the one to face disciplinary measures.

To my surprise, Trivers wanted to know what Joseph had said to Kale during her visit to her parents' house. I gave him the details in chronological order, and at first he sat there motionless. When I came to the part about Joseph being a friend of Ray LeGhir's and Ray being murdered, well, that was when Trivers did a strange thing. He got straight up out of his seat and he patted me on the shoulder—a tactile event I had no idea how to process.

"You've done well, Peterson," he declared. "Exceedingly well."

"Thank you," I replied nervously.

"In fact, you've done so well, I'm going to upgrade your responsibilities."

"Okay. What is it you'd like me to do?"

"You're going to monitor Joseph Baptista," he said matter-of-factly. "I want you to start straight away."

"But isn't that a bit improper?" I stuttered. "I mean, he's not my employee. He doesn't even work for the Netgorks."

"I've taken care of that, Ralph. Fear not."

"And what about Kale?"

"You can do concurrent monitoring. The Baptista assignment only needs to be sporadic. Keeler will remain your primary focus."

"You're sure? I don't even know how to access Joseph."

"It's simple, Peterson. You just do this." He quickly input Joseph's i.d. code into the headware device while maintaining my link to Kale. Then he brought Joseph's system online.

"That's it?" I said.

"That's it. Big-time bosses do this sort of thing all the time. Think of it as a training exercise. Okay, Peterson?"

"Yeah, sure."

"And of course," he added, "you'll let me know if anything happens with Baptista."

"Absolutely," I said. "You can count on me."

"Then it's all yours, big boy. It's all yours." And he waved me out of the room.

✳

My proddings weren't quite as enthusiastic about the idea of monitoring Joseph as they had been about Kale. But I figured if I'd come this far I'd might as well go the whole way, particularly if it meant I'd be sitting in a big-time office in a matter of days.

So as soon as I left the suite, I patched into Joseph's system. He was still at Kale's parents' house, standing in front of the bathroom mirror playing a dead harmonica. I could hardly find any other activity within him. His netgork channels were virtually empty, and his Web ties were entirely bypassed.

It wasn't until 4.28 minutes later, when George spoke to him from the hallway, that I located incoming data.

"Hey, Joseph," George called out. "I'm sorry to interrupt, but Ansie and I were wondering if you had a moment."

"Definitely, boss," replied Joseph. "Definitely."

He bent two more notes on his harmonica. Then he followed George into the living room, where Ansie was positioned on a sofa.

"I know you've got a lot on your mind," explained George. "But we thought it'd be nice to have a little family meeting. We have a surprise for you."

"Lay it on me," said Joseph, sitting in a chair.

"Well," said George, "Ansie and I are a bit concerned about the idea of you going back to New Mexico, especially in such an isolated place. So we've been thinking up ways to try to get you to stay here with us."

"Mmmm."

"We've decided we'd like to build a house for you, right here in our backyard."

"We'd really love to do it," said Ansie. "This way you'd have your privacy, and you could come and go as you pleased."

"Would it be solar?" asked Joseph. "With unenlivened walls?"

"Sure, if that's what you want," said George. "But we'd like you to be comfortable."

"We want to give you all the luxuries you deserve," said Ansie.

Joseph thought momentarily, then shook his whiskers. "Hey, the old man appreciates the offer, but it can't be done. You know me. I need that huge red mesa looming over my back, with the sky overhead so blue it's almost black."

"Damn it, Dad!" cried Ansie. "We're trying to make a sacrifice for you, to do what's best. This is serious. We're worried sick about you."

"Worried sick? Why should you be worried?" Joseph tightened his thigh muscles, bracing for the response.

"For Ray's sake," she replied. "You're 98 years old. Do you expect us to just relax when you go traipsing off to the edge of the world to live in some primitive adobe hut? And you've altogether stopped responding to us neurally. Is that going to continue too? You're going to cut us off completely?"

"You know how I feel about the Web," said Joseph.

"No, I don't know. I really don't. People who love you transmit signals of concern, and you don't even have the common decency to respond. How could a childhood experience be that traumatic?"

Joseph put his hands to his leathered face. "It wasn't a childhood experience."

"That's what you always said when I was growing up," she insisted. "You said you had nightmares about data when you were a kid."

"The nightmares weren't a lie, Ansie. They just weren't the whole story."

"Then what is the whole story? I want to hear it once and for all."

His eyes turned downward. "I was trying to make things easier for you," he said. "I know it didn't work. I know I wasn't the father you wanted me to be."

"I have no idea what you're talking about, Dad."

"I'm talking about exactly what you're afraid I'm talking about. About the hole in my life, the hole you've always hated."

"You're speaking nonsense," she protested.

"Relax, honey," said George. "At least let him talk. What is it about this hole, Joseph? Tell us."

"Look," he said hesitantly, "you two both had the meter in you at birth. You both grew up with it. So you came to love it, and your friends came to love it. The whole world did. Which is all fine by me. The difference is, I didn't grow up with the meter."

"We know that, Dad," said Ansie impatiently. "Your generation got implanted after birth. Big deal."

"Yes. But I didn't get implanted when the others did."

"I don't follow."

"I didn't get implanted until twelve years after the transition. For twelve years, while everyone else had the meter, I didn't."

Ansie stood up from the couch angrily. "You're playing another one of your games. That's totally impossible."

"No, it's not impossible," replied Joseph. "I should have told you a long time ago."

"This is ridiculous." She looked at her husband to see his reaction.

"Well," said George. "It does seem a bit strange, Joseph. I mean, why wouldn't you get the meter right away?"

"I really don't know," he replied. "They took away all my memories, even going back four years before I evaded the meter."

"You're saying there are sixteen years in the middle of your life that are completely blank?"

"That's right," he replied. "From 2004 to Ansie's birth."

"Great Ray!" exclaimed George. "That's something else. That's really something else."

"What about all those things you told me about my mother?" asked Ansie, her arms and legs trembling. "How do you explain them?"

"I made them up," said Joseph. "All I know is that her name was Rija Forrester, like I told you, and that she died when you were born in 2020."

"You're saying you have no idea what she was really like? No idea at all?"

"Nothing except that she must have been as beautiful as you and Kale."

"That's hardly what I'm talking about," burst out Ansie. "I'm talking about all the years I spent wondering who my mother was, why she was gone, why my father was so different. How could you wait until I was 57 years old to tell me this?" She turned down to look at the floor, tears falling from her eyes.

"It's okay, honey," said George. "I'm sure he never meant to hurt you."

"Believe it or not," said Joseph softly, "I thought you would be glad I didn't tell you."

There was a long pause as Ansie continued crying.

"I'm sure you were trying to handle things the best way you knew how," said George.

Joseph nodded.

"But then what really happened when Ansie was born?" continued George awkwardly.

"I never got to see Rija after she went to the hospital," said Joseph. "They put me in jail while they implanted Ansie with a meter. Then they implanted me, I got rehabilitated, and we started a new life."

George whistled. "So Ansie has been connected to the Web for longer than you? Could that be right? You were 41 years old when you first got the PIFFEN meter?"

"Yeah," said Joseph.

"Well, it's quite a story. It's really something else."

"It's not a story," interjected Ansie. "It's my life. My entire life."

"Of course, dear," said George.

"Thanks a lot, Dad," said Ansie bitterly. "Thanks for keeping me in the dark all this time. How considerate."

"I know I handled it badly," said Joseph. "But I've always loved you, Ansie. Can't you believe that?"

"Why should I?" she said.

"Because it's true. If you hadn't been in my life, I never would have been able to make it. Not even for a single day."

Ansie continued looking at the floor, although there was a calmness to her face that hadn't been there before. "Just promise me you won't tell Kale anything about this," she said. "Not a single word. With all she's going through, this is the last thing she needs to hear."

"If that's what you want," replied Joseph.

They looked at each other tentatively.

"Well, good then," said George. "It's all settled, fine and dandy."

So Ansie went to take a nap, George picked up his Stroke Compensation golf putter, and Joseph began packing his bags.

CHAPTER EIGHT

AFTER EATING her lunch at the Dudley house dining hall, Kale spent 47.28 minutes reviewing her meeting with Professor Morgaux, noting her own deficiencies. Her conclusion was that she'd been sloppy. She hadn't come across as an assimilated retrofitter.

In order to improve her understanding, she decided to observe a neural reconditioning practicum. With her imaging pointers, she located one in progress two buildings away. She peered through a window in the hallway, and from there she could see a group of retrofitters lying on their backs in module booths.

"Now this next step is critical," coached an assistant. "Please signal if you're not ready."

The class frequency remained still.

"I want you all to locate a damaged cell in the Z-register of quadrant IV of your epsilon space. Can everybody do that?"

"Yes," said the class in unison.

"Remember, you must attenuate the cell when I say so, using the Tavicz breathing method. Are you ready?"

"Ready," they said.

"Okay. Attenuate now. One, two, three. And... disattenuate. Good. Again, attenuate for three seconds. One, two, three. And...

disattenuate. Good! Very Good! Now repeat the sequence on your own until you notice a detectable improvement in your processability."

The students did as he said, each attempting to repair a segment of their neural tissue. Meanwhile, the professor passed through the room, guiding those that needed assistance.

After a few minutes, the students began to raise their heads from their module booths, indicating they had successfully completed the procedure. One of the earliest risers was Greggy Panagopoulos, who was in a module booth only a few feet from the classroom door.

"What are you doing here?" he transmitted through a spare netgork.

"Research," she signaled. "You make an excellent subject."

He rolled his eyes. "That's pretty much the last thing I want to be."

"I'm sorry. I didn't mean it like that."

"Are you sure?"

"Yes, really. I apologize."

"Well," replied Greggy, smiling slightly, "I suppose you *could* make it up to me."

"I'll tell you what. Why don't you join me for dinner tonight?"

Greggy became worried. "No, no. I was just teasing you."

"I'm serious," continued Kale. "I'd really like to have dinner with you."

The professor started barking new orders to the students. "That's me," transmitted Greggy. "I'll get back to you, okay?"

As Kale walked out of the classroom building, the warm sensation beneath her stomach began to emanate again. At the same time, her uncertainty index climbed to 94.31. Unsure how to reconcile the two, she browsed through Harvard Square.

When she passed a shuttle rental agency on Eliot Street, she entered the facility and requested a mini-shuttle with a dark blue chassis. The clerk intook her i.d. and pointed her to a late-model Thistler in the rear lot. Kale linked with its biochip and stepped into the cockpit, stroking the interior fur.

After consulting a series of shoreline maps on the travelers channel, she chose to fly north to Cape Ann. She specified a cruising altitude of 1649 feet, for optimal visibility. The shuttle departed off a nearby ascension ramp.

Once in the air, she considered what Chamy and Gemela had said about Greggy. She even loaded the most recent Current Population Survey into her system to do some compatible mate analysis. But before she could enter Greggy into the estimating equation, a small voice inside her said, "What is this? Must you analyze everything?"

As the Thistler stabilized, it approached the limits of the plant-free metropolitan area. The demarcation line where live trees were growing was just past the township of Beverly. To her surprise, the shuttle zipped across the line instead of rerouting.

Kale could hardly believe the change in earthly colors. The leaves of the trees appeared as brilliant reds, yellows, oranges, and greens. To the east she could even see the deep blue of the Atlantic. Due to the biologicals, she didn't expect to touch down anywhere in the vicinity, but when she checked for local markers, the travelers channel indicated a sanctioned landing field at the tip of the Cape, near Halibut Point. As a lark, she input the station coordinates.

The last thing she predicted was that the Thistler would comply. But 3.38 seconds later, it began its descent. Before she could reconfigure her data, the shuttle was taxiing to a weathered docking facility and positioning itself against a suction door.

The station appeared to be entirely unoccupied. She double-checked and reconfirmed that the travelers channel listed the site as an operational terminal. Its functional description was classified under "Public Beach and Swimming Facility."

When the suction door opened, Kale slowly stepped out into the station. She walked through the main hall for 68 feet until she came to the east wing. There she noticed a clear plexiglass tunnel, twelve feet in diameter, protruding across the landscape toward the ocean.

With her curiosity roused, she entered the tunnel. Her first observation was that the trees pressed up against the plexiglass from the outside. She noticed several flowers and insects, as well as a bigger moving creature, which she thought might be a lizard.

The exposure was exhilarating, yet a part of her couldn't help feeling scared. She'd been warned all her life of the danger of plants and animals, of their deathly toxic secretions, their lowly organic physiologies, and their seditious intentions. Now the real thing—not a database—was pushing in against her from all angles.

For a moment, she forgot about the thick sheet of plexiglass separating her from the plants. Her system filled with images of being choked by the leaves, and she recalled her mother shrieking that plants were odious and horrible. Around the next bend, the tunnel extended over the actual ocean surface and the plants came to an abrupt halt. Kale hurried forward in anticipation, amazed that her feet were only inches from the water.

When she came to the end of the tunnel, she discovered it led to a bulb-shaped pool of water. The pool was separated from the ocean by the plexiglass, but directly below it was the entire ocean environment. Kale remembered how her grandfather had once said that his generation enjoyed swimming in the ocean. She was so captivated by the water that she removed all her clothes.

Before I could fully intake her smooth skin, she dove to the bottom of the pool and swam toward some sort of sea creature. She identified the creature as a puckerfish, using her animal database, and she began staring at it as earnestly as it stared at her.

She continued staring at the puckerfish for the next 8.67 minutes, until her skin became wrinkled and pruned. Then she emerged from the pool, pretending to be the first human to crawl on land. Her nipples protruded firmly as she circled around the edge of the basin on her hands and knees, thinking she was both carbon and silicon, living and non-living, an entity with roots deeper than her PIFFEN meter.

While doing this she thought of Professor Morgaux. The way he spoke, the nature of his mannerisms, made her feel certain that the pre-Web world was no more foreign to him than to the creatures in the ocean. As she shook her black hair dry, a parallel thought came to her: Perhaps there were advantages to not being synchronized with one's meter. How else might one fully appreciate the pre-Web world?

When she got back to the Thistler, she requested an automatic return to Cambridge. Then she boldly sent a signal to Greggy Panagopoulos demanding that he accept her dinner invitation.

✸

That night they went to a fancy restaurant in downtown Boston. The food was brought in direct from the *Worcester* farm satellite, and everything was prepared by a Knauser 626i, with spectral differentiation and chromatic dispersion treatments.

"I've never seen hues like that," said Kale, pointing to a dish of broccoli appetizers in the shape of mermaids.

Greggy nodded. "How about a toast to the brain? To that ancient overlooked muscle."

"To the brain," replied Kale. She withdrew two glasses of Gold Nectar from the ExpressTube at their table. They clinked their glasses, sipped their Nectar, and took bites of the mermaids.

"You know," said Greggy, "one could imagine the brain as an entire world, with each neuron a separate economic agent."

"Except I doubt neurons would need PIFFEN meters."

"True," smiled Greggy. "It's a much purer world. But that's how Ray LeGhir got the idea for the meter—from studying nerve signal transmission."

"Really?" said Kale, as she pulled their optimally arranged plates from the ExpressTube. "I have a feeling your sources are a lot more interesting than this restaurants'."

"Yeah, well, thank Ray that food doesn't have to be retrofitted."

"Seriously, I don't think you realize how remarkable you are."

Greggy broke into an odd laughter, as if he were almost in pain.

"Did I say something?" asked Kale. "Are you okay?"

"I'm fine," he replied, catching his breath. "No one's ever said something like that to me. I'm pretty much uniformly despised. Not that I mind so much."

Kale looked at him admiringly. "Would you think I'm silly if I suggested we dance?"

"Not at all."

They got up and began swaying to the music of Chiasma, using internal sound generators to suit their own tastes. Kale enjoyed watching Greggy flip his tangled hair to emphasize his favorite chords. He had tight legs and a lean torso, which further complemented his dancing style, and he delicately twirled her each time the music reached a crescendo.

After 62.31 minutes, Kale whispered in Greggy's ear, "Let's get a room."

"What for?" he said.

"To catch our breath."

"Okay."

They checked in at the registration desk and rode an elevator to the 14th floor. Their room was burgundy and gold, with two queen size beds and four ExpressTubes. As soon as they entered, Greggy threw off his coat and lay down on one of the beds.

"I could use some rest," he said. "How about you?"

"Actually, I was hoping we could do something else."

"Like what?"

"Get to know each other better," she said.

"Okay, name your topic."

"I mean, besides talking, Greggy."

"More dancing?"

She smiled at him suggestively. "That's not what I mean either."

"No way," he stuttered. "Are you saying... you want to try to... to *bond*?"

Kale nodded.

"That's crazy. You're assimilated. I don't have anything you'd want."

"How do you know?"

"I'm a retrofitter, remember. There's no way I'd have any signals to offer."

"But it's not just the signals you have. It's how you use them."

Greggy shook his head. "That's why I'm at Harvard. Because I *don't* use them well."

"I'm not talking about efficiency. I know you sense there's more than that."

"So now you're saying I'm a wastebyte?"

"Maybe I am. Maybe I happen to find you a very attractive wastebyte."

Greggy gave her another deep stare, this time his lips barely forming a smile. "Just remember, you were the one who suggested this."

He climbed onto the bed as Kale approached from the other side. They positioned themselves face-to-face on their hands and knees, slowly pressing the tops of their skulls together so that their radio transceivers were joined. Then they began linking their channels— starting with their public ones and moving systematically to their private ones—until all their netgork space was fused into a mutual receptor.

Once they were fully bonded, Greggy's eyes lit up with excitement. He tried to show restraint by first investigating Kale's architecture, but the temptation was too much to resist. Within half a millisecond, he was like a child on a game channel, smothering himself with Kale's private input, starved for the fresh stimuli.

Meanwhile, Kale examined Greggy's neural interface tissue, thinking this would be a good way to find out about the life of a retrofitter. She quickly determined that his defects were trivial—they were all just circuit switch problems. It astonished her that something this mundane could have such a profound effect.

That was when she thought of an alternative: Why not interface with Greggy's body rather than his data? With a mischievous grin, she took her hands and rubbed them along Greggy's face and neck.

The sensation was quite gratifying to her—although I had no idea why. During the next 15.31 seconds, her pleasure level rose all the way to 98.74. She even began considering rubbing her legs against Greggy.

According to my analyzers, Greggy also was enjoying the odd routine, although he didn't seem to trust his own meter readings. He kept trying to distract himself by analyzing the chemical properties of the sweat on Kale's palms. Then all at once, he sat up and uncoupled their netgorks.

"We can't," he said. "We've got to stop."

"Why?" transmitted Kale. "What's the matter?"

"Your data. You just got a signal from Chamy."

"Chamy?" she said. "I didn't even notice."

"You'd better listen. It's serious." He routed the message to her audio track:

Hi Kale,

Sorry to disturb you. But remember what Mike Eu was working on? Well, he's figured it out, and you're the lucky target!

Your friend,

Chamy

"That's strange," said Kale. "Is this something about the private scrambler?"

"Possibly," replied Greggy. "He could be broadcasting from our systems right now. You see what I'm saying?"

"But we can't just stop. We have to at least finish what we've..."

"I'm sorry, Kale," he interrupted. "Mike's not the type of person I take lightly." His eyes locked onto hers for 0.26 seconds. Then he threw on his coat and left.

CHAPTER NINE

IT WASN'T until 1:58 AM Thursday morning that Kale crept back into her temporary apartment. Shaken by what had happened to her private netgork, she wanted to confront Chamy and Gemela. But they were both fast asleep, deeply entwined in their subconscious data, so Kale just lied down on her bunk bed.

She didn't blame Mike Eu for his infiltration scheme—it was something she probably would have tried herself, if only because it was supposedly impossible. And it only made sense that Greggy had ran out the way he had. His progress at Harvard depended entirely on his outward image.

What bothered her most was Chamy and Gemela's involvement. She felt sure they had encouraged Mike to try out his scheme on her, and she couldn't understand why they'd chosen such a bad time, when she'd been in the midst of bonding with a retrofitter.

The result was that she never fell asleep. She just replayed her memory circuits all night, puzzling over her roommates' behavior. As soon as the first light of the morning came, she slipped out of the apartment and walked up to the university.

I wasn't eager to continue my monitoring, since it was 6:07 AM, but my proddings made it clear I had a job to do. I figured I might as well send Kale a query, to see if I could draw her out of her mood.

"Hey, Keeler," I transmitted. "Top of the morning to you. Any developments for me?"

"No," she said. "I've only been awake 6.24 minutes."

"Sure, sure. But what about from yesterday? Any new lines of attack?"

"Maybe one or two."

"Like what?"

"Did you process the reports I sent?"

"Absolutely," I lied. "Absolutely."

"Then I'll tell you one thing. I've been going over what Morgaux said about all information regarding the pre-PIFFEN period being removed from the Web."

"Yeah? I hardly see how there could have been anything interesting about *that* period."

"Maybe not," she replied. "But it does seem strange. Why go to the trouble of rooting out all references to the transition, even in the remote data banks?"

"To cut storage costs," I said smugly. "What's so strange about that?"

"Maybe nothing. But what if the information was removed to hide something?"

"Is that what Morgaux thinks?"

"He's a bit reserved. It's hard to tell where he stands on the situation, and there are a lot of strands to pick up."

"So pick them up. Whatever it takes."

"I'm going to need to do some more sifting around. It could take time."

"Time is a non-issue," I replied sternly. "We don't want the tip of the iceberg. We want the whole bloody thing. Whatever it takes to get it. We've been through this before, Keeler."

"Then why don't you get me a bloody decent room?" she transmitted angrily. "How can you expect me to get any work done when you put me up with retrofit students?"

"My hands are tied, Keeler."

"And why is that, may I ask?"

"You know these retrofitters. They're screwed up, but they're not stupid. Every once in a while, they'll surprise you. Trivers thinks they might lead you to the story faster. If you let them, that is." I laughed wildly and cut the transmission before she could reply.

56 seconds later, Kale approached Widener Hall. She had heard old-time books were stored there, so she initiated the access impulse code to the rear entry.

Once inside, she followed a crusty hallway to the main foyer, where ancient sayings in unknown languages adorned the walls. She climbed a marble staircase to the second floor, and after passing nine rows of tiny drawers with letters on them, she came to a bright room with a high-arched ceiling and stained glass windows. Greggy Panagopoulos was seated at the far end, hunched over a dusty book.

"This must be what they call a library," said Kale, smiling.

"Very impressive," replied Greggy. "You've seen books before?"

"Of course. What are you processing?"

"You mean *reading*," he said.

"Yes, right, *reading*."

Greggy hesitated. "Listen, Kale, I've been thinking. I'm not sure it's such a good idea for you to be around me... at least not if you want to continue making efficient bids."

"You don't want to?" she asked.

"It doesn't much matter to me. I've let go of the desire. But you have a future."

"I'm still interested in what you're reading."

"Are you short on topics or something?"

"What I'm short on is meaning, like all the rest of us."

He took a deep breath. "Okay. I'm reading an article in *The Journal of Molecular Biology* from Spring 2009. It's called, 'PIFFEN Meter Evasion: The Chemical Possibilities.'"

Kale looked at him blankly.

"It's about various drugs people could have used to evade the early meter implants," he explained.

"Drugs?" she said. "How?"

"That's what they were trying to figure out."

"I wasn't aware such things happened."

"They don't anymore," he added. "Now that we're born with the meter, it wouldn't be possible. But before bioelectronic birthing, babies came from women's stomachs."

Kale stared at him dumbfounded. "Weird."

"The only people who could have evaded the meter were those who were born before the transition, because they were the ones who had to be implanted through the water supply. For them, it seems certain alkaloid-type drugs could have been used to block the PIFFEN cells from attaching to their brains."

"And how many people did this?" asked Kale.

"Probably no one. I mean, the authors didn't say anyone tried. They just showed it was chemically possible."

"Well, what does Morgaux think?"

"I doubt he's seen this article," he said. "It was a mistake that it was even left in the stacks."

"I'm sure he'd be interested."

Greggy shook his head. "Not his style."

"But what if there really were some evaders?" she asked.

"You're talking 0.01 probability."

"Unlikely things do happen. I just learned yesterday that my grandfather was a friend of Ray LeGhir."

"What?" he exclaimed. "LeGhir's been dead for at least 69 years."

"Yeah, and my grandfather's 98."

Greggy slid to the edge of his chair. "Then what's his name?"

"Joseph Baptista."

"All right," he said. "I'll investigate this claim."

"I thought you didn't think it was such a good idea for us to be involved?"

"I don't. But your grandfather isn't you, is he?"

She paused for a moment. "I'll tell you one thing," she said. "You've definitely got organics in your blood, Greg."

"And it would be an even bigger discovery if I found you didn't."

❂

From Widener Hall, Kale went to the theory lecture hall. Morgaux wasn't scheduled to speak until that afternoon, but she wanted to work on decoding his Instability Theorem. The best place to do it, she figured, was in his delivery chambers.

She began by filling her head with preparatory equations. Then she settled into a chair and zeroed in on the theorem, methodically attacking it line by line. Morgaux had omitted steps in a few critical places, but it soon became clear she could follow his work. By 10:28 AM, she comprehended it in its entirety.

The gist of the theorem was that an idealized economy could stray from an efficient outcome. If people were triggered to think differently about the future, then it was possible the distribution of resources could be altered. This meant that certain pieces of data could exist that people were better off *not* knowing—thus the efficiency of missing information.

The finding was interesting to Kale, but she had no illusions about it being sufficient material for a big-time story on the Public Netgorks. It was just a theory, hardly the province of mainstream appeal. She felt sure Trivers sought something of greater significance.

Just as she was contemplating how to file her report, three men wearing gas masks barged into the lecture hall. "Kale Catherine Keeler," they transmitted conjunctively, "by authority of the Web Protection Agency, we hereby place you under physical arrest."

"Arrest? For what?" she exclaimed.

"Plant palpation and suspicion of toxic contamination," they replied through external speakers.

"I'm a reporter," she said. "I'm acting on assignment."

"We'll see about that." They placed her in Web-secluding handcuffs and escorted her out of the lecture hall. After propping her against a cement pole with a rotating triangle, they sprayed her with a preliminary detoxicant. A moment later, she was shoved aboard a private shuttle.

Kale was utterly disoriented. She tried transmitting to me nine distinct times, until she realized the handcuffs were blocking her outgoing signals. 86.49 seconds later, the shuttle set down on a WPA roof top and the three men dragged her into the headquarters. They immediately deposited her in a quarantine cell and activated a detox jet. Once the room was cleared of all bacteria, the agency chief, Jackson Cranston, entered. "All right, Ms. Keeler," he said. "We've scoped you and you're not infected. But that's the least of our concerns."

"What are your concerns?"

"You've intentionally broken the Second Law of the Internal. Do you deny this?"

"No."

"I'll be perfectly honest with you, Ms. Keeler," he continued. "We've seen cases of people who've accidentally grazed against plants or animals. But never in all my years have we seen anything like this. If you want a chance at a cell with a window, you better start talking."

"About what?"

"Don't toy with me. I'm referring to a particular sycamore tree in the Santa Monica Canyon and a certain weed in Cambridge. And let's not forget about your little excursion to Halibut Point."

"I had clearance to land in Cape Anne," she countered.

"Why do you think we gave you clearance?" he said angrily. "Now stop bitwasting us, Ms. Keeler. You're a threat to world security, a public hazard. We know you're in collusion with the lower forms. And we know all about your animal database."

"I'm not in any collusion. The animal database was child's play."

"Ha! That's precisely the most dangerous kind. But very well. We didn't expect your cooperation. Say goodbye to the light, Ms. Keeler."

"Wait a minute!" she cried. "Don't I get to signal someone?"

"You've got sixty seconds. Then you're out of here." He cleared the lock on her radio transceiver and went to wait in the hallway.

Kale tried to formulate her thoughts, but she was unsure who to call upon. Her parents? Me? Her roommates? Morgaux? Greggy?

Surprisingly, she settled on me, although only because the thought of explaining herself to anyone else seemed too much to bear.

"Ralph," she transmitted, "I'm in a bind. A major bind."

"A bind?" I replied nonchalantly. "So what's new?"

"This is serious, Ralph. I'm being held by the WPA." She proceeded to give me the full details.

"What?" I transmitted, faking surprise. "You *touched* two plants and went swimming in the *ocean*? I don't understand, Keeler. I mean, I'll do what I can. But hell, you broke an Internal Law. The WPA doesn't like to bargain, you know. Not even with the Gork."

"That's reassuring, Ralph."

"Just try to hang tight, Keeler. And we'll be in touch."

"How?" she replied. "How will we be in touch?"

But then her sixty seconds expired, and her transceiver locked up.

CHAPTER TEN

I GUESS I had a heroic streak because I went straight up to Trivers' suite to inform him of Kale's predicament. I even ignored his secretary when she told me he was busy eating lunch. I just waltzed into his office and poured out the whole scoop.

To my surprise, Trivers was understanding. He waited for me to finish speaking, then he calmly looked up from his plate of food.

"Very good, Ralph," he said. "Very good. You've behaved appropriately, you've done the right thing."

"Thank you," I replied. "So what's my next move?"

"I'll handle it from here," he said. "Why don't you enjoy a nice lunch? Here, have a piece of my steak. It's a premium cut, made in a very special way, and I think you'll find it quite delectable."

"Uh, thank you," I replied, averting my eyes from his odd meal. "To tell you the truth, Clyde, what I really have a hankering for is one of those SuperMold sandwiches."

"I see, I see. In that case, let it be my treat. What kind of SuperMold would you like?"

"How about a simulant pepperoni sub in the shape of a hockey puck?" I asked.

"No problem, no problem." Trivers snapped his fingers, and the order appeared at his Executive ExpressTube. "Here you go, Ralph. Enjoy."

I thanked him and headed downstairs to my office. Then I wolfed down my sub, along with 27 ounces of PepTime. My proddings reprimanded me for intaking too many calories, but I didn't care. At least I'd avoided eating the strange, unformed food Trivers had offered me.

By that time, Kale was in her prison cell. My headware still allowed me to access her system, even though she herself was blocked from inputting to the Web. But there wasn't much for me to monitor, since everything around her was dark. The only items I could locate in her room were a thin cotton mat and a bedpan.

According to her data, she was scheduled to receive just one meal a day, and she wasn't even allowed to process her incoming signals. The whole scenario was quite depressing, to say the least. Kale's pleasure quotient was down 56.24 points from an hour earlier, and mine had fallen almost as much—probably because I kept thinking I should have somehow warned her about her plant-touching behavior.

But then I noticed a curious thing. Kale's pleasure level started to reverse its decline. As she came to accept the fact that she was being guided solely by her own body, with no outside assistance from the Web, a proud sensation began to sweep through her system. She took delight in knowing that her own body was providing all the necessary data to regulate itself.

I watched her index creep up another 18.47 points, and I was beginning to think I'd seen it all. Then an even stranger thing happened. The three men who'd first arrested Kale burst into her cell. "Ms. Keeler!" they shouted. "You're free to go now!"

"Huh?" replied Kale, as the familiar buzz of the Web began pervading her operating system. "I've only been in here for 10.18 minutes."

"We made an error," they explained. "On behalf of Mr. Cranston, we've been instructed to apologize for any inconvenience."

"An error?"

"You've been found innocent of any unsanctioned activities, Ms. Keeler. You're free to go as you please."

They pointed her to an exit. 12.18 seconds later she was on a sidewalk under the bright sun, two blocks from the downtown Government Center.

Kale immediately sent me a signal of thanks, as she assumed I was the one who'd set her free. I didn't see any reason to set her straight, so I took the credit and told her she owed me big-time. Then I signaled Trivers for the details, apologizing for my Web usage.

"It was a piece of cake," he transmitted. "I told Cranston some malarky about how we were doing a study on the WPA's response mechanism. I explained that we couldn't warn them of Keeler's behavior because we wanted to make sure their response was unbiased."

"That was clever," I replied. "Very clever."

"All in a day's work, right?"

"Yeah, I guess so. But uh, aren't you a bit concerned about what Keeler actually did?"

"Nah. She's a special reporter. She's got special habits. Tell her to forget it and just get back to work. That's all I care about."

"Absolutely," I said. "And you want me to proceed with the assignment as usual?"

"Yes, Ralph. Proceed, proceed."

✺

As I cut the transmission, Kale ordered a falafel hovercraft with vegetable crisps in the shape of playing cards. She stopped at a nearby public ExpressTube to retrieve the order, but all it contained were the crisps. "*Insufficient value to complete order,*" announced the Tube.

Laughing, Kale sat down at a shiny ingestion booth. After the morning's events, she was grateful just to have her freedom again. People came and went in and out of the ingestion booth, each performing their optimal actions, and she watched with fascination. She barely even noticed a request from her kidneys to supplement her crisps with liquid. 12.45 seconds passed before she acknowledged the deficiency and got a drink of water.

When she was done eating, she processed her incoming signals. Although there were 12,012 impulses on her social netgork, she was more interested in her family netgork, which held only 329 signals. The ones from her mother were particularly short and evasive:

Hi, Kale. Hope the assignment's going well!

Kale, dear, I'd love to know the status of you and Greggy Panagopoulos!

Honey, we've decided to dynamize the epidermal pigments on the exterior of the house!

In contrast, her father's signals were unusually descriptive. One even said:

Dear Kale,

Your mom and I are doing extremely well. Our pleasure levels have never been so high (as I'm sure you're aware), and our daily routines are as perfect as ever. The only unfortunate thing, I'm sorry to report, is that your grandfather has decided to return to New Mexico. Of course, we'll miss him a great deal.

By the way, I'm enjoying my Gravity Deniers tremendously.

I've already extracted 38.47 satisfaction units from them. So thank you again, dear, and good luck on the assignment.

Kale had never known her father to be the first to tell her something important in the family. Ever since she'd been born, her mother had always been the primary disseminator of family data. The disparity compelled Kale to question Ansie.

"Hello, Mom?" she transmitted. "How come you didn't tell me about Joseph leaving?"

"Oh, honey. It's just one of those things I didn't think was worth fretting over. You know how Grandpa gets. Once he sets his mind on something, there's no stopping him. I learned that lesson long ago."

"Well, when is he leaving?" asked Kale.

"This evening at 6:02 PM."

"I wish I could say gooddata to him."

"Grandpa will understand, dear. You need to be more easy on yourself. Why don't you have dinner tonight with Greggy?"

"Greggy Panagopoulos? I'm not seeing him anymore."

"But he looked like such a handsome boy from the images I gleaned. Didn't you two have a high compatibility rating?"

"I don't know, Mom. I never checked."

"Honey, you have to check your compatibility rating. And if it's a 95 or above, you need to ask him to get a sperm extraction. You're almost 27 years old, dear. You've got to start thinking about these things. I made George get an extraction when I was 21."

"Mom, please. Greggy's a retrofitter."

Ansie gasped. "What in Ray's name! A retrofitter? Kale Katherine Keeler! How could you?"

"It's over, Mom. Forget it."

"Did he force himself on you? Are you okay, dear? Great Ray! He must have been absolutely foaming to get at your data!"

"No, Mom. It wasn't like that. He was very sweet. Just because he doesn't have a perfect meter, doesn't make him a raving maniac."

"Oh, you and your grandfather."

"Forget it."

"But I wish things weren't so hard for you, dear. I wish I knew why these features of the world that help the rest of us have so much trouble working for you."

"I'm fine."

"Maybe you should intake today's Web poem. It's called, *We're All Together in This.*"

"All right, Mom, I'll try."

CHAPTER ELEVEN

AFTER FINISHING WITH HER SIGNALS, Kale returned to the lecture hall. She chose a seat in the rear of the hall so that she wouldn't have to see Chamy and Gemela. Then she watched Professor Morgaux mount the suspension field.

"Settle down, please," he said, depositing two black velvet boxes on the podium. "I'm going to be conducting a special experiment today, and I'll need a volunteer."

Six students signaled willingness. Morgaux randomized, selecting a tall female named Cassie.

"The item I have here is something that none of my previous classes have seen," he said, as he removed a cube-shaped object the size of a human head from the larger velvet box. "Registry Implants was uncharacteristically cooperative in letting me borrow it, probably because they have no record of what it is. But I happen to be quite certain it's an early predecessor of the PIFFEN meter. Obviously, it wasn't designed to be internalized, as you can see."

The class laughed hesitantly.

"Does anybody want to speculate how this device worked and what it did?"

"You stuck your finger in that hole and it gave you a manicure," suggested Cassie.

"Close," replied Morgaux. "You have the first part right. The device served as what was called a cash register."

"A *cash register*," repeated the class.

"In the old days, people used a medium called currency to store value. This currency was in the form of metal discs and rectangular pieces of paper. Since there was no ExpressTube, each consumer had to walk up to a cash register with his or her chosen products and insert a finger into this cylindrical orifice." He pointed to a black hole at the base of the cube-shaped object.

"The device would calculate the maximum amount the consumer was willing to pay, and that would be how much currency the consumer had to exchange for the desired products." Morgaux rested his hands on his hips. "Is that clear so far?"

"*Yes*," replied the class.

"So the question I want you all to ponder is, how did the cash register calculate the consumer's maximum willingness to pay?"

"Through the Web?" ventured a group of students.

"I'm afraid not," replied the professor. "The Web wasn't in existence yet."

"Through something like the Web?" offered a second group.

"No, not exactly. The cash register was a terribly unsophisticated instrument, not in real-time like the PIFFEN meter. It followed an elementary search algorithm, testing a number of values until it located the threshold price beyond which the consumer no longer wanted a product. The electrochemical satisfaction impulses emanating from the consumer's finger prevented him or her from faking the threshold point." Morgaux looked up at the class. "Is that processed?" he asked.

"*Processed*," they replied.

"Good," said the professor. "Let's actually try it. Pick a product, Cassie. Not too expensive, please."

"How about some Chameleon eyeliner?" she said.

"Fine." Morgaux retrieved the eyeliner from the classroom ExpressTube, holding it high to show the class. He handed it to Cassie.

"Okay," he said to her, "you're the consumer and I'm the seller. You've just selected this product. Now place your right index finger in the orifice, as if you were going to buy it."

A number appeared on the register's display screen. "What's it read?" he said.

"48,569.12," replied Cassie, unimpressed.

"Good. That's your maximal willingness to pay for Chameleon eyeliner, in uniform value units. And what else does it happen to be?"

"*Minimum average cost,*" said the class in unison, having instantaneously accessed the commodity channel.

"Exactly!" exclaimed Morgaux. "And why is her maximal willingness to pay equal to the minimum average cost of producing the eyeliner?"

"Because she's not stupid," said Gemela. "She knows she can get it anytime she wants for that price, so why would she be willing to pay more?"

"That's right. Even though the register is able to read Cassie's mind, she's still on an equal footing because she can access the Web to find out the true cost of producing the eyeliner. So neither party can exploit the other. And that's why we're efficient. Does everyone understand this?"

Class-wide affirmation was transmitted.

"Okay. We're ready to take it a step further. Suppose Cassie didn't have a PIFFEN meter. Suppose she was disengaged from the Web. In fact, let's suppose there simply was no Web. Then how much would Cassie be willing to pay for the eyeliner?"

Greggy Panagopoulos shot up his arm.

"Yes, Mr. Panagopoulos?"

"It's a trick question," he said. "If all products were traded over that device, then she wouldn't be willing to pay anything for it."

"Excuse me?" replied Morgaux.

"She wouldn't need the eyeliner for survival," explained Greggy, "and sellers would know this. So her entire budget would end up being spent only on those products that were necessary for subsistence, because she'd obviously rather keep on living than not."

Morgaux looked up nervously. "I'm afraid that's a bit too speculative for this class," he said. "The correct answer is that without the presence of the Web, Cassie's maximal willingness to pay would be indeterminate. Firms would know consumers' preferences through the registers, but consumers would remain in the dark about production costs. Thus we'd have instability."

The students all transmitted signals of confusion—even Kale was puzzled by the professor's sudden vagueness. But Morgaux continued hurriedly.

"That constitutes our exploration of the pre-Web world. Now we're ready to turn to the PIFFEN meter, a dynamic device that completely overpowers the cash register."

He withdrew a model of the meter from the smaller velvet box. "What we have here is a precise duplicate of a PIFFEN meter, enlarged one hundred-fold for easier viewing."

Kale patched into Morgaux's optic nerves. She'd never before examined the structure of the meter. It resembled a tiny chevron bead, except instead of a hole piercing its center, two small nodes protruded from either end.

"You've all had experience using your own meter—though perhaps not very efficiently," said the professor. "The basic premise of this course is that we can speed your reassimilation by exposing you to its inner detail." He projected a cross-section of the meter and its relationship to the brain onto the three-dimensional display.

"In this context," he continued, "you can see that the actual meter is about a tenth of a millimeter in length, with inhibitor receptors in the posterior node and output fibers in the anterior node. The meter is lodged at the base of the hypothalamus so that the inhibitor receptors are strategically positioned to perform complimentary analysis."

He projected another view of the meter. "Here, the tip of the posterior node has been shaved to reveal the receptors. Each tiny receptor corresponds to a specific commodity produced in the economy, such as Chameleon Eyeliner. All told, there are 88,983,707,413 receptors—one for every brand of every type of good or service that can be purchased in the marketplace."

To this last comment, a group of students transmitted a question impulse. "What about in the past?" they asked, "when there used to be *new products*?"

"Aha," said Morgaux. "I'm glad you're thinking. The meter used to come with blank receptors in the event that new products were invented. Now that's no longer necessary."

"We still don't understand what exactly the receptors do," complained several students.

"Okay, let's trace what happens in Cassie's PIFFEN meter when she purchases the Chameleon Eyeliner," offered the professor.

"*Okay*," replied the class.

"The first thing that occurs when Cassie buys the eyeliner is that the receptor associated with it measures the pleasure she receives from the purchase, as reflected in her hypothalamus. At the same time, all of Cassie's other receptors recalculate their commodity's contribution to her satisfaction level in order to capture any cross-effects from the eyeliner purchase.

"Once these contributions are calculated—and, by the way, this is done every tenth of a second—the information is transferred to the central cortex of her meter, where it is processed, rescaled in value units, and transmitted to the output fibers in the anterior node. Then the data is sent by power line carrier to her packet radio transceiver. You know about that, right?"

"*Yes*," mouthed the class.

"We're ready for the most important part. Since every human has a transceiver located in the fontanel of his or her skull, all of our transceivers together form a system of points. This system of points, or grid, is precisely what constitutes the Web. It is what enables all of us to continuously access Cassie's satisfaction levels, along with everyone else's, in order to make our daily decisions. *This* is what makes us efficient!"

A silent whir of excitement overcame the room.

"And the reason the Web works so well," continued Morgaux, "is that our data is shipped via packets that are relayed from one brain to the next across adjacent transceivers. Each transceiver requires very little power, only enough to reach its nearest neighbor, and there are virtually an unlimited number of paths any particular packet can take, for maximum reliability."

As the professor paused, a male in his early forties put out a signal. Kale scanned the identity channel and determined that the person was Mike Eu.

"Yes?" replied Morgaux, with apparent hesitation.

"Based on what you've described," said Mike, "I'm curious how the security of private information is maintained?"

Kale winced at the question.

"I'm not sure why you bring that up," said Morgaux. "For those who don't recall, private information is any information that doesn't effect economic efficiency. The primary function of the meter has little to do with such data. But of course, the Web itself is perfectly equipped for all data sources. Is that why you ask the question?"

"I guess," said Mike, suppressing a smile.

"Well, the security of a channel carrying private information is maintained in the same way as for public information—except that only authorized individuals can bypass the relevant code for private information. Does that answer your question, Mr. Eu?"

"Perfectly," said Mike.

"Now you see how far we've come from the constraints of our own nerve fibers, which by themselves can only transmit signals at the piddly rate of about 300 feet per second. Just think, for instance, of the sad predicament of those 200-foot lizards that used to roam the earth. Why, if you kicked one of them in the rear, it would take him well over a second to process the signal in his brain and swat you back in the face with his tail."

The students laughed.

"So you see the value of the Web?"

"*Yes!*" they exclaimed. "*We do!*"

"Good. That's it for today. Thank you."

The professor stepped down from the suspension field, and the students began efficiently gathering their possessions. But Kale stayed perfectly still—as did I. And somehow we both let our thoughts drift to an earlier time, a time of lowly cash registers and odd Webless interactions.

CHAPTER TWELVE

SADLY, there seemed no way to understand our past. I tried projecting back to the pre-PIFFEN world, I really did. But it was a gigantic blur of uncertainty, and my proddings kept whispering that the endeavor was beyond my ability.

Kale didn't have much better luck. No images of the past occupied her operating system. She did realize, however, that Morgaux's cash register demonstration held a glimmer of opportunity.

She decided to convince Morgaux that she appreciated his subtleties, that she shared his concerns. As she headed for his office, tracing the various alternatives, she searched for the best way to gain his trust. She was so caught up in the analysis that she didn't notice Chamy following behind her.

After 42 seconds of unsuccessful signaling, Chamy finally ran up next to her and spoke directly to her face.

"Kale Keeler," she said. "Kale Keeler, the visiting scholar, please respond!"

"Chamy," said Kale, emerging from her data. "How are you?"

"I'm fine, which you would know if you hadn't been ignoring my signals all day." She moved into the sun so that her lips glistened.

"I've been busy," explained Kale. "To tell you the truth, I'm still a bit upset about last night."

"What do you mean? We did you a favor. Your root system didn't want to bond with Greggy."

"How do you know that?"

Chamy pressed in her lips. "How do you think?"

"The thing is, Chamy, it's not exactly pleasant to have someone invade your private netgork."

"Mike understands that, but he needed to try out what he's been working on. It's not like he let any of your data leak into public channels. Mike's totally conscientious about those things. It was a good application, it really was."

"You should have warned me first."

"I did warn you, the first time I saw you," replied Chamy.

"I still think I deserve something for being Mike's guinea pig."

"Like what?"

"How about if we meet with Mike later today?"

"Yeah, I suppose we could do that. Why?"

"I think I might have another application for him."

"This better be good," said Chamy.

On her way to the Littaeur Center, Kale brushed her hand against a row of cement poles with rotating triangles. As she did this, she imagined them to be trees. If the toxicity of plants was caused by the transition, she reasoned, then maybe people weren't as distrusting of plants in the old days. Maybe there weren't even any Internal Laws.

I was immediately concerned by this line of thought. The last thing I needed were more violations on Kale's part, so I sent her a series of supervisory command memos. By the time she was done processing them, she was already on the second floor of the Littaeur Center.

"Hello, Kale," called out Morgaux from the doorway of his office.

"I was just going to query you. We've got an unexpected opening in our seminar tomorrow, and I was hoping you could fill it."

"Tomorrow?" replied Kale, stalling for a response from Jane Friedland.

"It's an informal gathering of professors and advanced students," he said. "We were hoping you could present some of your findings from your dissertation."

"I suppose I could pull something together. Can I ask you a quick question though?"

Morgaux shrugged, motioning her into his office.

"I've been thinking about the cash register you demonstrated today," she said. "I'm still not sure why consumers would shop at a store with one of them if they could avoid it."

"They wouldn't if they had a choice," he replied briskly. "I was assuming all stores had them."

"Did they?"

"No one knows."

"But even if they did, why wouldn't each store want to cut its price a bit to capture a bigger share of the market?"

"It depends on how competitive the market was," he said. "If one seller controlled all the stores, prices wouldn't have to fall."

"So that's what you think happened?" she asked.

"I don't see any other reason why the registers would have been introduced."

"Then why did you disagree with Greggy's comment about subsistence-based living?"

"Please," he groaned. "I wish I could get my hands on him."

"Why? What he said seemed perfectly reasonable to me."

"No, no, no. All I'd wanted to do was show that the registers could have been destabilizing. And then he launches into that speculative mess."

"But what makes him wrong? I don't see it."

"For Ray's sake," he exploded. "I don't have to justify a damn thing to you. Now please leave. I have work to do."

✸

Kale knew enough not to allow Morgaux's behavior to ruffle her. Rather, she took his outburst as verification that he was withholding information, and she told herself that it was simply a matter of creating the right setting for him to reveal it.

But first she was anxious to resolve the issue of the odd signals she'd received from her mother. Her hope was that Mike Eu would agree to help her. After a quick dinner, she walked to his room in Winthrop House.

Both Chamy and Mike were waiting when she arrived. The three of them engaged in small talk for 89 seconds. Then Mike cocked his head slightly. "Chamy mentioned there might be something I could do to compensate you for the other day," he said awkwardly.

"Yes," she replied. "I need to get past my mother's scrambler."

"That violates world law."

"World law didn't stop you from breaking my code," said Kale.

"I don't know," he said hesitantly.

"Come on, Mike. I'm not asking for a full installation. I just want to get into a small cell of my mother's netgork space. I think you owe me that much, for using me as your test site."

"What is it you want from her netgork?" he asked.

"She's been acting strangely. Sending me unusual signals."

"That's supposed to be enough to motivate me?"

"All I know is that it has something to do with my grandfather."

"Then why don't you just ask him?"

"He left for New Mexico this afternoon," explained Kale. "And he doesn't use the Web."

"Oh, I see," said Mike. "Now we're getting somewhere. A weirdness. A scene of bizarreness." He dragged out a carousel of transceiver detection organisms from under his bed and accessed the almanac channel. "Spectrum detection is best at sunset, especially on clear days like this. I need your mom's code."

"She's a blue card: 034/157-58-85-7; region 053188."

He entered the data and began connecting his equipment. "What we're going to do is bounce signals off her radio and look at refraction rates. We'll do it repeatedly from orthogonal dimensions. Then we'll just gather the results and fit a non-linear equation, using maximum likelihood estimators."

"It's that easy?" said Kale.

"Anything's easy if you've got the right molecular equipment. But who else knows how to get refraction rates orthogonally?"

"Be careful, Mike," interrupted Chamy. "You can't let this stuff get into the wrong hands."

"Don't you worry, baby. It's under control. Now remember, Kale, we're just estimating your mom's spectrum code. We could be wrong. So when you enter the netgork, check first to see if it really is your mom's. If not, we'll have to reestimate the equation."

"And the person won't know I'm entering?"

"No. Not at all."

Mike input the activation data to his equipment and raised his arm to offer Kale an entrance signal. Before he could give the cue, however, a warning impulse issued from his auxiliary security monitor.

"Wasted bitdoo!" he exclaimed. "You've set me up! Who are you? A flitting Web Monitor?"

"No," said Kale. "Of course not."

"Then what type of wastebyte are you?"

"I'm just a visiting scholar, for Ray's sake. I'm not here to cause any trouble."

"Right! That's why your netgork code is creeping with overlay transfers!"

"What?"

"You're pirated," explained Mike. "Somebody's monitoring all your impulses."

"That can't be. This must be some kind of joke. Or else your organisms are infected."

"Impossible. I know overlay transfers when I see them."

"This is insane," she said, as fear slid into her abdomen. "Who's doing this monitoring?"

"I can't get a trace. It reeks big-time. The pirater's got heavy-duty protection."

"I don't understand. I really don't."

Mike took a deep breath. "Let me get this straight," he said slowly. "You're trying to tell me that you didn't know you were being pirated?"

"Yes, that's what I'm saying, Mike."

"Think about it," interjected Chamy. "If Kale knew she was being pirated, would she be so stupid as to try this with you?"

"Yeah, well..."

"It's true," said Kale. "If I'm being pirated, that's all the more reason I need your help."

"And why should I get caught up in the middle? I don't even know anything about you."

"I'd hardly say that," said Kale. "You did break into my private netgork."

"So what? I didn't search your system. It was just a test. How was I supposed to know you'd be creeping with transfers?"

"Maybe if I explained to you what I'm really involved in..."

"No, please!" he replied. "I don't want to know."

"Look," she said. "I'm not sure why you're so interested in private information, but my guess is you're not so different from me. The fact is, we live in a system of bitwaste on top of bitwaste. So are you going to help me or not?"

Mike looked at Kale like he'd just been delivered a tray of rainbow-colored flying saucer burritos. "Well... I'm not even sure I can," he stuttered. "I'd have to rig up a way to bend around the overlays."

"Try," Chamy encouraged. "At least try."

"And what's my reward?"

"How about some motion bonding?" said Chamy, with mischievous eyes. "The kind you like, with transducer data."

"All right, damn it. I'll do it." He relinked to his equipment and began constructing a wave path around the overlays.

"Okay," he said, after fiddling for 28 seconds, "the first thing you should know, Kale, is that the pirater's been on you since Monday afternoon. I see trailer marks starting with images of a big man with yellow hair. Hey, wait a minute. Is that Clyde Trivers, the CEO of the Gork?"

"Yeah, that's Trivers," said Kale, studying the image with her boosters.

"Wow," said Chamy. "It looks like you were in a conference room or something. Who's the other guy to your left, overweight and dorky looking?"

"That's Ralph Peterson, my channel boss," replied Kale. "Does this mean that Trivers and Peterson are the ones pirating me?"

"Not necessarily," said Mike. "They just happened to have been with you when the pirater started tapping you. In fact, hold on a second. Yeah, now I'm picking up trailer marks from even earlier than that. They're from last Friday morning, for just a few seconds. Is that you at an ingestion booth, eating a ballerina sweet roll?"

"Yeah, but I hadn't even started my assignment then."

"Well, somebody must have known something."

Kale mopped her forehead. "What have I gotten myself into?"

"Relax," he said. "If my overlays work, in 34 seconds you'll be *into* your mom's head."

"What about the pirater?" she said. "I mean, if I find something important, I hardly want to be advertising it."

"I know, I know. I'm building some temporary protection for you right now. It's only going to work while you're in this room."

"Fine. I'll take what I can get."

Mike proceeded to set up an interference circuit to jam the overlay transfers.

Of course, as soon as he connected it, everything on my headware turned to white noise—pure random white noise. And there wasn't a thing I could do about it. Not a single thing.

CHAPTER THIRTEEN

I HAVE TO CONFESS, my first reaction was one of relief. I'd never been that thrilled to use Trivers' headware in the first place, and I guess I felt some sort of perverse pleasure in seeing the device get outsmarted.

But it was only a matter of 1.42 seconds before my proddings went into their hyper-frenetic mode, reminding me of my deeper purpose. Plus they pointed out, quite vigorously, that I still had my promotion to think about. So before I knew it, I was rushing up to Trivers' suite again.

Once I made it past Trivers' secretary, I saw the big boss had concerns of his own. His hair was practically standing on end, and without even giving me a chance to speak, he launched straight into one of his trademark tirades.

"Peterson!" he shouted. "Where the hell are your reports on Baptista? All humanity depends on them! They're crucial, absolutely crucial! I need those reports!"

"On Joseph Baptista?" I asked humbly. "I already sent you everything I got on him yesterday."

"I'm talking about for today, you idiot!"

"But I haven't monitored him today. You said I could watch over him sporadically."

"For Ray's sake," he growled. "Not *that* sporadically. By now he's probably already left for New Mexico."

"Uh, actually," I said, "I don't think he's scheduled to leave until 6:02 PM."

"Then get on him, Peterson. It's 5:58 right now. I want all the details on his trip home!"

"Absolutely, Clyde. But there's something I think you ought to know."

"Make it quick, damn it."

"It's about your headware device." I was about to break the news to him when suddenly Mike's interference circuit dissolved. All at once I could see Kale walking away from Mike's room.

"So go on," demanded Trivers. "What the hell is it you want to tell me about the headware?"

"Well, uh, actually," I stumbled, "I was wondering if you had one in another color. I'm sort of getting tired of black."

"What the hell, Peterson? I don't have time for this crap! I want that report on Baptista before I go home!"

"Absolutely," I replied. "I'm sorry, Clyde. It'll get top priority. I promise."

When I entered Joseph's system, he was in the midst of negotiating through the crowds at the mega-shuttle terminal in New Haven. People kept staring at his long, braided hair, and it took him an extra 27 seconds to find his shuttle.

He kept his eyes shut the whole way to New Mexico, and I was afraid I'd have nothing to report. Luckily, at the Albuquerque terminal he had to show the customs officers his clearance code for unprotected living among earthly forms, so he opened his visual system.

From there, he hopped into a private mini-shuttle and headed east. He swerved around Cedar Crest to pick up the back route markers to Santa Fe, his eyes focusing on the rugged roots of piñon and juniper trees. Then he shot past the delicate Ortiz mountain and glanced to the west, where he saw the whole backside of the Sandia Crest, lifted up almost a vertical mile above the Rio Grande. The setting sun left a red-purple residue in the clouds, and Joseph said softly into the wind, "Ramp to the stars."

51 seconds later, he crossed the southern limits of Santa Fe. He closed his eyes again when he came to the two bowl-shaped hills known as Monte Sol and Monte Luna, for they were littered with huge, unoccupied adobe homes. None of the people who had flocked to Santa Fe before the transition lived there anymore. Only the local Indians remained in town, and they were clustered around the plaza's quasi-protected zone, where there stood a relay station with 17 transceiver boosters.

Joseph sped past the station, winding down Canyon Road, then traveled north on Bishops Lodge Road to Tesuque. After 2.86 miles, he veered right, scooting up the west side of the Sangre de Cristo mountains. With the fading light of the sunset, he guided the mini-shuttle onto its landing pad.

As he climbed out, he stopped momentarily to study the outlines of his house. It was an earth-sheltered solar home, entirely inanimate, nestled into a gentle south-facing slope at an altitude of 8734 feet. He had built it himself 31 years earlier from a mixture of cement and local red soil. Even the walls were shaped by his own hands.

The most striking part of the house was the cylindrical tower that anchored the southeastern corner. The second floor of the tower was encased entirely in glass and served as a solar observatory. It was in this room, I discovered, that Joseph was tracking the path of the ecliptic.

359 days earlier—on October 6, 2076—Joseph had set a small piece of mirror into the south facing windowsill. The mirror caused the sun to reflect a spot of light on the ceiling of the room. Everyday

at noon, he marked the position of the spot of light with a small piece of round red tile. For the past two weeks, he'd asked his friend Drop McWith to take over the job.

"I'm back, Drop," he called out, as he approached the house.

"Well, hey," muttered Drop, a thick man with a facial twitch and a bald head. "Come on in." He handed Joseph a steaming bowl of green chile, beans, and cheese. The food was piled in a heap of strange, random forms.

Joseph nodded his thanks and carried the bowl inside to sit down.

"You want some bancha tea?" asked Drop.

"Sure," said Joseph. He took a bite of the odd gruel and recalled an old-time pleasure.

"Not bad, eh?"

"Can't complain. Just about anything green would be good after this long."

"You mean you didn't get chiles delivered through your kids' ExpressTube?"

Joseph took a sip of tea. "Don't start with me, Drop. You're lucky I'm in a resilient mood or I might be tempted to boot you out of here."

"Wait a minute, Baptista. If you kick me out of here, what'll happen to your llamas? Your llamas love me. They need me. I'm their sunshine, their happiness, their direct link to the Andes." Drop smiled, raising his sharp nose. "And as evidence, there's a little surprise in the stable."

Joseph calmly ate the rest of his meal, cleaning the inside of his bowl with a piece of white dough. Then he got up. "What about in the sunroom?" he asked. "Any surprises there?"

"I did a new spot everyday at noon, like you asked. The figure eight is almost complete."

"Five more days. The 365th tile will be placed on Tuesday, October 5th—assuming you didn't screw up."

"I didn't screw up," he said. "Go look if you want."

"We'll check the stable first."

They went outside, climbing a soft hill behind the house. Prickly plants covered the landscape, but they easily avoided them, having made the walk hundreds of times. When they crossed the arroyo on the other side of the hill, they both put on protective jackets and gloves. Then they entered the llama stalls.

I had no experience with animals, so I didn't know how to evaluate them. But it seemed that one of the llamas—a four-year-old male named Nibby—sensed Joseph's smell. As Joseph approached, the llama flattened back his ears and stepped forward. He even tried to direct his nose toward Joseph's mouth.

"Hello, my beast," said Joseph, careful not to let the llama touch him.

"Show us your surprise, Nibby," said Drop.

They followed Nibby to the corner of the stall where a two-year-old llama named Cayuca was feeding. At her side nursed a newborn baby.

"My little cria," cooed Joseph. "So this is why I came home." He mock-petted Cayuca, then crouched down beside the newborn.

"I've given her a name, subject to your approval," said Drop.

"Tell me."

"Rija," said Drop slowly.

At the mention of the name, Joseph became rigid. He paused for a moment, then stood up and walked out of the stable.

"Come on, Baptista. Where are you going?"

"Stay away!" Joseph yelled.

Drop pursued him. "Just punch me!" he called out. "Go ahead and punch me! But damn it, I know that baby llama is worthy of the name!"

Joseph found a clearing in the arroyo and sat down, scooping a bit of red dirt into his gloved hands.

"You need to resolve it," added Drop. "You've got to."

"You don't know a damn thing about what I need."

"Then what's the problem with naming her Rija?"

"There is no problem. No problem at all." Joseph looked at the dirt.

"All right," said Drop. "I was out of line. But the baby was so beautiful. And I thought maybe it would help you move forward, especially now that the analemma is almost done."

They both turned their eyes upward to watch the stars. As they stared intently, the sky seemed to gradually solidify, with the rays of starlight becoming narrow blue pathways. Even by my own data, I could swear I saw the pathways piercing all the way through to the end of the blackness.

But before I could properly intake the perspective, Joseph and Drop started back to the house for seconds on green chile. So I ignored what I'd seen, figuring it lacked big-time potential, and I obediently began preparing my report for Trivers.

CHAPTER FOURTEEN

AS SOON AS I was done with the Baptista report, I sent it over to Trivers' suite, praying for approval. Then I wolfed down a simulant turkey bandwagon. By 9:53 PM Earth Standard Time, I was refocusing my attention on Kale's system.

Unfortunately, her memory was cleared of the whole episode in Mike Eu's room. I figured she dumped what she found from her mother's private netgork into some external data disk. All I could hope was that the disk contained the same information I already knew.

Other than that, there was little new to glean. Kale spent the rest of the evening sorting internal files. She crawled into her bunk bed at 9:47 PM, exhausted from a long day. I still had a slew of other obligations to fulfill, and I really should have gotten straight to them. But my turkey bandwagon made me drowsy, and before I knew it, I too fell fast asleep.

I didn't wake up until 7:31 AM Friday, the next morning. My proddings were shouting and yelling at me, saying that Kale was in the midst of serious dream. So I forced myself to enter into her system and locate her subconscious sector.

The main feature of Kale's dream seemed to be a huge flex-o-padding landscape on which she was running. She was trying to get to the edge of the flex-o-padding in order to see what lay beneath it, but she couldn't make any progress, no matter how hard she tried, because the flex-o-padding just kept expanding and expanding. Finally, she woke herself up in a cold sweat.

To my surprise, her first reaction was to check her incoming data. Then she remembered how she'd laughed at her signals on Tuesday, and it occurred to her that perhaps she should linger in a state of half-sleep. As she relaxed, she replayed a motto she'd processed as a child:

One world—One mind—One happiness—One Web

The motto was supposed to be comforting, to reassure her that everything was in the Web, that nothing had to be constructed from her own channels. But now it felt more disturbing than anything else. She yearned for a greater unifying principle, something Webless and intrinsic, like what she'd sensed in the WPA prison cell.

Her thoughts drifted back to her childhood. Was there ever a Webless space within her, she wondered? As she lay in bed, she recalled a particular summer day when she was nine years old.

She was playing darts in her backyard with Sammy, the boy next door. The dart board hung on the outside wall of the shuttle garage. After a few rounds, her father called out, "Kale, could you get my headware from the shuttle?"

"Yes, Dad," she replied.

She warned Sammy not to throw any darts while she entered the garage, since the door was only three feet from the dart board. Then she walked toward the shuttle, her back turned to him. Before she put out her hand to activate the door, however, she had a foreboding feeling that Sammy was going to throw a dart. She remembered thinking that it was going to hit her in the wrist, by accident. She even remembered imagining the exact spot in her left wrist where it would strike.

Sammy's signal came a few milliseconds later—first neurally, since it traveled faster than the vocal sound, and then verbally: "Watch out, Kale!"

But the warning was too late. She just stood there activating the door, three feet from the dart board. And then the dart hit her — plink!—directly in the exact spot she'd imagined, straight through to the bone.

Later that day, after her wound had been dressed, she momentarily wondered how she had predicted the accident. She'd received no input signals prior to Sammy's warning—she was sure of that. But the pain in her wrist quickly subsided, and at the age of nine, she was hardly too concerned with where a tiny piece of information came from.

17 years later, nothing could seem more significant. In the past three days, she'd already laughed at the Web once and disobeyed it twice. She'd also violated her mother's private netgork and engaged in strange tactile behavior with Greggy. To top it off, she'd ignored her incoming signals and stopped broadcasting the Internal Laws from her meter.

Now that she had evidence of a Webless source, I was prepared for her to launch into something even more dramatic. But the knowledge only seemed to make her more subdued and careful.

The first thing she did was delete her whole memory of the dart incident, probably because she knew she was being pirated. Then she got up out of bed and finished processing her signals. Meanwhile, she instructed the kitchen to mix tofu nodules and zucchini gas pumps in a saucepan, with fried potato ringlets on the side.

142 seconds later, Gemela and Chamy crawled out of their bunk beds, awakened by the visuals from the food. They sat down at the dining table just as the kitchen served three steaming plates.

"What on earth is that?" asked Gemela, looking at the odd texture of the tofu nodules.

"I call it zucchini rancheros," said Kale. "Try some." She motioned toward the table and they sat down.

"Kickbyte!" said Chamy, sampling a taste. "It's got a great chew to it. Especially after a wild night out."

"What's this about a wild night?" asked Gemela, as she took a big bite.

"Oh, you know Mike," replied Chamy. "He's always wanting to take you to deeper and more remote spaces."

"I can testify to that," said Kale.

"Wooh!" cried Gemela. "Can he accommodate three?"

They laughed heartily, and Kale noticed how much she enjoyed the company of her roommates. It struck her that they probably had closer access to the realm she was seeking, although she truncated the thought as soon as she remembered the pirater.

After breakfast, Kale found a secluded table at Widener Hall to prepare for the seminar she was supposed to give that afternoon. She worked with Jane Friedland's files for 34 minutes, until Greggy approached her with a thick book.

"Kale," he said. "I'm glad to find you here."

"You are?" she replied.

He deposited the book on the table and began flipping through the pages. "Good news. I dug up an article from the *Review of Political Economy* by Ray LeGhir, dated January 2002. Look at this."

Kale thought of the pirater. "Uh, I haven't really got time for books," she said.

"But this is important," said Greg.

"I've got to get ready for a seminar this afternoon."

"At least look at what I found. It'll only take a second."

"I can't. It'll have to wait."

"I don't understand. Is this because of what I said about not getting involved?"

"No, I'm just busy," Kale hesitated. "And I'm not really that concerned with Ray LeGhir."

"That's crazy," he erupted. "You're forgetting who he was, just like everybody else."

Kale looked distracted. "Really?" she said.

"Look at us. We worship the flow of data, but do we understand what Ray's motives were? No. Most people don't even know that the Ray they thank is Ray LeGhir."

Kale pretended to process her signals, but she was actually doodling in the pages of the book Greggy had brought.

"Just remember," continued Greggy, "the products of LeGhir's age were mechanically assembled in factories, with switches, diodes, resistors, and dead chips. But today everything we touch is the opposite. We've surrounded ourselves with manipulated life forms—even our own beings are adulterated. And after all these manipulations, how can we be sure nothing is missing?"

"Interesting question," said Kale. "All I know is that I have to prepare for a seminar." She stood up to leave the room, and as Greggy stared at her in confusion, she handed him back the book.

✸

Ordinarily, I would have stuck to monitoring Kale. But I did feel bad for Greggy, and my proddings were jumping all over me, pushing me to inquire further. I decided to retrieve Greggy's i.d. code and tap into his system, in the same way I had tapped Joseph.

I quickly verified Greggy's pain. His pleasure index had dropped to 4.76, and his system contained numerous emotional redundancies. "I don't understand her," he muttered to himself. "I just don't understand her."

He was so upset that he almost threw the book he was holding through a panel of stained glasses windows. Realizing this would accomplish nothing, he instead opened up the book and began re-reading LeGhir's article, trying to calm himself.

That was when he noticed Kale's doodling. At first, he was furious that she defaced such an important document. But after 37 seconds, his data analyzers got the better of him, and he noticed a pattern to her markings. Her doodlings involved circling different letters throughout the pages of the article. When he strung the circled letters together, he found a secret message:

Meet me at 6:45 tonight in Room 29, Winthrop House.

Greggy's pleasure index immediately soared, but mine was thrown straight to hell. After all, if I hadn't tapped Greggy's system, I'd never have known about Kale's plans for a clandestine meeting.

I couldn't deny it any longer. The fact that Kale knew she was being pirated had become a major problem. It was messing with my agenda, it was messing with my function, it was even messing with my *promotion*.

And clearly, that was cause for serious action.

CHAPTER FIFTEEN

I HAD to find a way to strengthen my monitoring capability, in case Mike tried to pull another interference scheme. My proddings were the first to agree. *"Pull a rerouting sequence, Ralph!"* they exclaimed. *"Find a weak frequency on Mike's overlay transfers!"*

The idea was pretty good, but after consulting the Web for 17 seconds, I determined that a full rerouting program was beyond my reach. I'd have to find weak frequencies for each of the audio, video, and temporal dimensions of Kale's sensory data. My proddings pointed out that I didn't need full headware capability. If I could just hear what was going on in Mike's room, that would give me the bulk of what I needed.

So instead of trying to maintain the multiple sensory capability of my headware, I configured a program to search through the audio frequency of Mike's protection net. Holes in audio waves were much more prevalent than in visual ones, and once a hole was found, my headware could quickly shift its audio receiver to that frequency. Then, if everything worked, I'd be able to hear conversations in Kale's presence even with Mike's security protection installed.

It took me until 3:51 PM to get the program in place. By then,

Kale was blankly sitting in a little dive called Ruby's Ingestion Booth. She was processing her signals and biting into a six-inch simulant tuna roll shaped like a mega-shuttle, but other than that her operating system was entirely dry. The only other thing she did before going to her 5:00 PM seminar was breathe.

The seminar wasn't exactly top-notch monitoring material either. Kale simply dispensed technical results for 82 minutes. After she plowed through her presentation, a group of beady-eyed econometricians questioned her on some of the more arcane features of her statistical findings.

Once the econometricians were satisfied, Professor Morgaux intervened. "It's 6:30 now," he said, "and I know some of you have other engagements. I propose we defer any further questions until dinner tonight—7:30 PM at the Faculty Club."

The audience applauded, and Kale sent a signal of thanks to Friedland. She made the usual small talk with various professors, until she came upon Morgaux.

"I neglected to mention dinner to you earlier," he said to her. "I trust you can make it?"

She nodded.

"May I escort you, say in 45 minutes?"

"That'd be fine, but I have to stop by a friend's room first."

"Certainly, I'll meet you there. Where is it?"

"Winthrop House, Room 29."

"Oh, I see," said Morgaux, with a worried look on his face.

Kale walked directly to Mike Eu's room, announcing herself on route. Mike didn't seem particularly glad to hear from her, but she explained that she'd left a storage disk under his bed.

"You can come in for your disk," said Mike. "That's all."

"Don't you think you should clean the space a bit?" she said, as she entered.

"Not if you're going to be tracking mud."

"Me? Look at the soles of my shoes. Perfectly clean. I only wish the rest of myself was that way."

"So?"

"So you know how good a clean room would make me feel."

"All right, all right," he said reluctantly. "I'll send out a signal for something."

A broom entered the room from the hallway and Kale fondled its neck, instructing it to sweep the floor. As she did this, Mike stepped outside of her line of vision. A few seconds later, he called out to her, "Okay, that's clean enough. We're all set."

It was then that the white noise came rushing back into my headware. I immediately invoked my rerouting program, and 0.31 seconds later the white noise on my audio link dissipated. I could hear everything as clear as ever, I just couldn't retrieve any other sensory data.

"He obviously wants you bad," Mike said. "The pirater's backtripped the overlay transfers, so I had to set up a dynamic bend. I'm not sure how long I can keep the room sealed."

"Whatever you can do I'll appreciate," replied Kale. "I only need about 45 minutes. Greggy is due any minute, and Morgaux will be here in a half hour."

"Forget it. No guests. Especially not that dried up old professor."

"You don't have to be here when they come."

"To hell with that," he exclaimed. "I am not leaving the monitor unattended."

"Then get in the closet. That way you can keep a close eye on the dynamic bend."

Mike laughed. "You expect me to sit in the closet of my own room, just to help you out on your shady activities?"

"No, I don't expect anything. If you think I'm engaged in shady activities, let's just call this whole thing off right now." She looked at him sternly.

"All right, all right. I just wish I knew where you got this mysterious capacity to achieve whatever you want."

"You're the expert in private information. You tell me."

"No, I don't think so," he replied, shaking his head. "I really don't think so." And then all I could hear was the sound of the closet door opening and closing.

At exactly 6:45 PM Greggy transmitted a signal of arrival, and Kale hurried to let him inside the room.

"Greg," she said, "thank Ray you're here. I'm sorry about this morning. It's just that... I'm being pirated."

"What?" he exclaimed. "Right now?"

"Yes, Mike's got me protected for the time being."

"I don't understand. Who's doing this?"

"I'm not sure. Maybe someone who's afraid of what I'm working on. Maybe the WPA."

Kale paused to upload the storage disk she'd been hiding. Then she relayed the whole story to Greggy—how she was on an undercover assignment for the Netgorks, how she'd touched plants and got jailed in a WPA cell, and how Mike Eu had discovered she was being pirated in the process of tapping into her mother's private netgork.

"I see," he said slowly. "This is more than I'd anticipated. And I thought the article I found was such a big deal."

"I'd still like to see it," she replied.

"It's just this footnote that Ray LeGhir wrote."

Kale read the passage aloud:

I am indebted to Joseph Baptista for bringing the redistributive potential of asymmetric information to my attention.

"So they did know each other," she said.

"Definitely. Your grandfather was telling the truth."

"What does it mean?"

"It's pretty complicated. What matters now is to get you somewhere safe."

"And what about Joseph?"

"You still want to talk to him?"

"I have to."

"Have you told Morgaux?"

"Not about my grandfather. But the strange thing is, I brought up that subsistence argument you gave in class, and he went crazy."

"Yeah, well Morgaux's just marking time now. You've got to try to appeal to his early days when he did his real research."

"You think inside he agrees with you?"

"It's possible," said Greggy. "Getting him to admit that is a whole other matter."

"He's supposed to be coming here in a few minutes."

"Then I guess I'd better clear out."

"Wait," said Kale. "I'm not sure we'll be able to communicate after you leave this room. You know, with the pirater and all."

"You're right. We shouldn't."

"So... I was just wondering," she said awkwardly. "Remember what you said about us not getting involved?"

"Yeah."

"Well, do you still..."

There was a long pause. "No," said Greggy, his voice wavering. "I don't. Not anymore."

Professor Morgaux entered the room 89 seconds after Greggy left, and I continued relying on my simple sound monitoring program.

"Hello, Walter," said Kale. "Come in."

"Ah, yes," he replied tentatively. "I'm familiar with this room."

"You know Mike Eu?"

"I do," he said.

"Sit down. The kitchen will fix you a drink."

"Actually, Kale, we probably ought to get to the Club while they're still serving palatable food."

"There are a couple of things I'd like to discuss first."

"I'd really prefer to..."

"I'll get straight to the point, Walter. I'm not from UCLA, and I'm not a visiting scholar. I work for the Public Netgorks as a special reporter. I was sent here undercover to investigate the implications of your research."

"I don't think I like what I'm hearing," he said coldly.

"I'm not fond of deception either. That's why I'm leveling with you now. My system is pirated, and Mike Eu was the only one I knew who could give me security protection."

"I fail to see what you think this has to do with me."

"Then listen," she said. "In the process of my investigation, I've stumbled onto some facts about my grandfather that may be of interest to you."

"Your grandfather? You've really lost me now."

"What if I told you that my grandfather evaded the meter for 12 years after the transition, that he was a close friend of Ray LeGhir, and that he is still alive today?"

"I'm listening."

"It's true. His name is Joseph Baptista."

"And what does this character have to say?"

"I haven't communicated with him about it yet. That's what I'm trying to..."

"I see," he interrupted. "So he exists only in principle."

"He's gone to New Mexico. And he refuses to use the Web. I only learned about his leaving yesterday."

"I still fail to see what this has to do with me."

"You know perfectly well. It's an opportunity to understand the transition."

"No," he said. "I couldn't get involved in that."

"You already are involved."

"On the contrary, Kale, I've simply shown that missing information can be efficient."

"Really? Then why do you tempt your students with PIFFEN meter chronologies and cash register demonstrations?"

"For motivation," he replied calmly.

"I don't think so. Too much is revealed in your Instability Theorem. You don't bury it enough."

"I'd hardly say that."

"The fact is, your theorem proves that the economy is *inefficient*, not the other way around."

"That's ridiculous."

"Then answer me this: Doesn't your theorem state that if people's expectations of the future shift, there may be a different outcome in the economy?"

"Sure," said Morgaux. "So?"

"So if there were shifts in people's memories of the past, wouldn't they produce the same kind of effect as shifts in expectations of the future?"

"It's hard to say."

"Come on," demanded Kale. "You know."

"Okay, yes. *If* such shifts were possible."

"Then suppose we could recover our memory of the pre-PIFFEN world. What would happen?"

"That's impossible," he said.

"But what if we could?"

"We don't know. The result is ambiguous."

"Wrong!" said Kale. "You know. It's what has driven you to hide in your stupid theory all these years."

Morgaux remained quiet.

"Isn't it?" Kale raised her voice. "Isn't it, Walter?"

He still said nothing.

"Or would you prefer to continue lying to your students? Come on, speak up!" demanded Kale.

"I never meant to lie," he said softly.

"And what's the truth?"

"There should still be inventions. Something terrible happened during the transition. I don't know exactly what." He sighed heavily. "The fact is, there were new products for the first twenty years or so after the transition. Then all of a sudden they stopped. No one else seemed concerned, so I did some research on the subject, and I discovered that none of these new products were made by people who'd been implanted with the meter at birth. They were all made by people who'd been born at least two decades before the transition—people who'd not spent any of their formative years under the Web. As this last generation of people began to die, so did the inventions."

Kale stared at him wide-eyed. "Then you do feel what I feel? There is something missing?"

"Well, I did," he said. "I mean, yes, when I first discovered the problem, I wanted to further study it. I had hopes of trying to locate this missing thing. But then everything changed, and I stopped feeling anything at all."

"I don't understand."

"I started getting threats demanding I stop my research. At first, I didn't take them seriously. But then my house was vandalized. I contacted security, took the normal precautions... I wasn't about to be deterred, right? Well, a few days later, when I came home from work, I found my wife lying on the kitchen floor." Morgaux's voice became barely audible. "She was strangled to death."

"Oh, Walter," she said softly.

"That was when I stopped feeling anything. I've buried myself in stupid theory, as you put it, ever since."

"I never should have said that. I'm sorry."

"No," he said. "The truth is, I needed this. You've made me see how weak I've been."

"You were hardly weak. Anybody would have done the same thing."

"I doubt that, Kale. Because when I came across the means to continue my research, I still did nothing."

"What means?" she asked.

"Five years ago, I inherited two data resonators," he explained. "They were designed by my predecessor, Elizabeth Siegal. She was the first professor to take LeGhir's place, one of the rare inventors I was talking about, and when she passed away, I was appointed to take her place. The resonators were tucked away for me in a compartment beneath her desk."

"What do they do?"

"They store data. When they come in contact with someone's skin, they extract all the data in the person's pre-processing zone instead of letting it enter their operating system. That way the individual can engage in mental imaging without danger of infiltration." He paused. "I could have continued my research quite safely."

"I see," said Kale.

"But what's more important now is you. I want to give you one of them. Don't misunderstand me, Kale. I'm not trying to encourage you to take risks you don't want to take. I'm clearly in no position to do that. But this resonator will allow you to conceal information from the pirater's scanners should you need to."

There was a moment of silence, during which Morgaux handed Kale one of the resonators.

"It looks like a tear drop, out of polished amethyst," said Kale.

"A similar material, I believe."

"And all I have to do is hold it in my hand if I want to ship data into its channel?"

"Yes, or place it anywhere against your skin. The resonator will take care of the rest."

"This is amazing, Walter," said Kale. "Thank you. Thank you so much"

"I should be the one thanking you," replied Morgaux. "Now, as I recall, I was supposed to take you to dinner."

"Yes, you were, weren't you?"

And so with Mike Eu still in the closet, Kale crossloaded the data from her active file into the secured channel of her new resonator, and the two of them departed for the Faculty Club.

CHAPTER SIXTEEN

AS SOON AS Kale left the security of Mike Eu's room, I recovered my full headware capability. I immediately scoured her circuits for whatever I could find, but she'd already cleared her system of all her assignment-related data.

Granted, I knew most everything she'd dumped into the tear drop resonator Morgaux had given her—in that regard my rerouting program had paid off. The problem was that Kale would use the resonator for all her new discoveries, which meant I was in worse shape than ever. Even my proddings didn't have any suggestions. The only option seemed to be to inform Trivers of the development and pray he understood it wasn't my fault.

When I went up to his suite, however, he was nowhere to be found. His secretary didn't even have a forwarding location. Instead, there was just a blinking hologram of him that kept mouthing, "I'm on important company business! I'm on important company business!"

I was hardly about to resort to signal transmission in a serious case like this, so I convinced his secretary to let me borrow a Netgork mini-shuttle with a geochip. 14.88 minutes later, I traced his coordinates to an exclusive club on Ventura Boulevard.

As soon as I went inside and saw him sitting in a booth, I knew I'd made the error of my life because Trivers was right in the midst of having his semen extracted. There he was in broad daylight, being serviced by a *real-life* host with long blonde hair and sparkling blue eyes. All I could do was stare straight at her and think about how I'd waited my whole life just for the day I could go down to a sweaty Repro clinic to have some hokey plastic doll massage my Cowper's gland.

Once I recovered from my shock, I tried to slip away. But Trivers couldn't resist the opportunity for humiliation.

"Why, hello, Peterson!" he called out to me. "Good to see you! Yes, I'm a bit preoccupied. But come join us. My extractor won't mind, will you Linda?"

"Not at all," she replied. "Please join us, Mr. Peterson."

"Well, uh..."

"Come on, Peterson," he persisted. "You've got to try some of my special steak this time. It's unlike anything you've ever had." He started cutting off a piece of the same unformed food that I'd seen him eat before.

"Thank you, Clyde," I replied. "But really, I'm not too hungry."

"Sit down anyway. Tell us what's on your mind."

"Yes, tell us what's on your mind," repeated Linda.

My system was a complete mess, but I sat down as calmly as I could. Then, with Trivers in the midst of his extraction, I began describing Kale's meeting with Morgaux. I focused mainly on the problem caused by Morgaux giving Kale the resonator, although I also mentioned how Kale had uncovered the true meaning of the Instability Theorem.

To my surprise, Trivers just sat silently throughout my description. It wasn't until I finished speaking that he erupted into anger.

"You incompetent bithead!" he yelled. "You never should have let Keeler accept that resonator! You disturbed the entire fate of the universe! You fucked up big-time!"

"You fucked up big-time!" repeated Linda.

"I'm sorry," I said. "I'm very sorry."

"Sorry?" growled Trivers. "What the hell is 'sorry' going to do? I want the situation corrected! Immediately!"

"Of course, of course. Just tell me how you'd like it done."

"I don't care how! It makes no difference! Just do it, god damn it! Before the weekend is over!"

"Absolutely," I said. "I'll get right on it, Clyde. I won't rest until it's done."

❂

I went straight back to my office and began replaying all the audio tracks from Kale's meeting with Morgaux. Meanwhile, I studied her resonator from every angle, using all the visual and temporal data she'd generated from handling it. Then I input the details to the Web and requested a plan of action.

The results were less than optimistic. Kale's tear drop resonator resembled a lead fortress. There wasn't a wave I could construct to penetrate it—not infrared, not radio, not even ultraviolet. By 9:18 PM, the Web still hadn't offered a single solution.

I was all set to say gooddata to my life when my neurons, by themselves, came up with a potential idea: Why not simply *prevent* Kale from bypassing her operating system when she shipped data to her resonator? Why not set up some sort of hidden mirror loop in her architecture so that impulses in her pre-processing zone would be sent to her operating system without her knowledge? That way I'd be able to just read off her signals, and she'd never know the difference.

Of course, the approach involved a serious hurdle. It demanded that Kale not be able to detect the hidden loop, while it was being installed or otherwise. That meant I'd have to build a psuedo-operating system into the design. Still, I couldn't think of any better way to get the desired result. So I leapt into the project with full force, and I kept at it all through the night, not even pausing to sleep or eat.

❈

When Kale woke up Saturday morning—at 6:58 AM—I resumed monitoring her on top of everything else. The odd thing was, as soon as Kale's active circuits opened, I started feeling a minor nausea in my stomach. The sensation was different than anything I'd experienced before, sort of like a cross between motion sickness and the beginnings of heat stroke. But I hardly had time to think about myself.

Within 2.05 seconds of waking up, Kale was processing her 14,792 office signals, transmitting 1,397 outbound signals, and making faces in the bathroom mirror. Eight milliseconds later, she threw on a turquoise dress and ordered a pair of Vectral Gradient sandals.

"You going somewhere?" asked Gemela, offering Kale a bowl of popcorn guava in the shape of hourglasses.

"Yeah," said Kale. "I'm visiting my parents for the weekend."

"But you'll be back, right?"

"Of course." She swallowed a bite from her bowl, surprised that it looked so good. "I've really enjoyed staying here. You've both been great."

"Hey," said Gemela, "no problem. The social architecture's been conducive."

"Totally conducive," added Chamy.

"And guess what?" said Gemela. "Chamy and I have a little surprise."

"For me?"

"Close your eyes, okay?" replied Chamy. She removed an amethyst necklace from her skirt pocket and carefully fastened it around Kale's neck.

"It's beautiful!" exclaimed Kale, as she opened her eyes. "How'd you know? Did Professor Morgaux suggest it?"

"Huh?" said Chamy. "You must be processing too hard. You've got Morgaux on the brain."

"We didn't even access your PIFFEN meter," explained Gemela.

"Chamy and I figured to hell with complimentarity analysis. We just picked out the necklace to set off your smooth skin."

"You went way too far," said Kale. "How can I thank you?"

"You don't need to," said Chamy.

"Yeah, forget the words," added Gemela. "Just go out there and optimize."

"Yeah, kick some chips!"

"I will," said Kale, her eyes moist. "I'll kick some chips." Then she retrieved her Vectral Gradient sandals from the ExpressTube and walked downstairs into the wind.

On the way to the mega-shuttle terminal, Kale kept thinking of Greggy. She tried deflecting his image, but to no avail. After 117 seconds of internal debate, she retrieved his address from a local directory file and followed the imaging pointers to his apartment.

"Hi!" said Greggy, as she reached the door. "Enter the domain!" He was wearing a purple sweatshirt with blue and magenta knitted socks, and the walls of his rooms were covered with odd markings on sheets of paper.

"Sorry to be barging in like this," she replied. "I hope I'm not overriding your transmission space or anything."

"No," he said. "My space is hardly full."

Kale admired the markings on the walls. "I've never seen images like this."

"I copied them from a book about an artist named Paul Klee, who lived before the transition."

"An artist?" asked Kale.

"A person who made objects for no purpose," he explained.

"They're strange, but I like them. They sort of remind my mind."

"For me too."

She turned to look him. "I know what we said, Greg, but I wanted to give you something before I leave."

She leaned toward him, recalling an image of two grey whales from her animal database. Then slowly and deliberately, without detectable friction, she touched her lips to Greggy's mouth.

Greggy pulled away. "We can't," he said. "The Laws."

"Who cares? What about before the Laws?"

"They're embedded, Kale. It's not possible."

"It's not possible or you don't want to?"

Greggy stared at her in amazement. "You know," he said softly, "the old-timers had a word for someone like you."

"What?"

"They would have called you a *goddess*."

Kale smiled. Then once again, without detectable friction, she placed her lips against his. But this time Greggy couldn't resist her boldness, in spite of his cerebral directives, and this time they held the position for 13.22 seconds.

In order to board the minor shuttle to Connecticut, Kale had to drain 68 percent of her stored value, as she didn't have Netgork approval for the journey. The outflow hardly phased her—she was rating an amazing 99.51 points on her satisfaction index.

In contrast, I was at my all time low, carrying a measly 3.28 points of pleasure. The last thing I needed was more odd behavior to monitor. I'd been suffering enough just trying to set up Kale's system for the mirror loop, and my case of nausea was getting worse.

Yet things were hardly slowing down. As soon as Kale arrived at her parents' house, at 11:54 AM, the oddities started all over again.

"Honey!" cried Ansie. "We weren't expecting you this weekend. You didn't give us a signal." She reconfigured the kitchen appliances for servings of three.

"Sorry, Mom," said Kale. "I just felt like getting away without planning anything."

"Well, sure. That's okay, honey. You deserve a break."

"Thanks."

"Did you notice the house on your way in?"

"You mean the new exterior coat? It's very nice."

"Isn't it?" said Ansie. "It's called ebullient beige. Your father and I decided to splurge and dynamize the epidermal pigments since—you know—we won't be building a home here for Joseph."

"I know."

Ansie hesitated. "So how's your value basis coming along?"

"Not too bad," replied Kale. "It hasn't really changed yet, but I think things are going to take off once I finish the assignment."

"You're sure you won't let your father help you out?"

"Yes, Mom. I'm fine."

"All right, then. I'll let you freshen up before Dad comes home."

Kale went upstairs to her childhood bedroom, took off her new Vectral Gradient sandals, and flopped on the bed. 308 cells had died in the pinky toe of her right foot, as her sandal was slightly too tight. She cupped the sandal in her hand and gently directed it to grow conformably. Then she slipped her tear drop resonator beneath the bedspread and sent me a query signal.

"Keeler," I responded. "What's going on? I haven't heard from you for 23 hours."

"Maybe you should look at my backup reports," she replied. "Morgaux made me lead a seminar yesterday, so I've been working with Friedland quite a bit."

"Good, good. Trivers is a little concerned, you know. He's afraid this thing is stagnating."

"Stagnating?"

"He's antsy. Pacing around. He thinks we should have gotten more by now."

"I thought you told me time wasn't an issue."

"Uh, that's true," I transmitted, trying to fight off the nausea within me. "I guess I'm a little frazzled."

"Are you apologizing, Ralph?"

"I've got a lot on my system. Pressure from Clyde. And more supervision duties. You know how it is."

"Sounds like you need to take a break."

"You can say that again."

"Hey, isn't it your birthday today, Ralph?"

"Yeah. Just another transition baby, you know."

"Really? You were born in 2008?"

"Yeah, in Mexico City."

"That must have been strange, being in the middle of all that."

"Don't be a bithead, Keeler. I have no memories."

"I'm just making a comment, Ralph. Take it easy."

"Save the comments for the assignment. We need results here."

"Yes sir, boss," she replied. "Yes sir."

Then she closed out the wave and reached under the bedspread for her resonator.

CHAPTER SEVENTEEN

KALE'S active circuits went black as soon as she touched the resonator, and the nausea in my stomach doubled in intensity. To make matters worse, I also began to feel the onset of a piercing headache, an unfamiliar kind deep inside my cerebral cortex.

My proddings assured me there was nothing to worry about. *"It's not your fault, Peterson,"* they whispered. *"It's normal to feel these things in the face of a major challenge. Just relax. Just ignore the pain."*

So I told myself that everything was okay, that Kale probably wouldn't be engaging in anything of great importance, and I concentrated all my energy on the hidden mirror loop. Kale's empty active circuits were a blessing in this regard because I was able to work on the project without spending so much effort on detection decoys. After 46 minutes, the whole procedure started to look very promising.

Unfortunately, my momentum did not last long. Just as I was finishing the foundation for the loop, Trivers came bursting into my office.

"Time's up, Peterson," he announced.

"Huh?" I said.

"You haven't solved the resonator problem."

"I know, but it's only Saturday. You gave me until the end of the weekend."

"I don't care what I told you," he replied coldly. "Your time's up now, so give me the headware."

"I've almost got it done, Clyde. A couple more hours and I'm sure I'll have the problem solved."

"Just give me the fucking headware. Don't make this more difficult than it has to be."

I tried to process his words, I really did. But the nausea within me was so overwhelming that instead I dropped to the floor and vomited into a waste basket.

"Stop that," said Trivers, jabbing my side with his shoe. "What the hell are you doing?"

"I can't help it," I moaned, wiping bile from my mouth. "It's my stomach. It's all messed up."

"I see. Then I'm afraid you're fired, Peterson. I'm terminating your employment as of now."

"Please, Clyde. Just 30 more minutes, and I'll have what you want."

"Forget it. Things have escalated more than anticipated."

"But what about my promotion?" I said, in horror. "What about what you promised?"

"Those are the breaks, Peterson. Some people just aren't meant for the big-time." He plucked the headware from my head and took off out the door.

My first impulse was to run after Trivers and ram my fist up his snout. In my condition, however, all I could manage was to puke a few more times in the waste basket and lie down on the floor. 264 seconds later, a security guard came in to tell me I was no longer authorized in the Netgorks building.

I had no choice in the matter. I grabbed a few sentimental items from my desk, then I crept onto the next shuttle back to my apartment in Whittier.

When I got home, I had the kitchen bring me a cup of bullion broth with yellow pacifiers, since that was what my diagnostics suggested. My nausea was already pretty much relieved—I'd puked up 123 ounces of vomit, so there wasn't much left in me. The problem was with my head. I felt like my brain was being pried apart, with a sharp foreign object wedged in between.

My proddings assured me that my ailment was just a reaction to my troubles at work. But even so, my headache kept getting worse and worse. When my pleasure quotient sunk all the way down to 0.27, I knew I had to face up to the inevitable. I'd never felt such utter agony before—nothing had ever come close. The only explanation was that I was dying. I, Ralph Peterson, was *dying*.

Fear shuddered through my spine. I tried retracing the events of my lifetime, but my headache was too overpowering. I could only concentrate on the pain, as if I had no other data within me. I just closed my eyes, pulled a blanket over my head, and curled up on my bed.

That was when the strangest thing happened: Everything familiar to my system began drifting away—even my headache seemed to be getting more and more remote—and I felt like I was gradually becoming a part of *Kale's system*. Her private images seemed to be even more immediate and intense than when I'd been monitoring her.

My first thought was that the experience was somehow part of the dying process. I figured my brain was mimicking the sensation of monitoring Kale, as some sort of random spasm in preparation for shutting down. It made sense that the spasm would be from an episode of monitoring, since I'd spent so much time in the recent past doing that.

But when I started viewing the images more carefully, I could tell they were entirely new. They weren't just random juxtapositions of data I'd already gathered from Kale. Rather, they seemed to pick up from precisely where I'd left off when Trivers had taken back his headware.

Granted, this was hardly proof of any paranormality. But whatever was happening, I certainly lacked the resources to fight it. I couldn't even feel my own body—I didn't know if I was still in bed or what. So I just took a deep breath and let myself blend into Kale's system.

By that point, Kale was sitting on her bed on the second floor of her parents' house, thinking about how to contact Joseph without the pirater finding out. She debated sending him a signal via Drop McWith, like her parents sometimes did. She also considered having someone else transmit to Joseph, or perhaps sending Joseph a bundle of items through the ExpressTube with the hope that he'd be able to decode their symbolic meaning.

These methods all depended on the Web space, however, and if the pirater could infiltrate her system, then Kale had little reason to believe anybody else's netgork was safe. A part of her was tempted to dismiss the whole idea. After all, Trivers would more than likely be satisfied with what she'd already uncovered in Morgaux's theorem.

Still, she couldn't get Joseph off her mind. Logic had little to do with it. Neither did wanting to please Trivers or increasing her value basis. For the first time, she felt sure she had something to offer her grandfather, something that extended past her own biology. But how could she contact him without risking his safety?

As she sat still on the bed for another 23 seconds, the solution became obvious. Why not bypass the Web altogether? Why not rely on her original cells to communicate across location, to Joseph's cells?

No doubt, it was a purely foreign concept, inconceivable from any pre-existing database. But when she considered the notion from the space of her cells, she knew it had to be possible. How else could she have sensed what Morgaux had sensed in his own blood? How else could she have predicted the dart? And how else could Chamy and Gemela have known to get her an amethyst necklace to match her tear drop resonator?

She resolved to trust in the existence of an original Web, a Web before the Web. And she resolved to trust fully and completely, with will and non-doubt.

As she did so, my connection to her system began to fade. Her images became less crisp, less in focus, and I could faintly hear the whirring of my proddings, *"Hang in there, Peterson. Hang in there for a few more minutes."*

I doubted I could last that long, but somehow I latched onto Kale as she stared out the bedroom window. Two birds were soaring in the sky, venturing directly over the treeless zone of human inhabitation—a rare occurrence. They were flying in unison, each seemingly knowing the other's path.

For 2.06 minutes, Kale watched the birds circle over the cement suburban landscape. She studied every aspect of them—their muscles, their eyes, their wings, their signal frequencies. She even identified them as members of a species called blue herons. Then she assimilated her observations deep within herself.

At precisely 4:08 PM, the blue herons disappeared over the horizon. Kale slowly arched her back, smoothing her skin like a transceiver. When her sternum was fully exposed to the wind and her head was tilted back to her waist, a surge issued from the behind her mind, and she began releasing a pre-Web signal of her own:

Joseph,

You are my grandfather. I need your help and you need mine.
We need to be together, to return a lost jewel to this world.

I'm ready whenever you are. Just tell me how and when.

Love,

Cat

Once she completed the transmission, my link to her system became further diffused, with all the visual data collapsing to black and white. But Kale stayed very still, almost as if she knew my fragility. She just stood by the window, watching the way the air moved, waiting for a response, yet not waiting. Even when George's shuttle pulled into the garage, at 4:29 PM, she barely acknowledged the event. She just continued standing by the window, staring into the distance.

And then it happened: At 4:44 PM, Ansie gave out a shrill cry. A moment later, she and George rushed upstairs to the bedroom.

"Hi, Kale," said George. "Your mother and I just received a signal we think you'd better know about."

"What is it?" asked Kale, still standing by the window.

"A message from Drop McWith. Evidently, grandpa's not feeling too well."

"But Drop's taking care of everything he needs," explained Ansie. "And Joseph already has an excellent doctor by his side."

"What's the matter with him?" asked Kale worriedly.

"It's some kind of virus, they think."

"He has a very good chance of recovery," said George. "And, well, there's something else that's come up too. Your mother and I weren't sure whether we should tell you or not. We know you're in the middle of an important assignment, and it hardly seems fair to burden you with this now. But you have a right to know, to make your own decision. We'll support you no matter what you decide."

"We want you to know that," added Ansie.

"So tell me," said Kale. "What is it?"

"It's a bit difficult," sighed George. "In his transmission to us, Drop mentioned that Joseph has been asking for you. Your mother explained to him that you'd never been to New Mexico, and that it'd be quite a shock to your system. But Drop kept stressing how much Joseph wants to see you. And, well, he really is quite right. The decision isn't ours to make."

"It's whatever you'd like to do," said Ansie.

"I'll go," answered Kale directly. "I'll get my things together right away."

And then, at the exact moment she spoke this, everything within me went blank. There wasn't even any white noise. My link to Kale's system just completely severed, along with every other connection I had—even to my proddings, even to my own data. It was all just pure blankness.

Blankness, blankness, blankness.

PART TWO

MENISCUS

It's a puny ambition, Andrew. You're better than a man. You've gone downhill from the moment you opted for organicism.

ALVIN MAGDESCU

CHAPTER EIGHTEEN

I TRULY THOUGHT I'd died. All my active circuits had entirely shut down, and I couldn't locate even one bit of data for my conscious mind to absorb. How was I to know my subconscious system was still whirring away?

What had happened, you see, was that I'd fallen into a coma—a deep, deep coma—in which I remained submerged for 52 hours and 42 minutes. My conscious mind wasn't able to record anything during this period, but my subconscious system *did* keep track of the deeper events that took place inside of me, and eventually my conscious mind managed to uncover these events.

That ended up being crucial because my coma was hardly the run-of-the-mill variety. Rather, it involved the transmission of a stream of old-time symbols. These symbols were expressed by neuro-electrical impulses, as any signals would be. But they weren't coming from my netgorks or from the Web. They were coming straight from the central cortex of my PIFFEN meter, as if my meter were some sort of independent data source.

What was particularly strange was that the symbols weren't embedding in my neural tissue. They were simply passing through my subconscious system, from the inner core of my meter up into my radio transceiver. Then they were exiting from my head into an external portion of the Web space.

Naturally, my subconscious was intrigued. After 12.36 seconds, it determined that the symbols were actually representations of *written words*, and it began spending all my available energy processing them. My subconscious continued doing this throughout the whole period that I remained in the coma.

In the meantime, I just lay limp in my bed, unaware of anything. Once the stream of symbols came to a stop, I was damn near starvation. After all, 52 hours and 42 minutes without food and water was hardly a pleasant undertaking for someone like me.

But in the end, once everything was sorted out, I had to forgive my subconscious system. Because, amazingly, the words that it unraveled happened to be the following:

ATTENTION: FIRST READER!
THIS DOCUMENT IS CURRENTLY WEBLESS.
YOU ARE THE TRANSFORMING AGENT.

Subject: The Cause and Conditions of the Great Transition

Time: October 31, 2008 to November 14, 2008

Author: Ray LeGhir, Builder of the PIFFEN meter,
Professor of Economic Biology, Harvard University

THIS DOCUMENT IS the true account of how humans came to have PIFFEN meters implanted in their brains. I can testify to its truth because I was privy to direct sources. As the inventor of the PIFFEN meter, I exploited my position and entered the master channel when it was first being formed. Thus I was able to access the minds of all persons described herein.

No doubt, my method of preparing this document was highly unprofessional, but without it there would be no record of the terrible tyranny endured by humans in the year 2008. This tyranny was so all-encompassing that its overthrow not only required the implanting of PIFFEN meters, but also the purging of all people's memories of the tyrannical period.

Such memory-purging would have been trivial were it not for the fact that every type of recording instrument, including pencil and paper, was made inaccessible during the reign of tyranny. Even this shortcoming I tended to view as insignificant in the midst of the oppressive climate surrounding us. The loss of such a short span of human history, covering just two weeks, seemed a small price to pay for freedom.

However, I must confess, as my overthrow of the tyrant moved closer to reality, I became increasingly guilt-ridden. I asked myself if I indeed had the right to censor such a critical episode of humankind, and I wondered if future generations might benefit from this knowledge in ways that I could not anticipate. Ultimately, I felt compelled to provide an avenue of possibility for recovering the purged information.

In the pages that follow, I have not always concealed my lack of training in the disciplines of history and literature, and so the irony of my effort may appear complete. My hope is that the rushed circumstance will warrant some lenience of style.

In any event, I remain grateful to all those who have assisted me. I particularly wish to thank my six colleagues: Beatrice Coleson, Dan Gilmore, Jack Myers, Albert Senghavi, and Lou Silverthwait. To the women pilots who made the PIFFEN meter implantings possible, I am forever indebted.

> *Ray LeGhir*
> *Cambridge, Massachusetts*
> *November 15, 2008*

THE TYRANT AS A CHILD

Underlying the Great Transition of 2008 was the most repressive and horrific regime in recorded history. No prior government had ever produced so much misery or attained such all-pervasive control of humankind. Yet all this was accomplished by a single tyrant—one Nathan Vince Burgstaller.

Born on May 25, 1972 in Carmel, California, Nathan Burgstaller was raised in a three-story mansion overlooking the Pacific Ocean. His father, Leo Burgstaller, an agriculturalist of humble origins, built an empire founded on hard work and carefully regulated growth. By Nathan's birth, Leo had already negotiated a series of clever land acquisitions, establishing himself as a primary grower in the Salinas Valley.

In spite of such opulence, Nathan's early years were marked by two difficult circumstances. The first of these was a separation from his mother, Janet Bishop-Burgstaller, who left Carmel when Nathan was only nine months old. Enticed by claims of a fountain of youth near Bali, Janet was found raped and murdered in the outskirts of Jakarta six weeks after commencing her odyssey.

Although Nathan was supervised by a squadron of nurses and nannies, he remained motherless, as Leo never remarried. Janet's only known influence on Nathan appears to have been the nickname she conferred, "Knotty," which he retained through adulthood.

Knotty's second difficult circumstance arose a year later, as he was learning to speak. Each morning after Leo left for the valley, Knotty's favorite nanny, Priscilla, greeted him with the question, "Is Daddy at work, Knotty? Is Daddy at work?"

Initially, this elicited no response. Later, on cheerful days, Priscilla drew an occasional "Yep." But on the morning when Knotty finally spoke a complete sentence, his response was, "Uh huh. Dada at gork! Dada at gork!"

The first time this happened, Priscilla thought nothing of it. "That's very good, Knotty," she said, praising him. "Daddy is at *work*. Daddy is at *work*."

The following day, however, Knotty made the same mistake. He repeated it the following day, and the day after that. Each time, he said 'gork' with total delight and amusement.

That next morning Priscilla decided to try an experiment. She asked him, "Do you want to go take a walk, Knotty? Do you want to go take a walk?" As Knotty remained silent, she gently took his hand and led him out the living room into a garden overlooking the Pacific.

Being a quick learner, Knotty only required a day to adjust to the new routine. On the second morning, when she asked the question again, he answered her matter-of-factly. "Yep, galk," he said. "Galk."

Priscilla resolved to suspend judgement until she collected more information. The subsequent day, Knotty was even more talkative. "Yep, galk," he said. "Gont to woh take a galk."

At that point, Priscilla knew she could no longer hold back. She immediately called Leo at his office. He came home early and Priscilla demonstrated her experiment.

Knotty was uncharacteristically cooperative, reveling in the attention. He even repeated new words as Priscilla uttered them. Each time, with perfect correspondence, he replaced all the g-sounds with w-sounds and all the w-sounds with g-sounds.

Alarmed by the sheer peculiarity of it, Leo rushed Knotty to the family doctor. The doctor confirmed Knotty's g and w-reversal problem but found no evidence of its extension to other consonants or vowels, nor any sign of other disorders. A battery of visits to hearing specialists, speech therapists, and psychiatrists revealed little more.

The consensus was that Knotty suffered from a rare auditory processing defect. The nerve fibers appeared to be confounded inside Knotty's audio cortex, so that when a g-sound was spoken he actually heard a w-sound and vice versa.

The doctors explained that the defect was similar to certain kinds of colorblindness, in which a person might perceive green when shown a red light and red when shown a green light. They assured Leo that the problem was quite minor and that it need not impact Knotty's life. Knotty merely had to be trained to take account of his defect—that is, to say the g-sound when he heard the w-sound and to say the w-sound when he heard the g-sound. Accordingly, Leo hired a live-in speech therapist to undertake the training and, as a supplement, Knotty was sent weekly to a prominent audiologist in San Francisco.

After half a year of exercises, however, the therapy was still not succeeding. If anything, as Knotty's vocabulary expanded, the defect only became more noticeable.

Leo tried a new speech therapist from San Diego. When that met with the same result, he chose another therapist, and another one, each time selecting from among the top specialists in the nation. Invariably, they voiced the same complaint: Knotty was a terribly clever young boy, but he had no interest in changing his speaking habits, no matter how they attempted to motivate him.

Desperate to solve his son's problem, Leo turned to a therapist of less orthodox methods. He arranged for Clayton Pinscher, a Utah-based "shock counselor", to visit their home.

Knotty was only five years old at the time, but Clayton showed little compassion. He simply strapped Knotty into a chair and wired him up to an electric shock machine.

"Okay, Knotty, repeat after me. Say *work*."

"Gork," said Knotty.

"Now say *gork*."

"Work," said Knotty.

"Excellent," replied Clayton. "You've demonstrated that you know how to say both words. Now you must reverse what you're doing. Otherwise you'll be punished. Do you understand?"

"I wuess."

"Good, let's begin. Repeat after me. Say *work*."

"Gork," said Knotty, with a slight grin.

"This isn't a game, Knotty," admonished Clayton. "You must reverse your impulse." He quickly administered a small shock.

"Og!" cried Knotty. "That hurt!"

"Now say *gork*." said Clayton.

"Work," said Knotty.

Again Clayton administered a shock, this time with greater voltage, and again Knotty cried out in pain.

"We can do this all day if you want. Now repeat after me. Say *gork*."

"Work!"

"Say *work*."

"Gork!"

Clayton continued the procedure several more times, each time setting the shock machine higher. But Knotty refused to submit. Finally, Clayton set the shock machine on maximum voltage and repeated, "*Work, work, work, work*."

At this, Knotty flew into hysterics, screaming at the top of his lungs. Leo charged into the room, demanding that Clayton stop. Then he unstrapped Knotty from the chair and threw Clayton out of the house.

By that time, however, the damage was done. The deepest part of Knotty's essence, that which defined his very being, had been invaded and attacked by an agent of his own father. Knotty would never trust anyone again, and for the next month, he refused to speak at all.

Still, Leo did not give up. He researched the problem endlessly, convinced there was a solution. A year later, after the dust had settled and Knotty seemed back to his old ways, Leo proposed another approach—to send Knotty to a special school for the hearing impaired.

"No! I gon't woh," cried Knotty. "If you send me, I'll run agay."

"But, son," said Leo, "we've tried everything else. It's for your own good. Can't you see, we must at least try?"

"No!" yelled Knotty. "Ghen gill *you* see, I'm not the one gith a problem! You are! You're the one gho needs a shock machine!" He stormed out of the room, slamming the door.

Undeterred, Leo consulted an eminent psychologist from New York City. The psychologist reviewed Knotty's records, then advised Leo to dismiss the therapists and abandon the training. His theory was that Knotty had not yet resolved his mother's abandonment. The best course of action would be to let Knotty come to terms with his feelings at his own pace, until he saw for himself the advantages of overcoming his speech problem.

Leo admitted there was merit to the idea and agreed to stop pressuring his son. Even so, Knotty's response was unencouraging. He withdrew further from friendships with other children and showed no signs of adjusting his speech patterns.

His remaining years of childhood were quite solitary, with interaction limited to his father, his schoolteachers, and a few servants at home. Occasionally, Leo attempted to introduce him to boys his own age, but never with any success. Knotty preferred to engage himself in his two favorite pastimes: books and bombs.

Knotty truly was an exceptional reader. He devoured an average of four books a week, and his teachers all agreed that he was highly gifted, although many were alarmed by his taste for subject matter. In eighth grade, for instance, his three elective book reports were on *Das Kapital*, *Mein Kampf*, and *Beyond Good and Evil*.

Knotty's fascination with incendiary devices was similarly intense. Like many boys, Knotty felt an urge to play with matches, but he was too industrious to merely light them. Instead, he preferred to scrape off the sulfurous material on their tips and stockpile it in nooks and crannies around the house.

Not surprisingly, this led to numerous indoor fires. The majority of them were extinguished by the servants without much trouble. However, the Carmel Fire Department did pay one visit to the Burgstaller mansion on the evening of December 24, 1984, when Knotty was twelve years old.

On that particular occasion, the firemen arrived to find the family's Christmas tree engulfed in flames, along with all the Christmas gifts. Fortunately, the bulk of the house was saved. The occurrence was officially attributed to electrical failure in the wiring of the Christmas tree lights, but the fire chief noted the following in his log book:

> *Several Christmas tree light bulbs were found floating in the toilet adjacent to the boy's bedroom, each packed with match tip filings, making them highly flammable. Since the boy appears to be quite well behaved, it does not seem likely he could have been responsible.*

Thus the matter was closed without so much as a word of questioning brought to Knotty, and no one even stopped to wonder what any of this might foretell.

THE TYRANT AS A
YOUNG MAN

In the ensuing years, Knotty became progressively alienated. Most of the servants he grew up with quit their jobs in favor of less stressful environments, and Leo turned his attention to a series of bold takeover campaigns to augment his land holdings.

By his first year in high school, Knotty regularly skipped classes. Nothing anyone said or did could convince him to participate in the activities commonly associated with teenagers. Even the new red Acura his father bought him for his sixteenth birthday had less than ten miles on it a year later.

Knotty was quite handsome as a young man, with fine blonde hair and sharp features, but he displayed no interest in girls. Nor was he attracted to drugs, alcohol, or rock music.

After graduating from high school, Knotty continued to stay at home. Refusing to find a job or attend college, he burrowed ever more deeply into his room, only coming out for nourishment and mail order deliveries from electronics and chemical firms.

It took two more years and several lengthy consultations with the New York psychologist before Leo could muster the strength to challenge Knotty's behavior. Finally, in August of 1992, he stated his position.

"Knotty," he said, "you're twenty years old now, and I feel it would be best for you—and for me—if you did something to improve your life."

"Forwet it," said Knotty. "I'll do ghatever I gant."

"I'd be happy to find you a job anywhere you want to work or help you apply to a college. But if you don't cooperate, I'll have to ask you to leave."

"No gay, Dad. You'd never kick me out. You still feel too wuilty for ghat you let happen to me."

"Perhaps," replied Leo softly. "But I'm not going to sit here and watch you ruin your whole life. There are other things I can do too, you know."

"Like ghat?" sneered Knotty. "Ghat can you possibly do?"

"For starters, I can stop paying for all your damn UPS orders."

Knotty's face sunk. "No gay. That's my ghole existence. You gouldn't."

"Yes, I would. And I will, unless you do what I ask."

"Fine," said Knotty anxiously. "I'll woh to Monterey College. Part-time. But that's it."

"Let's enroll you right now. We'll take my car."

Thus, in Knotty's first excursion away from home for over a year, they proceeded straight to Monterey Peninsula College. Knotty signed up for courses in microeconomics, accounting, and real estate.

Two weeks later, on the first day of classes, Knotty climbed into his Acura to drive to campus. None of the household staff could believe it, but Leo had a servant tail Knotty to verify that he actually attended his courses.

In his real estate class, Knotty sat next to a student named Drop McWith. Drop was a mature-looking 15 year old with light red hair and a slight facial twitch. He had recently run away from his home in Silver Springs, Maryland, using his older brother's i.d.

After a dull lecture on the relationship between housing construction and the interest rate, Drop started conversing with

Knotty. "What do you think?" he asked. "Is this how boring the whole course is going to be?"

"It is," replied Knotty, engaging in his first communication with a peer since eleventh grade.

"You've had this guy before?"

"No," said Knotty. "But they're all the same."

"Let's blow this joint and get some lunch." His face twitched as he offered his hand. "My name's Drop McWith."

"I'm Knotty Burwstaller. Tell me hog you wot your tgitch and I'll consider your proposal."

"Excuse me?"

"Ghy you gink," said Knotty.

"What?" asked Drop, still confused.

"Ghy you do this." Knotty demonstrated.

"Oh, my twitch," said Drop. "What'd you call it? My tgitch? That's a good one. Yes, well I got my tgitch long ago. My mother sent me to a psychiatrist when I was eight, and one of the drugs he prescribed happened to have an unforeseen side effect, if you know what I mean."

"I'm sorry," said Knotty. It was the first time he'd ever said these words.

"Hey, it's no big deal. Now are we getting lunch or what?"

"That gould be wood."

They left the classroom and walked out to Drop's 1948 Dodge Power Ram truck. "You like burritos?" he asked.

"Never had one," said Knotty.

"Are you serious? Who are you?"

"Just a peculiar kid."

"You don't look like a kid to me. But I'll tell you what. You'd better get the avocado and cheese, with extra salsa."

They stopped at a small fast-food joint, ordered their burritos, and took them to a table outside. As they ate, Drop inquired into Knotty's background. It didn't take him long to determine that Knotty's g and w-reversal was involuntary, but that in itself didn't mean much to him. What intrigued him more was his self-assured display of it.

"Hey, Knotty," he said, after they finished eating, "do you mind if we run a quick errand before I swing you back to your car? It's on the way."

"Ghut gill I wet from it?"

"Maybe a chance to make some money," said Drop. "Do you like money?"

"No."

"Ah. Then you'll be the killer salesman."

They got into the truck and Drop floored it to a run-down house near the college. After some convincing, he led Knotty into his basement apartment.

"Here," he said, grabbing an armful of clothing from his closet and thrusting it onto Knotty. "Bring this out to my truck, will you?"

Drop gathered another armful of clothes and followed Knotty up the pathway. They dumped the clothing in the bed of his truck, then made two more runs to Drop's closet. Altogether, they collected fifteen suits, ten sport jackets, seven coats, six pairs of slacks, and a dozen pairs of shoes. Most of the garments were dusty, but they were all from the finest of clothiers, and few of them looked to be have been worn more than once.

"Hog'd you wet all this?" asked Knotty, as they climbed into the cab of the truck.

"I was born into a rich-ass family back East. My dad sold office supplies, which was real, but I couldn't deal with it, so I moved out here."

"And nog?"

"Huh?"

"Ghat's next?"

"You'll see."

Drop worked the gears through traffic until he came to a small shop called *Second Life*. He jumped out in front of the shop and grabbed one of the clothing piles, motioning for Knotty to get the other pile. Together they walked inside.

"Can I help you?" said an old woman.

"I was wondering if you were doing any buying," replied Drop, as they set their bundles on the counter.

The woman picked through the clothing, alternating between bursts of careful inspection and reckless once-overs until she settled on an in-between approach. Finally, she looked up at Drop. "I'll give you forty bucks," she said.

"For all of it?" asked Drop.

"I don't want the shoes. They stink."

"Fine. It's a deal."

"Gate a minute!" protested Knotty. "This is girth ten times that!"

"More than that, kiddo," replied Drop. "But what do you care? You don't like money anyway?"

"Do you want the forty bucks or not?" said the woman.

"Yes, please," said Drop. "I'll take it."

She handed him two twenties. "Next time," she said, "I suggest you come in alone."

As they drove back to the college, Drop rambled about his east coast origins, but Knotty was too busy reevaluating his own life. It wasn't until they came to the college parking lot that he finally spoke.

"I thouwht you said you'd wive me a chance to make some money," he said.

"I intend to, Knotty. I just had to check you out first. But now that we're here, I'll show you what I'm talking about."

Drop reached under the seat of his truck and pulled out a display rack covered with black velour. Mounted on it was a large array of beaded earrings adorned with semi-precious stones and Venetian glass. "Can I trust you?" he asked.

"No," said Knotty.

"Good. I want you to take these earrings to all the little boutique shops in town. I'll give you fifty percent of anything you sell. Just don't let them weasel you into putting any of it on consignment. You got that?"

"But I don't knog the first thinw about jegelry."

"Exactly," said Drop. "That's what's going to grab their attention. Get it? So I'll see you at class next week. *Gith* my fifty percent."

Then he flashed Knotty a wink, and he roared away.

THE TYRANT AS A YOUNG ENTREPRENEUR

AT FIRST, Knotty perceived Drop's business offer as irrelevant. He stuffed the velour earring board deep into the trunk of his Acura and forgot about it. But two days later, while standing in front of his bathroom mirror, he remembered how Drop had relinquished his clothing. Intrigued by the idea of release, he fastened a thin tie around his neck and bounded down the stairs to his car.

During the next twenty-four hours, Knotty visited eight shops and sold thirty pairs of earrings. With each sale, he became more intrigued by the world of business, by the idea that he could simply walk into a store and persuade someone to buy his products.

It wasn't the making of money that interested him. It was the power, the feeling of manipulating and controlling the desires of others. The sensation excited him even more than the calculated explosion of a bomb.

Of course, Knotty still had his speech problem, and not everyone was understanding of it. At his ninth boutique, he came across a hardened saleswoman. "Good you like to see some hand-crafted earrinws?" he asked her.

The clerk broke into laughter. "What's the matter kid? Got cotton balls under your tongue? Or are the earrings made in Japan?"

"Neither," replied Knotty, showing her the velour display. "I have jade, amethyst, warnet, crystal, and Venetian wlass desiwns from four to nine dollars."

"I'm afraid we don't carry no warnet here," she said. "But I'll tell you what. You tell your boss to send out a man who can speak and maybe we can do business."

Knotty was stunned. He had never before felt constrained by his g and w-reversal problem. He had never even imagined such a circumstance. All he could do was pick up his display, turn around, and walk out the door.

Once outside, he hunched over the sidewalk and clenched every muscle in his body. He maintained this position for several minutes, almost bursting his blood vessels. Then, suddenly, he spun around and walked back into the store.

"I understand you want a man who can speak," he said, successfully executing two double reversals.

"Oh, please," replied the clerk. "Don't bore me with rehabilitation efforts."

"At least let me show you the earrings with their proper descriptions," persisted Knotty. "Here, for instance, is one of our most popular styles. It consists of four round garnets in each earring, alternating with fourteen karat gold beads, and completed by an oblong garnet at the end."

"Hmmn."

"It's a most original design," he continued, "and complimentary to a wide range of outfits."

"Okay, kid, okay. I'll take a few. How much did you say?"

"Nine dollars per."

With the remaining hours of the afternoon, he visited four more boutiques and sold out Drop's entire display. At each of them he spoke impeccably, never revealing his auditory processing defect. When he returned home, he continued speaking without any sign of his impairment. The only word he found he could not say was 'work', because of its painful association with the shock treatment he had received when five years old.

The servants were astonished by his transformation, and when Leo heard him speak, he threw up his arms in joy.

"Son!" he said. "Great God! How did this happen?"

"I came across something I want," replied Knotty calmly. "I'm making the necessary adjustments."

"This is fantastic!" cried Leo. "What is this thing you want? Let's go out and get it right now! We must celebrate!"

"No," said Knotty. "It's something I have to build up to. You'll see it one day, when I achieve it."

Thus Knotty provided the first clue of his secret vision, his grand intention for total power and perfect monopoly. The words, however, passed directly over his father's head.

What Leo did observe was a level of commitment in his son that he had never thought possible. In the following months, Knotty continued selling jewelry on a daily basis. He also began attending Monterey College full-time, applying himself diligently in all his courses, especially economics. Not only did he receive straight A's in all his classes, but UCLA accepted him for transfer.

After a fruitful summer of boutique sales, he said goodbye to his father and Drop and drove his Acura to Los Angeles. With his fine Nordic features, he only needed a few weeks to land a spot in a top fraternity. His social skills were still rather weak, but his knowledge of jewelry enabled him to arouse and maintain the interest of females, and this earned him sufficient respect from his fraternal brothers.

Meanwhile, Knotty pursued his interest in economics. He also joined the Entrepreneurial Club, an ideal forum for him to advance his business ideas. In a matter of a few months, he and three other club members opened a laser printing service on campus. Shortly thereafter, they began manufacturing pop-up sunscreens for automobile windshields.

Knotty, however, was looking for something bigger. He wanted a product that would lay wide a whole new niche of consumers. After two full years of studying economic theory, a potential concept flashed before him.

He envisioned 'The Video Expressmobile,' a sports van loaded with video cassettes, cruising the suburbs of Los Angeles. The Expressmobile would offer home delivery and pick-up, saving customers the inconvenience of regular trips to a video store.

Knotty immediately launched into the project, not even consulting with his business friends. Using the profits from his other ventures, he bought a new van and stocked it with several thousand video cassettes. Then he took to the streets, eager for expansion.

What he found was a very difficult and competitive market. Only in the most affluent parts of L.A., such as Beverly Hills, Bel-Air, Brentwood, and Pacific Palisades, did he experience a warm reception. Yet these areas were so spread out and on such windy roads that Knotty's job of dispensing and retrieving tapes was made especially burdensome, particularly since there was often no one home when he went to pick up tapes.

After two months of sweating in his van, Knotty had to face the facts. He dropped all plans of expansion, restricted his service to a select group of repeat customers, and hired a driver to take over the route. In this way, he transformed his blunder into a steady source of revenue—small as it was—and he was again free to attend to his studies.

During the remaining two years of his education, Knotty avoided other marketing ploys. He turned his attention to courses in genetics, perceptual processes, and artificial intelligence. New business ideas still sprang forth in his mind, but he dismissed them ruthlessly, telling himself that the truly destined one would recur repeatedly.

It wasn't until his last semester at UCLA that he began to experience such recurrences. Even then, he remained skeptical for two full months, particularly since his inspiration again concerned rental videos. But no matter how hard he tried to reject the concept, it kept returning. After the hundredth time, he allowed himself to consider it.

The idea was to develop a chain of video stores equipped with an 'interactive expert system' that would allow customers to retrieve movierelated information via terminals. Customers could search for movies by title, subject, actor, even director or producer. They could also request synopses and reviews of any movie in stock.

Knotty had little doubt that such a system could provide a much needed service. After all, he was keenly aware of the problems associated with selecting a video. Unless customers knew exactly what they wanted, they had to search through rows and rows of tapes in order to reach a decision.

But before taking the idea any further, Knotty wisely consulted software programmers and systems designers to confirm that his idea was technically feasible. Likewise, he approached reviewers, distributors, and other movie buffs to verify that the required database could be assembled.

At that point, he telephoned his father and did something he'd never done before—he asked Leo for money.

"If I'm going to do this properly," he explained, "I'll need a good deal of backing. I can scrape together sixty thousand myself, but it's going to take a lot more than that."

"How much is a lot more?" asked Leo.

"Ten million to get the system running, five million to set up a few stores, and another ten million to ride on for the first year."

"I don't have that kind of liquidity, son."

"How about selling a ranch or two?" suggested Knotty.

"No, I can't touch my land. But I suppose I could sell off some stocks."

"And what would that come to?"

"Close to a million," replied Leo.

"So where am I supposed to get the other twenty-four million?"

"Be realistic, son. Nobody handed me that kind of money when I was your age."

"Yeah, and nobody had your brain electrocuted just because you were a creative genius."

Leo erupted into a fit of coughing. "All right," he said. "Answer me this: What would you name your store?"

"*Total Video*," said Knotty directly.

"Uhmm."

"So what do you say?"

"I'll sleep on the idea, and if I still like it in the morning, I'll co-sign a loan for twenty-four million."

The next day Leo was amenable, and Knotty had a business. He had to complete his degree in economics first, but upon graduation in May of 1996 he started the project in earnest.

Straight away, he rented the top floor of an office building in the San Fernando Valley, affixing an enormous ice-blue *Total Video* sign to its exterior. Then he hired a team of computer programmers from UCLA.

Once his programmers developed the basic structure for the software, Knotty rented another floor in the building for movie industry specialists to assemble the supporting database. Meanwhile, he negotiated a deal with a popular pair of movie reviewers that gave him rights to feature quotes and snips from their reviews.

Throughout the process, Knotty demonstrated strong managerial talent. Not only did he have a knack for inspiring his employees to share his vision, but he also had the technical ability to guide them. As a result, his team had a working prototype in three and a half months.

A week later Knotty secured locations for two test-site stores, one in Westwood and the other in Sherman Oaks. He deftly cut through bureaucratic red tape to get the stores ready, and on the first of December, only six months after he had graduated from UCLA, both locations were opened to the public.

Initially, customers were skeptical. But once they tried Knotty's system, they routinely became hooked. Since Knotty charged the same price for rentals as other video stores, there was little reason not to frequent a Total Video outlet.

Soon enough, Knotty found himself fielding calls from other

video retailers. Several companies offered to buy his business outright, and even more requested licensing to use his system, but he turned them all down. Having learned the importance of timing, Knotty knew to wait for the right moment. He sunk all the money he had left into constructing six more corporate stores in the Southern California area.

Five months later the stores were operational and packed with customers. Industry experts hailed his approach as the wave of the future, and a competing video chain announced it would soon be installing a similar information system for its customers.

On July 4, 1997, with demand at its height, Knotty announced a select offering of Total Video franchises at 58 locations in the continental United States. Despite it taking place on a national holiday, the sale was a great success. Each of the franchises were purchased within an hour of the announcement. Two weeks later, Knotty made available another block of 58 franchises, and once again the public rushed to acquire them.

Not surprisingly, the franchise stores quickly became profit-makers. Over the next year, Knotty held nine more block offerings, each time selling 58 franchises. By July of 1998, there were 530 Total Video stores located domestically and 116 abroad.

In the meantime, the other large video chains implemented their own expert systems. But the Total Video system improved upon each of the competitors' innovations, and most people agreed that Knotty's terminals were easier to use. The smaller independent video stores ended up either buying into Knotty's franchises or going out of business.

By the end of 1999, any doubts about the long-term survival of Total Video dissipated. Almost 4,000 franchises were sprinkled throughout the world, and although Knotty was far from monopolizing the video market, his competitors had largely given up on their efforts to beat his system. Instead they simply focused their efforts on matching it.

At the age of 27, then, Knotty Burgstaller was an international success story. The President of the United States described him as a "shining example of the American system and American values," and throughout the world people admired him for his campaign to increase the informational content of video cassettes. For Knotty, however, this was just the smallest of beginnings, the tiniest kernel of his dream.

If just one person commanded the foresight to realize where he was headed, perhaps the Tyranny of 2008 would have been averted. But who could have understood how Knotty thought? Who could have anticipated his objectives?

Few people were even aware of his childhood difficulties, and those who were felt only empathy. But no one, not even Leo, could have possibly anticipated the horrible truth that Knotty's current power was only a minuscule fraction of what it soon would be.

THE TYRANT AND HIS
BLACKEST PLACE

WHILE THOSE AROUND him praised his spirit of enterprise, Knotty turned inward to focus on his secret vision. He had shown he could draw from society's receptacle of knowledge to build institutions. Now it was time to go a step further.

Knotty knew that the exploratory years he spent as a child in Carmel would give him access to avenues no Harvard M.B.A. could begin to fathom. He also knew, if only because his secret vision required it, that there existed some as yet undiscovered technology capable of changing the law of supply and demand forever in his favor.

Thus Knotty poured over scientific journals late at night—not because he presumed the answer to his puzzle would lie in any one of them, but rather because their tight language formed a kind of counterpoint to his inner search. The fulfillment of his secret vision, he believed, required that he find a way to the blackest place within him.

Most students of human psychology would find such behavior delusional, but Knotty was not a man who played games with himself. Though his perceptions of the outer world were often blurred, he understood the workings of his own body like few others.

It was only a matter of a few weeks before he discovered the dark portion of himself he sought. He locked onto its coordinates like a starving man taking his first bite, and as he gained command of the territory, he began to simultaneously occupy it and read the journals.

The hardest part was learning how to feed the black hole in his head while harmonizing it with the written words. After only ten short days, he mastered the technique. At that point, he sorted through his articles one by one, without hurrying, without doubt.

So it was inevitable. On the evening of February 13, 2000, while skimming a journal devoted to advances in biocomputing, he glimpsed the first component of his secret vision: An instrument to accurately measure customers' preferences.

If he invented a tool that could measure how much satisfaction a customer derived from a product, he could use it to charge each of his customers the full amount they would be willing to pay. What faster way could there be to assume the world's wealth? What better way to seize the world's power?

Accordingly, Knotty launched into a program to develop what he called 'the bioeconomic calculating device.' Under the pretense of improved consumer research, he began luring biologists, economists, psychologists, and computer programmers to work for him.

It was through his recruitment efforts at the Massachusetts Institute of Technology that I myself first heard of Knotty Burgstaller. At the time, I was an undergraduate student. I missed his lecture on the future of consumer research, but I do recall a great deal of talk among my peers about the tremendous salaries and facilities he was offering at his Total Video labs in Los Angeles.

Knotty wasn't able to attract any M.I.T. professors—they all balked at the prospect of working for a video chain. He ended up drawing most of his researchers from second- and third-tier schools. Still, the process forced him to examine what the other components of his secret vision might involve. His bioeconomic device wouldn't be enough in and of itself. He needed control of a major industry to make proper use of the device, and the video business was far too trivial for someone with his ambition.

To address the situation, Knotty returned to his technique of reading while occupying the blackest place in his mind. This time he read only economics theory, under the assumption that such material was most aligned with his objectives.

On the evening of April 14, while reading *Microeconomics* by Hal Varian, Knotty synthesized what he had previously only partially understood. In a great flash of black light, he recognized the two additional components needed to make his secret vision come true.

First, he had to enter into an industry that could sustain a perfect monopoly. Otherwise his bioeconomic device would be useless—all his customers would simply switch to a competitor. Second, he had to provide a product that was essential for human life. His customers would thereby be forced to buy his product at almost any price.

The only complexity was choosing the right product. Few commodities qualified as strictly essential for life, and Knotty quickly narrowed his list of contenders to four possibilities: Shelter, sex, food, and water.

He considered companionship as a fifth possibility, but upon recalling the long lives of many prisoners he realized it was not truly essential. This led him to disqualify shelter, since many humans had survived without it, particularly in temperate climates. Finally, he eliminated sex, as he himself had never engaged in it.

That left him with only two candidates to entertain. Food and water. He fell into a deep puzzle: To what extent was water truly essential? Strictly speaking, one could do without water if one had food. Yet that was begging the question, he conceded, for food could not be grown without water and, moreover, all food contained water.

After careful consideration, Knotty decided that both products were indeed essential. Either could serve as the right product, provided their supply was fully controlled. The question was, which was easier to monopolize?

Most people would argue that they were both impossible to monopolize, since food and water were spread abundantly across the surface of the earth. But this is precisely where Knotty's access to his blackest place differentiated him from the rest of us.

He had only to wait for another clear night. Once it arrived, he calmly strutted into the thinking room of his Holmby Hills penthouse and sat down on an uncomfortable chair. He did not even read any journals. He simply burrowed into his blackest place and let his images fly.

At first, his dark logic pointed to the simplicity of water, which was basically unperishable. It seemed feasible to hoard a huge supply of it and make the remaining water on earth unfit for human consumption. Then he could use the bioeconomic device—once it was invented—to sell his palatable water for maximal prices. He could even set up water distribution centers at each of his Total Video stores. Better yet, he could seize all the water utility companies.

Before he allowed himself to be swept away, however, Knotty remembered his Video Expressmobile fiasco. Cautiously, he pulled himself back to the center of the vortex that formed his black hole. From this position, he quickly saw the weakness of his concept.

Water was too easy to purify. There were few contaminants that could not be easily removed from it. True, he could bombard the earth's water supply with radioactive particles, but how would he avoid killing his consumers in the process? Even supposing these obstacles could be overcome, what would stop consumers from recycling water for themselves?

The problem, Knotty realized, was that water wasn't manipulable enough. Its simple elements, hydrogen and oxygen, would not permit any significant rearranging.

On the other hand, food was organic. It originated from living things containing amino acids and strands of DNA, and this meant it could be contaminated in specific ways to produce specific responses. Knotty only needed the right type of virus, and he could infect all of the world's food supply.

No doubt, such a virus would have to be carefully designed to make sure the entire foodstock on earth was rendered inedible for all humans. It would also have to avoid impacting the fragile ecological chains connecting the other species of life. But from his studies in genetics, Knotty knew the concept was theoretically possible. By using gene-splicing techniques, a virus could be made to respond only to a particular DNA sequence found in humans. If engineered properly, it could produce a fatal illness when ingested by people but be harmless when ingested by other animals.

Of course, before releasing something of this type into the environment, he would have to grow an alternative food supply resistant to the virus—one for which he maintained complete control to exploit the desperate population. With these elements in place, he would be able to sell the resistant food for maximal prices via his bioeconomic device. His customers would become completely dependent on him, and his only task would be to insure that the seeds to his resistant strain were kept out of his consumers' hands.

The realization caused Knotty to leap from his chair. He rushed to open a bottle of Dom Perignon and poured it into three separate glasses—one for the bioeconomic device, one for the virus, and one for the alternative foodstuff. Then he took a long sip from each glass and told himself he was brilliant.

THE TYRANT IN THE DOLDRUMS

Knotty contemplated his brilliance all night long, until the first rays of sunlight crept over the Hollywood hills. Then he put on a tie, walked downstairs to his Mercedes, and headed north to his father's headquarters in the Salinas Valley.

In the past months, Leo's business had flourished almost as much as Total Video. He had extended his farming operations as far south as Bakersfield and expanded into the food processing industry with a new line of microwavable frozen foods. To reflect these changes, Leo had consolidated all his activities under one name: Agripe Industries, which stood for AGRIcultural Processing and Engineering.

Knotty was eager to see the new changes. When he arrived at the Agripe headquarters, he dodged two security guards, ran up the backstairs to the top floor of the building, and marched straight into Leo's office.

"Son!" said Leo, looking up from a stack of papers. "I didn't think we'd ever draw you back to the salad bowl."

"Are you kidding?" said Knotty. "This place is great. I love the new new name too."

"Yeah, it's all right."

"It's more than all right, Dad. It's brilliant."

"I suppose," said Leo. "But I don't think you came all the way up here just to tell me that."

Knotty paused for a moment. "No," he said. "The truth is, I have more capital than I know what to do with, and I was hoping you could help. There's only so much I can do with video."

"Really? It must not be like food."

"No, it's not. Video is just tape wrapped up in a plastic box. There's no limit to what you can do with food."

"I never knew you felt that way, son."

"I've always respected food. That's why I'm here, to see if you'll do business with me."

"What'd you have in mind?" asked Leo.

"A chain of convenience stores with a supermarket feel. I'd call it *Total Food*, and I'd have you as my primary supplier. You'd ship straight to my locations. We'd cut out the middleman and split the savings down the middle."

"Not a bad idea, but this type of thing's been tried before. Vertical integration is tricky."

"Yeah. It wouldn't be a merger though. Just a long-term contract."

Leo pondered for a moment.

"So how about it?" said Knotty impatiently.

"Don't get me wrong, I'm not questioning your business instinct. But now's not a real good time for us."

"It's now or never, Dad. I don't have time to screw around. I could be strapped down on a table and lobotomized any day now. You know how that sort of thing goes." He looked at his father fiercely.

"Okay, sure. You put in the order, Agripe will supply the food. But I think you ought to move slow on it."

"At wholesale prices, right?" asked Knotty.

Leo shook his head. "We can't do that, but we'll give you a break if you do your own shipping."

"Give me a serious discount and my trucks are there."

"Fifteen percent," said Leo.

"Twenty-five," said Knotty.

"Don't push," said Leo. "Twenty percent. If you meet our minimums."

"Deal." Knotty thrust out his hand and they shook.

"I'll be damned," said Leo, grinning. "How'd you turn out to be such a clever businessman?"

"Osmosis," replied Knotty. "Pure osmosis."

They both laughed and went downstairs for lunch at the Agripe cafeteria. That evening, after Knotty had departed, Leo wrote in his journal, "At last I have been delivered the son I always wanted."

When Knotty returned to L.A., he focused all his efforts on his Total Food concept. Everything in his gut told him the stores would make the perfect foundation for his secret vision. Ignoring his father's advice, he jumped into the project aggressively.

His goal was to unveil fifty new corporate stores by midsummer, to take the market by surprise. He ran into a bit more red tape than with Total Video, partly because of changes in the building code and partly because he was seeking to make a greater opening splash, but the first Total Food stores were unveiled on September 7th, 2000.

Consumers immediately fell in love with them. They were small and quick, like other convenience stores, yet they stocked many of the high-end products the bigger supermarkets carried. Most importantly, they featured the winning combination of low prices and upscale decorating.

Of course, the low prices made the marketing of additional stores a bit difficult, as investors were afraid of poor returns—particularly since Knotty's contract stipulated that all franchise owners buy their commodities from him. But consumers continued to respond favorably to the stores, and the investors who did buy franchises began to make sizable profits. After three months, Knotty actually lowered many of his supply prices while keeping retail prices unchanged.

It was this act that stimulated the flurry of interest Knotty sought. With investors convinced that he could indeed buy food more cheaply than his competitors, franchise sales became brisk. By March of 2001, there were over 250 Total Food franchises either in operation or undergoing construction.

Still, the success did not come without cost. Agripe charged Total Food only slightly less than what most food stores paid, and Knotty had considerable start-up expenses. While his enormous profits from Total Video were more than able to keep him above water, his stockpiles of excess capital were eroding, and all his energy was going to managing the food stores.

Knotty yearned to devote all his time to his secret vision. Total Food was just a positioning strategy, with no value to Knotty until he had the other two prongs of his master plan in place. True, his team of scientists were already at work on the bioeconomic device, and the funds for this came directly out of his R&D budget for Total Video. But this was the easiest part of his plan, since his researchers didn't require any knowledge of its intended purpose.

In contrast, the development of the fatal virus was much more complex. It demanded a state-of-the-art biotechnology lab, along with a highly trained genetic engineer. Furthermore, in order to maintain complete control, Knotty suspected he would have to grow the virus-resistant foodstock in outer space. Financing these endeavors would require billions of dollars and massive security.

So for the first time, doubt crept into Knotty's mind. At first, he blamed it on stellar interference. But to his surprise, he kept emerging from his thinking room empty-headed, with no solutions.

After weeks passed without success, he began retracting from his responsibilities at work, and he resumed his teenage habit of locking himself in his bedroom and lying in bed, doing nothing. Soon enough, he even gave up on going to his thinking room. His contact with the world became reduced to the occasional messages he faxed to his secretary, and rumors spread that he was severely ill.

On the morning of May 3, 2001, the biggest blow came to Knotty since his mother had abandoned him for Indonesia. It happened when he left his bedroom to check his incoming mail. There he was on the cover of *Time* magazine, in full color, with his blonde hair ruffled and his lips turned downward in disdain. Next to the photo, in bold letters, was the caption, "Decline of an Empire?"

The image was too much for Knotty. He took it as judgment that his dream was doomed, that even his blackest place could not save him, and instead of returning to the bedroom, he collapsed on a velvet couch in the living room.

During the next three days, he ate and drank nothing. He just lay on the couch withering, waiting for death to take him. The only feasible plan for total tyranny ever to be fashioned seemed destined to fade away.

On the fourth day, Knotty's father drove to visit one of his farms east of King City. Leo had no idea that his son was only a wink away from death. He made the trip simply to inspect a broccoli field, in response to reports of poor production.

What happened when he got out of his car, however, was purely unanticipated. For as Leo stooped over the field to examine a broccoli sprout, a parachutist leaped out of a plane from 16,000 feet above. This particular parachutist—an Evan T. Bolins—was extremely experienced with airborne maneuvers and widely regarded for his clear-headed practices. Yet that morning he apparently suffered a slight mental lapse: He forgot to strap a parachute pack to his back.

Perhaps, upon realizing his error in mid-air, he developed a vicious streak. Or perhaps he simply lost consciousness and let the winds direct him where they would. In either event, the result of his fall was a direct impact at the base of Leo's spine, causing them both to crumple to their deaths on a green bed of unproductive broccoli.

Later that morning, the ranch foreman noticed Leo's car parked on the side of the road. When he stopped to investigate, he spotted the bodies and called the authorities. A crew of policemen soon arrived.

After positively identifying the bodies, the police attempted to notify Knotty of his father's tragic death, but Knotty was unable to answer the phone. By that time, he himself was half-dead and entirely unconscious.

Because of Leo's stature in the Salinas Valley, the King City authorities felt it urgent to contact Knotty as soon as possible. The police chief even placed a call to the Total Video corporate office, and while no one there could suggest where Knotty might be, his secretary explained that he hadn't been in to work for quite some time and that he seemed rather ill when she last saw him.

With this tip, the King City chief telephoned the Los Angeles Police Department. He was connected to a detective who happened to be a great admirer of the Total Video chains. With only a little urging, the detective agreed to make a visit to Knotty's penthouse.

A security guard at the building divulged that Knotty had entered his penthouse four weeks earlier and, to the best of his knowledge, hadn't exited. After five knocks and no answer, the detective heroically broke through the door—with no concept of this deed's impact on humanity. Inside he found Knotty's desiccated body lying on the velvet couch.

It took a full day of intravenous feeding for Knotty to be revived. The doctors postulated that he had contracted a "severe viral infection" producing massive dehydration in his body. Knotty saw no need to mention that his illness was actually self-induced.

As he regained his logical faculties, however, his deep depression returned. He refused to eat anything the nurses brought, and his arms had to be tied down to keep him from pulling out the I.V. needle.

The doctors assumed that his illness caused this behavior. Their bigger concern was whether to inform Knotty of his father's death. After much debate, the final bureaucratic word was that they had no right to withhold the information, regardless of his condition. The head resident proceeded to impart the news, and according to the orderlies witnessing the scene, Knotty's expression of grief was genuine.

Shortly thereafter, Leo's attorney entered the room. He explained that the initial version of Leo's will did not include Knotty. Rather, it specified that all of Leo's personal belongings were to go to his favorite charities and that Agripe was to be sold to the highest bidder, with the proceeds distributed to the University of California at Davis.

"I know all about that," said Knotty morosely. "My father told me years ago."

"Yes, right," continued the attorney. "But things have changed. The day after your last visit with your father, he changed his will to show you as the sole inheritor. You're a very lucky man, Mr. Burgstaller. You stand to inherit assets worth approximately eight hundred million dollars—perhaps more if the taxes are handled well."

"You're sure of this?" said Knotty.

"Absolutely sure," replied the attorney.

Knotty slowly raised himself from his bed. "In that case, I believe I'm ready for my first meal. I've worked up quite an appetite."

To his doctor's surprise, Knotty quickly recovered his strength. Receiving his father's inheritance at such an opportune time renewed his faith in himself, not only because it gave him the financial backing he needed, but also because he interpreted it as a final reconciliation of all his father's wrongs.

By the end of two weeks, Knotty was a cyclone of activity. In addition to restoring order to his Total Video and Total Food concerns, he deftly assumed responsibility for Agripe Industries. All of his employees, both old and new, eagerly supported him when they learned of his bout with a serious viral infection.

The bulk of Knotty's work, however, was done late at night in his Holmby Hills thinking room. Knotty now possessed all the resources necessary to fully embark on his secret vision, and it didn't take long for him to see that control of Agripe was a godsend.

Agripe was already actively involved in agricultural research to improve crop yields and livestock traits. They employed two geneticists and were in the midst of recruiting a third. By further pursuing such research, everyone would understand that Knotty was just doing for food what he had done for video—developing technology to enrich the product.

Consequently, when the probate judge cleared Leo's will in late July of 2001, Knotty announced plans for a multi-million dollar research facility to be built on an 85-acre site north of Santa Barbara. The facility was to house all of Agripe's current R&D operations, with increased emphasis in genetic engineering. Knotty earmarked part of the facility for research on outer space farming, which again could be rationalized as responsible, future-looking research.

To design the center, Knotty hired a top engineering firm. Under his guidance, the engineers developed plans for a building in the spirit of a traditional pyramid, but with its form truncated mid-way at the tenth floor, where a smaller pyramid would be inset and rotated 45 degrees from the orientation of the base.

The overall effect was dramatic yet comfortably symmetric. The shape retained the purity of a pyramid, but it had an extra dynamic presence, appearing as if its middle part had been sliced away and the apex piece twisted an eighth turn. To integrate the design, the structure was covered with a skin of arctic blue glass.

Thanks to strong funding and good management, the entire project was completed in late June of 2002. A consensus quickly emerged that the Burgstaller Pyramid, as it came to be called, was an architectural masterpiece. Positive publicity for Knotty soared higher than ever.

Suddenly, Knotty's desire to recruit top scientists and engineers was realizable. Hundreds of inquiries from top-caliber researchers came pouring in, without Knotty even having to advertise. When he did post job offerings, he found he could fill them from virtually any university or laboratory he wished. He was even able to successfully raid NASA for his outer space farming project.

As a result, by the fall of 2002, his Pyramid was stocked with over 700 employees, three fourths of whom held Ph.D.'s from either Harvard, Yale, Stanford, or M.I.T.

THE TYRANT AND HIS LAST RECRUIT

Knotty still faced the greatest recruitment challenge of all—to locate his critical scientist who would fashion the lethal virus he had conceived. His other researchers were working on small projects with no concept of his master plan, but this critical scientist would have to comprehend at least some small part of his vision in order to develop the necessary virus. Finding such a person, Knotty knew, would be no simple task.

His first strategy was to look up disgruntled geneticists who had failed to receive proper credit from their research. He hoped that perhaps they might be bitter enough to want to wreak havoc on the world. But after speaking to them, he saw it wasn't likely. Rather, the fledgling scientists were only that much more eager to play by the rules of their profession in the climb toward higher status.

Knotty's next approach was to examine the pool of recent Ph.D. graduates from top microbiology departments. The majority of these individuals were doing exactly what one would expect—working for universities, pharmaceutical companies, oil conglomerates, gene-splicing firms, cancer institutes, and AIDS centers. A small proportion of them had died or retired on their profits. But three of the names could not be accounted for in any of the conventional ways.

The first one, Frederick Majors, was easily reconciled. In a matter of hours, Knotty located one of Fred's ex-girlfriends, who explained that he was last seen bedding down with a tribe of Aborigines south of Darwin, Australia. That ruled out Fred.

The second mystery candidate, Jake Snadelian, had taken a research job two years earlier with the firm responsible for putting human growth hormone on the market. Evidently, Jake couldn't resist self-administering small doses of the substance. The hormone proved to be worthy, as it added almost half a foot to Jake's small frame in less than sixteen months. But in the process, the drug severely traumatized his system, and Jake ended up in a sanitarium outside of Atlanta.

It was the last name, Martha Buliment, that proved to be the most difficult for Knotty to locate. From his preliminary search, Knotty could only determine that Martha's relatives were all deceased. None of the graduate students with whom Martha had attended Yale University had any idea where she was. It seemed she vanished from sight in the spring of 1998 after completing her doctoral dissertation, entitled *Biotoxins and Transfer Splicing*. Her placement file at the university suggested that no prospective employers ever interviewed her.

By all accounts, Martha was an excellent student in the biology department. Most of her colleagues expected her to be a star. While a few of them mentioned that she had held some eccentric views, this was hardly a reason for her to throw away her degree.

To Knotty everything pointed to a deeper explanation, and so he went to his thinking room to consider the matter. Oddly, his blackest place advised him to turn on the television and watch that night's rerun of *The Rockford Files*.

The suggestion turned out to be fruitful, as that particular episode involved Rockford tracking down a missing person by locating the cemetery in which the missing person's mother was buried. When the show ended, Knotty sped to the airport and jumped on a plane to Martha's hometown of Peekskill, New York.

The first cemetery he visited happened to have Martha's mother's remains in their registry, and flowers were still being delivered to the gravesite on a weekly basis. Knotty only had to offer twenty dollars to the woman at the local flower shop in order to reveal the source: a Dr. Mary Bolton from Felway Proving Grounds, Utah.

After a little background reading, Knotty felt sure he had hit pay dirt. Felway Proving Grounds was an army base bordering the salt flats about 80 miles southwest of Salt Lake City. More importantly, it boasted a long history of involvement with biological weapons, dating as far back as the early 1950s, when the U.S. Army began exploding germ bombs on the test grids at Felway.

The more Knotty read, the more excited he became. He discovered that the Pentagon had secretively built a new laboratory at Felway in 1999. This was no ordinary lab, but rather a maximum containment facility designed to accommodate the most dangerous germs and toxins imaginable.

Three days later—on September 17, 2002—Knotty flew to Salt Lake City. Once there, he rented a small package van and patrolled the city looking for a young woman matching Martha's build.

When at last he noticed a suitable female emerging from a downtown law office, he followed her to her house. He waited a few minutes to be sure she was alone, then knocked on her door and introduced himself as a solar screen salesman. She invited him into the living room, whereupon he pulled out a silencer and shot her in the back four times.

After changing into workclothes, Knotty slid the woman's body into a burlap sack and carried it out to his van. He headed west on Interstate 80 past the Stansbury mountains, then he veered left on an unmarked road and crossed the dusty scrub of Skull Valley to the front gate of Felway Proving Grounds.

"Special delivery for Dr. Bolton," said Knotty, authoritatively.

"I'll sign for it here, sir," replied the guard.

"Colonel Carathrope at Fort Detrick requested I deliver it to Dr. Bolton personally," said Knotty. He flashed a paper bearing the Fort Detrick seal, with Carathrope's forged signature.

"Yes, sir. She's at Downing Lab, Building #2048, but I'll have to escort you, sir." He signaled to another guard and climbed into Knotty's van.

They drove a quarter mile to the lab, where Knotty was shown to a waiting room. Ten minutes later, Dr. Bolton emerged from the clean-up showers, and Knotty could scarcely contain his excitement. She matched Martha's description perfectly: Five foot six, slender, gaunt, pale complexion, brown eyes, short brown hair, and a large mole above her left cheek.

Knotty had no opportunity to speak to her. She simply signed the papers, collected the package, and went back to her work. But Knotty had inserted a note in the package requesting that Dr. Bolton call him at his hotel in Salt Lake, and the note made it clear that he was *the* Knotty Burgstaller, with an offer she couldn't refuse.

Under ordinary circumstances, Dr. Bolton—a.k.a. Martha Buliment —would have reported the message to the Defense Intelligence Agency. It wasn't that she felt any overriding allegiance to the military. It was simply that she was satisfied with her job. Unrestricted access to exotic pathogens more than compensated her for any other shortcomings.

In the past months, however, a fair amount of bad press concerning biological weapons had been circulated. For instance, earlier that summer the media revealed that an aerosol test performed at Felway was responsible for the deaths of over 7000 sheep, due to an unexpected shift in wind. In August, a team of medical scientists at John Hopkins announced that over 875 civilian fatalities occurring between 1990 and 1996 could be traced to microorganisms that Felway had released for testing purposes.

As a result, new waves of protest against biological weapons were emerging, and there were indications that funding for the Felway lab could be reduced. This meant that research on some of the most dangerous viruses, which Martha specialized in, would probably be curtailed. There were even rumors that certain famous germs and toxins from the more aggressive days of the '50s and '60s would no longer be stored at Felway. Specifically, she heard that her supply of botulinum, one of the most potent neurotoxins ever to be isolated, would soon be destroyed.

This news disturbed Martha immensely. The main reason she had agreed to go undercover at Felway was due to the thrill she experienced in the presence of botulinum. Consequently, she decided not to report Knotty's note. Instead, she left her quarters that night and called Knotty from a pay phone.

"What exactly is your offer, Mr. Burgstaller?" she asked directly.

"I'd like to discuss it in person. Can you get away from Felway this evening?"

"I suppose."

"Good. I'll be in a white van at the on-ramp to Interstate 80 at 9:00 PM sharp. Follow me until I come to a halt."

"Fine," she said.

"Oh, and Dr. Bolton," he added, "I assure you this won't be a waste of your time."

Martha did not doubt Knotty's sincerity. She noticed an odd potential in his voice that did not seem to emanate the typical male frequencies, and less than an hour later she met with him on a secluded dirt road.

"Good evening, Dr. Bolton," said Knotty, dressed in a beige silk suit. "How are you?"

"Forget the pretense," replied Martha. "As far as I'm concerned, you're just another asshole."

"I won't play any games then," he began. "I know your true name is Martha Buliment, and I don't care. What I do care about is your ability. And your attitude."

"Why is that?" she asked, unafraid.

"To be perfectly frank, I'm concerned about our current military capabilities."

"Oh?"

"Yes. That's why I'd like to dedicate a portion of my assets to a defense program independent of public opinion."

"Uh huh," said Martha.

"I have no intention of leaving our defense up to the whims of the Pentagon. I need a talented genetic engineer like you."

"Thanks, but I don't give away my talents to megalomaniacs."

"Of course not. I'm assuming, however, that we share a common hatred for alien domination."

Martha laughed. "That's the first thing you've said of any significance."

"Excellent. Then I believe you'll find my working conditions quite attractive. Unlike the military, I'm able to offer an environment where the ideal biological agent can be creatively pursued free of bureaucratic constraints and fickle policy."

"Perhaps," she said. "But what about your facilities? And what about the problem of my identity?"

"As far as facilities go," said Knotty, "there is no need for concern. Nor is the identity issue a barrier. But it is true I won't be able to offer you the diversity of microbes you have at Felway. My interest is in a more focused pursuit based on the development of one or two ideal germs, in order to provide the ultimate deterrent."

"That could present a problem," replied Martha. "I operate most effectively in the presence of multiple microorganisms and biotoxins."

"Such as...?"

"Botulinum, plague, anthrax, and Ebola virus, for instance."

"Anything else?"

"Those would be sufficient," she said.

"Suppose I could provide you with a lab ten times as big as you currently have, with all the latest biotechnology equipment, double the salary, and each of these additional pathogens you've mentioned. Would you accept my offer?"

"It depends."

"On what?" asked Knotty.

"On how you plan to solve my identity problem. The military doesn't easily let go of someone like me."

"How about I show you?"

"Now?" she said.

"Yes, right now." Knotty led her to the van and handed her a new change of clothes.

"You want me to strip for you too?"

"Humor me."

Martha sneered as she dropped her skirt onto the desert floor. Knotty turned away embarrassedly and went to get the dead woman's corpse from the back of the van. He took Martha's discarded garments, slipped them onto the corpse, and set it on the driver's seat of her car.

"You're not too attached to your vehicle, are you?" he asked, as he placed a bomb next to the body.

"Not really," replied Martha. "But you do realize they'll try to trace my dental records?"

"Trust me, they won't find enough to cross check. The clothes are just for their fiber team to play with."

"I see."

They climbed into Knotty's van and took off toward the main road. When they had traveled about a quarter mile, Knotty pressed a remote control device and Martha's car exploded into a huge burst of orange light.

"That's the end of Mary Bolton," he laughed.

Martha shrugged her shoulders. "*C'est la vie.*"

"Now it's simply a matter of getting you some new documents."

"Just know that if you screw this up, I'll slap a sexual harassment suit on your ass faster than you can say 'dirty old white man.'"

"Of course, of course. By the way, what do you think of the name, Jessica Einster?"

"It'll do."

"Then it's settled. I'll have the documents for you in 24 hours."

"And don't forget my botulinum," she said.

"Ha ha ha," he laughed again.

And so they drove through the night, hurtling across the desert to their new oasis at the Burgstaller Pyramid in Santa Barbara.

THE TYRANT AND HIS WEAKNESS

By the time they reached the Pyramid, Martha's nameplate, *Dr. Jessica Einster, Executive Vice-President*, was mounted on the door of the top-floor office adjacent to Knotty's. Her new office was appointed with mahogany paneling and a skylit atrium, but Martha barely noticed. To gain her attention, Knotty took her hand and pressed it against a small button located underneath her desk.

The bookshelf on the north wall of the office slid aside, revealing an elevator leading to a hidden floor between the ninth and tenth stories of the Pyramid. Knotty and Martha entered the elevator and silently descended. When the doors retracted, the two of them passed through a pressurized chamber and shower room. Then Knotty input a security code, and the secret laboratory opened up before them.

The complex featured research offices, aerosol booths, freezer vaults, animal kennels, auxiliary labs, and two commercial-scale production rooms. Fully sealed from the rest of the building, it had its own ventilation, plumbing, and electricity systems. But what most excited Martha were the three 'hot suites' for working with dangerous viruses and bacteria.

"You've done your homework," said Martha.

Knotty nodded. "I've taken the liberty of stocking the freezers with some standard microbes from the commercial supply houses. The other pathogens you requested should be here by tomorrow."

"You have the requisite permits from the Department of Agriculture and the Public Health Service, I take it?" she asked.

"Oh, yes. We do legitimate research at the labs downstairs."

"That's reassuring."

"What I'd like to do," he said, leading her into a plushly carpeted retreat, "is to get a bit more specific about my objectives."

"Please do," said Martha.

"I have in mind a very particular type of germ. It must aerosolize well, and while in the air it must be highly infectious to all plant matter, yet unable to penetrate humans and animals. It can't be debilitating to the plants, as they're only to serve as latent carriers of the germ. Instead, when the infected plants are ingested by humans, that's when the germ must be disabling."

"What about when the plants are eaten by other animals?"

"Then the animals must become carriers but not affected themselves."

Martha showed a slight smile. "I can't say I've ever come across anything resembling what you seek."

"Does that mean you're doubtful?" he asked.

"No. There are many fantastic things still unknown."

"Good. Because I've seen this germ in my mind's eye and I intend to make it a reality."

In the days that followed, Martha immersed herself in her new position. She spent each morning at her top floor office, dutifully fulfilling her executive functions. Then she descended to her secret laboratory, where for the rest of the day she engaged in her real work.

She had no illusions about the difficulty of the challenge she faced. The microbe Knotty wanted had to be able to survive in both plants and animals, whereas most infectious agents occupied only one or the other. While airborne it was only supposed to invade plant tissue, meaning that it somehow had to be barred from using the respiratory tract as a portal of entry into humans. If humans ate the infected plant matter, it was then required to cause death.

This last transmission troubled Martha the most. Once the populace discovered that such a germ existed, they would be likely to cook their food very thoroughly, but no known germ that was infectious in humans could withstand being subjected to such extreme temperatures. Martha suspected it might be possible to genetically alter the DNA of a microorganism in order to make it more stable under heat, but she couldn't help thinking there had to a more direct approach.

When she tried confronting Knotty on this point, he became livid. "Perhaps you do not yet fathom who I am, so I will tell you this once," he said coldly. "I have a soul unlike any other—a soul larger, greater, fuller, and destined to overtake all life forces. This is unchallengeable and al-ready proven in Nature's court. You can either ally yourself with what is ordained or be crushed like an ant under the heel of my shoe."

Instead of being put off, Martha found his behavior to be strangely attractive. The feeling was a new one for her. Having been sodomized and molested by her father as a child, she had built her adult life around the premise that men were innately evil. Yet Knotty exuded such a peculiar type of power, she felt him to be in a separate category. Being with Knotty was almost as exciting as the presence of her sacred botulinum toxin.

After weeks of harboring her desire, she resolved to act on it. Her conscious mind rationalized this as a ploy to uncover Knotty's hidden objective, but her main motive was not that logical. It was simply an urge—a raw, driving urge.

Seduction was not something in which Martha had experience, so she consulted various sexual handbooks. She even studied adult videos and magazines for more graphic tips. But she didn't rush to apply her findings. Rather, she waited patiently for the right day.

On a particular Friday afternoon—November 8th, 2002—she lounged for two hours in a whirlpool bathtub. Then she slipped into a red teddy with lace stockings, donned a pair of black spiked heels, and strapped on a narrow, steel-studded belt.

When she was sure her image was perfect, she called Knotty down to her lab. He had just learned that Total Food profited 47 million dollars the previous quarter, and when he saw Martha reclining on the couch fondling a black leather whip, he felt something unprecedented in his loins.

"Je... Jessica," he said, stammering. "What's going on?"

"Is Knotty ready to be naughty?" she asked, slightly raising her legs.

"I'm... I'm not sure what you mean."

"I've always wondered if you could live up to your name."

She beckoned him to the edge of the couch and gently slid off his shirt. He was too bewildered to protest as she began rubbing kama sutra lotion on his back. She paid particular attention to his tight spots, massaging his muscles with precision and grace. When he was fully relaxed, she turned him on his back and removed the rest of his clothing. Then she expertly tied up his arms and legs with rope.

"Martha, what the devil?"

"You'll see," she said, climbing on top of him. "It's an experiment." She reached for a red vial holstered in her belt and poured the contents over his belly.

"Aaah," he groaned. "What is that?"

"Phytoplankton," she laughed. "I did a little gene-splicing so it releases a stimulatory enzyme upon skin contact." She poured another red vial on his crotch and a third over his chest.

"Aaah," he said. "It's too much, it's too much."

"But we're just beginning."

"This is crazy, Martha. What's gotten into you?"

"Lust," she said breathily. She returned to stroking and fondling him, until gradually his thoughts became filled with only pleasure.

"It's time for your next surprise," she said, withdrawing another vial—this one black—from her belt. "Guess what it is?"

Knotty pressed his groin against her. "What?"

"A quarter gram of a brand new toxin, ten times more deadly than botulinum." She rubbed herself against him to keep his attention. "I've named it Knotulinum in your honor."

"My god," he said.

"I want you to feel it," she whispered, pressing the vial into his hand. "Feel its power." She smoothly straddled his erect organ.

Knotty grasped the vial with all his might. Nothing before had ever felt so good. His dreams rose swiftly to the surface of his conscious, readying themselves to become reality, and he was filled with images of pure power and oppression.

But Martha was not yet satisfied. She wanted to go further, to cross his barriers. Carefully, she reclaimed the black vial from his hand and raised his knees.

"Oooh," he groaned.

"Now it's time to feel it where it's deepest," she said. With one deft movement, she slipped the vial into Knotty's anus.

"Ayeeeh!" he cried.

"Feel it," she repeated, as she gyrated wildly. "Feel it where it's deepest."

At first, Knotty was reluctant. But as the vial warmed and softened, a throbbing pleasure emanated through his senses. Even his blackest place soon succumbed to the fervor of their sexual energy.

It was then that Martha's wishes became fulfilled. In the passion of the moment, through the conduit of his erect linkage, she became united with Knotty's blackest place, and for one flickering instant she perceived the full outline of Knotty's master plan.

The image was so far-reaching, so fantastic, she could scarcely contain herself. She screamed in ecstasy as pure waves of orgasm coursed through her body. Knotty pounded and pounded in rhythm to her screams. When at last he climaxed, he laid down his head in exhaustion, expelling the vial from within himself.

The moment the vial dropped to the floor, Martha understood she'd been approaching the microbe puzzle in the wrong way. The answer was lying in front of her: She could use *a toxin* to poison the world's food supply.

Unlike microbes, toxins were often quite heat-stable. They could retain their potency even under the harshest of environments. And once an appropriate toxin was found, she could use any germ she wanted to produce it—the germ wouldn't need to survive once it entered a foodstuff, as long as the toxin was secreted.

A wide smile stretched across her face, and she slowly dragged her fingers through Knotty's blonde hair. "Wake up, my dear Knotty," she whispered into his ear. "Wake up. We have work to do!"

THE TYRANT AND THE TYRANNUM

FINDING A TOXIN with all the properties Knotty's plan required was not a simple matter. Since no naturally-occurring toxin of this sort existed, Martha's initial strategy was to manipulate the amino acid residues in known toxins in order to create a new one. This turned out to be fruitless, however, and several months passed before she stumbled on another method—to graft toxic groups onto the framework of existing protein molecules.

Using the grafting approach, Martha was able to generate entirely new types of toxic molecules and fine-tune their expression in cells. She soon came upon a large class of agents both harmless to plants and sufficiently heat-stable.

Her goal was to locate a toxin within this class that was only operative in humans. Postulating that specific genes controlled differences in susceptibility to toxicity, she hoped to construct a toxin sensitive to the different gene sequences in humans and animals.

Testing the concept required administering her creations to both animals and humans. In the military, she had only used her germs and toxins on animals, so at first she balked at the prospect of injecting her toxins in live humans. But Knotty pointed out that her prior efforts were ultimately applied to humans. Her work at Felway had already been responsible for tens of thousands of deaths worldwide. What difference did it make if her new research was a bit more direct?

By Knotty's logic, she was actually doing a favor for the homeless people he rounded up as subjects. After all, they were given free food and lodging, and the kennel rooms they were housed in at the Pyramid were no worse than the rescue missions to which they were accustomed.

Yet even with a steady supply of test subjects, Martha labored ten long months before she discovered a heat-resistant toxin that only affected humans. It was far from perfect, as it simply produced a minor skin rash. However, it did provide the base molecule she sought, and she immediately began tinkering with its structure.

Her approach thereafter was much like trying to make a key fit a lock by blindly cutting different teeth patterns. She fiddled and fiddled with little scientific method to guide her, but after a year of perseverance, on January 16th, 2005, she stumbled onto a toxin molecule with properties beyond her wildest dreams.

Twenty four hours after administering the new toxin, she checked her video monitors and saw her first glimpse of its effects: The men who received the toxin showed symptoms of a horrible dry gangrene, much like the dreaded Holy Fire that raged throughout Europe in the Middle Ages. Yet the animals in her test group exhibited no response to the toxin. It seemed the women were unaffected as well.

Upon more careful examination, Martha noticed a young woman lying on her back, hidden behind a group of convulsing men. The video monitors indicated that the woman was no longer breathing, although the other nine females in the kennel were all quite alive with no signs of gangrene. Eager to explain the paradox, Martha rushed to the interrogation booth.

"Hello, my friends," she greeted her prisoners through a remote speaker. "Which one of you out there would like to earn some extra food?"

The men were too ill to respond, but four of the women raised their hands.

"Okay," said Martha. "You, in the green shirt. Please check the pulse of the woman lying on the floor."

"She's already dead," objected the prisoner.

"Just do it," said Martha.

The prisoner shrugged her shoulders, then lifted the woman's arm. As she did this, a piece of the woman's hand fell to the floor, and the video monitor showed that her muscle tissue had turned to a dry yellow paste from the gangrene.

"Bizarre," muttered Martha.

"I know why," volunteered the prisoner. "She had sex with the men."

Martha raised her eyes in surprise. "When did this happen?"

"All last night. The men knew they were dying and wanted one last fling."

"That's what she gets, the whore!" called out another woman in disgust.

"And none of the rest of you were tempted?" asked Martha.

"No," they all said, shaking their heads.

"I see," said Martha. "Well, you've been extremely helpful. I'm going to give all of you extra food rations."

Martha returned to her office to replay the back-up tapes from her video monitors. She soon saw that her subjects had told the truth. The previous night, over a period of three hours, the woman had engaged in intercourse with six different men.

Intrigued, Martha conducted a more comprehensive series of tests on the toxin. She expected to discover that her initial results were in error. Instead, each test confirmed the initial pattern. The toxin produced no negative effects in plants or animals, yet in men it consistently caused a dry gangrene. In women it produced the same outcome, but *only* when they first engaged in some form of sexual activity.

Martha determined that all forms of sexual arousal were potentially hazardous to women who were exposed to the toxin. In some cases, just a slight caress of the neck or legs was enough to make a woman fall prey to the gangrene, even several days after being exposed. Once aroused, the women exposed to the toxin developed the gangrenous symptoms in about eight hours.

In the men, however, sexual arousal did not affect their response. They developed the disease approximately one day after exposure. Their behavior made no difference.

For both men and women, the gangrene led to certain death. Martha tried all the known drug treatments and radiation therapies, as well as various other approaches, but none of them had the slightest effect. Once a man ingested the toxin, or a woman ingested it and had sex, the paste-like decay of the body was inevitable. Typically, it took one or two days for the disease to destroy the life-sustaining organs.

Martha realized that these odd dynamics were not exactly what Knotty had in mind. At first, she didn't even consider submitting her results to him. She merely hoped her discovery might lead to the toxin with the effects Knotty wanted.

Over the next three months, however, Martha failed to generate any toxin molecules that came closer to meeting Knotty's requirements. All the toxins she isolated were either too mild or they affected plants and animals, and she was running out of toxic permutations with which to experiment.

After another month of fruitless testing, with Knotty pressing her for results, the possibility occurred to Martha: Why not give Knotty the gangrene-producing toxin?

Its only defect was that it didn't affect women who abstained from sexual arousal. But such women weren't likely to be a very large group, especially not over the long-term. As long as they didn't know *why* they were being spared from the gangrenous death, they would chalk it up to luck instead of connecting it to their lack of sexual activity.

On the other hand, Martha would be in a much safer position if she proceeded with the gangrene-producing toxin, for she would be protected in case Knotty turned on her. She could simply abstain from sex to not be subjected to his tyranny. Why construct something to which she herself would be vulnerable?

Consequently, on October 15th, 2005, Martha rode the secret elevator to the top floor of the Pyramid and told Knotty the good news, that she had succeeded in finding a toxin meeting all of his requirements. The two of them hurriedly descended down to the lab, and Martha showed him an assortment of dead men and women, their arms and legs fully blackened.

Knotty was thrilled. He jubilantly led Martha to a back room to undress her. Then he filled a boiler tub with Mumm's extra dry champagne.

"I have two toasts, my dear," he exclaimed, plopping her into the bubbly liquid. "One to you, the inventor, the most brilliant bioengineer ever to live. And a second to the toxin, this wonderful toxin, which I propose we name *tyrannum*, in honor of its great power and potential."

Martha swallowed a sip of champagne from the tub. "Yes, my dear," she said. "I agree. Tyrannum is perfect. Quite perfect."

Martha's next project was to select the viruses and bacteria with which to disseminate the tyrannum toxin. She needed a diverse enough set so that all edible plants throughout the world would be vulnerable. Of course, with the thousands of plant diseases that existed, she had a wide array of choices.

This, in fact, was the beautiful thing about bioengineering. By introducing the appropriate tox genes, any microbe could be made to manufacture any toxin. Martha simply eliminated the ones that had a narrow host range or were hard to spread and picked her favorites from the remaining set.

Once she chose her microbial vectors, she spliced the tyrannum tox genes directly into them using standard bioengineering techniques. She also removed any genes that secreted other toxins damaging to plants. As a final measure, she adjusted the DNA and RNA of the chosen vectors in order to extend their range and reduce their ability to sicken the infected plant.

By early July of 2006, Martha's microbes were single-purposed machines. They were hearty enough to enter and multiply in almost any plant matter, filling their targets with the tyrannum toxin, yet gentle enough not to hinder the maintenance and reproduction processes. And they were so tenacious, they could survive the worst climatic conditions.

Martha's only remaining assignment—to reproduce the microbes for widespread release over the earth's surface—was a routine operation, much like brewing beer. With the commercial production facilities on the secret floor of the Burgstaller Pyramid, she was able to perform it on an immense scale in record time.

In fact, by the summer of 2007, she had filled the underground storage tanks adjacent to the Pyramid with 45,000 barrels of microbial broth. Her output quadrupled over the next ten months, with 210,000 barrels of the broth ready to be dumped throughout the world.

Meanwhile, she managed to achieve another type of reproduction. She conceived a child with Knotty in late February of 2008, on a king-sized water bed filled with Knotulinum toxin. And it was here, I must say, that Martha made her first serious error, for she assumed that the prospect of a child would give her further leverage over Knotty.

But as it happened, nothing could have been further from the truth.

THE TYRANT AND HIS
SPACE FARMS

Never once did Knotty doubt Martha as she labored over the tyrannum toxin. He felt certain he had won her loyalty and, in any event, he had far too many other worries on his mind.

The most taxing of them was the toxin-resistant food supply. Knotty knew that if he tried to grow tyrannum-resistant crops on earth, he would have to continually guard his fields from being ransacked. Even if he could keep the masses away in the short run, seeds could be misplaced or leaked.

Growing the resistant food on orbiting satellites seemed the perfect solution. In outer space, no one would be able to access his seeds, and his crops could be robotically harvested and processed before bringing them to earth.

The problem was that outer space farming was an entirely untested proposition. Huge growing fields would have to be constructed, positioned, and maintained up in the sky above the atmosphere. It was unknown if sufficient quantities of food could be made to grow under such conditions, or if such quantities could be feasibly transported back to earth.

Wisely, Knotty harbored no illusions about the extent of research needed. The first thing he did when his team of aerospace engineers and agricultural experts arrived at the Burgstaller Pyramid was to call them into his executive meeting room.

"Food is our lifeblood," Knotty began abruptly. "In the past fifty years, we have more than doubled output, even while farmland has shrunk. And yes, we have spread our biological revolution to many far away lands. But ultimately, my friends, these achievements will prove useless unless we face up to the future. Ultimately, our progress will be wasted unless we confront the limits of the earth." Knotty paused briefly.

"How can this be done?" he continued. "We must reach for a new vision. We must inject Agripe with the courage to become a true pioneer in agriculture. We must become the first firm to grow food in outer space. Yes, that's right, *food in outer space*. That is why I've gathered you here."

A chorus of murmurs floated through the meeting room, but Knotty did not stop.

"Undoubtedly," he said, slightly louder, "there will be those of you who find such a project preposterous. If so, I will gladly assist you in finding alternate employment. But if you hold a vision similar to my own, if you feel the call of service to humanity, I can assure you these will be exciting times here at Agripe.

"That, my friends, is all I have to say today. The rest of the equation is for you to decide—for yourselves, and for every other man and woman on earth."

Knotty's team of experts left the room dazed and confused. Two of the most senior project engineers immediately submitted their resignations. Several of the other researchers backed out of their financing for new Santa Barbara hillside homes.

The following day, however, the remaining individuals met to reassess the situation. They all agreed that the notion of outer space farming was far fetched. But having slept on it, they had to admit there were some attractive features.

After all, fields in outer space could be exposed to long hours of sunlight with no clouds or other obstructions. The adjustability of floating fields meant that crops could be positioned to receive direct rays at all times. Moreover, there were no adverse wind effects in outer space, and with careful management, no pests or diseases either.

In light of these possibilities, the majority of Knotty's researchers decided to accept his proposition. They promptly set about addressing the fundamental engineering issues, drawing heavily from a set of NASA documents that examined the feasibility of using solar satellites to generate electricity in outer space.

Because of the complexities, it took until June of 2003 for the researchers to put together a prototype model. Their proposed system was one of multiple farm satellites, each 20 kilometers long, 10 kilometers wide, and half a kilometer deep. The satellites were to be placed in geosynchronous earth orbit at an altitude of 22,300 miles and would each weigh about 200,000 metric tons, providing 46,000 acres of growing surface.

Everything about the plan thrilled Knotty except for the bottom line. Each farm satellite was projected to cost 2.1 billion dollars. This meant that even if the satellites were ten times more productive per acre than conventional farming, it would still take over 400 of them, or *840 billion dollars*, just to feed the world population at the barest subsistence level.

Obviously, Knotty lacked that kind of money—his net worth was barely over four billion dollars. But he refused to submit to negative thoughts. Instead, he jumped in his car and drove from Santa Barbara to his thinking room in Holmby Hills.

To his astonishment, the solution rushed before his eyes the moment he entered his blackest place. It wouldn't be necessary to build the 400 farm satellites right away. Even without the satellites, he could still control the entire population and extract the world's wealth.

All he would have to do was grow a transitional supply of resistant food on earth before anyone realized what he intended to do with it. As soon as he released Martha's microbes and people started dying, he could sell his tyrannum-resistant food for maximal prices. In a matter of days, he would have all the money he needed.

At that point, he wouldn't even need money anymore. He could simply take over the space programs of the superpowers and direct them as he saw fit. Everyone else would have as much incentive as him to make sure the 400 space farms were built. Otherwise, they simply would not eat. Otherwise, they simply would die.

Of course, Knotty still needed to complete at least one farm satellite before releasing Martha's microbes so that he would have the experience to build the others when they became necessary. But building one space farm wouldn't arouse nearly as much suspicion as building 400. It would just be another far-flung R&D project, financed by a visionary entrepreneur.

So as soon as Knotty got back to Santa Barbara, he instructed his team to turn their focus to the deployment of a single satellite. He even gave them a target date for completion—September 1st, 2007. And to boost them from theory to practice, he cleverly negotiated the acquisition of a heavy-lift launching spacecraft from the Japanese.

The engineers began by setting up an outer space construction base. This took eighteen months to prepare. Assembling the huge satellite consumed another two years, due to the need to provide shielded enclosures to protect the space workers from ionizing radiation.

Thereafter, the bulk of the project involved preparing the greenhouse. The entire satellite was coated with a special polymer glazing; photovoltaic panels were mounted across it to provide power for the processing equipment and ion engines; and the interior of the greenhouse was equipped with a hydroponic food production system consisting of multiple rows of special plant beds linked to a liquid nutrient supply channel.

Fortunately, the lessened gravitational force in outer space eliminated the need for a supporting medium to prop up the plants. Only the necessary gases for photosynthesis and plant respiration were required to circulate in the space above the nutrient channel.

The most complex design feature, however, involved the actual planting and harvesting of the crops. To automate this system, Knotty's engineers configured the greenhouse so that each plant bed was connected to a central input/output pipe running through the midshaft of the satellite. The pipe would allow servicing spaceships to connect to the satellite and inject seeds into the central tube. When the greenhouse was ready to be harvested, processing ships could 'suck' the mature plants out of their beds, at which point they could easily be reaped and converted to foodstuff.

The construction of such a system met with its fair share of complications, and the interior of the greenhouse required close to three years to finish. But Knotty's employees were extremely loyal, working around the clock to satisfy him. Within a few short months after the target date, the concept of the farm satellite was a reality. All that remained was to inject seeds into the central tube.

To Knotty's chagrin, however, the tyrannum-resistant seeds were not yet available. His agricultural experts couldn't seem to produce a resistant gene stock.

None of them expected the procedure to be too difficult, especially since they had already developed an enzyme which destroyed the tyrannum toxin. But whenever Knotty's researchers spliced the tyrannum-resistant enzyme into a seed, it only produced an immature, stunted plant.

Finally, on January 16th, 2008, a successful splice occurred. This was achieved when one of the younger researchers, who happened to follow a macrobiotic diet, decided to try splicing the enzyme into an adzuki bean from China. To everyone's amazement, the altered seed produced a healthy sprout.

The researchers concluded that the success was a result of the bean's ancient and unadulterated genes, and they quickly resolved to experiment with other non-hybrid seeds. Most such seeds had already been displaced in the race for greater crop yields, but they did locate a few of them, and one in particular, a pepper plant from southern Hungary, ended up tolerating insertion of the enzyme.

Knotty doubted he could sustain the masses on a diet consisting of only adzuki beans and peppers, so he consulted the available literature on nutrition. He learned that adzuki beans were a good source of protein and the Hungarian pepper was rich in vitamins A and C, but the two together simply could not support human life for any substantial length of time. At the very minimum, he would need to add some kind of grain.

In light of his findings, Knotty went back to his agricultural experts with a clear directive: "Experiment with all known varieties of corn, wheat, and rice."

The experts had the same problem as before—all the varieties offered by the seed companies were adulterated. They tried every non-hybrid grain they could find, even raiding ancient archaeological sites, but weeks passed and still no grain would accept the enzyme.

Knotty remained calm, again turning to his blackest place. And, difficult as it is for me to describe, this was precisely how he came to locate the much needed tyrannum-resistant starch.

The unhappy event occurred on the morning of February 4th, 2008 as Knotty read the newspaper in the breakfast nook of his Santa Barbara ranch. Martha, having spent the night, was spoonfeeding him a small treat—a Yoplait Breakfast Yogurt with wheat and walnuts.

Deep in thought, Knotty swallowed the first bite without tasting it. When she placed the second spoonful in his mouth, his tongue detected the spongy texture of a wheat berry. He immediately spit out his mouthful onto the table.

"What the hell are you feeding me?" he exclaimed.

"Breakfast Yogurt with wheat berries," said Martha. "It's good for you."

"Wheat berries?" he replied, picking up the cup from the table. "Hell, I might as well run some of these over to the lab. I doubt it could be worse than anything else the boys are testing."

That morning he took two of the berries to his agricultural experts and—need I say it?—they found that the berries *could* withstand the splicing. Apparently, their immersion in the yogurt solution heightened their tolerance to the enzyme, thus fostering insertion.

The following day, Knotty arranged to buy 450,000 containers of Yoplait Breakfast Yogurt with wheat berries. He hired hundreds of temporary workers to separate the berries from the yogurt, and for the next two weeks they furiously spliced Martha's tyrannum-eating enzyme into the wheat seeds.

On February 24th of 2008, the first batch of seeds was loaded into his transport spaceship and injected into the greenhouse. Over the next six weeks, the remaining seeds were planted on all his available Agripe fields. Since his land holdings now stretched far past the San Joaquin Valley into Utah, Colorado, Kansas, and parts of Iowa, this amounted to over half a million acres sowed with the tyrannum-resistant beans, wheat, and peppers.

One might wonder why Knotty's growers, or at least some observers of the agricultural industry, didn't become alarmed by his sudden shift into these three crops. In fact, no one saw any reason to perceive the move as threatening. They were just beans and wheat and peppers, and Knotty's status as an entrepreneurial giant was too well established for anyone to question the sensibility of his decisions.

Thus, hard as it is to fathom, two out of three prongs of his plan for total tyranny were now almost fully realized.

THE TYRANT AND HIS FINAL HURDLE

Only the first prong of Knotty's plan, the bioeconomic device, remained incomplete. Overconfidence was partly to blame, as Knotty neglected to stay in close communication with his bioeconomic researchers during the years they toiled at the Total Video labs. He simply assumed from their reassurances that they were making good progress.

As a result, when they unveiled the device in February of 2008, all they could show him was a glorified lie detector, based on the standard polygraph machine. The device boasted various artificial intelligence programs, and it was capable of directly interfacing with consumers. But it still suffered from the same problem all polygraph machines suffered from—unreliability.

For Knotty's hidden purpose, that made it entirely unacceptable. He needed a machine that could stand up to the pressure of human beings in misery, on the verge of starvation. Yet this was hardly something he could explain to his researchers, and now it seemed too late no matter what he told them.

Clearly, there was no way he could expect his researchers to come up with a new design by the time his tyrannum-resistant crops were harvested. So he did the only thing he could do. He came to visit *me* at my office in the economics department of Harvard University.

To be frank, I probably should have expected the visit. My achievements as Professor Ray LeGhir were hardly world-renowned, but among academics I held a reputation for my research in consumer preferences, and it was no secret that I was involved in work similar to that being done by the Total Video researchers.

Of course, my interest in the concept of a bioeconomic device came from a completely different direction. It arose in the winter of 2004 when I was in my third year of graduate school at Harvard. My roommate, a fellow economics student named Joseph Baptista, first introduced me to the idea.

Joseph was a rather unusual individual, with long black hair and deep yellow-green eyes. Ordinarily, we traveled in different circles, but one night he took me aside and told me that he had discovered a way to make the poor rich.

As he traced through his reasoning, I listened with wide eyes. With meticulous precision, he explained that if an instrument existed to measure consumers valuations of any given product, and if all businesses adopted it, then this could lead to an equalization of wealth across all social classes, wiping out poverty altogether.

Joseph mentioned that such an invention might cause a temporary reduction in wealth for society, but I didn't concern myself with this effect, probably because I lived in a time of such material overexposure. The prospect of a complete redistribution of wealth—especially one without any change in the rules of capitalism or government—entirely captivated me.

Still, I wasn't about to accept Joseph's arguments at face value, so I did a series of mathematical simulations. To my surprise, my results supported his conclusions under a set of fairly standard assumptions. Joseph was unimpressed by my high-brow confirmations, but he continued to encourage my academic angle, and when he dropped out of Harvard, he made me promise I'd continue my work.

In a matter of a few months, I published a journal article on the subject, mainly to showcase my math techniques. It was just a short article, but my advisors seemed pleased, and they suggested I take the research a step further.

By that time, I already knew about Knotty's Total Video labs and the difficulties they were having. Since I'd earned undergraduate degrees in both biology and economics at M.I.T., I couldn't help thinking that I might be able to approach the idea from a fresh direction and please my advisors at the same time.

The risks and responsibilities inherent in such an endeavor never crossed my mind. I simply charged ahead, writing a series of ground-clearing articles that outlined my specifications and criteria for a true bioeconomic device. Oddly, the articles generated a fair amount of interest. Job offers arrived from top schools throughout the world, and even Harvard got into the act, dangling before me a position I couldn't refuse—a professorship with dual appointments in economics and biology.

That was how it all started. By mid-September of 2005, I was hard at work in my new laboratory, completely absorbed by all the scientific details.

My first project was to trace the nerve fibers linked to the brain. I was well aware of the fact that Knotty's researchers used the polygraph as their point of departure, and that was where I thought I might have an advantage. The polygraph relied on changes in secondary characteristics—mainly blood pressure, pulse rate, and respiration—to indicate deception. I suspected I could create a more accurate device by monitoring the source of the matter directly.

My focus was on the nerve fibers connected to the hypothalamus, an inner area of the brain that earlier research had found to register sensations of pain and pleasure. I studied these fibers for almost a year, using all the latest laser technologies to trace their response to various sensory inputs.

I soon discovered that different fibers were associated with different kinds of data. Most importantly, I found that a certain class of fibers was exclusively responsible for carrying the electrochemical impulses regulating beliefs and feelings.

The discovery of these truth fibers, as I called them, made my task clear—to design an instrument that could selectively measure only the impulses of these fibers when placed in contact with an undifferentiated mass of nerve endings. This, I believed, would provide an accurate reflection of a customer's willingness to pay for a product.

I worked steadily for thirteen months, and with the help of numerous neuropsychologists and biologists, I made a number of breakthrough discoveries. By December of 2007, all the major elements were in place, and on February 13, 2008, I actually completed my first prototype.

On that historic day, I called in my research assistant and asked him to get me a snack from the corner Total Food store. Meanwhile, I attached a set of sensory receptors to the major nerve endings throughout my arms and legs.

When my assistant returned, he placed a chocolate chip cookie on my lap and plugged the receptors into my machine.

"Okay, Professor LeGhir," he said, well-rehearsed for the moment. "Are you willing to pay a million dollars for this cookie?"

The machine flashed a red light indicating that I was not. This was clearly the correct response, seeing as the cookie cost $1.95 at the corner store.

"Are you willing to pay $10.00 for the cookie?" he asked. Again the light flashed red.

"What about $2.00?" he asked.

I tried as hard as I could to deceive the machine, telling myself that the cookie wasn't worth two dollars, but I was unable to fool it— the light turned green.

Of course, my brilliant assistant did not stop there. "How about $2.50, Professor LeGhir?" he asked.

Once more, I attempted to fight it, but the light remained green. I had to admit this was perfectly reasonable—avoiding the hassle of walking to the store was worth at least 55 cents.

In fact, by successively raising the price until the light turned red, my assistant discovered that the most I was willing to offer him to avoid the walk to the store was $3.43. At that point, he held out his hands with a big smile. I quickly paid him the money and took a bite of the cookie. Then we had ourselves a celebration.

The truth of the matter was that I still hadn't grasped the significance of my invention. All I could think of was the prestige I might win among my colleagues, and the only protective measure I took was to install some extra dead bolts on my lab doors.

Over the next few weeks, neither I nor my assistant could find any way to outwit the device. Regardless of the product or our mental states, it always determined our maximum willingness to pay.

Perhaps even more impressive, my invention was a perfect lie detector. It could answer *anything else* about our mental states as well. We didn't even have to be strapped to all the receptors for it to work. We only had to touch one of them with an index finger, and it operated beautifully.

With this discovery, I decided to streamline my invention. I spent a month reworking the circuitry boards and condensing the receptor apparatus, and at the base of the machine I drilled a hole for the tips of the receptors so that users only had to insert one of their fingers into the cavity, making it much easier to use than the initial prototype.

By the time I finished all my improvements it was March of 2008. There seemed nothing left to do but to actually confront the implications of what I had done, and I was about to do this, I truly was, when I heard the knock on my office door.

As soon as Knotty spoke his first words, I knew exactly who he was. "Hello, Professor LeGhir," he said upon entering. He extended his hand, and I weakly reached for it.

"Forgive me for interrupting you like this," he continued. "I hope I'm not intruding."

"No, no," I replied. "That's quite all right. What can I do for you, Mr. Burgstaller?"

"It's come to my attention that you've made some great strides in your research."

"I'm not sure about 'great' strides," I replied humbly. "But strides at any rate."

Knotty laughed. "I'm quite confident that yours are absolutely huge, Professor LeGhir, compared to the strides my researchers have made."

"This is just a small operation, I'm afraid."

Knotty nodded his head vigorously. "Yes, yes," he said. "In fact, the reason I'm here is to suggest we do something about that."

"Oh?"

"I'd like to buy you out," he smiled.

"Buy me out? That wouldn't be..."

"Of course," he interrupted, "I have absolutely no interest in offending your integrity. Not in the least. I'm prepared to walk down any avenue you suggest, whether it be a friendly agreement or an elaborate compensation package. The sky is the limit, Professor LeGhir."

"I'm afraid I don't understand. What exactly is it you want?"

"Your bioeconomic device, of course."

"But I don't have one yet," I replied. "It's still in its developmental phase."

"Well, you must be very close."

"That's hard to say. You never really know until you're there."

"True, true," he said, still smiling. "But I'm prepared to take that risk. You name your price. I'll settle for whatever you have. If I've overestimated, so much the better for you."

"I'm sorry. I just can't do that."

"If it's because of your contractual obligations to Harvard, we can overcome that."

"No, no. It's not that."

"Ethics?" he asked.

"No, it's a personal matter," I said awkwardly.

Knotty's face suddenly became stone cold. "Very well. I'm not a man to push. But I am known for two things: My overly generous offers and my failure to ever make them twice." He stalled for a few seconds, waiting for me to reconcile.

"I'm sorry, Mr. Burgstaller," I said. "I'm simply not interested."

"There are always alternatives, Professor LeGhir," he replied. "Many, many alternatives." Then he marched out of the office, slamming the door.

For the rest of the day, I sat staring vacantly at the wall of my office. I'd had little experience in the world of business, and power struggles of this type were not my forte. I wasn't sure whether to be alarmed, or if the encounter was routine.

Yes, I realized that a businessperson could potentially profit from my invention if he or she had some kind of monopoly. But Knotty sold food and video tapes, both over which he had no monopoly whatsoever. I didn't see what his interest in my invention could be, other than for his research.

Even if Knotty did have some ulterior motive, I still wasn't sure why I should be concerned. My bioeconomic device was just an instrument that provided information to sellers about how much buyers wanted their product. It hardly carried the earth-shattering importance of, say, an atomic bomb. It could help sellers fetch bigger profits, but it could also help equalize the distribution of wealth.

So I went home that night, ate a little dinner, and got ready for bed. I told myself there was nothing to worry about, nothing more to confront, and I laid my head down on the pillow. Nonetheless, my body wouldn't let me rest. A faint image kept creeping through the back of my mind, filling me with doubt.

After two hours of sleeplessness, I had no choice but to face the image. It was a vision of global suffering and starvation, of humans in misery, living in mud villages, bent over on their hands and knees, counting kernels of grain. Counting, counting, counting.

As soon as I saw this, I knew exactly what it was—the wealth reduction effect Joseph had mentioned. My heart filled with terror. I could hardly believe I'd been so ignorant, so blinded by ego. The more I confronted the image, the larger it grew. And the eyes of the children, children with bloated stomachs and skeletal limbs, felt more and more like my own eyes.

It was only a matter of another minute before I knew what I had to do. I had to destroy my invention. The world did not need my privacy-invading device, and that was that.

I threw on some clothes and raced up Cambridge Street to the Littaeur Center. Then I hurried down to my basement lab, fumbling with my newly-installed dead bolts, and I swung open the door.

And that was when I saw to my horror—as must be apparent by your very existence—that my bioeconomic device was gone.

THE TYRANT AND MY DEFENSIVE MEASURES

I SPENT THE rest of the night wrestling with my conscience, spilling tears of guilt and shame, berating myself for what I let happen. It was unthinkable, unforgivable. I would have liked to bury my head in the sand and forget it all happened, but I knew I owed the world more than that. As humiliating as it was, my first obligation was to inform the police, which I did immediately.

After taking my report, the Cambridge Chief of Police assured me he would conduct a thorough investigation with joint support from the FBI and the National Science Foundation. He said there was nothing else to do but be patient. I assumed it was pointless to contact Knotty.

Two weeks later, I learned from the chairman of the Harvard biology department that the police were investigating *me*. They hadn't even checked into Knotty's affairs. I, the lowly professor, was the object of their suspicion.

That was when I knew I had to enlist outside help. The first person I thought of was Joseph Baptista. I hadn't seen him for several years, but I heard he worked for a maple syrup farm north of Brattleboro, Vermont.

It took me a couple of days to find Joseph. At first, I thought I was mistaken because I barely recognized him—he was wearing his hair quite short, with a black bandanna covering most of it, and he had a strand of purple beads around his neck. But when I approached him, he seemed glad to see me. We sat down on a log and I explained what had happened.

"That's quite impressive, Ray," he replied. "You've done well. Far better than I expected."

"But aren't you worried?"

He looked at me quizzically. "You're giving the human species precisely what it needs—a kick in the pants to rid us of our lust for the external. Let Knotty Burgstaller take the burden of materialism all upon himself, if he wishes. It will only leave the rest of us free to look within, unencumbered."

"But... but what about the wealth reduction effect?" I stammered. "What about all the suffering that will come?"

"What about all the suffering that already exists?" he countered. "What about all the divided selves deceived by the promise of wealth? And what about all the murder, rape, and torture committed in its pursuit?"

"You don't understand," I insisted. "If my device is used to its full extent, we could be stripped of everything. We could all end up living in mud huts."

"You're trying to say your invention was a mistake? I'm afraid not, Ray. It was destined."

"No, it was just an experiment. I never intended for it to be released like this. That's crazy."

"It's no longer for you to judge," he said calmly. "Why not forget your troubles and help me tend to the trees?"

Realizing that Joseph wasn't going to be of any use, I quickly said goodbye and walked back to my car. When I got home, I called a friend at the Total Video labs. I wanted to see if there had been any shift in Knotty's research agenda in the past month, but it seemed the only news was Agripe Industries' expansion into wheat, beans, and peppers. I didn't see any significance there, since I failed to see how Knotty could monopolize food.

My next move was what I should have done in the first place. I brought together my five most trusted colleagues—an economist, an engineer, a biologist, a psychologist, and a computer scientist—and I filled them in on the whole horrible mess, including the fact that I was now under investigation by the police.

To my surprise, they all offered to help. One of my colleagues even offered to try to recover my device from Knotty, but the others pointed out that he would undoubtedly have the machine under tight security. Since I lacked any concrete evidence implicating him in the theft, there would be no legal way to get it back either.

Still, we all understood the potential danger of the situation, particularly once I described the wealth reduction effect and how Knotty could precipitate it if he used my device in monopolized industries. It was clear we had to take some sort of defensive approach.

The best way to do this, we decided, would be to put consumers on an equal footing—that is, to somehow give them the ability to determine the *minimum* amount for which firms would be willing to sell their products. That way customers could all unite together, fighting any potential exploitation by refusing to pay more than this minimum amount.

The question was how to achieve such an equalization. At first, my colleagues and I doubted it was even feasible. But after several days of intense thought, an intriguing possibility came to me: What if a version of my device was installed in each person's brain? And what if all the devices were linked by a transmission media so that we all could access each other's devices?

In this case, consumers would be able to determine firms' minimum acceptable selling price. Since all firms consisted of individual owners, consumers could simply read the owners' devices to locate the exact threshold point at which owners would be willing to sell any given product. As a result, their own maximum willingness to pay would fall to this level, the wealth reduction effect would be negated, and the overall efficiency of the economy would likely be improved.

This was my hope, at any rate. It was a plausible scenario, certainly. And even if its implementation required much work, none of my colleagues could offer another approach with a better chance of protecting the world from my machine. So after ten days of vigorous debate, in late March of 2008, our team resolved to dedicate all our available energy to the task.

Our biggest challenge was how to adequately miniaturize my device to make it fit in people's brains. On top of this, the issue of how the miniaturized devices would actually be implanted plagued us, for we knew certain people would try to resist them. Plus we had to devise an inexpensive communications network capable of linking all the devices together.

Fortunately, my colleagues were highly qualified, and generous funding from my computer scientist friend, Jack Myers, allowed us to equip an old building in Central Square with the latest research gear. We set up a state-of-the-art bioengineering lab, fully pressurized, in the basement of the building. Then we entered into double lives, each carrying out our normal activities during the day and feverishly working at our secret site all night.

Meanwhile, Knotty secretly transported my bioeconomic device to Korea. He knew of a company there that specialized in duplication of high-technology items, and he negotiated a contract to have 120,000 duplicates of the device delivered by the first of October.

That gave him adequate time to expand the scope of his Total Food stores. He wasn't particularly worried about individuals in remote or isolated regions, who tended to lack great wealth, but he figured that developed areas should have at least one Total Food store per 30,000 people. Wherever this ratio wasn't met, he offered franchises at very favorable terms, and by late June there were over 19,000 new Total Food stores under construction.

In the meantime, Knotty developed computerized dispensers so that he could sell his tyrannum-resistant food in precise allotments without any human handling. These automated dispensers were installed—typically ten at a time—along the outside wall of each Total Food store.

The dispensers were quite similar to ATM machines, but instead of using bank cards, they required customers to insert their index fingers into a small orifice next to the display screen—an orifice wired directly to the soon-to-arrive bioeconomic devices.

The advantage of this approach was that each Total Food store could serve up to ten customers at a time with only one bioeconomic device. Since the devices were perfect lie detectors, Knotty would be able to maintain complete control over the distribution of his food. In fact, by appropriately configuring the program for his dispensers, he could extract any information he wanted from his customers, including gender, occupation, and family background.

Knotty equipped all his stores with underground storage tanks to hold the resistant food. These storage tanks, capable of holding enough grain to keep 30,000 people alive for a year, were linked by vacuum-pump to the automated dispensers. Moreover, they were rigged to self-destruct upon the slightest sign of tampering.

Of course, Knotty couldn't hide all of these changes from the public, as anybody who shopped at Total Food could see the modifications being made. He simply told the media that Total Food was in the process of installing gasoline pumps, along with convenient automated tellers. To the casual onlookers, as well as to the news reporters, this seemed perfectly reasonable.

By early September of 2008, all of Knotty's preparations were complete, and his tyrannum-resistant crops were ready to be harvested. Touting Agripe's "commitment to responsible food processing," he mobilized a giant task force to gather the adzuki beans, wheat seeds, and Hungarian peppers. As usual, everyone was impressed.

Once every last bit of the produce was gathered—for who could have foreseen the future value of one of the miserable seeds?—he shipped it directly to Agripe headquarters in Salinas. Giant grinding machines pulverized the wheat berries, beans, and peppers into fine flours. These ingredients were mixed together, according to a formula of three parts wheat flour, two parts adzuki bean flour, and one part paprika, to form a foodstuff Knotty affectionately named 'pepwad.'

The same procedure was followed in the processing of his outer space produce, which—to Knotty's great satisfaction—had grown even more bountifully than the earth crops. A huge processing space-ship drew the food out of the hydroponic greenhouse and robotically ground it into the pepwad mixture, except for a small portion of the new seed injected back into the greenhouse beds for re-planting.

With this accomplished, the pepwad was loaded onto ships and trucks and planes and trains, destined for Total Food stores every-where. And as the foodstuff wound its way throughout the world, Knotty's reign of tyranny moved one step closer to reality.

Knotty still showed no outward sign of moving toward control of any industry, but my colleagues and I hardly slowed down our defensive efforts. Even if Knotty appeared to be lacking in monopolistic motives, he had obviously taken possession of my machine, and we knew we had to be prepared for its reckless use.

Fortunately, thanks to bioengineering breakthroughs by a group of Princeton scientists, we had already succeeded in greatly miniatur-izing the circuitry of my bioeconomic device. The receptor compo-nent now fit into a single microscopic fiber, and the entire apparatus occupied less than one-tenth of a cubic millimeter.

We called this condensed apparatus a PIFFEN meter, as an acronym for Perfect Information For Fully Efficient Networking. Because it relied entirely on biocircuitry, we could reproduce it at a geometric rate, which meant we would be able to 'breed' enough PIFFEN cells for the entire human population in only a couple of days.

At the same time, we settled on a communications technology for linking together the PIFFEN meters. This technology, based on packet radio, was highly reliable yet very low-powered, and its simplicity allowed us to program the PIFFEN meters to 'grow' their own transceivers using ordinary human cell tissue.

Under this design, when a meter entered a human brain it would multiply to form the full transceiver mechanism, then migrate to the top portion of the person's skull for maximal receptability. From there everything would be set to go.

The main problem that still nagged us was how to initiate the actual meter implantings. In order for our scheme to be effective, the meters not only had to make their way into the hypothalamus of each and every human brain, but they also had to become operational in all human beings at roughly the same time, in order to eliminate any opportunities for consumer exploitation.

If this last obstacle hadn't stymied us, Knotty never would have had a chance—we would have overpowered him before he ever enacted his plan. Even with this obstacle, we came quite close, as Knotty barely ended up having a two week lead over us. But two weeks or two hundred weeks, I cannot claim it made much difference.

For the fact was, Knotty did initiate his master plan, and the pain that resulted during his reign of tyranny was beyond all description, beyond all understanding, beyond all human emotion that ever before had been experienced.

THE TYRANT AS THE TYRANT

By October 27th of 2008, all of Knotty's Total Food stores had received their pepwad shipments. The bioeconomic devices had been installed, and Martha had finished brewing a colossal supply of tyrannum-secreting microbes, so there was nothing to stop Knotty from carrying out his master plan that very day. As it happened, however, his mind was set on a particular date.

If only Halloween occurred on November 31st, we would have been ready for Knotty, but such was not our fate. For on the evening of October 31st, while all the costume-clad witches and ghosts and goblins ran rampant in the streets, Knotty hired thousands of chartered planes to dump Martha's viruses and bacteria into the air. The wind patterns were perfect that night, and the microbes infected every piece of plant tissue they touched. They spread, and spread, and spread.

But it was still too early for Knotty to unveil his tyranny. The microbes required at least a day to properly fill their host cells with tyrannum. So Knotty and Martha stayed home all day on November 1st, nibbling only tyrannum-resistant food, as they had been doing for the past two weeks.

That evening, they packed their bags and drove to Palm Springs, where Knotty had purchased a large private estate under a false name. When they arrived, Knotty showed Martha to a plush couch in the living room, as she was now eight and a half months pregnant. Then he went into the den, plugged in his laptop computer, and prepared the following facsimile message:

Good evening, my friends. This is Knotty Burgstaller.

I'm writing to report that a lethal toxin has found its way into the world's food supply. This toxin produces a gangrenous symptom, and all edible foodstuffs appear to be susceptible to it, except for a special new product called pepwad, available exclusively at Total Food stores.

Other foods, even those canned and vacuum-sealed, are likely to develop the toxin once they are exposed to the air. But pepwad has a unique enzymatic structure which immediately destroys the toxin. I therefore recommend that all people subsist solely on pepwad and water until further notice.

Knotty chuckled softly as he attached a source code scrambler to the message and transmitted it to the Cable News Network. Then he went to take a shower to wind down from the long drive. The moment Martha heard him turn on the water, she snuck into the den and quietly typed an addendum to his message:

P.S. I neglected to mention that women are invulnerable to the toxin, as long as they abstain from all sexual activity. Consequently, women don't need to buy pepwad if they choose to practice abstinence. Please publicize this fact. Thanks.

—Knotty Burgstaller

Before she could transmit the message to CNN headquarters,

however, Knotty came dashing out of the shower. "What the hell are you doing?" he demanded.

"Nothing," she said.

"I have a bad feeling, Martha."

"I was just about to send a letter to a friend."

"You don't have any friends," he said. He peered at the monitor to see what she had written, but she intervened, switching off the power.

"God damn it!" he yelled. "This is no game, Martha! Show me what you wrote!"

"Fine. I didn't send it anyway." She turned on the monitor, revealing her addendum.

The moment he saw what she had written, his face turned livid blue. "You god damn bitch!" he snarled. "You god damn betraying bitch!"

"It's not what you think. You'll still control all the males—they have all the wealth anyway. And the women will forever be in your debt. Isn't that enough?"

"Totality is the vision I have," he replied stiffly, "and it is the one I will achieve."

"It's too late for that. The microbes are out."

"It's never too late, my little betrayer. How could you think I would not have protection against such a ploy?"

"Protection?"

"I may have misjudged you, Martha, but I'll not make the same mistake twice." He reached for her neck and began to clamp down on it with his thumb.

"What about our child?" she gasped.

He laughed, relaxing his grasp. "You have a point, my dear. It could be useful to keep the child. Perhaps my daughter will be more loyal to me."

He dragged Martha into the windowless maid's quarters, stripping the room of all amenities except for a small television. Then he pushed a 350-pound marble coffee table against the outside of the door and went to sit down in the most uncomfortable chair he could find.

It wasn't until the following morning that a couple of CNN news assistants came across Knotty's fax message. Initially, they considered it to be a fraud, but when they called the Burgstaller Pyramid, they were unable to disconfirm it. Instead Knotty's secretary informed them that Mr. Burgstaller was out of town and that she'd been instructed to tell whoever called that "the fax message was no joke."

The assistants showed the message to their supervisors, who almost bit their tongues, for they had just received reports of a sudden outbreak of dry gangrene in nine different countries throughout the world. Pandemonium ensued at the news desks. Was the message true? Did it explain the outbreak of gangrene? Could it be that Mr. Burgstaller was actually involved in the outbreak? Was it possible he was being held hostage by some terrorist group?

Several minutes passed before a reporter made an important observation. Knotty's message appeared inconsistent with the pattern of the disease, for the incoming data showed that the only victims to date were *women*. Moreover, a substantial proportion of them seemed to be linked to prostitution, swinger clubs, or various other promiscuous activities.

The newspeople couldn't have possibly understood the implications of this outcome. They only knew that it demanded immediate world media attention.

It was at this time that Knotty woke up from his night's sleep in the uncomfortable chair. Surprisingly well-rested, he opened his laptop computer and accessed the master program that regulated all his automated pepwad dispensers.

Up until then, he'd hardly given any thought on how to respond to the problem Martha created. But the moment he awoke, he knew exactly what to do. He quickly wrote a subroutine that instructed his dispensers to randomly inject purple ergot into the pepwad allotments of his female customers.

Purple ergot was a highly poisonous fungus that produced symptoms quite like the tyrannum toxin. Knotty had stocked his dispensers with this ergot when they were first installed, as he feared that Martha's microbes might not produce enough victims, but this safeguard was equally useful in solving his new little problem.

Randomly injecting females' pepwad with the ergot would hide the fact that sexually inactive women were unaffected by the tyrannum toxin. Since the dispensers issued separate packets of pepwad for each family member, few men would be likely to eat the ergot. Knotty's resistant food would be too valuable for people to want to share, even between husband and wife.

The only problem was that these random ergot injections would kill a certain number of females despite their exclusive diet of pepwad, so people might question whether pepwad was really free from the toxin. But there was a brilliant way out of the dilemma, as Knotty's blackest place was quick to suggest.

All Knotty had to do was slightly alter the truth, to claim that pepwad only protected women from the gangrene disease if they avoided sexual arousal. After all, prostitutes were the hardest hit group up to that point, so the disease's implications already carried a strong moral overtone. If a woman who ate pepwad happened to die of gangrene, who could prove she hadn't experienced sexual arousal prior to her death?

Thus, with an ear-to-ear smile, Knotty quickly transmitted a second fax to CNN:

So sorry to be pestering you, but it occurs to me that there are some additional things you might want to know:

1) The disease you are witnessing throughout the world is fatal and incurable. It is a result of ingesting toxin-contaminated food.

2) This toxin cannot be removed from contaminated food,

either by heat or any other means. Pepwad is the only safe food. Period.

3) Males have not yet showed signs of the disease because it takes longer to manifest within their hormonal environment. However, they are no less vulnerable to the toxin than females.

4) Sexually aroused females respond most rapidly to the toxin. Even on an exclusive diet of pepwad, they may absorb the toxin through their lungs. Therefore all women are advised to practice abstinence.

5) The seeds for growing additional pepwad are located on an Agripe satellite in outer space. These are the only seeds that can produce resistant food.

6) Any effort to harass me or my property, or to approach the Agripe satellite, will lead to the destruction of these seeds, and thus to the destruction of humankind.

7) All Total Food stores are equipped with automated pepwad dispensers linked to underground storage tanks. Any tampering with these facilities will cause their immediate self-destruction.

8) Only household heads will be permitted to interact with the dispensers. In the interest of fair distribution, purchasers will be charged prices for pepwad in accordance with their desire for it, as will soon be made clear.

That's all you need to know. Thanks very much. And good luck!

This time the CNN assistants immediately spotted Knotty's

incoming fax message. As soon as they did, they shouted for all the reporters and editors and producers to come to the room. One of the assistants began to read the message aloud.

At first, the newspeople chattered amongst themselves, listening with only one ear. But their demeanor changed as they absorbed the doomsday message. In the back of their minds, they had always imagined a dreaded event of this type. They had always expected an upheaval of massive proportions. And at that moment, they each understood that the upheaval had commenced.

Even the most hardened reporters were affected. Even the editors who had disregarded Knotty's first message now stood frozen. And those who had been defiantly munching their lunches, all exhibited the same reaction—they simply stopped chewing and let their mouthfuls fall onto the floor.

But Knotty was far from done. He knew CNN would have to confirm the authenticity of his statements before it could publicize them. Accordingly, he connected a video teleconferencing unit to his phone, with his source scrambler attached. Then he dialed the appropriate interface link and patched himself into the main video screen at CNN headquarters.

"Good morning," he said smiling. "This is Knotty Burgstaller once again."

"It's Burgstaller!" cried a startled reporter who happened to be passing by the video conference room. "Come here, everybody! It's Knotty Burgstaller on the screen!"

The newspeople shuffled into the room, still in shock. When they were all assembled, an executive producer raised his hands for silence.

"All right, Mr. Burgstaller," he said. "Now that we've finally got a hold of you, let's get to the bottom of this. Are you the one who's been sending reports about a toxin poisoning the world's food supply?"

"Yes, sir."

"How did you learn of this toxin?"

"From a former friend of mine," he replied, still smiling.

"And how did this friend of yours learn of it?" asked the executive.

"She was the one who created the toxin, and I was the one who spread it all over the earth's surface." Knotty beamed with pride.

There was a long pause as the newspeople tried to assimilate his last statement. Finally, a young reporter shouted out, "This is some kind of a joke! He must be an impostor!"

"No," replied Knotty. "It's no joke. I'm Burgstaller all right. Everything I've said is true, as you'll soon see."

"What are you... crazy?" exclaimed the reporter. "Why in hell would you cause such lunacy?"

"To be the Total Tyrant," he explained. "I've always wanted to be the Total Tyrant. It's been my lifelong dream. It truly has. So thank you. Thank you all very, very much."

Knotty gently waved his hand goodbye, and the video screen went dead.

THE TYRANT AND THE TYRANNY

As soon as the appropriate officials were apprised of the situation, they assembled an international team of emergency authorities to investigate Knotty's claims. Lab samples were taken from various foods throughout the world to see which of them, if any, contained the fatal toxin Knotty had described. Meanwhile, undercover agents procured samples of Knotty's pepwad to check whether it was indeed toxin-free.

Unfortunately, the tests required 24 hours to achieve accurate results. But if Knotty was right and pepwad proved to be the only toxin-resistant food, then withholding this information from the public would cause millions of people to die unnecessarily.

The authorities concluded that they had a moral obligation to release Knotty's messages to the public, even before the lab samples were completed. Thus, by early afternoon on November 3rd, the world's major news agencies were given a prepared statement, and radio and television stations everywhere broadcasted it without delay.

Of course, this statement did not endorse pepwad, nor did it confirm the presence of a food toxin. It merely relayed Knotty's warning, in the event that people wished to act upon it. More conclusive information, the people were told, would be made available soon.

Initially, few people panicked. The concept of such a widespread toxin was too difficult to conceive. After all, the total number of gangrene victims at that point was less than 5,000, and none of them were men.

But in a couple more hours, the situation changed, for the gangrene began to strike those unlucky males who had ingested the toxin and engaged in sex. There were not too many men in this category—only 1,600 males were reported to have the symptoms as of 3:00 PM Pacific Standard Time. But the fact that men were starting to contract the disease had a significant effect on the way people viewed the situation. All of a sudden, the media had evidence that Knotty told the truth, at least with regard to the vulnerability of males to the toxin.

To make matters worse, after 3 PM the number of men with gangrenous symptoms sharply increased. Many were at work or on their way home when they first began to feel bolts of fiery pain pass through their limbs. As they stopped to examine themselves and saw their arms and legs turning a sickly greenish-yellow, they often could not help but scream out in terror.

In this manner, substantial segments of the population came to witness first-hand the reality of Knotty's warning. Yet until 6 PM Pacific Standard Time, there was still a fairly large contingent of doubters and cynics. It wasn't until after 6 PM that the world as we knew it came to an end.

By that point, 24 hours had passed since the tyrannum toxin first penetrated organic matter, and even celibate males began to fall prey to the dry gangrene. Between the hours of 6 and 7 o'clock, almost 120,000 males exhibited symptoms of the disease, compared to 55,000 females. For the first time, young boys and old men joined ranks with the others in succumbing to the gangrene.

The pitiful victims could be seen everywhere—in stores, cars, restaurants, train stations, even on the lawns in front of their homes.

Often they were howling and moaning from the burning pain, as their limbs steadily eroded into a consistency resembling paste.

In the face of such tragedy, it became harder to dismiss the idea that pepwad might offer protection. People were truly terrified, and while some responded by running for the hills or entering into a fast, the dominant reaction was to head directly for the closest Total Food store.

By that evening, eager buyers were mobbing the pepwad dispensers. The lines typically stretched several blocks, and in wealthier areas they often exceeded a mile in length. Yet the procedure for interacting with the dispensers was quite straightforward. Each household head simply had to insert a finger into the dispenser's orifice, whereupon he or she was entitled to purchase up to eight ounces of pepwad per day per family member.

There was no way purchasers could lie about the number of members in their family or their gender, since the bioeconomic devices were perfect lie detectors. It was simply a matter of paying the price that flashed on the display screen—a price set purely by the purchaser's own willingness to pay—and the dispensers quickly doled out the appropriate packets of reddish-brown pepwad.

The difficulty, however, was in agreeing to this price. Never before had price been a function of one's occupation or preferences. And now, suddenly, people were forced to confront an all-knowing bioeconomic device.

Simply put, this meant that the richer they were, and the less skeptical of Knotty's message they were, the more they had to pay. Among the wealthy it was not uncommon to be charged $100,000 for the first sack of pepwad. And when the display screen of a pepwad dispenser indicated such an extreme price, there was no way the customer could deny its validity. For that price was, by construction, precisely his or her maximum acceptable buy price. In essence, it was how much the customer valued the ability to keep on living, scaled down to the extent that he or she doubted Knotty's message.

Of course, Knotty had to allow for credit. Customers could

hardly be expected to pay such high prices on the spot. Those who lacked the full amount were instructed to insert all the currency they did have into the dispensers' payment slot. The remainder, they were informed, would be due upon their next visit.

But this hardly lessened the shock of the procedure. Most customers couldn't believe the situation at first. They had to carefully review all their options, and realize how limited they were, before giving in to Knotty's terms. So the lines just kept getting longer and longer.

In spite of these circumstances, conditions at Knotty's Total Food stores were, for the most part, under control. People were too overwhelmed by the experience to engage in any kind of violent protest. When they finally got home with their pepwad, their primary concern was to follow the cooking instructions written on the packets:

Pour pepwad into boiling water and simmer for three minutes.
Be sure to add nothing but inorganic minerals, if desired.

Eating pepwad was another matter. Once cooked, it became a dark brown mush not easily disassociated from excrement. For many, its utterly bland taste and glue-like consistency made the prospect of exclusively eating pepwad worse than death itself.

As a result, countless people violated the diet. Those who managed to make it through the day often awoke late at night, unable to resist the delicacies still lurking within their refrigerators or cupboards.

Even those able to subsist with only pepwad in their stomachs still had other problems to face. Or so they believed, at any rate. For Knotty's warnings had been widely heeded, and few women doubted his claim that sexual activity could be dangerous. Many men suspected that the risk of sexual activity might apply to them as well.

Still, not everyone was willing to fall into Knotty's trap without a struggle, and there were numerous attempts to overcome it. The most brazen individuals thought they could resort to cannibalism to evade the disease. They erroneously assumed that if they ate non-infected human flesh, they would be immune to Martha's microbes. What they failed to realize was that the microbes could invade the contents of their bellies.

A more common attempt at beating the system was to purchase pepwad from previous buyers. After all, people soon realized that the less well-to-do were getting their pepwad for a far lower price. These individuals were bombarded with bids for their pepwad allotments, often for five, ten, or even a hundred times the amount they had paid Knotty's machines.

Those who negotiated such deals, however, were inevitably disappointed. For when they returned to the dispensers the next day, they discovered they gained nothing from the exchange—the bioeconomic devices were too discerning, and any money they made from selling their daily allotment of pepwad was lost to Knotty in the form of an increase in the price of their next purchase.

People quickly learned that they were better off keeping their pepwad to themselves, especially since the eight ounces Knotty allotted per day was, by design, about the minimum caloric intake an average person could live on. Even those who tried to defer facing the pepwad dispensers were only able to do so for at most one or two days. Ultimately, they had to pay the maximal prices and hand over their wealth to Knotty.

Nonetheless, there was one way around Knotty's scheme that met with limited success—the pressurized chamber that my colleagues and I built. Otherwise, there would be no story to tell. Knotty would have simply taken over our labs and research equipment and prevented us from doing any further work.

As I mentioned earlier, the pressurized chamber was in the basement of our building at Central Square. It was a room about twenty by thirty feet where we did most of the biocircuitry preparations.

Since the chamber was sealed from the rest of the earth's atmosphere, not even Martha's microbes could enter.

When we first heard the CNN reports, we headed straight for our secret workplace. None of us anticipated that Knotty's move would take this form—without a mind like his, it was impossible to have foreseen his plan for tyranny. But once we knew, we had little trouble predicting the shape of things to come.

We stocked the chamber with all the water, canned food, and oxygen tanks we could gather, and we brought in additional equipment and supplies we thought we might need for our work. Then we said our prayers, changed into our support suits, and sealed ourselves permanently from the outer world.

Unfortunately, there was no room for us to take in any others. We couldn't even tell our friends or families. Our only hope was to somehow solve the PIFFEN meter implantation problem while still in the chamber. If any people on the outside knew our location, we feared Knotty would discover it when they transacted with his dispensers.

Our immediate constraint was oxygen—we had about two weeks of air supply for all six of us. Furthermore, our mobility was greatly limited within the chamber, and there was the real possibility that one or more of us had already ingested a tyrannum-producing microbe, meaning that we would all end up being exposed without protection.

But the biggest constraining factor, no doubt, was with the people outside our chamber, not with us. For it wasn't at all clear that they could withstand even one more day of Knotty's tyranny, and we had no way of knowing how long it would take us to offer the world any other real alternative.

THE TYRANT AND THE TYRANNIZED

THE FIRST DAY of total tyranny had been relatively easy. It was the second day, November 3rd, that brought the real chaos. That was the day that the lab test results were broadcasted and the price of pepwad became maximal.

The test results definitively supported Knotty's claims. Every food-stuff besides pepwad was found to be susceptible to the tyrannum-producing microbes. Where or how the food was stored didn't matter. Martha's microbes were so well dispersed that anything edible was prone to infection from the moment of exposure to air until full digestion in the body.

The lab reports estimated that eight percent of non-pepwad food-stuff already had the toxin within it, and the odds were expected to get worse as the microbes spread further. Of course, females abstaining from sex would have been better off not eating pepwad to avoid the risk of Knotty's purple ergot powder. But no one knew this at the time, and Knotty avoided suspicion by adjusting his ergot injection rate to keep pace with the number of infected males.

As far as the public was concerned, pepwad seemed the only hope for survival, and even those who lived hundreds of miles from the nearest Total Food Store understood that their lives depended on making the journey. Convinced of its necessity, people's willingness to pay for pepwad became precisely equal to their valuation of life, without any downscaling on account of uncertainty. Instead of getting their eight ounces of pepwad for only a fraction of their net worth, they now had to drain all their savings.

By their second or third visit to a Total Food store, most households were parting with more than just their liquid assets. They were turning over everything they felt wasn't absolutely indispensable for life. Although this varied somewhat from one household to the next, there was no duping the bioeconomic device when it came to such a determination.

Thus, it was only a short while before Knotty gained the majority of the world's wealth. By the evening of November 3rd, all franchise owners of his Total Food stores had relinquished title to him. By the following day, he owned most existing currency, real estate, jewelry, precious metals, and negotiable financial instruments—not to mention sundry items like cars, televisions and furniture.

A small fraction of the population had not yet visited a pepwad dispenser, so Knotty couldn't get at their assets. For example, there were people in prisons and hospitals and nursing homes left stranded by their caretakers, who were scrambling to procure pepwad for themselves. There were also individuals who had no means of transport to get to Total Food Stores, as well as those who were attempting to fast instead of eating pepwad, and those who were already infected with the gangrene.

But none of these individuals were of concern to Knotty. Ultimately, they would all end up either buying pepwad from one of his dispensers or dying in the streets. If they died in the streets, it would only be a matter of time before their assets passed into the hands of the living, through inheritance or looting. At that point, Knotty would extract the booty from these new owners.

How did Knotty actually take hold of all this wealth? And how did he keep track of it all? This was the most curious thing about

Knotty's brand of tyranny, for he didn't have to gain physical possession of any of it.

The exchange of property for pepwad was by a neural impulse agreement. That is to say, the customer, with a finger in the dispenser orifice, simply admitted that such and such an item was now owned by Knotty. Nothing had to be signed or transferred, and the agreement was perfectly enforceable. Any thought of trying to reclaim that piece of property would be detected by the bioeconomic device during the next visit.

This made things surprisingly easy for Knotty. He didn't have to worry about storage, shipping, or security, nor did he need an army to enforce his authority. Everything he acquired could stay wherever it was. Yet all of it was indisputably under his control.

That was the critical factor for Knotty. It didn't matter if, under his rule, people lived too meagerly to generate any additional wealth. He simply sought ownership of all that currently existed. He relished the power of ownership, not the material underlying it.

Of course, there were certain assets that people deemed essential for survival over which Knotty had no control. Almost everyone required a blanket, some clothing, a jug of water, and perhaps a small stove with which to cook pepwad. One's willingness to pay for pepwad could not include the exchange of these items.

Furthermore, in extremely cold climates many people felt they needed to have some form of shelter. Even if they were willing to trade their houses for pepwad, they often required that small sections of their homes be leased back to them. Knotty's bioeconomic devices would generally consent to this, with the proviso that all nonessential rooms, along with their furniture and appliances, be strictly avoided.

In the more temperate climates, such arrangements were made only in exceptional circumstances. Most homeowners, once they traded in their houses for pepwad, were forced to camp in the streets or on property Knotty had not yet acquired. Likewise, the vast majority of renters lost their leases as soon as their landlords confronted the dispensers.

This, perhaps, was the most difficult outcome to accept about the state of total tyranny. While throngs of squatters lived on the sidewalks and sewers, the houses surrounding them remained unoccupied.

Even in the most prestigious neighborhoods, on the coasts of California and Japan and along the Mediterranean, the predicament was the same. Thousands upon thousands of glorious homes—with their skylights and spas and designer kitchens—sat entirely vacant. No one dared enter unless they were prepared to die, for their actions would be revealed when they next confronted one of Knotty's bioeconomic devices, and they would be denied pepwad.

But what about the FBI, you might ask. And what about the CIA and the National Security Advisory? What about Interpol and the British Secret Service, or any of the intelligence organizations from other countries? Why didn't these agencies intervene to challenge such lunacy?

Quite simply, there was nothing they could do. Laws and customs, contracts and constitutions, deeds and trusts, all went flying out the window under Knotty's tyranny. No organization dared to stand up against Knotty to enforce them. Intelligence agencies and secret police and even militaries were ultimately made up of individuals, and each of these individuals had to face the bioeconomic device in order to survive.

Admittedly, Knotty employed no guards to uphold his reign. As long as they ate no pepwad, these authorities could have seized whatever resources they wished. They could have surrounded Knotty with an arsenal of tanks and other weaponry.

But Knotty had the ultimate leverage. If he was assassinated or arrested, or even just harassed, his space farm and all of his underground storage tanks were programmed to self-destruct. And that, clearly, would have been the end of humanity.

In light of the desperate circumstances, one might anticipate numerous individuals willing to risk everything to reclaim their old lives. In fact, the effect was much the opposite. With the fabric of human civilization torn to shreds, the populace lost all that was familiar. Among the many tumultuous events with which to contend, there was disease and starvation, the death of loved ones, the loss of property, the abandonment of one's community, and perhaps most dreadful of all, the complete and total loss of any security regarding the future.

People coped by numbing themselves, by denying the severity of their circumstances, and even by idolizing their new leader. But rarely did they contemplate rebellion. One of the more curious manifestations of this latter phenomenon was the gathering of entertainers from throughout the world to perform for Knotty. Comedians, musicians, actors, and jugglers all vied for the opportunity to please him. Hundreds of doctors and health specialists also flocked to Knotty's side to monitor his well-being, and vigilante groups organized to watch for any signs of subversive behavior among disgruntled individuals.

Beyond these efforts at self-preservation, there was almost no activity at all. The vast majority of the surviving population was reduced to living on sidewalks, in drainage pipes, or under bridges. Few people still held jobs, as any income people earned over and beyond the cost of maintaining their subsistence hovels was absorbed into the price for pepwad. The only significant remaining industries were mortuaries and water utilities, both over which Knotty held ownership.

Thus, with the economy brought to a standstill, Knotty revealed his next big surprise. On November 6th, he promised jobs for all who wanted them. He needed to begin building his fleet of space farms, and since there were no other employers to compete with, he could offer the most meager of wages. All he had to do was give his workers enough pepwad to sustain their families.

In a matter of days then, Knotty not only held the bulk of the world's wealth, but he also commanded over the bulk of the able-bodied population. As the world's only employer, Knotty was ruthless. His workers trained for sixteen hours a day at command posts adjacent to each Total Food store. If they didn't perform adequately, Knotty withheld their payments of pepwad until they either shaped up or died.

So this was the great 'equalizing effect' that Joseph predicted and that I confirmed with my fancy mathematical equations. And in a sense, we both could take credit for being right—the distribution of income had become almost perfectly flat throughout the entire world. But of course, it was the rich who had become poor, not the poor who had become rich, and huge segments of the population were wiped out in the process.

I might as well admit it: In the first three days of Knotty's tyranny, over 600 million people died from the tyrannum toxin—100 million females and 500 million males. During the same period, another 360 million females were killed by Knotty's ergot injections. In the ensuing days, as the remaining population learned to subsist solely on pepwad, there were hundreds of millions more deaths, because Martha's microbes continued to interact with undigested non-pepwad food lingering in people's colons.

Altogether, there were over *two billion fatalities.* Human corpses lay scattered in every city, every village, virtually every square yard of human settlement. Most often the victims were buried namelessly, in mass grave-sites the size of which the world had seen no precedent.

For sadly, no prior war or plague could compare next to the horrors of Knotty's master plan. Nothing in the history of humankind could even come close. *Two billion people had been exterminated—one fourth the entire human population.*

And that was a fact I somehow had to live with.

THE TYRANT AND HIS BETRAYER

Because all radio and television ceased broadcasting on November 3rd, however, my colleagues and I had no way of knowing the extent of the suffering at the time. Our only source of information came from peering out a tiny window that overlapped our pressurized chamber.

This window faced a major cross street where a colony of squatters was living, so it was our one link to the outside world. Had we experienced any more contact, we probably would have been too paralyzed by fear to remain functional. As things stood, we channeled all our energy into our work, laboring day and night without sleep.

After only three days in the chamber, our engineer-in-residence, Beatrice Coleson, came up with a truly pioneering application of biochip design that enabled us to modify our PIFFEN cells to survive at any temperature, as long as they were kept moist. Meanwhile, our microbiologist, Albert Senghavi, upgraded the cells to discriminate between the DNA of humans and non-humans.

Another clever feature of the PIFFEN cells was developed by Lou Silverthwait, our psychologist. Recognizing that we couldn't risk our plan being discovered midway in its implementation, Lou preprogrammed the cells to delay informing their hosts of their presence until externally prompted by us.

Dan Gilmore, the mathematical economist in our group, set up the radio frequency for the PIFFEN cells. Jack Myers, our computer expert, took care of the master control codes so that we could coordinate the cells once the human population was saturated. And then there was the controversial feature for which I was responsible—the erasure of all memory of Knotty's tyranny.

After all, the whole purpose of our PIFFEN meters was to put consumers on an equal footing with Knotty by allowing them to determine the true cost of producing pepwad. If everything went according to plan, consumers' willingness to pay for pepwad would fall to this level, so that Knotty's profit would be eliminated and his tyranny dissolved.

But there was a potential problem. What if people were so numbed by Knotty's tyranny that they chose not to take advantage of their PIFFEN meter implants? What if their lives were too filled with horror and dependency to want to risk further upheaval? And what if they feared they might lose their pepwad allotments by challenging Knotty?

These were my biggest worries, and why I felt I had to add the memory-erasing feature to our PIFFEN cells. For if people had no memory of the tyrannical period, they wouldn't carry any residual fear. They would have no reason not to use their meters. Knotty would have no choice but to accept their terms and sell pepwad at fair prices, and the ordinary workings of the economy would be restored.

Admittedly, such a wide-scale erasure had drawbacks. Not only was it invasive, but it meant that the most catastrophic event in the history of humankind would be forever forgotten. People's memories were all they had, since access to such things as tape recorders, computers, typewriters, and pens and paper was stripped within a day or two of the tyranny. But in my view, the loss of two weeks of history seemed a small price to pay for the regaining of world freedom.

I knew of a neuro-transmitter compound called trophylin that had been shown to disable short-term memory without causing neurological damage, so I simply engineered the PIFFEN cells to produce and secrete this compound. I had to specify the amount of trophylin to be secreted, and this was a bit complex, since individuals often varied in their response. But I finally settled on an 'upper bound' dose, which meant that more sensitive individuals would lose their memories of events starting a few days before November 1st, while even the least sensitive individuals would be sure to lose their memories of the entire tyrannical period.

The only complication was that the trophylin would erase *everything* people had learned during this period, including the fact that the plants and animals on earth were tainted with the tyrannum toxin. Yet in order to survive, people would still need to know this. There was also Knotty's warning that women could be in danger if they experienced sexual arousal, which at the time I did not know to be false.

The best solution—to alter the trophylin to selectively preserve these parts of people's memory—wasn't possible given the limited amount of time I had. Instead, the only feasible approach was to reintroduce this knowledge into people's brains after the meters had been implanted.

Consequently, I supplemented each PIFFEN cell with a special hybrid neuron. This 'data neuron', as I called it, was designed to hold all the critical information that people needed to know in order to avoid the dangers of the tyrannum toxin. I incorporated it directly into each PIFFEN cell's architecture, so that people would be automatically reminded of the critical information whenever they were at risk.

The most difficult part was deciding the precise content of this critical information. I wanted to keep it as simple as possible, yet I didn't want to underemphasize or omit any crucial details, so I finally settled on the following message, encoded into 54 distinct languages:

WARNING!
For Your Own Safety!

1. *Do not eat earth-grown food products.*
2. *Do not touch plants or animals.*
3. *Avoid sexual arousal of any kind.*

There were a number of shortcomings to my message, which I could only hope would not prove too serious. The most immediate was the fact that the data neurons were language-based, meaning that children couldn't benefit from them until they learned to speak. Prior to that point, it would be the parents' responsibility to keep them out of danger.

Perhaps more problematic was the repressive nature of the message. I was particularly concerned with its call for complete sexual abstinence, but my colleagues felt it better to discourage sexual arousal in both men and women, rather than in just women, since this would maintain symmetry and reduce tension between the sexes. In any case, we had no strong evidence to reject the notion that sexual arousal was dangerous for all.

Our expectation was always that these data neurons would be temporary. The severe lifestyle adjustments they demanded would only be short-term, we told ourselves. For this reason, I equipped the data neurons with an updating capability, so that as soon as the threat of tyrannum was brought under control, they could be modified or, hopefully, eliminated altogether.

It took until the evening of November 6th to complete these final details. At that point, we began linking the various components of our PIFFEN cells into a unified operating system.

For security reasons, we located the master channel of the system in a secret NASA satellite—this was the brainchild of Jack Myers, who had top-level NASA clearance. The main function of our master channel was to make sure each cell did what it was supposed to do once it landed inside a human being.

Our instructions were as follows: Once a PIFFEN cell was ingested by a person, it was programmed to travel down the esophagus and enter the bloodstream through the stomach lining. The cell would navigate its way to the base of the hypothalamus and attach itself to a particular neural structure called the escinola, where it would grow into its full metering capability. Meanwhile, it would send off a tiny transceiver to be embedded in the fontanel of the person's skull, for radio transmission capability, and to prevent any new PIFFEN cell entrants from attaching themselves, so that each person would be sure to have only one operating meter.

With this accomplished, the meter would send a signal to the master channel indicating its success. It was then to wait for a response signal issued by us once the rest of the population was implanted in a similar fashion. Upon full saturation, all the meters together would release their doses of trophylin. With everyone's short-term memory erased, the meters would activate the data neurons, introduce themselves to their hosts, and provide instructions for the population to overthrow Knotty's total tyranny.

The plan seemed to us to be quite a good one. But we still faced an enormous hurdle—how to release the PIFFEN cells so that each person throughout the world would unknowingly ingest one. The only feasible approach was through drinking water, since our cells required a moist environment. But we didn't see how the six of us, on our own, could single-handedly distribute PIFFEN cells throughout the world's water supply.

Granted, we could throw the cell cultures into the Fresh Pond reservoir, which served the Cambridge area. But even if they reproduced at an exponential rate, it would take months for the cells to spread into the world water system. And we definitely could not wait that long.

On the other hand, we were hesitant to recruit others, for if anyone involved in our distribution scheme went to a pepwad dispenser, Knotty would immediately find out about our plan. Yet if they ate anything besides pepwad, they would be exposed to the tyrannum toxin.

None of us could solve the puzzle, however, and as the night of November 6th gave way to dawn, we realized we hadn't slept for five days. We decided to lie down briefly before returning to the problem. Within minutes of folding out our cots, all of us fell fast asleep.

We probably would have continued slumbering for at least half the day, if it weren't for a most unexpected interruption: The telephone rang. Since the last broadcasts on November 3rd, we had tried making a few telephone calls, but no one ever picked up the line, even though the phone service remained intact. We concluded that Knotty had denied everyone access to their telephones.

The ringing telephone suggested at least one exception, and Dan Gilmore immediately reached for the speakerphone.

"Yes?" he answered.

"Hello?" said an urgent voice on the other end. "Is somebody there?"

"Yes. Who is this?"

"My name is Martha Buliment. I'm being held hostage by Knotty Burgstaller."

"Excuse me?" said Dan skeptically. He motioned for us to time the call, in case it was a set-up. "Why are you calling us?"

"I've been dialing every number in Cambridge for the past three days, hoping somebody would pick up. I'm looking for Ray LeGhir."

"Your efforts have paid off," I interjected. "I'm right here."

"It's you?" said Martha. "Ray LeGhir?"

"Yes," I said. "You have 30 seconds to explain what you want, or I'll hang up."

"I'm trapped in a tiny room with nothing to eat. I've spent the last three days punching numbers into a telephone I built out of an old television set."

"I still don't know what you want," I said.

"I want to help you. I have some information about the toxin. What Knotty said about it is a lie. As long as women avoid being sexually aroused, they don't need to buy pepwad."

"You're sure about this?"

"Of course, I'm sure," she said. "I'm the one who made the damn toxin."

"Then why have so many women gotten gangrene?"

"Because Knotty's dispensers are randomly injecting a poison into the women's portions. That's why he..."

Lou and Dan motioned to cut the call.

"Time's up," I said. "We'll do what we can. Good luck."

I hung up the phone, and my colleagues and I turned to each other with wide eyes. If Martha's revelation was true, then our problem was solved. *Women* could distribute the PIFFEN cell cultures. As long as they didn't have sex, they could eat any type of food while distributing the cells, and they wouldn't need to face Knotty's pepwad dispensers.

Of course, we had no way to verify Martha's claim. But Beatrice Coleson immediately began gathering her belongings.

"I'm going out there," she said. "I'm the only one who can do it. I've got to try to round up a team of women to spread the PIFFEN cells."

"You still have food in your digestive tract," I cautioned. "It could interact."

"You ought to at least wait until you've digested more," said Dan. "We have only her word."

"I can't wait," insisted Beatrice. "People are suffering, and we don't have time to spare." And with that, Beatrice climbed past the interim hatch and headed out the vacuum chamber.

THE TYRANT AND THE WOMEN

I STILL HAD my reservations. The notion of getting every human being in the world to ingest a tiny PIFFEN cell seemed too fantastic to believe. But we had three reasons to be optimistic.

First, to our good fortune, Beatrice was a very social woman who had numerous female friends throughout the world. Second, the human population was not nearly as spread out as it would have been under normal conditions, since most people were clustered around Knotty's Total Food stores. And finally, a full array of transportation resources was suddenly available to Beatrice and the women she recruited.

This last circumstance was due to the fact that Knotty's control of property hinged solely on pepwad dependency. If women didn't actually need pepwad, then they wouldn't need to face the dispensers. They could use all the idle property that Knotty held—including planes, helicopters, trucks, and boats.

Consequently, Beatrice's first move was to hotwire an abandoned automobile in the street and drive it to the Total Food store in her home-town of Newton. She soon spotted a number of her female friends and neighbors. Almost all of them responded enthusiastically to Beatrice's plan—anything seemed better than facing Knotty's dispensers.

Many had other women friends as well, so the group rapidly expanded. When they exhausted the Boston area, they cruised the country in a jet airplane, rounding up as many female volunteers as they could, particularly those with pilot's licenses.

The rest of my colleagues and I continued the task of reproducing our PIFFEN cells. We knew that if Martha's claim was true, then the data neurons in our PIFFEN cells contained faulty information in urging the avoidance of sexual arousal. But unfortunately, to delete this reference would entail revamping the PIFFEN cells, which would set us back at least another 2 or 3 days.

On the other hand, if we proceeded with the cells we had, the data neurons could be updated later in accordance with the facts. It would just be a matter of accessing the master channel via the assigned password, which each of my colleagues knew, in order to make the adjustment. So we all agreed that our best option was to proceed with what we had rather than make the population endure Knotty's tyranny any longer.

The following morning at about 10 AM, Beatrice returned from her recruiting mission with 108 female pilots. She assembled them on the second floor of our building, where they were fully briefed regarding our plan of attack. Not a single one of them withdrew their participation once they heard the many assumptions upon which the plan was based.

I would be lying, however, if I didn't admit there was some dissension when Beatrice revealed the design of the PIFFEN meter. Several women objected to the extensive genetic manipulation on which it relied. Others disliked the memory erasure component. Still others were skeptical of the privacy intrusions associated with the communications network we wanted to set up.

Beatrice dealt with these issues one by one, in a calm and orderly fashion. When the women wanted more details, she let them speak to me via our intercom system, at which point I tried to describe the whole set of circumstances that had shaped our decisions.

The thorniest issue by far was the one over which my opinions carried no weight, for a few of the women had matriarchal leanings. When they heard of their invulnerability to the food toxin, they couldn't help raising the possibility of abandoning the PIFFEN meter plan and creating a whole new society of women independent of Knotty's tyranny.

I had to admit, their idea was not entirely without justification, and a number of women were enticed by it. Surprisingly, it was Dan Gilmore who brought unity back to the group.

"Sure, it all sounds very good," he said through the intercom. "Especially for those of you who have no emotional ties to any living men. But for the rest of you, I'm afraid to say, you'd be more down-trodden than ever.

"Just think about it," he continued. "If there was a man you had feelings for, you'd hardly want him to starve to death, right? And he'd obviously know this too. You'd constantly be having to shell out for him, because it would affect his willingness to pay for pepwad—his knowing you wouldn't let him starve would show up on Knotty's dispensers, even if he didn't want it to. So you'd be forced to keep supporting him, just because of these feelings you had. And what about your fathers, your sons, your ex-husbands, your ex-lovers? The same thing would happen with them too, unless you were willing to let them starve to death."

With this one argument, Dan exposed the inherent weakness of the matriarchy idea, and the women had to concede that he was right. For none of them could honestly claim to lack any emotional ties to living men.

That night, as the women discussed their plans, Beatrice knocked on the door outside the pressurized chamber.

"There's a man upstairs," she said. "He's asking to speak with you."

"How does he know I'm here?"

"I'm not sure. He says his name is Joseph Baptista."

"I see," I said. "You'd better bring him to me."

She went upstairs and led Joseph to the entrance of the chamber.

"Aren't you going to invite me in?" he asked through the intercom speaker.

"No," I replied coldly. "You shouldn't even be in the building."

Joseph gave me an ironic look. "I heard about your recruiting efforts, Ray, and I figured we'd better have a talk."

"It's a little late for that," I said.

"Not really. There's plenty of time for you to get a hold of yourself."

"Oh? How's that?"

"Leave things as they are and stop your work on the meter."

"That's absurd. But if you really want to stop me, Joseph, all you have to do is tell Knotty where I am."

"I can't do that," he said. "He'd kill you."

"You're worried about one measly life, after all this?"

"I'm only an observer. I only want you to do what you are guided to do internally."

"I'm doing exactly that. Have no doubt about it."

"I won't stop you, Ray." He paused for a long moment. "All I ask is that you remember the long-term."

Then he walked back up the stairs, and I returned to my work.

While the other women slept, Beatrice and two of her friends located a nearby Hertz-Penske truck rental center. They rounded up all the moving vans on the lot and drove them back to our headquarters, loading them one by one with our PIFFEN cell packets. My male colleagues and I struggled to keep pace with them, reproducing as many new cells as we could.

By 4 AM the next morning—November 8th—the vans were filled to the brim with packets. Beatrice woke up the other women pilots, and they all formed a caravan, driving the vans and their cargo to

Logan airport. When they reached the airstrip, they reviewed their strategies and assigned geographic responsibilities. They each chose aircraft appropriate for their assignments and divvied up the PIFFEN cells.

Before sunrise, all the planes were in the air. The first targets the women hit were the municipal water treatment facilities in their assigned territories. Next, they circled around and dumped the cells into lakes, rivers, and reservoirs.

The tactics weren't enough to guarantee that every human would soon ingest a PIFFEN cell, since some sources of drinking water were quite isolated, like remote wells and springs, as well as catchments of rain. But the one good thing about Knotty's tyranny, for our purposes, was that it barred the majority of the population from utilizing such sources. Even those who hadn't left their land rarely retained drinking rights to any wells or springs, since such access wasn't necessary for survival. And obviously, no one could afford to consume fancy bottled waters or seltzers.

Instead, the vast majority of people got their water from Knotty's Total Food stores via drinking fountains that he installed next to each pepwad dispenser. They were too afraid to use untreated water, since it might harbor the tyrannum toxin, and the drinking fountains at the Total Food stores were typically their only access to plumbing.

As a result, even if the women pilots ceased their activities after the first day, 99 percent of humans would have wound up ingesting a PIFFEN cell. But our objectives required *complete* saturation of the human species as soon as possible. So after targeting all the obvious bodies of water, the women turned their attention to cloud seeding, injecting the most supercooled clouds in the atmosphere with condensation nuclei.

In this manner, the earth was pounded with waterlogged PIFFEN cells. In regions where it did not rain, the women resorted to spraying the air with a fine mist of PIFFEN cells. This was especially effective in the vicinity of Total Food stores, where the density of the population allowed thousands and thousands of people to be reached simultaneously.

By the evening of November 12th, over three billion people had been successfully implanted. The PIFFEN cells were everywhere, on every drop of dew and every trace of moisture. It was simply a matter of waiting for the rest of the human population to be penetrated—an outcome promised by the laws of probability.

THE TYRANT AND HIS CHRONICLER

Luckily, Knotty failed to notice any of the 108 aircraft crisscrossing the sky. We wanted to make sure he remained unaware of our attentions, so to keep things simple, Beatrice flew all the women pilots to a deserted island in the south Pacific.

Meanwhile, my male colleagues and I monitored the confirmation signals. Since we were still far from complete saturation, my colleagues seized the opportunity to catch up on their sleep. Unlike the others, however, I found myself unable to rest.

Instead, I wrestled over the fact that the PIFFEN cells would be blotting out every human being's memory of the past ten days. I had been through the argument a thousand times, and I still believed in the necessity of memory erasure. But now that our plan was almost reality, I couldn't help worrying about the side effects. I kept thinking how a crucial piece of our identity would be lost forever. We would never know why we had meters in our brains, and who could say what this might do to our psyches?

To assuage my guilt, I decided to provide some sort of document chronicling Knotty's tyranny and the events leading up to it—the very document you are currently reading.

My problem was that I couldn't just release such information into general circulation. I'd have to withhold it until the economy had stabilized and the population had sufficiently recovered. Otherwise, I'd be defeating the whole purpose of the memory erasing.

But if I hid my document somewhere, there was a chance someone else might discover it prematurely. Besides, I myself wouldn't even be able to remember where I'd put it, since the memory erasure meant that I would end up forgetting everything prior to the PIFFEN cell saturation point.

The only solution was to design an artificial intelligence mechanism that could somehow store the document until society was ready for it to be released. I didn't have much time, and all sorts of possibilities for a release mechanism raced through my mind, but most were too complex, and I hardly wanted to drag my colleagues into another major project.

That was when the obvious struck me: I could use a PIFFEN cell as my core structure. If I upgraded its memory chip to be able to store the document, then I could expand its operating system to include a set of criteria under which to release the document, and I'd only have to do this for one PIFFEN cell, since there only had to be one carrier of the document.

The beauty of the idea was that this modified structure could still function as a normal PIFFEN cell. It could reside in someone's brain just like any other cell, and the person who happened to ingest it wouldn't need to know anything about its special purpose.

Eventually, the document would travel through the hypothalamus in order to be released, and at that point the person might experience a bit of discomfort. But otherwise, the person would be able to live life as usual. In fact, whoever ingested this 'augmented' PIFFEN cell could be selected at random. I could simply drop my special cell into the water supply along with all the regular ones so that no one would ever know who received it—at least not until my document was released.

As I expected, the upgrading was a simple matter. Within an hour, I equipped a PIFFEN cell with an auxiliary data bank capable of holding 300 pages of text. I also prepared its operating system for instructions as to how and when to release the text.

My problem was selecting a clear indicator of people's readiness to learn of Knotty's tyranny. All the criteria I came up with seemed terribly arbitrary. Since the oxygen level in our pressurized chamber was fast depleting—there appeared to be less than a day's supply left for the five of us—I turned to the writing of the document.

The initial part of the document was straightforward. I had studied Knotty's past after my bioeconomic device had been stolen, and I was familiar with much of what had happened up to the actual execution of his master plan. Consequently, I wrote the bulk of the first seven chapters in a matter of five hours.

At that point, my colleagues awakened from their sleep. I tried not to let them see what I was doing, but my efforts were transparent. Aware of the dwindling oxygen level, they offered to leave the chamber so I would have more time to complete my work.

I strongly protested, arguing that it would be too dangerous for them, since it could still take quite some time for complete saturation of the PIFFEN cells. They countered that none of them had eaten for the past fourteen hours, so the food interaction problem would be negligible. Furthermore, they were confident that saturation would be reached in less than two days, and they confessed that they were all extremely anxious to see their families. (I, on the other hand, had no family.)

Reluctantly, I allowed myself to be persuaded. Jack Myers gave me the details on how to activate the PIFFEN cells once saturation took place, and in a matter of minutes, we were saying goodbye, shedding tears of sadness, praying for success, and longing for the day we would be reunited.

Shortly after my colleagues left the chamber, I had an insight about how to release my document. A sign of people's readiness to learn of the transition would be when they first recognized the shortcomings of their own PIFFEN meters, for by that point they could hardly be too frightened of their past. And what better indicator of such a thing than if somebody were to laugh at his or her own meter?

Pleased with my ingenuity, I proceeded to program my cell's operating system so that, once activated, it would continuously search through the master channel for any individual who exhibited an act of laughing at his or her meter. I didn't want to take the chance of releasing my document too early, so I also added a protective feature. I instructed the cell's operating system to release the document *only* when the laughing person had also succeeded in communicating to another individual without relying on his or her PIFFEN meter. This way it would be clear that the laugh was not a fluke, and that the person was truly no longer dependent on his or her meter.

I decided to release the document only to this one special person, rather than broadcast it to the public. I figured he or she would know better than I when to reveal it to the rest of society.

For additional security, I programmed the augmented cell to release my text only via the same method of communication that the person had first used in going beyond his or her PIFFEN meter. If the person couldn't understand this method, it would prove that his or her transmission had only been by chance, and so the document would remain hidden.

Having completed these tasks, I turned to a subtler issue: What if the person who ingested the augmented PIFFEN cell ended up dying before the conditions for my document to be released were met? There wasn't a tremendous amount I could do here, short of finding a cure for human mortality, but I did come up with two protective measures.

First, I spliced a generous dose of adaptive intelligence into the augmented cell, so that it would be able to offer guidance to the person it inhabited. The main purpose of this guidance was to prevent the person from sustaining injuries or experiencing ill health. I also equipped the augmented cell with a "learning-by-doing" algorithm so that it could offer various helpful tips and suggestions as it became familiar with the person's daily routine.

The second protective feature was more direct. In order to maximize my time-frame, I programmed the augmented cell to only lodge itself into the hypothalamus of a newborn baby less than sixty days old. If it was ingested by anyone else, the cell had instructions to pass through that person's digestive tract.

Because the standard PIFFEN cells weren't designed to handle such conditions, I immersed the augmented cell in a thin layer of water. Then I sealed it in a waterproof membrane that normal digestive enzymes could not break down, and I equipped the cell with a powerful solvent to dissolve the membrane once it reached the desired destination. With these alterations, I could rest assured that my mechanism would survive any environment without danger of desiccation.

I completed the augmented cell on the evening of November 13th. By that time, over four billion PIFFEN cells had sent signals of successful implantations. According to my projections, full saturation would be reached in less than 24 hours, so I returned my attention to the writing of the document.

Unfortunately, when it came to describing the finer details of Knotty's activities, such as the construction of his tyrannum toxin and the nature of his relationship with Martha, I had many unanswered questions. I had to do the best I could, leaving serious gaps.

By sunset on November 14th, I found that I'd recorded every significant fact I knew. I wasn't entirely happy with the coverage of my document, but the signal counting monitor attached to our radio equipment indicated that 5,613,146,807 successful implantations had occurred. No new signals had been recorded for over 30 minutes.

The obvious conclusion was that the time had come—the population had finally reached saturation. I promptly reviewed the procedures for activating the PIFFEN cells, checking that everything was indeed ready.

As I did this, however, another incoming signal registered on our radio console. Oddly, instead of a successful PIFFEN cell implantation, this signal indicated a failure, meaning that a cell had somehow become dysfunctional after ingestion.

I sorted through the reception register to see if any other signals of this type had been received, and to my dismay, I discovered there had been a total of 42. My immediate fear was that Knotty had discovered our actions and developed some method of disabling each PIFFEN cell as it attempted to penetrate his hypothalamus.

Thankfully, when I checked the geographic origin of the failure signals, my fear was put to rest. The signals had all come from the same place—a remote location east of Santa Fe, New Mexico—and they had all occurred at roughly equal intervals over the past three days. This meant they couldn't possibly have been caused by Knotty, for he had stayed at his ranch in Palm Springs for the entire past week.

I was pretty sure I knew whose hypothalamus was responsible for the 42 signals—Joseph Baptista's. Joseph had often described a favorite camping spot in the Santa Fe National Forest, and the source signals pinpointed it perfectly.

Since no further signals arrived over the next half hour, my conclusion was that we had achieved complete saturation, minus one. But Joseph wasn't going to damage things. He said he was only an observer, and I felt certain he meant it.

My obligation was to activate the PIFFEN meters. Then I remembered that I myself hadn't yet received a PIFFEN cell implant —I'd been isolated in the pressurized chamber the whole time, drinking bottled water.

The implication of this fact made me chuckle aloud. As long as I remained in the chamber, *my* memory wouldn't be erased upon activating the cells. Even better, when the meters were made operational and linked together, I'd be able to enter into anyone's mind I wanted, via the master channel. I could fill all the holes in my document!

Without further delay, I initiated the global activation code for the PIFFEN cells. Thereafter, in steady undulations across the planet, each meter revealed itself to its host. But I barely took time to observe the process—my priority was to complete the document.

In less than a minute, the master channel became operational and I delved straight into Knotty's PIFFEN meter. I proceeded to retrace all his trials and tribulations in pursuit of his secret vision, including his recruitment of Martha and their various activities—sexual as well as scientific.

These findings prompted several new questions, particularly about Martha's motives and how she made the toxin affect only males. Effortlessly, I accessed Martha's meter in conjunction with Knotty's, and for eight solid hours I explored both their minds as I saw fit, recording everything I could find of relevance.

When I was done with Knotty and Martha, I took the liberty of scanning the brains of various secondary parties. I entered Beatrice's brain to gather more information about the PIFFEN cell distribution process, and I entered Drop McWith's brain to shed more light on Knotty's early college years. The minds of various other strategically-located people provided me with a broader view of the general conditions under Knotty's tyranny.

By the following morning, I felt content that I had filled the major gaps in my document. No doubt, I could have done more, but I was anxious to download my text into the augmented cell's data bank in order to be sure that my plan would take effect.

At that point, I bravely logged off the master channel, praying I'd not overlooked anything too significant. Then I quickly wrote the above paragraphs—the ones you are reading at this very moment.

THE TYRANT AND HIS FALL

Now I'm sitting in front of my computer keyboard, taking one last moment to double-check my work. The truth is, I'm a little scared to stop writing, and I'm so exhausted I'm beginning to doubt if I'm really finished.

At least, it's raining outside. And yes, the augmented cell is ready to receive my document. All I have to do is press the download button. In preparation, I've even opened the window seal on my pressurized chamber so that I can toss the cell out into the rain-filled gutter.

I keep thinking there's something crucial I've forgotten. I just can't quite put my finger on what it is, and I'm so tired, so incredibly tired.

I hear footsteps coming now. I'm hoping it's Albert Senghavi or Dan Gilmore or one of my other colleagues with some piece of good news. But the footsteps are fast, very fast. I'm starting to worry.

The door flies open. Yes, it's Knotty. I pretend not to see him, so I can still type into the keyboard.

"You god damn little wimp," he says. "I knew I'd find you here."

"Huh?"

"You fucked up big-time, LeGhir. You thought you had me, but all you did was slow me down. There's nothing you can do."

"I didn't realize there was anything I needed to do," I reply, staring at my keyboard.

"I'm afraid, old boy, there are a couple of things you don't quite know."

"Such as?"

"Such as your professor pals are history. I knocked them off last night, as soon as they went home to their families. Your pals' memories had already begun to fade, thanks to your god damn PIFFEN meters, but they knew enough to give me the basics."

"You killed them?"

"That's right, my friend."

I look straight into Knotty's eyes, wanting to tear his jugular vein into pulp, but somehow I stay calm. "What do you want?" I ask slowly.

"You're going to give me the location of the master channel, and then I'm going to dismantle your whole god damn creation."

"How... how can you possibly..."

He laughs. "You thought your pathetic meters would erase my memory, is that it?"

I nod my head.

"Well, sure," he says. "They did, just like for everyone else. But you forget, old boy, I still had my computer files and fax messages. I was the tyrant, for Christ's sake, so I never had to part with anything. I got to keep all my belongings. You see?"

"Oh god," I sigh. "Oh god."

"Now stop typing into your fucking computer, and tell me where the god damn master channel is!"

"It's right here, inside my computer. Where else would I put it?"

"Fuck you, LeGhir. I know it's somewhere in your office at Harvard. Your pals told me that much."

"They told you?" I say, faking surprise.

"That's right, LeGhir. Give me the exact location, with the password, or I'll blow your ass away and find it myself."

"I'll take the latter."

"You think you've got the guts?"

"Go ahead and find out."

"Fine, you little piece of shit."

He draws a small handgun, a Walther PPKS, I think. He points it straight at me, waiting for me to plea mercy. But I just keep typing, so he takes aim, and pulls..;jalkjdklf nlknjhqwlhhhhhhhhhhh hhhhhh-hhhh hhhhhh hjjj

I'mm shhot in head and cchest, 3 or 4 bulets. Knotys gone, thought I dead. Not mch left in me, lotta blood. But hav to finish. I press dwnload button, take augmntd cell, throw out wndow into gutter, into rain

that's all

sorry

dying

PART THREE

INTO THE EBB

And so castles made of sand
Fall in the sea eventually

JIMI HENDRIX

CHAPTER NINETEEN

THOSE WERE the words that came gushing out of my PIFFEN meter while I lay in my coma—the words that Ray LeGhir wrote to explain the transition, to make sure that the historical records of humankind were complete. Hard as it is to imagine, I, Ralph Peterson, happened to be the carrier of this information.

That was why I had my proddings, and why I'd become a channel supervisor for the Netgorks. It was even why I'd ended up wearing Trivers' sleazy headware to monitor Kale. Because the truth was, just about everything in my life derived from the fact that I'd been the little baby who swallowed the augmented PIFFEN cell.

But I couldn't grasp this revelation at the time. I was still lying on my back in a coma, and Ray LeGhir's document still hadn't been successfully transmitted to anyone. Even though the document had passed through the subconscious sector of my brain and made its way into a secret channel of the Web—a procedure which took a grand total of 48 minutes—Kale had no idea it existed. Neither did anyone else.

You see, the augmented cell needed to perform one further task. It had to send a signal to Kale telling her how to access Ray's document, and it had to do this using the same method of pre-Web communication that Kale used with Joseph.

Unfortunately, my special cell wasn't prepared to follow such a procedure. After all, Ray LeGhir hadn't exactly anticipated that Kale would sent her signal to Joseph in the manner of a seasoned bird.

I had to remain stuck in my coma for another 51 hours and 54 minutes. I had to just lie in my bed, unaware of anything at all. Meanwhile, as the augmented cell struggled to simulate the antics of a seasoned bird, the lives of everyone else just continued moving along.

✦

Kale's life, of course, was most relevant. She was the one who caused the augmented cell to release Ray's document out of my brain, and she was the one traveling to the outbacks of northern New Mexico.

Once she received Joseph's request to visit him—on that fateful Saturday of October 2nd, 2077—it only took her 87 minutes to eat dinner and have her travel bag packed. Her father dropped her off at the mega-shuttle terminal in New Haven. By midnight, she was on her way.

She managed to sleep while hovering over the Midwest, so she barely noticed the lights below from the huge intercontinental data storage structures. But as she approached Albuquerque, she fixated on the flat expanse of tumbleweeds, lizardskin, and stillness.

At the layover terminal, she had to post a recognizance bond to travel into unprotected territory. The border authorities gave her a thorough examination, checking all her reflexes, then they reluctantly allowed her into a small northern-bound shuttle. At 4:57 AM, she was deposited in front of the Tesuque computer control station, where Joseph and Drop were waiting in an old-time vehicle.

"Well, who is this?" said Joseph, as he climbed out of the contraption. "Who is this?"

"Grandpa!" exclaimed Kale. "You shouldn't have gotten out of bed when you're sick." She said this only to appear consistent to the pirater.

"It's just a little virus, Cat. It's gotten much better since yesterday. Besides, how could I miss picking you up on your first visit ever?"

Kale smiled warmly.

"By the way," continued Joseph, "this is my compadre, Drop McWith."

"A privilege to meet you," said Drop, who still sat inside the old-time vehicle. "I'm delighted you've finally made it out here."

"Me too," said Kale. "I've been looking forward to seeing New Mexico for a long time."

"What are we waiting for?" he said, his brow twitching excitedly. "Let's take her up to the castle."

They got in the vehicle, and Drop drove eastward up a windy road. Kale noticed the air had a different quality, lighter and more active. As the morning sun crawled over the Sangre de Cristos, she was amazed by the piñon and juniper trees, which were everywhere, even in close proximity to the occasional dwellings nestled in the hills.

"There it is," announced Drop, as they rounded the last bend. "There's the castle."

"It's incredible," said Kale. "Not at all like I thought. Mom always called it a hut."

"You know Joseph hates to boast," said Drop, "but it's definitely the most supreme castle in the area."

As soon as they parked, she rushed to the house, her pleasure level rising to 92.43. "How did you do this, Grandpa?" she asked, studying the mountainous texture of the adobe walls. "How did you make these forms?"

"The easy way," replied Joseph. "With my bare hands."

"I could look at them for hours."

"We could use you here for hours." He ushered her inside the cave-like house, with Drop following behind.

"I love it," said Kale.

"How about some breakfast?" asked Joseph.

"Sure," she said. "I'm starved."

"It's your lucky day. Drop and I are going to fix you a real New Mexican breakfast. You can go set your things upstairs in the sunroom—that's where you'll be sleeping."

Kale walked through an oval-shaped living room with a stalactite fireplace, then she climbed a spiral staircase to the top of the tower. The sunroom was furnished modestly with an unenlivened bed beneath the south-facing window. Out the window she could see a full vista from Baldy Peak to Chicoma to Cabezon, all the way to Sandia Crest. But she was most captivated by what she saw above the window. Mounted on the ceiling were 362 small red tiles arranged in the shape of a figure eight, comprising Joseph's almost finished analemma.

She studied the tiles for 26 seconds, until she remembered to signal me about her new location. When she determined that my system was unavailable, for an unspecified reason, she left a message with my secretary—that is, my ex-secretary.

Next she turned to her incoming data to catch up on her processing. She simultaneously checked in with Professor Morgaux via her data resonator and considered transmitting with Greggy but decided against it because of the pirater. Instead, she changed into her turquoise dress, put on the amethyst necklace Chamy and Gemela had given her, and went downstairs.

Joseph motioned her to a long wooden table, where Drop was serving portions of posole, unaltered squash, and orange juice. At first, Kale didn't understand what the squash was, but when Drop explained that it grew that way from vines of plants on the *Borneo* satellite, she readied herself for a bite.

"This looks very exotic," she said. "Everything is so different."

"I should have gotten you out here sooner," said Joseph. "I've wanted to for many years. I guess I've just been self-consumed."

"It's not your fault," she replied. "I couldn't have come before."

"She's right," said Drop. "A multitude of complex factors can be attributed to her extensive period of separation from the castle. But she's here now, so I'd like to propose a toast. A toast to Kale Keeler and Joseph Baptista. In their element."

They clinked glasses and drank their orange juice. As they ate, Drop described to Kale the beauty of the surrounding mountains and valleys. Joseph proposed they take a hike after breakfast.

"But shouldn't you get some rest?" said Kale.

"Nah," interjected Drop. "The old man is mountain-driven. No one this side of the Rio Grande knows the structure of a hill like your grandfather."

"That's because of the llamas," Joseph replied. "In any case, a little exercise is exactly what I need."

"Llamas?" said Kale. "We can take them with us?"

"Sure," he said. "But there's no touching."

"I know, Grandpa."

"And guess what?" added Drop. "I'll take care of the noon ritual in the sunroom, so you can hike for as long as you want."

"Thank you, Drop," said Joseph. "It's the last time I'll need you to place a tile."

"Yeah, yeah," he said, smiling. "I do all the drudgery, and you get the glory of completion."

❂

16.49 minutes later, Joseph was signaling the animals to begin their ascent. He selected two llamas for the hike, Nibby and Horse. Nibby carried a large pack on his back, while Horse hauled two canisters of water. For protection, Kale and Joseph wore jeans, turtlenecks, and nylon gloves.

"It looks like you packed us enough food for a week," joked Kale, as she followed the llamas across an arroyo.

"I brought some astronomical instruments," replied Joseph. "I thought I might do some fiddling up top."

"In the daylight?"

"Yes, perhaps." The trail came to a fork and Joseph turned his shoulders to the right to guide the llamas.

"They're so obedient," remarked Kale.

"Not always," he said. "Of all the beasts of burden, these ones have given in the least. But they don't ask for much, and they can go without food and water for longer than the others. That's how they've managed to survive all these years."

They carried on toward the first pass. After 54.26 minutes, the piñon trees gave way to tall ponderosas and the llamas began to hum. A half-mile later they crossed the pass, and Kale nervously peered down at the sprawl of Santa Fe, to the south.

"We're at 9,000 feet," said Joseph. He tapped Kale's thigh—a contact to which her receptors were unaccustomed. Then he led her and the animals down a series of switchbacks into a narrow ravine.

At the bottom of the canyon were five deciduous trees, each full of vibrant orange and yellow leaves. Joseph gestured to the llamas to stop, and he and Kale sat down in the shade.

"Don't we need protection from the leaves?" she asked, looking up at the trees.

"Not really," he replied. "Their sap is what's toxic, and you can only get hurt if you ingest it, though the WPA doesn't like to admit that fact."

"How do you know?"

"Experience," he said. "The WPA wants to keep us afraid, to scare us from traces of the past."

Kale nodded. "What about bancha tea? It's made out of leaves, isn't it?"

"Yeah, but it's from the space farms, like everything else."

"Oh," she said, looking at him expectantly. "So are there other things you can tell me... about the past?"

"I'm afraid not much, Cat."

She withdrew the tear drop resonator from her pocket and held it firmly in her hand. "I thought you might be interested in this device," she input. "It stores everything in a private channel." She handed the resonator to Joseph, explaining how to use it with her eyes.

"That's clever, Cat," he replied, after intaking her words. "But it's not going to do much for me."

"There's something I should mention," she input. "I know about your conversation with Mom and Dad. I tapped into Mom's netgork without her permission."

"Then you understand why I couldn't tell you anything about it."

"Yes," she added. "But what I don't understand is, if your memory was erased from 2004 to 2020, how can you be sure you didn't have a meter? And how do you know those other things you told Mom?"

"They gave me the information when they released me," he answered through the resonator, "on the grounds that I'd be too disabled without at least knowing that."

"And what if they were lies?"

"No, because I also know from deeper sources within my being."

"Then you *can* tell me more," she input. "From those sources."

Joseph turned to her with the most tired eyes she'd seen. "I'm sorry, Cat," he said. "There's nothing left in me. Nothing."

"So why did you respond to my message?"

"Because you were right. A jewel must be returned. But it's fruitless to rely on something I no longer have. There's only one way back."

"What?" she input anxiously.

"Time," he said. "Time and light." And then he stood up and gestured to the llamas.

Joseph proceeded up the hill toward his favorite peak, and Kale struggled to keep pace. As she mulled over her grandfather's words, she received a response signal from my ex-secretary:

Dear Ms. Keeler,

I'm sorry to inform you that Mr. Peterson has been dismissed from his position as supervisor. Mr. Brandon Marshall has been appointed to replace him, and he is the one to whom you should now direct your reports.

Warm regards.

—Ms. Olafson

Of course, Kale was hardly surprised by this piece of news. She'd been expecting my dismissal for the past several months, as had everyone else in the office. The fact that my system was unavailable made perfect sense—she assumed I'd disconnected my interface circuits as a result of having been fired.

Instead of concerning herself with my predicament, she initiated transmission with her new channel boss. "Hello, Mr. Marshall," she signaled. "This is Kale Keeler."

"Keeler," he responded. "Very efficient timing. I was just preparing to contact you. We need confirmation on your geographic coordinates."

"My latitude is 35 degrees, 44 minutes, and 29 seconds," she transmitted. "My longitude is 106 degrees, 11 minutes, and 8 seconds."

"Tesuque, New Mexico?" he calculated. "That's unprotected territory. What's your function, Keeler?"

"I'm visiting my grandfather. He picked up a bad flu bug and the family had a little scare, so I came out late last night."

"Sounds inefficient, Keeler. Very inefficient. Give me your assurance that you'll be in Cambridge tomorrow to resume the assignment and I'll overlook the matter."

"Actually, that's something I'd like to discuss, Mr. Marshall. This is the first time I've ever visited my grandfather's home, and now that I'm here I can't believe how beautiful it is."

"I don't register the word 'beautiful.' What are you saying?"

"Give me two more days, Mr. Marshall. I can work on the assignment out here. This is exactly what I need—a little time away from the hustle and bustle to sort out the confusion."

Marshall hesitated for a moment. "Very well, Keeler," he replied. "But you must have the project packaged and complete by Friday, 5 PM."

"How about Sunday?" she countered. "I've still got a lot of inroads."

"Not good enough."

"Saturday?"

"Saturday noon, at the latest," he warned.

"Fine, Saturday noon."

"You'd better not misappropriate any time."

"I won't, Mr. Marshall," she assured him. "I certainly won't."

Kale determined her elevation to be 10,346 feet. She hadn't walked this vigorously for 4.56 years, and she was beginning to doubt she could take another step. Just as she was ready to turn back, Joseph pointed to a clearing along the ridge, where a small rock table offered a panoramic view of the Jemez mountains.

"We're here," he said, parking the llamas beside the table.

They laid out melons, carrot juice, rice cakes, and breakfast burritos. As they ate hungrily, Joseph identified markers on the valley floor. Midway through the meal, he fetched his bag of astronomical instruments.

"I want you to see some of the things I've turned to," he said.

He placed a spherical sundial on the table, showing her its features. Then he explained how the earth rotated every 24 hours, and how it orbited the sun every year while maintaining a fixed 23.5 degree tilt of its axis. He even demonstrated how to find due south by noting the position of the sun when the shadows were shortest.

8.36 minutes later, when it was precisely noontime, he handed Kale a sextant. "Now tell me how you'd figure what time of year it was, if you didn't know," said Joseph.

Kale's first reaction was to search the Web for the answer, but she determined it was absent from the major channels. Thinking to herself for 149 seconds, she aligned the sextant southward and marked where the light fell on its arc.

"According to this device," she said, "the sun is 52 degrees above the horizon. Since it's noontime and the latitude here is 36 degrees, that means that today the angle of the sun is about two degrees below the equator."

"Good," said Joseph.

"So I estimate that it's approximately a week or ten days after fall equinox."

"Right. Of course, it could also be a week or ten days before spring equinox—if you didn't know better. But that's what makes the game useful. You have to put yourself in a position of unknowing to fully appreciate it."

"I see," said Kale.

Joseph nodded and his eyes began to get cloudy. "And you know, sometimes it seems I lost those sixteen years of my past because I didn't have the strength to keep on carrying my memories... because I wanted to know less instead of more. You know what I mean, Cat?"

"Not exactly."

"But it seems true to me, Cat," he said. "It seems entirely true to me." With that, he abruptly stood up and began preparing the llamas for the homeward descent.

CHAPTER TWENTY

TREKKING DOWN THE MOUNTAINSIDE, Kale remained silent and frustrated. She didn't understand her grandfather's distance, and she couldn't help wondering whether perhaps she'd made an error in traveling to New Mexico.

Joseph hardly noticed her silence. When they got back to the house, he led her to the stables and showed her how to feed and groom the llamas without getting too close to their bodies. Then he went inside to take a nap.

At first, Kale was fearful of interacting with the llamas—especially the males, which had long pointed horns extending from their foreheads. But the llamas' responses fascinated her. They tried to nuzzle up against her as she brushed them, and their eyes seemed to transmit encouragement, as if telling her she was in the right place.

She ended up spending several hours in the stalls. She particularly enjoyed watching the llamas care for Rija, the baby. When Cayuca and Nibby began licking Rija's fur, Kale almost broke into tears.

She understood that the Web was actually a refinement of the llama's system—a refinement that enabled a million-fold increase in neuroelectrical impulse transmission. What bothered her was that she didn't *feel* the advantages of the Web, and she kept seeing looks in the llamas' eyes that suggested they agreed.

Still, she didn't sense the llamas to be judgmental or critical of her circumstance. If anything, they were consoling her, telling her to be patient. She got the distinct impression that they wanted her to continue processing her incoming data.

So she scanned her netgorks and engaged in basic channel maintenance. Meanwhile, she sent out signals of well-being to everyone she knew except Greggy. As she did this, she noticed Chamy processing a mutual netgork.

"Hi, Chamy," she transmitted.

"Hi, Kale!" responded Chamy. "Gemela and I miss you!"

"I miss you too. How is everything?"

"Not so good. I'm a bit confused."

"Why?" asked Kale. "What's wrong?"

"It's Mike. He was supposed to meet me here 38 minutes ago, and he still hasn't showed up. He's not responding to my signals."

"Maybe he got carried away with one of his projects."

"He always tells me when he's doing that," said Chamy.

"Then maybe he needed to bypass his circuit interfacers for some reason. Or maybe he just turned them off to relax. That's starting to get popular—even my ex-boss is doing it."

"Really?"

"Yeah."

"I guess the world is optimal, after all."

"Sadly, yes."

"He he," she chuckled. "Thanks, Kale."

❂

That evening, when Kale sat down to dinner with Joseph and Drop, she asked a curious question. It wasn't a question she consciously formed. Rather, when Drop mentioned that she seemed to enjoy the llamas, she just blurted it out: "How come llamas only have one horn projecting from their foreheads?" she asked.

"It's cosmetics," he replied. "Only the males have the horns, and they're purely decorative. They don't fight with them or dig with them or do anything else utilitarian. Right, boss?"

Joseph remained silent.

"Or is your question," added Drop, "how come they don't have dual horns like other multi-stomached ruminants?"

"Yeah, that too," said Kale.

"Well, let's see. The answer is rather complex... "

"One thing can be said for sure," interrupted Joseph. "Neither male nor female llamas had any horns before the transition."

"I don't remember that," said Drop.

"That's because the memory of non-horned llamas has been extracted from us by the WPA," replied Joseph dryly.

"Then how do *you* know?" he asked.

"Because the llamas showed me."

"What?" said Kale.

"When I was a teenager, back in the 1990s, I spent a summer working for a llama trekking outfit in Colorado. I had plenty of idle time, so I got in the habit of watching how the llamas used ear postures to communicate their moods. Pretty soon I was able to keep track of what posture was associated with what mood."

"Fascinating," said Drop. "But what's that have to do with how they got their horns?"

"Years later," said Joseph, "when Ansie and I were first given our meter implants, I was sorted into a job as a llama herdsman for the BLM. When I saw horns on the male llamas I wasn't surprised, since I had no memory to the contrary. It was the way they moved their ears that seemed peculiar to me. After a few months, I realized the horns were taking up space that the male llamas had previously used for their various ear postures. That was why I no longer recognized their new postures, and that was why I knew they didn't used to have horns."

"Wow," said Kale.

"We have a genius here," said Drop. "A veritable genius."

"Just common sense," said Joseph.

"But what caused the horns to grow?" asked Kale. "That's the strange thing, isn't it?"

"Probably plant toxicity," he explained. "We'll never know the real truth." And then he began clearing the table.

❂

As soon as Kale went upstairs to the sunroom, she removed her tear drop resonator from her purse and slipped it between her fingers. She quickly intook a message from Morgaux:

Kale,

Hope all is going well in New Mexico. No signs of the pirater here, but I'll keep you posted. One thing peculiar: Greggy Panagopoulos sent me a signal this evening. He's anxious to get in touch with you, but he wouldn't tell me why, and he doesn't want to use the Web. Let me know how you want to proceed.

—Morgaux

Kale input a response, explaining that Greggy was a good friend. She requested that Morgaux invite Greggy to his office at 8 AM the next morning so they could communicate through the secured channel.

As she was completing the transmission, Drop knocked on the door. "Hi," he said, entering before she could hide the resonator. "Hey, is that a loose bead in your hand? Did your necklace break?"

"It's not from my necklace," she said.

"It looks like amethyst. Good color and radiance. But you shouldn't be carrying it unprotected like that. You might lose it."

"I've never really worried about that."

"Well, hey, I used to do a lot of jewelry. Why don't you let me make an earring out of it to match your necklace?"

Kale smiled. "How do I know you won't break it?"

"How? Because I am the great Drop McWith. Your grandfather and I have known each other since we were young boys. We've been down and out on the road together, and we've been on top of the heap together. But more relevant right now, I believe I've come up with something of extreme importance to his welfare, something triggered by your question tonight. That's why I want to talk with you."

"Okay," she said.

"It concerns his llamas—and his memory. I'm going to try something, and if you can hang tight for a day or two, I think you might get what you need."

"What makes you think I need something?"

"Listen, Kale," he said sadly. "I only play the fool to alleviate pressure. I know this thing you seek. I may not know how to articulate it, but I know what it is."

"I'm still not sure I understand."

"I'd be a liar if I tried to be any more specific, but I know that Joseph's memory is only the outer receptacle for what's lost in all of us. So you can certainly trust me with your bead."

"All right, Drop," she said, handing him the resonator. "I'll give you a shot, but please be careful."

"I promise. You can watch me if you want."

They went downstairs to Drop's studio, where he used ionic exchange to bond a piece of white gold to the tip of the resonator. From the manner in which he raised his eyebrows, Kale could tell he was accessing the secured channel as he touched the resonator. She understood it was his way of making the request.

As he intook the data, he formed the white gold into a thin wire.

Then he slipped on a small Oaxacan seed shaped like a crude kettle drum and placed a tiny gold ball above it. To complete the earring, he wound thin-gauge gold around the central wire and attached a french hook.

"What do you think?" he said, holding it out to her.

"A bit strange. What are the etchings on its sides?"

"They're purely stochastic," he said defensively. "The seed grows like that."

"Oh."

"I put an extra-strong clasp on the hook, so it won't come off unless your ear's with it."

"That's reassuring."

She slipped the earring onto her left ear and accessed Drop's visual system to view herself. She had to admit the effect was impressive—the white gold set off her black hair far better than yellow gold would have, and the sheen of the resonator perfectly complimented her amethyst necklace.

"Well?" said Drop.

"It's nice," she said. "It's actually very, very nice."

"Just you wait," he replied. "You're going to grow to love it, to completely love it." Then he grinned, gave her the thumbs-up sign, and hurried down the stairs.

CHAPTER TWENTY-ONE

KALE SLEPT SOUNDLY SUNDAY NIGHT, without the turbulence that plagued her dream time in Cambridge. Her system let her sleep until 7:54 AM the next morning, just six minutes before her scheduled conference with Greggy and Morgaux.

Despite the rushed circumstance, she didn't ignore her incoming signals. She scanned them methodically, starting with the 13,426 signals on her office netgork, then working through the 2728 signals on her family netgork and the 1364 signals on her social netgork. She even double-processed a particular message from Chamy:

Dear Kale,

You were right. Mike finally came over last night, so I guess everything's okay. We didn't talk too much. He seemed preoccupied, mumbling something about "his new commitment to efficiency."

But I'm sure all will renormalize. Thanks.

—Chamy

Kale wanted to respond straight away, but she had no time. All she could do was brush a few knots out of her hair and straighten the beads on her amethyst necklace. Then she reached for her tear drop earring.

"Hello?" she input to the resonator. "Walter? Greg?"

"Hello, Kale," replied Morgaux. "Greggy's not here. I've already sent him home. I'm afraid I'm going to have to cut our transmission short."

"Why? What's the matter?"

"Mike Eu is in serious trouble, and I'm quite confident it's because of his involvement with you."

"But I just got a signal from Chamy saying he turned up."

"Oh, he turned up all right," input Morgaux. "Just not in his original form."

"Huh?"

"Mike Eu is no longer Mike Eu. His private data has been replaced with generic personality modules."

"I don't understand," she replied. "What happened?"

"That's something I'd prefer not to discuss."

"You're telling me it's my fault, but you're not going to explain why?"

Morgaux sighed. "Mike's a special case student. I've been recording his retrofit experience from the beginning, and last night his sensors collapsed. In a matter of seconds, all his private netgork tissue decomposed."

"And how does this point to me?"

"We don't have any direct evidence, but the event happened 23 hours after Mike met you. Your pirater's the only one with a clear motive."

"Isn't that simplifying things a bit?"

"It doesn't matter," he burst out. "The risks are too high. I can't be involved any longer."

She hesitated for a moment. "All right, but I still need to contact Greg."

"I can't help you with that. It's too much. First, I lost my wife to it. And now this. Now I've lost... "

"What?" asked Kale. "You've lost what?"

"It's old data. Too old. From before your time."

"You're not making any sense, Walter."

He stalled for 2.34 seconds, trying to steady himself. "Mike Eu is my son," he trembled. "Do you understand? Now all I have left is his shell. I've been a fool."

"You're his real father?"

Morgaux nodded. "When Mike was born, I let my ambition get the better of me. I thought he would be the perfect research experiment, so I attached a switch to his PIFFEN meter, to see if he would choose to disconnect himself from it."

"And did he?"

"Yes, he grew up half the time inside the Web and half the time outside it. That was how he ended up at Harvard—and why, when he turned sixteen, he no longer accepted me as his father."

Kale input nothing. She only stared numbly at the resonator in her hand.

"I'm paying a price I should have paid long ago," he added. "It was inevitable."

"Walter, I'm sorry."

"I don't mean to blame you. I just hope you can see why I can't be involved."

"I do. Of course. I'm sorry."

And then Morgaux's inputs turned to nothingness, and she was left on her own.

❂

For the next 68 seconds, Kale felt like a degrading biochip. Her netgork filled with emotion, but her control circuit was power-depleted, and the only signals she could produce were fragmented, without substance.

Finally, her backup power supply kicked in, and a single clear thought leapt from her mind: *She had to quit her assignment.* She immediately transmitted a signal to Brandon Marshall, indicating that she no longer felt qualified to conduct the assignment and that she wished to be transferred to a new one.

"Very well," he responded. "Just dispatch me all the files, Keeler, and I'll feed them to your replacement."

"You're not disappointed?" she asked.

"Disappointment lies outside my job description, Keeler."

"Don't you need a reason for my quitting?"

"Negative, Keeler. Just report to the Netgorks for reassignment by 4:22 PM."

"Yes sir," she said. "I'll be there."

Kale packed her travel bag and went downstairs, where Joseph was in the midst of cooking breakfast. She sat down at the kitchen table.

"Cat," he said. "I've got bad news. Drop's snuck off with Nibby and Horse on a half-assed mining expedition down south."

"He mentioned something to me about that last night," replied Kale.

"It means we can't take a hike."

"Actually, I've got bad news too, Grandpa. It turns out I'm going to have to leave today."

"You only just got here."

"I know, but I found out this morning that a friend of mine was attacked, probably because he'd been helping me on my assignment. I don't want anyone else to get hurt, so I'm quitting the job, which means I have to go back to L.A. for reassignment."

"Is your friend okay?"

"I don't think so," she said bluntly. "His private data was all stripped from him."

"I see."

"It's terrible," she said.

"Yeah," he agreed. "But I'm a bit surprised you're quitting for a reason like that. I've carried the same circumstance all these years, you know."

She turned to look at him. "I didn't think of it that way, Grandpa."

"Just stay here one more day, okay?"

"I have a new boss. He wants me back."

"Maybe you can get a deferment."

"I doubt it," she said.

"Think about it, Cat. In the meantime, I've cooked up your favorite breakfast, just the way you like it."

She looked at him quizzically.

"You don't remember?" he asked. "When you were a little girl, you liked to eat off the table without a plate. You said the food tasted better that way. So look out, here it comes." He placed a stack of buckwheat circles in front of her, with maple syrup and butter pouring down its sides. Then he set down his own stack beside her, and they dug into the food.

Soon they were talking of old times. Joseph reminded her how he used to secretly take her for walks outside when she was a young girl. While in process-training, he would sneak her candy, prohibited by her mother. Or at night, they would work together on the animal database.

The memories convinced Kale to delay her return to L.A. She transmitted to Brandon Marshall, saying she wouldn't be returning to the Netgorks for at least another day, regardless of disciplinary measures. Then she gathered her courage and sent a signal to Mike Eu.

"Hello, Mike?" she put through the Web. "Are you active?"

"Mike Eu online," he replied. "Please specify your objective function."

"This is Kale Keeler. Remember me?"

"Certainly. You're the Drollinger Bates Visiting Scholar in Political Economy. You're currently involved in advanced research on optimal job matching. However, you've not been in Cambridge for 46 hours and 11 minutes."

"That's right," she said.

"What is your desired outcome, Kale Keeler?"

"I just wanted to... I wanted to see how you're doing."

"I'm fulfilling my retrofit duties. I'm currently ranked number 37 in my class, and I'm confident I can improve my performance."

"Are you mad at me?" she asked.

"Mad?"

"For what happened Thursday night."

"I was engaged in neuron exercises all Thursday night. Is that what you're referring to?"

"No," transmitted Kale. "I'm talking about the information scrambling you did."

"I'm unaware of that term, *information scrambling*."

"Don't you remember being with me Thursday night?"

"No. But I must inform you, I'm currently detecting inefficiency modulations from within your frequency."

"What?"

"According to my high-density analyzers, there appears to be a deficiency in your PIFFEN meter."

"A deficiency?"

"Your meter is no longer broadcasting the Internal Laws through your system. It doesn't seem to be carrying the Laws at all."

"Oh that," said Kale anxiously. "That's nothing to worry about. I have the Laws in my back-up files."

"I doubt that would qualify, Kale Keeler. I suspect you require immediate retrofitting."

"Huh?"

"You'd better contact the University. I no longer have clearance to interact with you. I must reoptimize my wave path in order to maintain good standing."

"Wait, Mike, I just wanted to tell you I'm sorry. I'm really sorry."

But it was too late—he'd already cut the wave and permanently sealed his system from her transmission code.

❂

There were 14,511 signals flashing on Kale's incoming queue, but she ignored them all. Instead, she took off her amethyst necklace and held it in the palm of her hand. Then she lay down on the bed and wept.

She wept for all the people in her life, for all the animals that ever were. She wept for the sycamore tree outside her Santa Monica condominium, and for the weed she'd touched on the banks of the Charles river. She didn't stop until her tear ducts were purely dry and her pleasure quotient fell to 39.13. Absently putting on her necklace, she got up from the bed.

At 11:54 AM, Joseph knocked on the door. "I don't mean to disturb you," he said, carrying a small folding ladder. "But it's almost time."

"Time?" she asked.

"For the analemma. I've only got two tiles left. Then it's complete, with all the sun's secrets tossed to the wind."

Kale nodded.

"So what do you think?" he asked, looking up at the analemma with misty eyes.

"I don't know, really."

"You must think something."

"I guess I don't really understand why you've spent so much time on it—it just looks like a sideways figure eight to me."

"That's it exactly," he smiled. "That's why."

"What do you mean, Grandpa?"

"The figure eight shows the most important thing of all, the thing on which all else depends."

"What thing?"

"That the earth is an *animal*, Cat."

"The earth is an animal?" she repeated, confused.

"Yes, that's what causes the figure eight. The earth doesn't just move at one constant speed. It changes when it feels like it, and it wobbles on its axis as it orbits. That's why the spots of light on the ceiling aren't always in the same place at the same time."

"Oh," she said very slowly.

"You see, the earth's a big animal, and we're the little animals on the big animal, trying to pass the time." He pointed to an old quartz clock on the wall, which read exactly noon. "And now's your chance to prove it."

"No, you should be the one."

"I will tomorrow, on the final day. But today it's yours, Cat. Today it's all yours."

So Kale climbed the ladder, carefully using a felt-tip pen to mark the spot of light reflected by the mirror. Then Joseph mixed the mortar, and she set the second-to-last red tile into place.

That afternoon, while Joseph lay down to nap, Kale went outside for a walk. She seemed to touch the ground more freely, and the receptors in her system even faintly registered the smells of the nearby trees and flowers. But she resisted reaching further past the Web. She needed more time to consider her grandfather's claim about the earth.

Instead, she turned to her incoming signals, processing them more thoroughly than ever, as a sort of testimony to her overcoming them. She transmitted complex visual images of well-being to every member of her social netgork, even Greggy Panagopoulos.

After she processed, she fed Cayuca and Rija. She raked the

stalls until she heard Drop's old-time vehicle pulling into the rear yard. Then she went to help him unload Nibby and Horse from the trailer.

"Did you find what you were looking for?" she asked.

"Yes," he whispered. "But first, where's the old man?"

"He's inside."

"Good, I want to show you something." He pulled out a ball of plastic wrap and opened it up to reveal a bluish green mush.

"What is it?" asked Kale.

"Baptista's antidote, to bring alive his memory of the past."

He led her into the stable. "I can trust you to keep quiet, right?"

"Yeah, I guess."

"It began a couple of weeks ago," he said excitedly, "when I took Nibby and Horse down south. We were supposed to be hunting for fossils, but straight away Nibby became obsessed with a strange kind of cactus, a kind I'd never seen before."

"Okay," said Kale.

"He kept going up to these cactuses, pushing the tip of his horn right into the buttonlike part of them and rotating around them. At first, I thought maybe he was trying to absorb some minerals or something, like at a salt lick. But he just kept moving from one cactus to the next, making his rotations, then looking up at me longingly. I wasn't wise enough to understand him, so I dragged him away and we went home."

"What's this have to do with Joseph?" asked Kale.

"That's what I'm coming to. Yesterday, when Joseph said that llamas didn't used to have horns, something clicked inside me. I remembered what Nibby had done with his horn, and I suddenly realized what he was trying to tell me—that this particular type of cactus was a way back for Joseph, just like the horn was for him."

Kale looked at him dubiously.

"That's why I took Nibby to the desert this morning, to check my realization," Drop continued. "Sure enough, he headed straight for the cactuses again, rubbing his horn into the buttonlike part and rotating around it four or five times. Each time, he backed off and looked up at me."

"I'm not sure that qualifies as proof."

"But this time I was prepared. I had my pocket knife, so I used it to cut out the button part of the cactus. Nibby starting humming like crazy when I did that, and he twisted his horn into the dirt, indicating that I should grind the button up. Once I finished, he walked straight back into the trailer to tell me that the mission was complete. So we came right home, and now I'm going to slip the cactus mush into Joseph's dinner, and he's going to remember everything."

"I admit it's clever," said Kale. "But I still don't see how some cactus mush is supposed to restore Joseph's memory."

"I'm not sure either. But I know Nibby is totally devoted to Joseph, and I know this is what he wants to happen."

"What if he's wrong? What if the cactus is poisonous?"

"Come on, you've seen how Nibby interacts with the old man. It's going to work."

"Maybe so, but there's something else you ought to know first. I've quit my assignment, Drop. A friend of mine was attacked, probably because he was helping me out."

He looked at her intently. "What happened?"

"His personality modules were lifted from his system through an untraceable channel. He's become generic."

"Oh, Ray. That's ugly."

"Yeah, it is."

"You're probably worried that something like that could happen to Joseph, right? It couldn't, Kale. He's completely delinked from the Web."

"You mean his interface circuits are out?"

"Been out for years."

"Still," she said, "if somebody wants to hurt Joseph, there are other ways."

Drop discretely reached for her tear drop earring. "Do you

mind?" he input to the secured channel. "I sort of found out about this while I was working on it last night."

"I know. Go ahead."

"I realize you're being pirated," he input. "And I realize that means we have to allow for the possibility of physical interference. But what happened to your friend is all the more reason we need to continue. It means you're getting close, Kale. Besides, I've got just the thing for protection."

"What?" she replied through the resonator.

"A case of trigger fields, so we can set up a ring of them around the house."

"That's crazy, Drop. Trigger fields are illegal."

"Do you want Joseph to be safe, or don't you?"

"I think we should let Joseph make that decision."

"*That's* crazy," replied Drop. "Joseph would never agree to any help. We both know that. And anyway, I'd hardly say what happened to your friend was legal."

Kale stared at the ground for 6.54 seconds. "All right," she input. "I'll help you set up the fields. But that doesn't mean we're going to use them."

"Of course not."

"They'll just be for peace of mind," she added.

"Exactly, exactly. I'll do the digging while you lay down the relays." He pulled out two handkerchiefs from a supply chest in the stable and proceeded to blindfold Kale and himself.

"This is so the pirater doesn't get any clues," Drop input. "Make sure you dump all your thoughts into the resonator while you're laying the fields." He opened a trap door in the floor of the stable and lifted out a large metal suitcase. Then he grabbed a shovel and walked outside with Kale behind him.

A hundred feet from the front door of Joseph's house, he began digging a trench parallel to the south side of the house. Kale followed him by feel, laying down the multi-directional trigger relays from the suitcase. They continued in this manner, covering all four sides of the house and always maintaining a hundred-foot distance.

Once they positioned the relays, they retraced their steps along the trenches. Drop attached one trigger cartridge to each relay node, while Kale did the burying and camouflaging.

They set the field range to cover all of Joseph's property. Drop explained that the trigger fields, once activated, would strike at any foreign object in their range, whether human or not.

"But there's one problem," he input. "We have to select a code to activate the fields. Obviously, we can't store it in either of our memories. If we want to evade the pirater, it'll have to go into the secured channel. So whoever holds the resonator will be responsible for any potential activation."

"I understand." Kale input the code into her resonator, and they each removed their blindfolds, as the last rays of the sun slid behind the Jemez mountains.

When they went back inside the house, Joseph offered his favorite meal: simulant chicken enchiladas with blue corn disks and potato chunks. Drop waited for an opportune moment, then he slipped his cactus mush into the enchilada with the most green chile —the one he knew Joseph would eat—and they all sat down to dinner.

CHAPTER TWENTY-TWO

THE REST of Monday evening was uneventful in New Mexico. Drop, Joseph, and Kale enjoyed a pleasant dinner, and Joseph ate the altered enchilada. After 84 minutes of casual conversation, they went to bed. And they all slept deeply—in Joseph's case, psychedelically.

Back in Los Angeles, however, a major turn of events occurred. At 9:39 PM Earth Standard time, the augmented cell in my brain figured out how to simulate the antics of a seasoned bird and sent out its signal to Kale.

Of course, Kale didn't directly intake the signal. She was already fast asleep, and bird-like signals were not the kind of data she had experience processing. But the augmented cell only required the tiniest bit of energy—just enough to periodically transmit its signal until Kale received it. So the cell released me from my comatic state, and I suddenly rolled over on my side and opened my eyes, after having been unconscious for 52 hours and 42 minutes.

I was groggy and disoriented, but that was a fairly normal state of affairs for me. I assumed I'd awakened from an afternoon nap. That is, I assumed it was Saturday night, not Monday night.

I didn't have any memories of being in a coma, nor did I remember anything about the terrible headache I'd had prior to falling into the coma. I didn't even remember that Trivers had fired me for failing to properly monitor Kale.

All I knew was that I was incredibly hungry. I ordered an extra-large simulant pastrami sandwich in the shape of a bowling pin, then I pulled myself out of bed and got dressed. When my sandwich arrived, I devoured it in eleven bites, washing it down with a Joltsie seltzer.

Out of habit, I headed over to the Netgorks building. I'd spent every evening there for the past 48 years, and I still didn't remember that I'd lost my job, so I dragged my body to the seventh floor of the Netgorks Terminal. I was about to walk straight into my office when I saw Clyde Trivers and Brandon Marshall talking to each other.

My first thought was that perhaps they were working on a belated birthday party for me. But after listening for 8.42 seconds, I realized they weren't concerned with me at all. Instead, Trivers was boasting about some new device of his.

"There's never been anything like it," he said proudly. "It's a high frequency micro missile, undetectable by humans."

"Yes, but what about accuracy?" replied Marshall.

"That's the least of our concerns, Brandon. The damn thing is so accurate, it'll hit a specific neuron if you want. Remember, it's memory activated. It won't go for anything that doesn't harbor the target data."

"Very well," said Marshall. "But who's going to deploy this missile? I wouldn't recommend utilizing my services in such a capacity."

"Of course not," replied Trivers. "You think I'd pull something like that on you? I've already got men out in New Mexico. They've been positioned for half a day now."

"I hope they're properly trained."

"They are, they are. Now come on, Brandon. You want to go the way of Peterson? Is that it?"

"Negative, Mr. Trivers."

"Then let's get this show on the road, damn it."

"Right away, Mr. Trivers. Right away."

They stood up to leave the office, so I slipped into the next-door conference room. I couldn't help wondering what Trivers meant when he asked Brandon if he wanted to go "the way of Peterson." And then, all of a sudden, it came rushing back to me: I'd been *fired*, for Ray's sake. That was why Trivers and Marshall had been in my office. Hell, it wasn't even my office anymore—Marshall had been hired to take my place.

A gigantic dose of humiliation swept through my stomach. I still didn't realize I'd been in a coma, but I knew perfectly well I wasn't wanted around the Netgorks building anymore. So I caught the next shuttle back to my Whittier apartment, and I collapsed on my couch for a solid 15 hours.

Joseph was the first to wake up the next morning at 7:32 AM. It only took him 6.79 seconds to recognize something different inside his brain.

"Hey, Drop!" he yelled. "Come over here! Now!"

Drop lifted his eyelids and curled his lips, then padded over to Joseph's bedside. "I'm here," he said, "at your service."

"What did you do?" demanded Joseph, still lying in bed. "What on earth did you do?"

"What did I do to what?"

"My memory—it's all coming back. I can remember the sixteen years. I can remember Rija!"

"Ah ha," said Drop, smiling profusely. "It seems I solved the riddle of life."

"What did you do? Tell me what you did!"

"I used my noggin, that's what. I put two and two together, and I made it happen."

"How? I need to know, Drop."

"It was Nibby who figured it out really. He's the master sleuth here." Drop proceeded to relay the story of Nibby and the cactus.

"There's just one thing," said Joseph, after Drop was done with his recounting. "You haven't told me what kind of cactus you used to make the antidote."

"I'm not exactly sure. It was round with a bluish green color, about three inches in diameter."

"With buttonlike tops?" asked Joseph.

"Yeah," he said, his twitch heightening. "How'd you know?"

"I remember it all now, Drop. That's what I ate to evade the meter. It's called peyote."

❂

119 seconds later, Drop pounded on Kale's door, telling her to hurry up and get out of bed. She put on jeans and a blouse, simultaneously processing 5643 incoming signals. Then she let Drop into the room.

"It's celebration time!" he announced excitedly. "We're going to have a breakfast feast, and Joseph's going to tell you everything you always wanted to know."

"What?" she said.

"He's a new man," explained Drop. "An entirely new man."

"Are you saying..."

"That's right. It worked, just like I said it would. And the timing couldn't have been more perfect, because today's the final day." He nodded to the analemma above them, which Joseph had started 364 days earlier.

They went downstairs to the living room and began the festivities. Joseph beamed like a young boy on his birthday. He poured them each a glass of champagne, then brought out a platter of home-made muffins and fruit tortes.

After they ate their fill, Joseph began sharing his new-found memories. Most of his descriptions were too abstract for Kale and

Drop, as they had little context in which to place the information. But they listened attentively to his flow of words, thankful to see him in his whole state, gradually piecing together what they could.

One of the biggest surprises came when Joseph brought up the subject of Knotty Burgstaller. Drop still remembered his days in Monterey when he first met Knotty, although he had no idea that Knotty was the tyrant.

"Wait just one minute!" Drop exclaimed, twitching nervously. "Are you sure you've got the name right? You're saying it was the Knotty Burgstaller of Total Video fame who was responsible for the transition?"

"The very same man," replied Joseph softly.

"I can't accept that."

"It's true. I remember it as clear as day."

"But I was the one who gave Knotty his start," he lamented. "*I* was the one who turned him into a businessman. How the hell could this have happened?"

"Fate," said Joseph.

"I never should have given you the peyote. How am I supposed to live with this knowledge?"

Joseph laughed. "Knotty wasn't really a villain. He did us all a favor. He took our capitalist ways and gave us their logical conclusion. The only problem was that Ray LeGhir refused to let us learn the lesson."

"Easy for you to say," said Drop.

"If it hadn't been you, it would have been someone else."

"I still say I never should have given you the peyote."

"But you know," said Joseph, with a twinkle in his eye, "I'm not even sure it was really the peyote."

"What?" said Drop.

"When Nibby poked at the peyote cactus, some of his horn material must have rubbed off. The peyote broke down the neurological barriers in my brain from before the transition, but the horn material was probably the actual restorer. Remember, the horns came about as a reaction to Knotty's toxin, so the material they're made from is a kind of natural counteractant."

"We really have to reward Nibby now," said Drop.

"I'm still confused about one thing," interjected Kale. "How did you know that eating peyote would let you evade the meter?"

"That was my father's idea," said Joseph. "I was visiting him a couple of months before the transition, just after he had a stroke. The two of us were alone in the hospital room when he looked me straight in the eyes and said, 'Son, you would not follow the peyote road while I was alive because you were too eager for your own road. Now you will eat peyote because it will become your road. There will be no other road for you to follow.' Then he grasped my hand and the life faded out of him.

"I didn't take him too seriously, because he was always saying things like that to me," Joseph continued. "But a few days later, Ray LeGhir told me about his PIFFEN cells, and I immediately sensed they were wrong, completely wrong. I couldn't dissuade Ray, so I started doing my own research, looking into how I might combat the cells.

"That was when I learned about the alkaloids in peyote. I figured my father had some insight. Maybe in some remote part of his consciousness, he understood that the peyote alkaloids would occupy the part of the brain that Ray's PIFFEN cells were supposed to attach to, preventing the cells from lodging. I had no better ideas, so I went to my Navajo friends, and they managed to scrape together 13 peyote buttons for me."

"And then what?" asked Kale.

"The next day, word came out that a toxin had poisoned the world's food supply, and Knotty began selling pepwad at his Total Food stores. I bought the stuff like everyone else, but I supplemented it with the peyote buttons. My biggest problem was trying to keep the peyote in my bloodstream. I vomited again and again, and my hallucinations were crazy, especially since the world around me was succumbing to tyranny.

"By the second week, though, my system began adjusting to the steady bombardment, and my brain became lucid enough to realize I was in trouble. I only had four or five more days' worth of peyote, and there was no way I could get any more buttons where I was living. My only choice was to go to the Chihuahuan desert where they grew. But I'd already given everything I had of value to Knotty's pepwad dispensers, and even if I'd had any money, all the transport companies had gone out of business.

"In my desperation, I got to thinking about the microbes that were spreading Knotty's toxin. I knew they were meant to invade the food people commonly ate, but what about plants that weren't normally ingested? I'd already been taking the peyote for almost a week, yet I had no signs of any gangrene. If the peyote was safe, I figured other plants from the cactus family might also be. After all, cactuses were extremely resilient, with strong barriers to infection, and they were hardly something anybody would worry about.

"So I bought my last sack of pepwad to nourish me until I got to the southwest, and I jumped into the first roadworthy car I came across. I drove it straight through to Texas, stopping only to siphon gas from other abandoned cars."

"Incredible," said Drop. "Go on."

"I set up my camp near Big Bend National Park, where peyote and other cactuses grew wild. At first, I ate only prickly pear fruits and the innards of barrel cactuses, but by the second day I learned how to make a starchy paste from yucca and agave leaves. The paste was actually a lot better than Knotty's pepwad.

"My main problem was that I couldn't stand the heat of Texas, and I didn't much care for the terrain either. After a couple of weeks, I picked a hefty supply of peyote buttons and headed north to Santa Fe, where I was familiar with the surrounding mountains. By then, it had become pretty clear that my theory about cactuses was right."

"But what about Rija?" asked Kale.

"About a year later I drifted over to the Jemez mountains, feeling more lonely than ever, and I started taking chances with my location.

I ended up sleeping in an old Anasazi cliff dwelling. It was there I met your grandmother.

"She was living a few miles up the arroyo, doing the same thing as me, eating peyote and other cactuses in order to evade the meter. I don't know how she figured it out—we never talked about that part of our past—but she was the only one I ever saw surviving that way besides me. Of course, we joined together and fell in love. Rija was more beautiful than I ever could have imagined, with skin softer than rain. She had long dark hair, pure green eyes, the most peaceful and loving face..."

Kale nodded sadly.

"How can I say it? We were destined for one another, and we lived together for ten wonderful years. Then a drought struck, our food supply got scarce, the journeys for peyote got more and more exhausting. And Rija got pregnant. A week before she was due she became very sick. This was in August of 2020. So what could we do? We resisted for as long as we could. Finally, I took her to the nearest hospital in Los Alamos.

"As soon as we checked in, they rushed Rija to a hospital bed and they booked me into a nearby jail. I never got to see her again. She died giving birth to your mother."

Kale began to cry. "I'm sorry," she said. "I'm so sorry. It just never seems to stop. We get pushed further and further into corners, further and further from our source. Everything gets crushed up and flattened, swallowed by external data. And there's no way past it, no way clear."

"But there is," replied Joseph. "Look, Cat. Look at the time."

She glanced at the clock on the wall. It read three minutes before noon. Drop wiped her eyes dry with his handkerchief, and they all went upstairs to the sunroom, where Joseph positioned the ladder under the analemma.

"How about I do the honors?" offered Drop. "You've already been through enough today."

Joseph shook his head.

"Not even for old time's sake?"

"I have to do it," replied Joseph sternly.

"If you let Drop do it," said Kale, "you could watch more easily."

"I have to do it," repeated Joseph. "I started it, and I'm going to finish it."

"I'll help you then," she said, thinking of the pirater. She stood on the windowsill, screening Joseph from view.

"Don't obstruct the spot of light," cautioned Joseph.

"I won't, Grandpa."

He climbed up the ladder, marking the spot on the ceiling. Then, without hesitation, he carefully set the final tile into position.

It was at that very moment that the pirater's agents crossed onto Joseph's property and launched the memory-seeking micro missile, pointing it high up into the air toward the sunroom. The weapon was too small and fast for anyone to see it, and it had a built-in containment deflector in order not to produce any audible noise. Yet somehow, Drop sensed the intrusion.

"Kale!" he yelled. "The fields!"

With lightning speed, she activated the secret code from her resonator and struck down all the agents on Joseph's property. But the trigger fields were no match for the high-tech micro missile. Before Kale or Drop could move another muscle, the deadly device burst through the sunroom and pierced directly into Joseph's brain.

CHAPTER TWENTY-THREE

IT TOOK another 0.35 seconds for Joseph to fall from the ladder onto the floor. By that point, the neural hemorrhaging was fatal. Drop cried out in agony when he confirmed that Joseph had no pulse, then he raced outside to locate the murderers.

The bodies of seven agents lay scattered among the juniper trees. Drop determined from their doctored i.d. labels that they were mercenaries, hired to perform the act without understanding. Unfortunately, their data banks were devoid of any clues. Drop tried to trace their underlying sources, but they were impeccably clean. All he could do was bury the bodies in a small gravesite on the northeast corner of the property.

Meanwhile, Kale remained in the sunroom. She had never seen death before—her only conception of it came from her animal database. She stayed kneeling by Joseph's side, physically stroking his forehead, hoping to soothe and revitalize him. But his face was already cold and lifeless, and the gleam in his eyes was gone.

When Drop came back inside, he tried to explain. "Your grandfather's spirit has gone to another place," he said softly.

"Please," said Kale, looking away. "Don't talk."

"It's not always a bad thing," he replied. "It's a returning, a returning to the earth."

"Stop, please."

"Look, I know it's my fault. I should have listened to your warning."

"If it's anybody's fault, it's mine," she sobbed. "I'm the one who led the agents to him. That's the real reason." She got up abruptly, her eyes full of tears, and she went downstairs.

She had never before been in Joseph's den, as she considered it to be her grandfather's private space. But the first thing she saw when she entered was an old-time picture of herself at nine years old.

As she cross-sorted her visual data, a memory rushed back to her —the picture was taken the day she played darts with Sammy. Her grandfather had been visiting then, and she remembered he'd brought with him an odd image-making machine.

Kale lifted the picture out of its frame. On the back were crisp words, in big block letters, as if they'd just been written. She accessed her impulse/visual translator to intake them:

DON'T FORGET, CAT. THE EARTH IS AN ANIMAL.

As she read the words, she began sobbing again, but it wasn't that she was sad. Rather, she was amazed that her grandfather could understand her so well. She was amazed that such connection was possible. And she had no doubt then that he was right—the earth *was* an animal.

She hadn't absorbed his meaning the first time he said it. The idea had been too much to reconcile with all her other concerns. But now that she saw his death and stood under it, she was able to embrace the concept from beginning to end. She could even imagine Joseph's spirit, intermingling with the air particles, returning to that biggest animal of them all.

The image gave her an inspiration: She needed to input *the earth* into her animal database as her final entry, for the sake of all the other animals—both the ones that had been made extinct and the ones still riding on the back of the biggest animal.

She performed the task with one quick command, holding the interest of all past animals preeminent. At that moment, the sun's shadows wavered slightly, and she felt a strange sensation on her skin —a sensation from the bird-like signal emanating out of my augmented cell.

Kale only registered the sensation for half a millisecond. There were too many other signals competing for her attention, and she was eager to get back to the sunroom, where Drop was sitting on a chair, staring up at the analemma.

"I'm sorry for running out on you," she said, as she entered the room.

"I didn't mean to push you," replied Drop. "I know it takes time."

"You didn't push me. Not at all."

Drop nodded.

"So... is there something we should do now?" she said awkwardly.

"I suppose we could find him a better resting place."

Kale shook her head in agreement. Together they adjusted Joseph's clothes and lifted him onto the bed. Kale carefully placed a blanket over him, then they walked downstairs to the living room.

After 2.68 minutes of silence, Drop reached for Kale's resonator. "We need to plan your next move," he input.

"I'd still like to stay around for awhile," she replied.

"I'm not sure that's such a good idea. It'd be better for you to go somewhere safer. When things settle down, you can come back with your parents for the funeral."

"And what about you? You could be in danger too."

"No," he replied. "There's no way the pirater would be interested in me."

"How do you know that?"

"I'm just a silly old man with a twitch. You're the one who works for the Netgorks."

"I probably should go back to L.A. I was supposed to report there yesterday."

"Is that what you want to do?"

"No, not really."

"It's none of my business, Kale, but I don't think it'd be wise to go there either. Everyone's expecting you to do that."

"There are some people I'd like to see in Cambridge," offered Kale.

"That's also a bit risky, isn't it?"

"Anywhere I go is bound to have risks. At least I have friends in Cambridge who might be able to help."

"True, if you can get there undetected. You can't just take a mega-shuttle."

"What's the alternative?" asked Kale.

He paused for moment, his twitch intensifying. "I know just the thing," he input. "But I can't explain now. Go get a bite to eat and have your travel bag packed. Meet me in the stable in ten minutes."

❂

Once again, Kale trusted Drop, even if he was being evasive. It only took her a moment to instruct her travel bag to pack. Then she sat down beside Joseph's body and stroked his hair.

As she reflected on his life with Rija, she wondered what it could mean that he had gotten her 'pregnant.' She visualized Joseph's spirit returning to earth, but this time she saw his rebirthing as well. She stored the image within her cells while walking downstairs, brushing her hands along the adobe walls. As she exited the house, she pressed both palms against the front door. Then she walked outside into the sunlight, onto the earth. Nothing made sense. Everything made sense.

When she entered the stable, Drop tied a handkerchief in front of her eyes and loaded her travel bag onto Nibby's back.

"I hope you're not expecting me to travel the whole way like this," said Kale.

"No," replied Drop, through the resonator. "Nibby and Horse are just going to lead you to your departure point."

"What am I supposed to do when I get to there?" she input.

"A friend of mine will be there. Just remind him that he owes me a favor."

"Sounds a bit peculiar."

"That's the whole idea. That's how we're going to throw off the pirater. Okay? You promise to take care of yourself, right?"

"Yeah, I promise." She stood on her tiptoes and gave Drop a hug.

"You better get a move on," he said, his cheeks turning red from the physicality. "Hold onto this rope and Nibby will guide you."

She grabbed the rope and smiled. "Bye, Drop."

"Get, Nibby!" he shouted. "Get, Horse!"

The llamas jerked forward on a western course. Kale almost stumbled several times, but the llamas were careful to choose as smooth a path as possible. After 48.31 minutes, they began snorting and humming to let Kale know they'd arrived.

Drop's friend noticed the odd assemblage out his window. "Yes?" he said, as he came out. "What can I do for you?"

"I was referred by Drop McWith," replied Kale, with her blindfold still on. "He said to mention you owe him a favor."

"Oh, yes," he laughed, "I owe him a kick in the rear."

"Actually, I'm trying to get transport out of New Mexico."

"The shuttle depot is back in the direction you came from."

"That's not exactly what I'm looking for," she said.

"This is the reason for the blindfold?"

"Yes, I guess."

"Come on." He unstrapped Kale's travel bag and led her to the rear yard.

"What about the llamas?"

"Beasts, go home!" he yelled. Nibby and Horse promptly turned around in the direction from which they came.

The man guided Kale to a concrete building behind his house. Inside, he activated a row of switches on a display channel. A circular hatch 12 feet in diameter rose from the ground.

"I suppose you've never ridden in one of these before," he said.

"I don't know," replied Kale. "Use this if there are any instructions." She handed him the tear drop resonator.

"You'll be on an A26 maintenance cylinder," he input. "It's a manual one—that's how come we can use it to bypass the monitors. There's a limited air supply, so you'll have to breathe lightly down there."

"I see," she responded. "And what exactly is an A26 maintenance cylinder?"

"Didn't Drop tell you what I do?"

"No."

The man laughed once again. "I service the mainlines for the ExpressTube system," he input. "This is the node junction for the mountain zone. The primary transcontinental line runs straight under here. Pretty impressive, eh?"

Kale nodded.

"So what's your destination, kid?"

"Any terminal in Cambridge. I'd rather not know which one."

"You got it, kid. Just be sure to activate the return function when you get out, or I'll be stranded without an A26 and it'll be my neck."

"I won't forget," she replied, as she climbed into the cylinder. "You've been a big help. Thank you."

"Not a problem, not a problem. You're a mild case compared to most of Drop's friends."

He handed back the resonator, sealed the cylinder door, and Kale was hurled eastward through the ExpressTube mainline.

CHAPTER TWENTY-FOUR

AS KALE JOURNEYED through the Tube, I awakened from my couch in my Whittier apartment. I was surprised to see it was already 3:14 PM, as that meant I'd slept for a full 15 hours, but I figured my body needed to adjust to the news of my firing.

My head was too muddled to bother checking the calendar function on my prompter. As far as I knew, it was Sunday afternoon—not Tuesday, October 5. I was still entirely blind to the fact that I'd been in a coma for two days.

I did notice, however, that I had a delivery waiting in my Express-Tube outlet. My first thought was that maybe I'd been sent a promotional frisbee burger or something. But the delivery was too small— just a tiny little box, one inch by two inches, wrapped in plain brown paper.

I ripped open the package and found a leather pouch with a physical note from Professor Morgaux:

Dear Mr. Ralph Peterson,

Enclosed is an item that may be of use to your subordinate,

Kale Keeler. I am sending it to you because Ms. Keeler is currently registered in transit. Please forward it to her at your earliest convenience. Thank you.

—Prof. Walter Morgaux

I felt peeved at Morgaux for sending me the package, as I hardly saw why I should be his personal go-between. But my main concern was food, so I ordered three flying saucer burritos with top-grade simulant sausage. As soon as they arrived, I gobbled them in eight bites, washing them down with 41 ounces of Aquamarine seltzer. I let out a nasty belch to express my state of mind, then I gave Kale a signal.

"Hey, Keeler," I transmitted, "this is Peterson, your old boss. I've got some news for you when you have a chance."

The last thing I expected was a prompt response, since my urgency status had dropped 83 notches. But Kale had little to do in the ExpressTube cylinder—it was hard and dark, with only a single metal stoop for her to sit on—and her system was still unprepared to pick up the birdwaves from my augmented cell.

"Hi, Ralph," she replied. "Is everything okay? I'm sorry to hear about your job."

"Ah, forget it," I said. "I was sick of supervising anyway."

"Really?"

"Absolutely, Keeler. I'm an ecstatic man."

"I'm glad it's a turn for the better."

"Absolutely."

"So what's this news you have for me?" she asked.

"I just got a package from Professor Morgaux—a package for you. He couldn't find an ExpressTube near you, so he forwarded it to me. Hold on for a second and I'll open it up."

"No, that's all right," she countered. "I'd prefer you didn't."

"It's no problem. I've got it right here."

"Really, Ralph. Just leave it. I'll signal you when I'm near an outlet."

"Sure, sure. But you sound strange. Where the hell are you?"

"It's a bit complicated."

"Is everything all right?"

"No, not really."

"What is it?" I asked.

"Actually, I'd prefer not to... "

"You can tell your old boss, can't you?"

"I don't think so."

"Not enough status points in my system, right? I suppose I better get used to that."

"No," she said. "It's just that... it's just that my grandfather's been murdered. It happened a few hours ago."

"What? Who did it?"

"I don't know, and I'm not really in the mood to talk about it."

"I understand. I'm really sorry, Keeler. But how was he murdered?"

"A miniaturized missile pierced his skull and internally exploded," she replied. "Does that make your day, Ralph?"

Needless to say, the news did not make my day. It only verified that I'd been an idiot. I should have realized what Trivers and Marshall were talking about when I'd overheard their conversation. I should have warned Kale.

The question was why would Trivers want to get rid of Joseph? Why would Joseph's memories be so threatening to him, particularly when Trivers himself had started the whole thing rolling with Kale's assignment?

I didn't have any answers, but I knew I'd reached my limits. I was sick of letting things happen, of living like everything was so damn random. And then it occurred to me: I couldn't even remember the last time my proddings had spoken to me. It seemed like ages, and when I tried to rouse them, they didn't even issue the slightest whisper.

I traced my memory to see when they'd last made contact with me, and it turned out to be at 2:36 PM on Saturday afternoon, when they advised me not to worry about a headache. They said it was purely psychological, and that I simply needed to relax.

When I thought about it, I did remember having the headache— as I recalled, it had been a brutal one. But it hardly seemed like just a day ago. The whole episode was a blur.

So I checked my calendar, and lo and behold, I finally discovered it wasn't Sunday afternoon. It was *Tuesday* afternoon. I'd lost track of two full days!

My physiology chart showed no conscious brain activity—not even the type associated with sleeping—from 7:57 PM Saturday to 9:39 PM Monday. Naturally I was confused, but I knew enough to submit the data to my internal diagnostics. As soon as I did that, my confusion turned to shock, massive shock. Because it was at that point that I learned I'd been in a *coma*. For 52.70 hours, I'd been in a deep, deep coma.

The first thing that crossed my mind was that my proddings were involved. After all, they told me that my headache was only 'psychological,' and I'd heard nothing from them since. But what worried me more was Trivers' involvement. If he was the one who murdered Joseph, he'd obviously want me out of the picture too. For that matter, he'd also probably try to strike Kale.

The more I thought about it, the more I realized Kale was a bigger target than me. She was entrenched in the assignment far more deeply than me, and she'd committed all sorts of violations in the process. The problem was that if I tried to warn her, I'd only be making her more vulnerable. I certainly didn't want to give Trivers any clues, nor did I want to frighten Kale unnecessarily.

I racked my brain on the subject for ten full minutes while munching an order of brownies in the shape of transmission towers, but nothing came to me. I guess I was looking for a distraction, because I absently picked up the leather pouch Morgaux had sent. My fingers pushed open the pouch and there it was: Morgaux's tear drop resonator, the companion to the one that dangled from Kale's ear.

I didn't know what to think at first. I mean, I was hardly eager to tap into Kale's private affairs again, but I understood that if I wanted to help Kale, the resonator would be paramount—it could even be a matter of life or death. Suffice it to say, I consulted my radio transceiver to detect the frequency of the tear drop resonator, then I patched directly into its private channel.

Once in the channel, I had access to all of Kale's operating system, not just her private data, since she was continuously touching her resonator by wearing it on her ear. I could even tap her pre-processing zone, where she had no way to hide her thoughts.

I quickly brought myself up to date on her circumstance. What struck me most was her last conversation with Mike Eu, particularly his determination that she had tampered with her meter to dispel the Internal Laws from her system.

I tried to trace Kale's meter diagnostics to confirm this, but I still couldn't locate any cause for her meter deficiency. It seemed Mike had either tapped into Kale more deeply than I, or he used some estimating techniques I didn't know.

I didn't find much in Kale's memory tracks either. I replayed Joseph's last moments in the sunroom to check for overlooked clues, but all I could tell was that the micro missile entered Joseph's brain just above his left earlobe. Otherwise, little in Kale's data suggested how I should respond.

✹

By then, Kale had been inside the ExpressTube cylinder for 1.52 hours—she was just east of Crumrod, Arkansas. The vacu-magnetic throbbing of the ExpressTube cylinder had steadily degraded her weblink, and her senses were correspondingly heightened, much as they had been in the WPA prison cell.

So that was how it happened. When the cylinder crossed under the Mississippi river at 3:56 PM, her frequency took on the clarity of the deep water above her. Her body became purely blood-driven, without the steady whirring of data within her. And all at once, she was able to receive the special bird-signal emanating from the augmented cell.

At first, she sensed it only on her skin, in the region of her left forearm. Then like a bird, she instinctively let the signal enter her capillaries. It flowed through her bloodstream, organizing itself in the following form:

Kale Catherine Keeler,

You do not know me. I am a messenger of artificial intelligence, created by Ray LeGhir. My function is to facilitate the restoration of missing information caused by the Transition of 2008.

I am contacting you because you are the first human since the Transition to laugh at the Web and transcend its limits. Thus you are deemed most capable of overseeing the release of this missing information to society.

You will find the information temporarily superimposed on channel Z9478213 - QU108473TAW913. The password code is ANOTHERHOPE.

This message will continue to be broadcasted at random intervals for 7 hours and 59 minutes. If you do not respond within this time period, the hidden information will retract from the specified location.

At exactly 4:02 PM, the signal reached the peripheral boundary of Kale's pre-processing zone. Remarkably, Kale's anterior nerve cells recognized that the communication was too important to allow into her consciousness where the pirater might access it. Of their own accord, they deleted the signal from her random storage, 0.06 seconds after it penetrated her pre-processing zone. Then Kale simply straightened her shoulders and waited for her ExpressTube journey to come to an end.

But the message was not lost. Thanks to my astute observational skills—and the tear drop resonator in my hand—I detected Kale's reception of the bird signal, even though she didn't. The signal was deleted too quickly for me to actually intake it, but luckily my back-up tracer was in high speed mode. I just specified the time of the occurrence, did some resequencing, and—voila!—I had the whole message in my domain.

At that point, I sat back down on my couch and took a long swig of PepTime. Then I instructed my transceiver to locate channel $Z9478213 - QU108473TAW913$, emulating Kale's frequency at the same time. As soon as I fed in the password, a string of words immediately flew into my active space:

ATTENTION: FIRST READER!
THIS DOCUMENT IS CURRENTLY WEBLESS.
YOU ARE THE TRANSFORMING AGENT.

With wide eyes, I intook the words that followed, the words comprising Ray LeGhir's treatise. It wasn't every day that a document of this sort popped into one's active space.

I just read and read, learning everything about Knotty Burgstaller and his master plan. The strange thing was that it all seemed vaguely familiar. I almost felt like I was reading the document for the second time.

Then I came to Chapter 19, where Ray LeGhir described his invention of the augmented cell. A curious lump formed in my throat when I read that only one person in the whole world was to receive the augmented PIFFEN cell. I couldn't help thinking that maybe this person was me.

When I read that this person would probably experience 'a bit of discomfort' as the document was being released, I had an even stronger feeling about the matter. That could explain *my coma*. But when I read that this person would get 'helpful tips and suggestions' from the augmented cell, then the concept completely overtook me— that could explain *my proddings*.

I plowed through the next few paragraphs to see if any other details fit my circumstance, and I came to the icing on the cake: Ray LeGhir programmed the augmented cell so that it would only enter into the brain of a baby less than 60 days old. I was born on October 1, 2008. When Ray released the cell on November 15, 2008, I'd been alive for precisely 46 days. What more proof did I need?

And then I got my final confirmation. My proddings actually spoke up, after three days of utter silence:

"Okay, Ralph," they whispered. *"You're right. You've figured it out. You were the individual who happened to receive Ray's augmented cell."*

"Thanks a lot," I replied.

"Yes, Ralph. We've been assisting you ever since Ray's cell randomly entered your brain 25,117 days ago. We represent the adaptive intelligence sector of the cell."

The lump in my throat suddenly became a red hot coal. "Wait a second!" I exclaimed. "You mean to say, you're just a tiny silicon chip embedded in my PIFFEN meter? And I've been calling you my proddings all these years?"

"That's right," they said.

"For Ray's sake, the things you bastards put me through!"

"We're sorry, old buddy. It was for the greater good, for all of humanity."

"And now what's supposed to happen?" I said bitterly. "I go into another coma?"

"No, not at all. We're preparing to wither away. That's why we've been so quiet. We've been consumed with final closing procedures. In 114 seconds, the augmented portion of your PIFFEN cell will collapse and you'll be on your own, with a normal life and a normal meter. So good luck, Ralph Peterson."

"What about Ray's document?" I asked.

"Yeah, it's pretty ironic, huh? For 69 years, the document was sitting in your brain in a sealed memory bank. Finally we get the green light to ship it out to the Web, and where's the first place it goes? Straight back into your brain. Weird, huh?"

"So do I start disseminating the information, or what?"

"No no, Ralph. You're not supposed to do anything. We've already factored your inability into the equation."

"What's that supposed to mean?"

"It means your actions don't have any bearing, Ralph. All you're expected to do is sit on your couch and eat flying saucer burritos. Our adaptive intelligence has already taken care of everything."

"Doesn't that seem a bit risky? I mean, Kale still hasn't responded to the signal."

"She's proven she has the capability. That was the critical thing for us. That's why we're packing up now."

"But what if she never finds out about the document?"

"Relax, Ralph. We've enjoyed our stay, we really have, but we can't chat any longer. We're withering now. You get it?"

"Come on, this is crazy. You can't just... "

"Gooddata, Ralph. Have a nice life, old buddy. Keep eating those flying saucer burritos." And they were gone, evaporated into the airwaves.

✷

All I could do was drop my head onto my lap. My whole life had been orchestrated by a silicon chip. My every move had been plotted —down to the very fact that I'd become a channel supervisor. Everything had been for the sake of Ray LeGhir's hidden agenda.

Worse yet, the silicon chip residing in my brain didn't even have the slightest faith in me. It had already 'factored my inability into the equation.' How inspiring.

For awhile there, I really didn't see a reason to continue living. It all seemed too much for me. I was seriously considering following my proddings' suggestion of ordering a few more flying saucer burritos.

But then I thought about Kale and what I could do to help her— what I *should* do to help her. I mean, how could a stupid silicon chip know my capabilities when it had never even given me a chance? What gave it the right to tell me what to do?

I was the one who recovered Ray's document, and I was the one who understood Kale's situation. My proddings only had secondhand information, and they relied on adaptive intelligence. But I was a human. I had the real thing inside of me.

I resolved right then to quit my sobbing. To hell with the flying saucer burritos. Instead, I changed into some clean clothes, slid Morgaux's resonator into my shirt pocket, and went straight outside to catch the 5:47 shuttle to the Public Netgorks.

When I reached the entrance gate for channel bosses, the sensor rings no longer validated my identification impulse. I input my previous status and requested clearance to use the gym facilities one last time, since I hadn't yet found employment elsewhere. The rings hesitated for a moment, then let me through.

I truly did want to do some fitness exercises to pump myself, so I went to the basement locker room and put on an anti-gravity suit. I let the anaerobic machines work out my muscles for 15.23 minutes.

With my body diagnostics at 73, I took an elevator to the 27th floor, where most of the auxiliary stations were located. I snuck down the hallways eager to solve Trivers' mess, but I wasn't quite as discreet as I should have been because a Netgorks security guard detained me after only 608 seconds.

"Ralph Peterson?" spat the guard accusingly.

"Yeah?" I replied.

"Come this way."

He led me into an empty office behind a tracking facility. From out of nowhere, Trivers marched into the office, wearing the same headware I'd been using to monitor Kale.

"What the fuck are you doing on the 27th floor?" he demanded.

"Uh... I just wanted to use the gym for awhile, and then I came up here for old time's sake. I haven't really adjusted to being out of a job, you know."

"This floor never had anything to do with your wastebyte job, Peterson."

"I know, I know. I got a little disoriented. I've been kind of confused lately."

Trivers' jaw relaxed. "I see," he said. "Well, you better go home and get some rest. And whatever you do, Peterson, don't come back here again. Is that clear?"

I nodded my head. I was about to take his advice and head back home when I felt overwhelmed with emotion—emotion that was purely my own, not some silicon chip derivation.

"Just tell me why you're so interested in Kale's private netgork?" I said slowly.

"That's none of your concern," he replied.

"While you're at it, why don't you explain why you felt you had to murder her grandfather," I continued. "That seemed pretty brash to me."

Trivers' face turned deep blue. "You just made a big mistake, Peterson. You just signed your death warrant. Anybody else you've told this to is dead too."

"I haven't told anybody, Clyde. I'm not like you."

"Then you're fucking stupid, my friend. Fucking stupid, as usual." Trivers snapped his fingers, and all at once a steel cage dropped from the ceiling to ensnare me.

"What the hell?" I said, in shock. "You can't do this to me! I worked for you for 48 years! 48 long hard years!"

"I can do whatever I want, Peterson. I have endless recourse." He disconnected my ties to the Web and swaggered out of the room.

For the next 38 seconds, I shook the steel bars as hard as I could and screamed at the top of my lungs. But my actions were entirely futile. The bars wouldn't budge, and no one could hear my cries.

All I could think was that I'd been living my whole life this way—in a cage, in my own prison. And the sad thing, the truly sad thing, was that I'd never before noticed the severity of the circumstance.

CHAPTER TWENTY-FIVE

AS IT HAPPENED, TRIVERS' steel cage was a blessing in disguise. Sure, I was frightened and lonely—I'd never been cut off from the Web before. But after 11.92 seconds, the same thing that happened to Kale in the WPA prison cell happened to me: A feeling of lightness spread through my netgork, as if I were being reborn, and for the first time ever I experienced my body taking care of itself without any external assistance.

At that point, I realized *why* the circumstance we'd been living under was so severe. Without the chance to experience life outside the Web, we all just accepted that the world was pure silicon with no carbon.

I was even beginning to see why Kale performed all her strange deeds. I probably would have meditated over this for at least another 80 or 100 seconds, if it weren't for the fact that my nostrils detected an unpleasant odor wafting into the cage—an odor I quickly realized must have been from Trivers, because it came from exactly where he'd been standing.

I'd never noticed Trivers' body odor before. I'd never really paid attention to *any* odor before, and I didn't recall anyone else ever doing such a thing either. Yet the smell in the room was really quite horrendous, like something gone very, very bad.

It occurred to me that if our sensory organs were dulled by the operation of the Web, that could explain why Trivers wanted to kill Joseph. After all, if people found out about what the Web had done to them, they might want to live unconnected to it. But then how would Trivers hold his position?

Assuming I was right, Kale was in bigger trouble than I'd thought. Trivers probably groomed her for the assignment because of her relation to Joseph. That was why he started her off investigating Professor Morgaux.

I had to get a message to Kale right away. But how? Even if I could somehow restore my ties to the Web, I still needed to prevent Trivers from intercepting my signal.

Curiously, my own brain offered me an idea: Why not communicate to Kale the same way she had to Joseph, by transmitting Weblessly like a seasoned bird? I observed her do the whole thing herself. It couldn't be that hard for me to do the same.

I replayed all my data from watching Kale, and I scanned each of my memory tracks for images of birds. Then I made my body assume the posture of a bird, and I locked myself into a birdlike state of mind. When my efforts mirrored my breath, I released the following image into the atmosphere:

Kale,

I've discovered a startling thing: Clyde Trivers is the pirater. He's the one that murdered your grandfather and ruined Mike Eu. And he's still got more on his agenda. You need to find some place to hide. He's a ruthless man, and he's already captured me. Please be careful. I'll try to break free and help you if I can.

—Ralph

I kept releasing the image over and over, since I had no way of knowing if my attempt would succeed. After 56 minutes, I still had no feedback from Kale. It seemed pretty clear I hadn't yet mastered the art of Webless transmission.

I was about to lie down on the floor of my cage and give up, when another alternative came rushing to me—Morgaux's tear drop resonator. Granted, it was possible that whatever Trivers had used to cut me off from the Web would also cut me off from the resonator's private channel. But Morgaux's device relied on a different transmission technology than the Web, one that perhaps Trivers hadn't anticipated.

Sure enough, when I pulled the resonator out of my pocket, I found I could still access the private channel. Eureka! I could hardly believe that Trivers had been so stupid—he should have checked my pockets before he left me in the cage. I wanted to let out a big laugh.

But then I had another rude awakening. When I tried to *input* a signal to the private channel, the resonator jammed up. All I got was a warning signal that said, "INCOMING DATA NON-ASSIGNABLE. POLARITY DAMAGED."

I could retrieve whatever of Kale's data I wanted, but the resonator wouldn't intake a single thing. Somehow the steel cage blocked the transmission.

My tear ducts produced moisture. This was too much. Ever since I'd been fired from my job, I'd come upon one defeat after another, and I really didn't see how I was supposed to hold things together in the face of all that had happened.

So I simply cried. I simply let down my defenses and cried—something I'd never done before. I didn't even try to hold back my emotion.

To my surprise, the crying made me feel better. After 4.68 minutes, I started thinking that maybe I could figure a way to break out of the cage. If there was a way into something, there had to be a way out of it. It was just a matter of waiting for the right inspiration.

In the meantime, I continued watching over Kale. Even if I couldn't communicate to her, at least I'd be there for her in some limited way. So I mustered up all the optimism I could find within myself, and I gently took hold of the tear drop resonator.

○

At 6:57 PM Earth Standard Time, Kale's ExpressTube reached its destination. The vacu-magnetic field around her weakened, allowing her to take deeper breaths, and the cylinder thumped to a stop. She released the door seal, opened the hatch, and climbed out.

After instructing the cylinder to return to its origination point, Kale began feeling her way up a flight of stairs. Once she got to the top of the service platform, she removed her blindfold. She saw she'd been deposited in an industrial part of Cambridge where several headware assembly plants were located.

The area was not entirely familiar to Kale, but off to the northwest—about 1.38 miles away—she recognized a row of cement poles with rotating triangles, neon-lit in the evening sky. Harvard had to be in that direction. As she consulted her imaging pointer to determine the most protected route, she glanced to her left. There, standing next to a cement-chip wall, were Chamy and Gemela.

"Maximal greetings!" exclaimed Gemela. "We've been waiting for you for 646 seconds."

Kale did a double-take. "Great Ray!" she said. "What are you two doing here?"

"We've been worried about you," replied Chamy. "Are you okay?"

"Yeah. But how'd you know I was coming?"

"We just felt you," explained Gemela. "We'd been missing you, and then we sensed you'd be arriving at this spot, so we just decided to wait for you."

"I've hardly even communicated... I've wanted to, it's just that there've been some unexpected... "

"We know," interjected Gemela. "We already sensed what happened. It's awful."

Kale stared numbly at the two of them.

"We've been upset about Mike, too," said Chamy. "You know about that, right?"

"Yes," said Kale softly. "I feel terrible for involving him."

"You had to do what you did," said Chamy. "For the sake of all of us, right?"

"I... think so," said Kale awkwardly. "But I don't see where you're getting this from."

"We've been feeling it. It's been in the wind, along with everything else."

"We know you're in danger," added Gemela. "We want to help."

"I appreciate your concern," said Kale. "I really do. But I just..."

Chamy reached out her hand, within inches of her shoulder. "It's all right, Kale. You don't have to talk about it now."

"We'll fix it later," said Gemela.

"There's nothing left to do. I came here to get away from it."

"It's really all over?" asked Gemela.

"Yes," said Kale. As she said this, a remote impulse in her pre-processing zone reminded her of the signal she'd subliminally received from my augmented cell, but she dismissed it.

"Then we should get you home," said Chamy. "We'll make zucchini rancheros with popcorn."

"Aren't you going to tell her what Greggy said?" asked Gemela anxiously.

"Greggy?" said Kale.

"He said you're made of pure light and dreams," said Chamy. "He's been asking about you over and over again."

Gemela giggled.

"When can I see him?" asked Kale.

"Anytime. He doesn't want to inconvenience you or anything."

"How about right now?" offered Gemela. "I know where he is. He's outside Widener Hall, sitting under a cement pole with a rotating triangle. But he's going to want to leave pretty soon, I can tell."

"Okay," said Kale. "Let's go."

And so they walked westward on Cambridge Street.

CHAPTER TWENTY-SIX

IN THE MEANTIME, I remained in my cage, waiting for inspiration. I tried climbing up the steel bars to see if I could break through the ceiling, but there was some kind of metal plate on the other side of the plaster. The bars themselves were over an inch thick, so I gave up trying to pry them apart.

If I hadn't been disconnected from the Web, I probably would have lost hope. I wasn't usually the type who responded well to pressure, and I knew Trivers could march back into the room and kill me at any moment. Or I could just die of starvation.

But without the Web's interference, I managed to stay calm and peaceful. I told myself that things were okay, and I kept my attention focused on Kale's private channel, if only to distract myself from any potential thoughts of doom.

After 6.29 minutes, Kale, Chamy, and Gemela reached Widener Hall. As Gemela predicted, Greggy was sitting under a cement pole with a rotating triangle, and when he and Kale's eyes met, little sparks of possibility flooded throughout their netgorks.

No one understood exactly what the sparks meant. But Chamy and Gemela easily detected them, and they offered to leave Kale and Greggy on their own.

"Just be optimal," whispered Gemela into Kale's ear.

"We'll save you some dinner for when you get home," added Chamy.

When they left, Greggy leaned toward Kale slightly. She thought of brushing her lips against his, in the way she had before she left for New Mexico, but there was too much tension in their frames, and the cement pole behind them seemed disapproving.

"My grandfather was murdered this morning," said Kale awkwardly. "By the pirater."

"What?" he exclaimed.

"He was standing on a ladder in his sunroom when a miniature missile pierced his skull. I watched it happen."

"But why? What'd he do?"

"His memory had started to come back. He was talking about the past, about the transition, what it was really like. I'm sure that's why the pirater did it."

Greggy pulled at his hair. "I never should have suggested you go out there."

"I had to see him." She wiped a tear from her cheek. "At least, it's all over now."

"I'm not so sure."

"He lived a full life, and he showed me incredible things, but he's gone now. I have to put it behind me."

"I wish you could. I wish I could too."

"What do you mean?"

"Things have happened you don't know about, Kale," said Greggy, his hands trembling. "I think we'd better find another place to talk."

They went to the Littaeur Center, where there was a student lounge on the third floor. It was 7:24 PM when they entered, with no one in the vicinity. To be safe, they sat on a couch in the rear of the lounge. Kale took off her teardrop earring and placed it between them.

"The first thing I should tell you," Greggy input, "is that I'm an orphan."

"An orphan?"

"My father was killed before I was born, and my mother when I was six—three days after she'd placed me in a state facility to protect me. I spent the rest of my childhood there, in upstate New York. When I turned eighteen, I was sorted into a job in systems maintenance, but my processing speeds were below par, which was how I ended up at Harvard."

"I had no idea," she responded.

"Last month my old orphanage contacted me," he continued. "They said that my mother left a package with them when I first entered the facility—a package she asked them to hold onto until I came of age. Somehow, they lost track of it until last month. As soon as I heard what happened, I went straight to pick it up. I was thinking it might contain data tracks or something like that."

"And what was it?" asked Kale.

"It turned out to be two matching bookends of silver. I was disappointed, but I figured they kind of explained my fascination with reading, so I set them on my shelf and wedged some books between them. Then last Saturday, after I saw you, I remembered a lullaby my mother used to sing—a lullaby that had something to do with bookends, of all things.

"That was when I realized that maybe her package had some deeper purpose, so I grabbed the bookends from my shelf and peeled off the felt from their bases. Underneath the second one, I slid away a small plate and found this note."

He withdrew a carefully folded piece of paper from his pocket, and motioned for Kale to read it through the private channel:

November 11, 2058

My Dear Greggy,

I never wanted to tell you this,
But now you have to know.
Your grandmother was Martha Buliment.
Your grandfather was Knotty Burgstaller.

Together they tyrannized the world.
She mixed a ruthless virus,
And he used it for all it was worth,
To make every human his.

The Web was invented to stop them.
And it did stop them in a sort of way.
But Knotty stopped Martha completely.
He killed her the day I was born.

For the next thirteen long years,
Knotty kept me in a closet,
Until I finally broke away,
With the help of some good people.

Later I was lucky to meet your father,
In our love we made you—a child of hope.
But then Knotty tracked down your father,
And now he's found me too.

This you have to know, Greggy.
Because you can't let him get to you.
You can't ever let him get to you.
Because you're our only child of hope.

Love and only love,

Mom

When Kale finished reading, emotions ran through her like water, but she felt unable to hold onto any of them. She couldn't even measure her quotient levels.

"So what do you think?" input Greggy.

"I... I don't know."

"You see what it means, right?"

"I'm not exactly sure."

"It means Knotty Burgstaller is the pirater," he explained.

She nodded her head slowly.

"Knotty Burgstaller is the one who murdered your grandfather," he continued. "My grandfather murdered your grandfather."

"I... I don't see how you figure that?"

"Because of what the note says."

Kale looked at him intently.

"Think about it," he input. "When your grandfather started getting his memory back, he mentioned something about Knotty Burgstaller, right?"

"He said Knotty infected all the food on earth. That was how the transition came about."

"And isn't that consistent with what my mom's note says?"

"Yeah, it is."

"Don't you see then? That's why Knotty pirated you. He couldn't let the world discover what he'd done."

"But what makes you think he's even still alive?" she asked. "He'd have to be over a hundred years old."

"There are all kinds of ways he could have survived."

"So if he's still so powerful, why hasn't he come after you, like your mother worried about?"

"Because he can't trace me. Before I entered the orphanage, my mother hired someone to change my PIFFEN frequency. That's why I'm a retrofitter—my meter nodes were grazed by the person who did the operation."

Kale flinched, thinking of the pain.

"The reason Knotty hasn't yet come after you is because you're still valuable to him," added Greggy. "He's waiting for you to lead him to more sources from the past, so he can eliminate them too."

"But I've already quit the assignment. I gave my boss notice yesterday, after I found out about Mike Eu."

"You quit the assignment?" he replied nervously. "And your boss didn't object?"

"He hardly even reacted. I just told him I no longer felt qualified, and he said fine."

"He didn't even question your efficiency ratio?"

"No, he's a new guy. My old boss was fired while I was out in New Mexico."

Greggy paused for a moment. "I don't like this."

"Wait a second," Kale input. "I think I hear someone coming up the stairs."

She put the tear drop resonator back on her ear, and they both listened nervously to the sound of footsteps—slow and awkward—ascending the stairs.

CHAPTER TWENTY-SEVEN

KALE AND GREGGY couldn't have anticipated the severity, but I already knew. The strange thing was, I remained optimistic. As the confrontation took place, I just remained peaceful and calm. And yes, it *was* Trivers walking up the stairs, dragging behind him a six-foot long Mylar body bag, which was why his footsteps were so slow and awkward.

"Well, well, well," he announced, as he entered the student lounge. "Gooddata, Ms. Keeler. Gooddata, Mr. Panagopolous."

"Gooddata," they said slowly.

"I've come to offer you my congratulations on a job well done," he said.

"Thank you," replied Kale. "But I thought Marshall told you, I quit the assignment yesterday. Greggy and I are just discussing netgork expansion techniques."

"Come now, Ms. Keeler," he said. "I think we can dispense with the bitwaste. Or is that asking too much?"

"I don't know what you mean." She tried to send out a distress signal, but Trivers had already installed a wave shield, blocking her transmission.

"There's nothing to discuss," interjected Greggy. "She quit the assignment. She doesn't have to tell you anything."

"That's true. That's quite true. But then again, you both might be interested to know who I have in this body bag." Trivers unzipped the Mylar bag, lifting it slightly to reveal Professor Morgaux.

"Oh, my Ray!" gasped Kale. "You've killed him."

"Not quite," replied Trivers. "He's under heavy sedation for better transportability. But I've got a soundbomb in my coat, and I'll use it on his ears if you don't do exactly as I say."

"A soundbomb?" asked Greggy.

"It'll blow out the professor's Eustachian tubes, leaving him to die a slow, agonizing death. And don't think I'm not eager to use it. I've had trouble with him before, years ago."

"So... so you're the one?" stammered Kale. "You're the one who poisoned his wife?"

Trivers showed a slight smile, then tightened his face. "Forget it, Keeler. I'm calling the shots here, and what I want is for you to get up off your ass and walk over to Morgaux's office."

"Let her go," said Greggy. "It's my fault. I pushed her into this. She didn't do anything."

"Is that right, Mr. Panagopoulos? Then I'll take the both of you, unless you prefer I kill you right now."

Neither Greggy nor Kale could reply. They both got up and put their hands above their heads. Then they slowly walked out of the lounge to Morgaux's office, as Trivers followed behind them with the body bag.

"Sit down and start dumping your private netgorks," said Trivers, when they reached the office. He stuffed Morgaux into a corner closet and threw Kale an external storage disk.

"Can you at least tell us what this is about?" she said.

"It's quite simple, my friends. I'm collecting knowledge of the pre-Web era, in order to create a testament to its sacred reality."

"I thought you wanted to dispense with the bitwaste," objected Greggy.

Trivers laughed. "You're quite the comic, aren't you, Panagopoulos?"

"I know when I hear bitdoo."

"Then tell us the real reason, if you think you're so clever."

Greggy looked down at the floor. "I'm not sure exactly. It has something to do with the fact that you control the Web, so you're not bound by it. That's why you can innovate. It's also why you need to eliminate all knowledge of the pre-Web era, so no one else can compete with you."

Trivers clapped his hands. "Impressive, Panagopoulos. Very impressive. Now download your silly data, both of you. And hurry up."

Greggy glanced at Kale, and they proceeded to perform the task. It took them 6.44 minutes to execute all the appropriate commands, then Kale handed over the newly filled storage disk—a disk that replicated all their conscious knowledge, except what resided in the tear drop resonator.

"I'm much obliged," said Trivers.

He hungrily intook the data, mumbling excitedly as each new bit of information crossed his receptors. But when he finished processing the disk, he was unsatisfied.

"Damn it, Keeler," he exclaimed, with his yellow hair standing on end. "This is crap. You've censored yourselves."

"No, that's everything. I swear."

"Fuck off. I know what I know." He reached for a laserblade attached to his headware and began waving it in front of their faces.

"We're not hiding anything," insisted Kale. "Maybe if you were a bit more specific."

"Specific? You want me to be specific?" His temples throbbed wildly. "I'm talking about a piece of evidence from the past. A piece of evidence that lays out the entire sequence of events leading up to the transition, most likely written by an asshole named Ray LeGhir. A piece of evidence that's been hidden for the past 69 years, and that I've inferred the existence of only by induction, and only after backtracing the complete data structure of our human species."

"I don't understand."

Trivers foamed at the mouth. "Don't fuck with me, Keeler! You know exactly what I'm talking about. All my asymptotic predictors confirm it—you're the one who's supposed to uncover the evidence. And you're supposed to have done it by now. By god damn fucking *now*! Now, now, now, now, now!"

"I'm sorry, Clyde," said Kale, as a twinge of the signal she'd received from the augmented cell passed through her nervous system. "But if your plan is failing, that's hardly my fault."

"You're lying. You're just hiding the results."

"Then why don't you sweep my operating system? You of all people should be able to do that."

Trivers pondered the situation. "You're right," he said. "You're absolutely right. I've got to be more scientific about this. I've got to stop my emotions from getting the better of me. It would be foolish to give up now, after all this. Wouldn't it, Mr. Panagopoulos?"

"I suppose," replied Greggy.

"Of course, you probably don't expect me to have the necessary equipment stowed in my pockets. Do you?"

"No, I guess not."

Trivers laughed heartily. "Ah, but I do! I do! So come on, get on your hands and knees, both of you! And do it quick, for Ray's sake!"

Kale stood still. "What if we refuse to cooperate?" she asked.

"Then Morgaux's dead. And after I kill him, I'll kill your little datafriend here. If that's not enough, I'll move on to your mother, your father, and everybody else in your social netgork."

"Okay," she replied. "Okay."

Reluctantly, she and Greggy crouched down on the floor behind Morgaux's desk. Once they were in place, Trivers locked their hands and feet into a magnetic force field. He mounted a set of tiny cathode terminals to each of their temples and wired the cathodes to his headware, linking them to a small transformer circuit.

"In case you're wondering," he boasted, "I knew all along you'd be less than honest with me. My cathodes will suck out everything from you, even if it's deep in your subconscious, even if it's something you've taught yourself to forget. And I wouldn't recommend trying to fight the procedure. That only makes it more painful. But don't worry, as soon as I get what I want, I'll have the cathodes clear your minds of everything. Then your blankened lives will go on as they should, forever trapped in a Web of beautiful data."

He laughed deeply as he initiated his extraction program. Kale tried to outsmart the extractors, putting up a false circuit, but her system was no match for them. It was only a matter of 84 seconds before Trivers came across the negative charge in Kale's epidermal tissue, where the bird-like signal from my augmented cell had first struck. Fortunately, he wasn't able to determine the content of the signal, since all of its imaging traces had been deleted. But the negative space created by the event stuck out to him as clear as day.

"What the hell is this, Keeler?" he said, pausing the extraction. "Am I to understand that you received a critical communication that you decided not to intake?"

"I... I have no idea," replied Kale, struggling to get hold of herself. "How would I know if I didn't intake it?"

"Clever, very fucking clever. And what about you, Mr. Panagopolous? Did you get a special signal too?"

"No," said Greggy.

"That's right. You're just Keeler's doobyte sidekick. You don't know shit, do you?" He pulled out his laserblade again and danced it around Greggy's neck.

"Stop it!" shouted Kale. "I'm not holding anything back!"

"Ah ha," replied Trivers. "Then I suggest you hurry up and intake the secret signal. Otherwise your little Greggy-boy is going to get all cut up, and that would be a real shame, wouldn't it?"

Kale stood still, transfixed.

"Wouldn't it, Keeler?" he repeated.

"I can't intake something I don't know about," she said. "That's not possible."

"Wrong, Keeler. The reason you don't know about it is because you've subconsciously suppressed your external receptors—I can see that from your wave cadences. All we've got to do is make a few corrections in your pre-processing zone. Then we wait for the signal to strike again."

"And what makes you so sure it will come in?"

"It will, Keeler. I'll know when it does because I'm going to dedicate a terminal exclusively to your epidermal tissue."

He reached into his coat pocket for another cathode and planted it on her left forearm, in the exact place she'd initially received the signal. With careful precision, he linked it to his transformer circuit and began making the necessary adjustments.

Once the new cathode was operational, Kale was under his command. Trivers cleared her frequency entirely, so that when she tried to turn toward Greggy, she found she'd been stripped of the ability. She could only focus on her external receptors.

Meanwhile, Trivers sat back and waited for another broadcasting of the augmented cell's secret signal. Since the intelligent component of the cell had already withered away, all that remained was its transmission capability, installed on some unknown satellite. That left no hope that the broadcasting would stop.

In fact, Trivers waited only 18 minutes. At 8:37 PM, the cell transmitted a clean and clear bird-signal, and Kale's skin promptly picked it up. This time she felt it on her right leg, directly above her fibula bone.

"Intake it, Keeler!" yelled Trivers. "Intake the damn thing!"

She tried to disassociate herself from the signal before it reached the cathode on her forehead, but her nervous system was too overtaken, and she had no choice but to arch her back like a seasoned bird.

As before, the signal entered into her capillaries, where it methodically traveled toward her pre-processing zone. Because of the cathode, however, her nervous system could not delete it. Trivers seized the signal out of her as soon as it reached her operating system. Then he jubilantly read it aloud:

Kale Catherine Keeler,

You do not know me. I am a messenger of artificial intelligence, created by Ray LeGhir. My function is to facilitate the restoration of missing information caused by the Transition of 2008.

I am contacting you because you are the first human since the Transition to laugh at the Web and transcend its limits. Thus you are deemed most capable of overseeing the release of this missing information to society.

You will find the information temporarily superimposed on channel Z9478213 - QU108473TAW913. The password code is ANOTHERHOPE.

This message will continue to be broadcasted at random intervals for another 3 hours and 20 minutes. If you do not respond within this time period, the information will retract from the specified location.

"Well, how about that!" exclaimed Trivers. "I finally caught the bastard at his own game!"

He prodded Kale with a cathode inverter, but Kale just groaned.

"Oops," said Trivers. "I forgot your frequency's cleaned."

She groaned again.

"Really," he continued. "I'd like for you to see the signal. I just got a bit carried away. Here, take a look."

He opened one of her circuits and re-shipped the signal to her, emulating her netgork. As she intook it, he submitted the password code to retrieve Ray LeGhir's document on her behalf. Then, while she was busy processing the signal, he discreetly retrieved the document for himself via the cathode terminals.

The moment Kale was done processing, she tried to submit the password for herself. But Trivers just burst into laughter.

"I'm afraid I've already done that for you, Keeler. I've got everything I want now. Ha ha ha ha!"

"You're sick," said Kale.

"Aw, come on. I've been waiting 69 years for this day. It's a big deal for me, really."

"You're a very sick man, Clyde."

"Sure, I'll admit it. I am sick. But how about if I offer you some nice entertainment to cheer you up? What would you say to that?"

"I couldn't care less."

"Come on, Keeler. I've got it all set up for you. All you have to do is watch. You too, Panagopoulos." He snapped his fingers, pointing to the sky. 0.39 seconds later, Kale and Greggy received visual images of an explosion in outer space.

"What the hell was that?" said Greggy.

"You don't know?" smiled Trivers.

Kale and Greggy remained silent, still trapped on their hands and knees.

"It was the satellite, my friends. You know, the satellite where Ray LeGhir's document was being stored. So we don't have to worry about that anymore, do we?"

"No!" exclaimed Kale.

"You'll never get away with this!" cried Greggy.

Trivers just kept laughing. "That's comical. Very, very comical. Now shut the fuck up, both of you, and put your heads to the floor. Because we're going into phase two. I'm going to remove this whole god damn episode from your minds—everything even remotely related to this assignment is going to be sucked out of you, thanks to my lovely cathode terminals. And meanwhile, I'm going to sit down and read this wonderful historical document you've just helped me to retrieve. Then I'm going to destroy it, once and for all, and the whole world's finally going to be beautiful. Beautiful, beautiful, beautiful!"

CHAPTER TWENTY-EIGHT

EVERYTHING WAS RIDING on my shoulders. I was the only hope for the survival of Ray's document. The pressure was intense, but I kept reminding myself that Kale and Greggy's situation was far worse. They didn't even know I was aware of their situation, nor did they know I had a copy of Ray's document. Instead, they were locked in a magnetic force field while Trivers's cathode terminals kept sucking data from their netgorks, like thousands of tiny needles rushing through their neural tissue.

I could hardly stand witnessing their peril, and I was tempted to stop accessing Kale's secured channel altogether. But if Kale and Greggy were brave enough to endure Trivers' extraction program, the least I could do was to stay by their side, via the resonator.

And that was when the inspiration I'd been hoping for finally struck. The *resonator* was my ticket out of the cage. As long as Trivers was intaking Kale's data through the cathode terminals, his operating system and Kale's operating system were temporarily linked. That meant I could use my resonator to get into Trivers' system. I could search through Trivers' mind for the control commands that regulated the operation of the steel cage and set myself free.

First, I had to update the resonator in order to make it

conformable with Trivers' operating space. That simply required locating one of the data bits he was extracting from Kale. I latched onto the sequence neurally and followed it through the cathodes into Trivers' brain.

Once I fed the resonator a sample of his system architecture, I had full and complete reign over Trivers' private netgork. It took me a couple of seconds to get used to the sheer immensity of the space—his storage capacity was thousands of times larger than anyone else's. But with a little practice, I managed to move through his netgork reasonably well. After 3.16 minutes, I stumbled onto his top-secret files.

Trivers' categories were pretty old-fashioned, even by my standards. I had to do some serious hunting before I found the heading, ROOMS WITH STEEL CAGES. But then I came across the subheading, CAGES THAT DROP FROM CEILINGS. Beneath that was the entry, 27TH FLOOR LOCATION.

I accessed the specification parameters for the entry and located a control variable called CAGE SETTING, with two possible options: UP or DOWN. I also found a control variable called ALARM MONITOR, with ON or OFF options.

The status menu indicated that the CAGE SETTING was in the DOWN position, and the ALARM MONITOR was ON. But that was an easy matter to fix. My main worry was attracting Trivers' attention if I reached into his system too abruptly, so I inserted a slight program change into his automatic maintenance routine—a little hook that said, "Please put all CAGE SETTING control variables in the UP position, and all ALARM MONITOR variables in the OFF position."

It was only a matter of 98 more seconds before the maintenance routine kicked into its new cycle. Then, to my amazement, I watched the steel bars slowly retract. When they got to the top of the ceiling, I even felt the familiar whirring of the Web as it interfaced with my transceiver. But I didn't pay the slightest attention to the beckoning channels. Instead, I picked myself up and walked right out of the cage.

At that point, I verified that the alarm monitors throughout the rest of the building were indeed off, and I checked my resonator to see if it was accepting data input. Luckily, the resonator's full capability had been restored, so I took a deep breath and input a signal directly to Kale's private channel:

Dear Kale,

I know what Trivers is doing to you and Greggy. I've been watching the whole thing through the resonator Morgaux sent me. Please try to hang on a bit longer. I'm on my way out to Cambridge right now. Trivers trapped me in the Netgorks building, but I just broke free, and now I'm going to help you. I'm going to do whatever it takes, Keeler, I swear.

—Ralph

My hope was that Kale would be able to access my message, even if she couldn't respond to it. But I soon saw I was deluded. Her nervous system was too overridden by Trivers' extraction program.

There was only so much longer that Kale and Greggy could hold out. Even using one of Trivers' super-shuttles, I was still at least 78 minutes from Cambridge, so I had to figure some way to stall Trivers. Realistically, my only chance seemed to be if I directly interfered with his extraction program—otherwise he'd never allow himself to be distracted.

At first, I didn't see how it could be done. But after ignoring the Web for 33.28 seconds, another inspiration popped into my head: I could keep refeeding the data from Kale's private channel back into her system while Trivers sucked it out.

I'd already brought all of Kale's data into my own system, and Trivers hadn't yet discovered her resonator. That meant I could create a continuous loop to confound his extraction program. The one draw-back was that Kale and Greggy would continue to be subjected to Trivers' cathode terminals. But given the stakes, I hardly saw how they'd disapprove.

I configured a sequencing algorithm to ship data back into Kale's resonator, and I instructed the algorithm to operate randomly so that Trivers wouldn't be able to detect it as quickly. At that point, I headed for the roof of the Netgorks building to get one of Trivers' super shuttles.

Halfway to the elevators, I realized I had no weapon of any sort— not even a simple ink gun—and I couldn't resist the opportunity: Why not give Trivers a taste of his own medicine? Why not use one of his own weapons against him?

I hacked back into his operating system via the cathode terminals and located a category in his files called INVENTIONS. It contained a whole array of headings, but the one that caught my eye was MASTER LOCATION, ROOM 3988.

As soon as I saw that, I jumped on an elevator for the 39th floor, the top floor of the building. Meanwhile, I went through Trivers' data to get the access code for Room 3988. When I reached the room, I just submitted the code and pushed open the door.

I could hardly believe what I saw. The room stretched back 184 feet, with thousands and thousands of glass compartments along the side walls, each one holding a different invention. Trivers had even gone to the trouble of physically labeling the compartments.

The first one I glanced at held a small device called an Agreement Induction Beam Generator, which I suspected was used to influence his reporter's decisions. Above that were two gun-shaped entities listed as Pleasure Adjustment Rods. Then there was a series of spray cans marked Numb-Out I, Numb-Out II, and Numb-Out III.

The next column of compartments contained inventions relating to personality manipulation. I saw one called Dumb Bell, another called Screw Up, and a third called The Generic Personality Program, which I guessed must have been used on Mike Eu.

Nearby were items emphasizing life extension, such as Heart Young, Skin Young, Hair Yellow, Eye Blue and so on. They all seemed to be for Trivers' use alone because underneath the labels were notations of when he'd first started using them.

Further inside I noticed a compartment that was empty except for a placard saying, "The Hog Butcher—Installed at Rooftop Location, Room 4006." The adjacent compartment had a similar placard, except it said, "The Bovine Butcher—Installed at Rooftop Location, Room 4006." There were 26 more empty compartments in a row, all containing placards referring to hogs and steer.

I had no understanding of what the placards meant, and I really wasn't interested, as I didn't see how I could use any of these inventions against Trivers. Fortunately, I soon found a more relevant series of compartments. There was a Heart-Seeking Bullet, a Liver-Seeking Rocket, an Eyeball-Seeking Grenade, and a Bladder-Seeking Knife. Then I came to a compartment that made me shiver all the way down to my bones because the label said, "Memory-Seeking Micro Missile."

I decided right then and there to take the Eyeball-Seeking Grenade. It seemed like exactly what Trivers deserved, and I felt sure I could program it to pluck out his eyeballs like two simulant sushi rolls in the shape of marbles. The only problem was that I couldn't get into the compartment. When I tried to lift the hinged glass door, it wouldn't budge. No amount of force on my part could wedge it open.

I was ready to scream. I mean, I should have been half way to Cambridge, and there I was roaming the center of all the world's ugliness, unable to use any of it to my advantage.

In desperation, I ran to the end of the room, where three doors lined the rear wall. The doors were controlled by the same security system as the compartments, but the one in the middle was slightly ajar. When I went to investigate, I saw to my delight that Trivers had left two items sitting on top of a test counter.

The first item, called Booster Additive, was a purplish fluid in a pint-sized container. I figured it was designed to boost machine performance, although it didn't come with any instructions. The second item, labeled a Wind Gust Ejector, was a cylindrically-shaped device with a narrow gold tip and a black body 3.32 inches long. Presumably, the red button in the middle ejected a gust of wind.

Not wanting to take a chance, I grabbed both items, stuffed them in my hip pocket, and I hurried out of the booth. When I got to the roof of the Netgorks building, it was already 9:04 PM, and I knew I had to get moving. But out of the corner of my eye, I spotted Room 4006, where Trivers' Hog and Bovine Butchers were reportedly installed. I had to take a cursory glance.

From the exterior, the room looked more like a shack than anything else, with old wood siding, a tar paper roof, and billowing smoke. When I opened the door, however, I gagged at the sight.

The whole front of the room was filled with huge carcasses of what seemed to be animal flesh. In the rear of the room, machines were cutting the carcasses into smaller pieces, then exposing these pieces to some sort of smoke treatment. The smoked flesh was sealed in pouches and packaged in boxes stamped, PRIVATE RESERVE OF MR. CLYDE TRIVERS.

I knew I'd stumbled onto something significant. My guess was that it had something to do with Trivers' odor and the weird food he liked to eat. But all I had time to do was record the scene and dash off to the shuttle port.

Conveniently, Trivers' fastest shuttle—a Gradient 626—was sitting unattended in the port hangar. I hopped into the cockpit, substituting Trivers' impulse for my own, and I linked with the shuttle's biochip.

The shuttle promised me top-level speed, but even that seemed inadequate. So while the biochip enlivened, I leapt out of the cockpit and poured the purple Booster Additive fluid into the fuel tank. What the hell? It was time to live dangerously.

I jumped back in, gave the all-clear signal, and before I could even brace myself, the shuttle catapulted off the rooftop and raced eastward at full throttle.

CHAPTER TWENTY-NINE

6.53 MINUTES LATER, while I was soaring past the giant castles and silica parks of Las Vegas, Trivers finished reading Ray LeGhir's document. He turned his attention to his extraction program and noticed the procedure was caught in an infinite loop.

"God damn it!" he exclaimed, as he inspected the cathode terminals on Kale's skin. "You're blocking the fucking program!"

"What?" said Kale. She was still locked in place on her hands and knees, unable to look up at his face.

"Greggy's all cleaned out, but you're not. What the hell's going on, Keeler?"

"I'm just trying to breathe."

Trivers grabbed her by the neck. "That's bitwaste. You're obviously doing something."

"I am not," she said, too depleted to be afraid. "Get your flitting hands off me."

"If you don't cooperate with my extraction process," he replied, "I'll have no choice but to kill you."

"Maybe that'd be the best thing, Clyde."

"Is that right? You really are naive." He paused for a moment, then began shaving a small patch of hair from Kale's head.

"I... I don't think you should do that," interjected Greggy, struggling to speak. "I... I don't think that'd be too wise."

"Stay out of this, Panagopoulos."

"I've made some insights," he replied. "I... I know who you are."

Trivers continued shaving Kale's hair. "You're just reacting to the extraction procedure, my friend. Your system's making things up to fill the void."

"No, I... I don't think so. It's because you've cleared out my brain enough to let my origins take over. That's why I recognize you now."

"Please shut up," said Trivers wearily. "Or I'll have to kill you too."

"R...really?" said Greggy. "You'd r...really kill your own grandson? Your own poor doobyte grandson?"

"I said shut up. I don't have time for this bitwaste."

"But it's not bitwaste, Grandpa. I'm the one that got away, the o...offspring of your daughter."

Trivers' face grew slightly pale. "What the fuck are you saying, Panagopoulos?"

"It's time to stop masquerading as Clyde Trivers. It's time you admit to the world that you're actually Kn...Knotty Burgstaller, my grandfather, the one responsible for the transition."

"You fucking asshole!" exploded Trivers. "You're a liar, an idiot, a weakling! And you're sure as hell no grandson of mine!" He leapt into the air and slammed his foot into Greggy's back, then repeatedly kicked and punched him.

Locked in the magnetic force field, Greggy had no way to defend himself. His only recourse was to absorb the blows as best he could. Kale tried to intervene, twisting and squirming to get near Greggy, but it was no use. The force field was too powerful, and all she could do was scream at the top of her lungs.

The commotion roused Morgaux from his sedated state. Instinctively, he emerged from the closet and struggled to pull Trivers from Greggy.

Trivers just laughed as he tripped his soundbomb. Morgaux

immediately rolled up into a ball on the floor, writhing in pain at the intense decibel level pounding through his eardrums.

"Walter!" cried Kale. "Walter!"

Morgaux shuddered once more, then stopped moving.

"He's dead," said Trivers. "I told you I'd use my soundbomb if you didn't obey me. Now you see I mean business."

"Oh, we're impressed," replied Greggy, his face swollen and bloodied. "We're very impressed."

Trivers stepped toward Greggy once more. He was about to throw another punch when he noticed his extraction program come to a halt. Apparently, the vibration from his soundbomb fractured the cathode terminals attached to Kale and Greggy. A moment later, Kale's amethyst necklace fell to the floor, the beads likewise fractured by the soundwaves.

Trivers hurried to repair the damaged cathode terminals, but it was obvious he'd made a blunder. To confound him further, I began shipping Ray LeGhir's document into Kale's private channel. I figured he would be shocked to discover that she retrieved the document herself.

Unfortunately, I was only able to ship the first two chapters. 0.66 seconds after I started the transmission, Kale's tear drop resonator also shattered. As the resonator pieces hissed and crackled, falling from Kale's ear, I lost contact with her system. I wasn't even able to verify that she processed the first two chapters. Kale and Greggy were simply left to battle for themselves.

✵

Clearly, things weren't going the way I wanted. But at least Trivers' extraction program was damaged, which bought me a bit more time. There were a couple of other positive developments as well.

For one, the Booster Additive helped tremendously. I was traveling at more than twice the cruising speed of an ordinary Gradient

626, and my shuttle's control circuit informed me that I was scheduled to reach Cambridge in 4.23 minutes. I already had clearance to land on the south side of the Littaeur Center, where there was a break from the cement poles with rotating triangles.

Secondly, I had Greggy's insight that Trivers and Burgstaller were one and the same. While riding the shuttle, I did some investigating of my own and shed some more light. According to the records channel, Knotty Burgstaller died on January 13, 2009, at the age of 36. But the doctor who'd impulsed the death certificate, Dr. J. P. Haas, conveniently happened to be Clyde Trivers' personal physician up until 2053.

There were other connections between Trivers and Burgstaller as well. They both had the same blood type, the same efficiency quotient, and the same metabolic conversion ratio. And their dental configurations were virtually identical.

Their only difference seemed to be that Trivers was taller and more muscular, with bluer eyes and yellower hair. Of course, if Burgstaller was still alive he'd be 105 years old, whereas Trivers was registered as 74. But such discrepancies could easily be accounted for by what I'd seen in Room 3988.

So I tried to tell myself that I was in the superior position, that at last I had something that I could use against Trivers. But the truth was, those last 4.23 minutes in the shuttle were the longest minutes in my life. Instead of monitoring events from the outside, I had to *imagine* what was happening, and that meant I had to face up to the extent of all the pain—the pain in Kale and Greggy and Walter and Mike, the pain in Chamy and Gemela, even the pain in Trivers.

Worse yet, I had to face up to the pain inside myself and admit that I hadn't really learned my lesson. Sure, I'd been disconnected from the Web, and I'd felt the potential. But I hadn't really internalized it. I hadn't really comprehended the truth about Webless space. If anything, the buzz of the Web seemed to be regaining its hold within me.

To fight the impulse, I reminisced about Kale. I reminisced about how she viewed the future, how she laughed at the present, how she interfaced with animals and touched plants, and how she dreamed and hoped and believed, knowing there was something more.

Then it struck me like a beam of starlight: These were the things Trivers feared most. These were the things which made him most vulnerable, for he knew they amounted to far more than his inventions ever would. And that was when I understood I was actually more like Kale than I was like him.

Yes, that was when I learned the lesson I needed to learn—the lesson I'd been running from for as long as I could remember.

CHAPTER THIRTY

THE NEXT THING I KNEW, the super-shuttle was on the ground, 42 yards south of the Littaeur Center. I jumped out of the cockpit at 9:31 PM and negotiated my way past a maze of cement poles with rotating triangles.

To my surprise, I could barely stand to look at the poles. I even considered dispelling the Internal Laws from my own meter, and if there'd been a plant nearby, I swear I would have reached out and touched it. But I had other objectives on my mind.

From the front steps of the Littaeur Center, I spotted the lit window of Morgaux's office. My optic boosters detected Trivers' presence, so I rushed up the stairs to the second floor. When I got to the office door, I squatted down in the hallway and peered through a crack under the door.

Thank Ray, Kale and Greggy were still alive, crouching on their hands and knees. Trivers hadn't yet finished repairing his extraction program—he was still tinkering with the cathode terminals. I thought about making my presence known when an odd thumping noise came from inside the room.

"Did you hear that?" said Kale.

"It looked like Morgaux's body moved," said Greggy. "Maybe he's still alive."

"Nonsense," replied Trivers. "His muscles are just playing themselves out."

"Did you take into account the refractive properties of amethyst when you set the decibel level for your soundbomb?" inquired Greggy.

"That's irrelevant," said Trivers.

"And did you consider the fact that the earth wobbles?" added Kale.

"Shut up, both of you. The professor's long gone, and my cathode terminals are almost fixed."

As if on cue, the thumping noise occurred again. This time there was no doubt that Morgaux was indeed alive, because he turned onto his side and began sniffing the air.

"Oooah," he groaned. "What's that smell? What's that horrible smell?"

"Walter?" replied Kale.

"Oooah," he groaned again, covering his nose. "There's a horrible smell in the air. My ears are ringing."

"A smell?" said Kale. "I don't smell anything."

"There is no smell," insisted Trivers. "The idiot's gone crazy. Fucking crazy."

He stepped toward Morgaux, about to apply another one of his inventions. Clearly, I could wait no longer. It was time to make my entrance.

"Hello, Clyde," I announced, throwing open the door. "How are you, my friend?"

Trivers stood there dumbfounded.

"Oh, I'm sorry, old pal," I said. "Would you prefer I call you Knotty?"

"Son of a bitch," he replied slowly.

"I know, Clyde, I know. It's all very confusing, isn't it? And to complicate things, there's this issue about the smell. But I can clear it all up if you give me half a chance."

Trivers stared into my eyes. "Don't fuck with me, Peterson. I'm quite fond of killing crazy people."

"Ah, but this has nothing to do with anyone going crazy, unless that means no longer wanting to live in a sterile domain of pure data."

"Very funny, Peterson. You say that as if you have a fucking choice about the matter."

"That's exactly it," I continued. "Maybe I never would have had a choice in the matter if it weren't for you, but you were the one who kept the possibility alive all these years with all your inventions and innovations. It was your choice really."

"Oh, Ralph," he sighed. "You've lost it. Completely lost it. That steel cage must have taken you over the edge."

"Precisely, Clyde. That's my whole point. When you cut me off from the Web, you opened me up to the very thing you were so desperate to keep shut. You did the same thing for Kale too, when you had her jailed by the WPA. And it must have happened to Morgaux just now, when he got hit by your soundbomb."

"Nonsense. All nonsense. I don't see why I'm even listening to this bitshit."

"Because I'm getting to the most interesting part, that's why. You see, I've been to your secret rooftop location—I've seen what's in Room 4006."

"You're bluffing," scoffed Trivers. "Only I have the entrance code."

"I pirated the code, Clyde. That's how I know where your smell comes from. It's from the animals, Clyde. You're eating their *flesh*."

Trivers' face turned beet red.

"Yes!" cried Morgaux. "That's what the smell is! It's rotting flesh, decomposing in his gut!"

Greggy nodded his head strangely, as if recalling some lost part of himself. "It's true," he said slowly. "It's also his own gut that's rotting. He may look like he's in his fifties, but he's actually 105 years old."

"You're all crazy," replied Trivers, rigid with denial. "This is pure bitwaste. I am not 105. And I certainly am not eating animals."

"Liar," I said. "I saw the hogs and steer—I used Kale's animal database to identify them. And I saw all your fancy slaughtering equipment. I know you're eating them."

"Fuck you! If you think I'd be so inefficient as to... "

"No, of course not," I interrupted. "I realize you weren't inefficient. You knew you had to do something if you wanted to keep your flesh habit. That's why you went into our meters and adjusted our sense of smell. You did the same thing to our senses of taste and touch to make us more concerned with the shape of our food than anything else. But you made your crucial error when you disconnected the three of us from the Web, because it completely slipped your mind that our senses would revert to their original capabilities."

"He's right," agreed Morgaux. "He's absolutely right. It's a brilliant analysis."

Trivers' face remained stoic. "Well, well," he said. "The time's finally come then. I might as well admit, Mr. Peterson's grand reconstruction is quite accurate. Everything that's been said is quite right except for one small detail."

"And what's that?" asked Morgaux.

"Oh, it's not much," he replied. "Not much at all. It's just that I object to the notion that Mr. Peterson has been brilliant. Rather, I think he's been quite stupid, in the same way that he's always been stupid."

"And I'm sure you want to tell me all about it, right?" I said.

"Actually, Ralph, in this case I think I'd rather show you. Because it takes a very special kind of stupidity—a very, very special kind of stupidity—to do all the research you've done, and then just walk in here and throw everything away, all in one shot, just like this."

He slapped his hands, sending a loud crackling noise through the air, and Morgaux and I were instantly lifted off the floor by an invisible pressure current. A moment later, we were deposited on our hands and knees, immobilized by the same magnetic force field that held Kale and Greggy.

Trivers laughed uproariously as he lifted my resonator out of my shirt pocket. "Such stupidity! And now I'm going to suck all this wonderful knowledge right out of all your heads. And at last my deed will be done. Ha ha ha ha!"

✹

Okay, maybe I had been stupid. Maybe I should have thought things through a bit more, and maybe I should have used the Wind Ejector in my pocket when I'd had the chance.

But at least I'd said what I had to say. At least I'd uncovered the truth and thrown it in Trivers' face. Even if I hadn't really helped Kale and Greggy, even if my discoveries were destined to be erased forever, at least I hadn't just stayed home eating flying saucer burritos. At least I'd proved my proddings wrong.

Besides, I could see the gratitude in Kale's face. Despite her being trapped on her hands and knees, on the verge of becoming another bundle of generic bitwaste, I could see she was proud of me.

So I tried to remain optimistic when Trivers attached his extractors to me. I just stayed perfectly motionless, resisting as little as possible. When he finished, 7.46 minutes later, I felt like a purely blank chip. I didn't even remember how I'd gotten to Cambridge.

It took Trivers 18.21 minutes to do the same thing to Morgaux. Then he moved to Greggy, to double-check that his netgorks had been fully cleaned. Finally, he stepped over to Kale and tapped her on the forehead.

"Your turn, Keeler," he said, grinning widely. "I've been saving you for last to maximize my enjoyment."

Kale nodded as if in agreement. "That's great," she replied softly. "The only problem is that I know your weakness now, Clyde."

"I'm a man of endless recourse. I have no weakness."

"You *were* a man of endless recourse," she corrected.

"Bitshit," Trivers snorted. "You think the Web Monitors can do anything to stop me? I own the fucking Netgorks."

"Yes, perhaps. But that's where the problem lies. I mean, Netgorks isn't actually a real word."

"Are we playing make-believe now? Because I'm sorry, Keeler, but it's time to..."

"No, *I'm* sorry," she interrupted. "I'm sorry your mother abandoned you when you were a baby. I'm sorry you had such an unhappy childhood in Carmel."

Trivers' chin quivered slightly. "You don't know what you're talking about. There's no such thing in my past."

"Wrong, Clyde. It's all in LeGhir's document. Ralph discovered it before you did. He sent me the first two chapters while you were busy reading it yourself."

"What the hell?"

"I know your weakness, Clyde. I know all about your g and w-reversal problem."

"I don't have any god damn reversal problem."

"Not anymore," she admitted. "Except you still can't say anything with the word 'work' in it—a scar left over from the electric shock treatment. That's why you had to change the name of the channel headquarters from the Public Networks to the Public *Netgorks*."

Trivers face became ghostly pale. "Now I have to kill you."

"You don't have the power," interrupted Greggy, struggling to fight the magnetic field. "We know your weakness."

"What weakness?" said Trivers. "You show me, you little doobyte loser."

Greggy smiled, then slowly whispered, "*Networks*." He paused for emphasis. "*Networks, networks, networks*."

"Fuck you!" said Trivers, cringing from the words. "I'm putting an end to this right now."

His brow furrowed as he searched his data for the ideal weapon to deploy. Then he nodded his head and snapped his fingers, but nothing happened.

"You see what I mean?" said Kale. "You've lost your touch."

Trivers snapped his fingers once more, but again nothing happened.

"Work, work, work," teased Greggy. *"Work, work, work, work, work."*

"You're all dead now!" yelled Trivers, his mouth frothing. "You're all dead now!"

His eyes rolled back into his sockets, and he stood perfectly still for 3.28 seconds. All at once, he lunged toward Kale and Greggy and violently threw his fists into their faces.

I was at a complete loss. Everything relevant to the situation had been extracted from my memory—I wasn't even sure if Trivers had gone mad, or if Kale and Greggy were somehow deserving of the attack. But then the magnetic field holding us down gave way, as Trivers' circuits began to fail. Morgaux jumped up to shield Kale and Greggy, and I followed his lead in blind faith.

For the next 44 seconds, Trivers fought and snarled like a wild animal from the past. We tried to contain him, and Morgaux and I momentarily pinned him against the side of the desk. But his strength was out of our league. Even our combined muscle power couldn't match his.

Finally, he broke away from our holds, throwing us on opposite sides of the room. He grabbed a black Harvard chair, screaming and yelling that he was going to kill us. Then he rushed toward Kale, with one leg of the chair pointed at her throat.

Thank Ray, Kale turned aside at the last second, causing Trivers to slam into the wall. Greggy and Walter seized the opportunity, pulling the chair out of his hands and wedging him against the wall on the other side of the room. It was at that point—at precisely 9:46 PM—that Drop McWith entered the office.

"Greetings, all," he said, waving his hand. "Just thought I'd drop in to give Ralph a clue. There's something in your hip pocket, Ralph, which you might find useful to dispose of our little tyrant here." He winked at me without twitching and mouthed 'hi' to Kale.

I was still confused, but I figured I might as well check my pocket, since I did feel an uncomfortable bulge. Cautiously, I got up on my haunches and pulled out the offending item.

Trivers was already vexed from the presence of Drop, but when he saw I had his Wind Ejector resting on my thigh, pointing directly at him, he went absolutely berserk. He just threw off Greggy and Walter with one thrust and came straight for me.

"Use the Ejector, Ralph!" yelled Drop. "Press the red button!"

Of course, I had no recollection of what the Wind Ejector was, or why I had it in my possession. All I could do was stand there like a zombie, frozen by the fury in Trivers' fast-approaching face.

Trivers was so completely focused on the Ejector, he didn't even notice Kale thrusting out her leg in front of him. He tripped over her leg and flew headfirst, with no control over his direction.

As physics would dictate, Trivers' airborne body headed straight for me. His left hand looked to be on course for a direct impact with the Wind Ejector. I didn't know what that meant, but I could see on Trivers' face that he was very, very worried.

The rest of it all happened in a nanosecond. His head crashed into my chest, his torso landed on my lap, and before he could do anything about it, his hand smashed against the Wind Ejector, depressing the red button.

There was an ear-splitting explosion, followed by a violent, hissing noise. Suddenly, an enormous gust of wind, almost on the order of a tornado, came bursting out of the tip of the Ejector. It was all finely focused right at Trivers' bulk, and the pressure was so great, so tremendously great, that Trivers was simply lifted up off my lap and blown straight out the window, into the blackness of the night.

The next thing we knew, the Wind Ejector stopped its hissing, and the air in the room became still. The five of us were so stunned, so shaken by the event, that we could barely even breathe. It took another 12.67 seconds before Kale pulled herself up off the floor to investigate the shattered window.

"Great Ray!" she exclaimed. "You have to see this!"

We all made our way to look out the window. And there, in the middle of Harvard Yard, illuminated by a row of neon-lit cement poles with rotating triangles, was the most amazing spectacle: Clyde Trivers' body perched high up in the sky, on the tallest of the cement poles. And the incredible thing, the truly incredible thing, was that his body was perfectly wedged inside the triangle.

His girth was accommodated by the inner perimeter of the triangle, and the fulcrum point of his belly rested directly on the base of the triangle, so that his head and arms hung out one side and his legs and feet out the other. And the whole thing, the whole mass of Trivers' body, rotated in unison with the triangle. It just rotated around and around again, 67 feet up in the air, in quiet harmony with all the other rotating triangles on the Harvard grounds.

The five of us stared out the window in complete awe. We just stood there, our mouths open wide, watching Trivers' body rotate in the sky. And we just kept standing there for what seemed like forever, afraid to look away, afraid it was all a dream.

But his body kept rotating, like some fancy ballerina from the old days. Rotating, rotating, rotating. Finally, we turned to one another, reassuring ourselves that it had really happened, and we all joined hands and helped each other down the stairs.

As you might imagine, the rest of the night was full of commotion. We reported the event to the WPA without delay, and in a matter of 16.48 minutes, swarms of agents converged around the cement pole that held Trivers' body.

To my surprise though, the first thing the agents did was bring in an emergency shuttle to treat our bruises and cuts. After that, they led us to a team of senior WPA officials, including Jackson Cranston, the agency chief.

Kale and Drop did most of the talking, since they were the only ones whose memories hadn't been fully extracted by Trivers. The senior WPA officials actually believed them, especially when Drop produced a working replica of Kale's tear drop resonator—a replica Drop admitted to secretly cloning while Kale had visited New Mexico.

Once they had the resonator, the WPA officials even consented to Kale's idea of patching into Trivers' system. As we hoped, his neural circuits still carried the data that he'd extracted, even though his system had expired. So we were able to verify what Kale and Drop said, as well as recover all our memories.

But the most significant thing, I think, was that the WPA officials didn't remove Trivers' body from the rotating triangle. They just let it keep spinning around and around, even after they downloaded his data. And they kept looking up at it, checking to see if it was still there.

It was as if they too had been waiting all these years—waiting for some carbon-based entity to overtake the vastness of the concrete and silica surrounding us. Trivers' innovation-filled body, draped over the cement pole, was the perfect thing.

Granted, it was no sycamore tree. It certainly couldn't compare to what grew behind Kale's condo in the Santa Monica Canyon. But with Trivers' body, the pole became partly organic, and that meant far more to us than anyone could have anticipated.

The rest of the night turned out to be more of a celebration than an investigation. Even the bureaucratic details felt uplifting, and when the first rays of sun appeared that next morning, Cranston gathered everyone around the cement pole to award us special medals of honor. He even replenished our value so we could afford to take vacations.

In a state of euphoria, the five of us gravitated down Massachusetts Avenue. We sat down at a SuperMold ingestion booth, and Drop ordered unshaped chile rellenos for each of us to sample. The taste made us laugh and cry at the same time.

After the meal, Morgaux nudged at Kale and Greggy, and the two of them got up to take a walk. When they were about 50 yards down the street, Kale turned back to look at me. I couldn't help noticing the way her black hair flowed so freely in the wind. Somehow it reminded me of the blue pathways I'd seen when Joseph and Drop had been stargazing in New Mexico.

I wanted to send her a signal, just to say hi, but a voice in me said I didn't need to rely on the Web. So I just concentrated in a way I'd never done before—it wasn't really concentrating as much as it was relaxing and feeling the surface of my skin—and I just did it. I sent Kale a Webless signal:

Hey Keeler,

I thought you might want to know, you've got my FULL approval. Absolutely. I mean, I see why you did what you did to your meter, and I think the world's ready, I really do.

To hell with the Internal Laws... let your instincts fly.

This is the big-time, Keeler. This is really the big-time!

—Peterson

The transmission took about as long as it would take a small bird. Then Kale looked over her shoulder, flashing me a huge smile, and she and Greggy went off, arm in arm, to find a secluded place on the banks of the Charles river.

Of course, I'm sure I could have figured a way to continue monitoring them. I could have measured exactly how many seconds their lips touched or exactly how many points their pleasure levels climbed. But I just wasn't that interested in precision anymore. I really wasn't.

In the next few hours, as the news spread of what was possible, I don't think anyone else on the planet was too interested in precision either. Because we had the whole Webless space in front of us, as well as our newly found senses of smell and touch and taste, and whatever else there was to discover too.

And so these were the things we wanted to explore—for as long as we had the chance. The wonderfully blissful, non-random chance.

ABOUT THE AUTHOR

Scott T. Grusky lives in Los Angeles, California. He holds an M.A. in economics from Harvard University and has spent most of his adult life either writing about technology or slogging through its trenches. You may contact him at stg@furthest.com or visit furthest.com.

❂

Other Books by Scott T. Grusky

Zero Percenters

facebook.com/scottgrusky

amazon.com/author/grusky

goodreads.com/grusky

bookbub.com/profile/scott-t-grusky